A MUSLIM SUICIDE

Middle East Literature in Translation
Michael Beard and Adnan Haydar, *Series Editors*

Other titles from Middle East Literature in Translation

Abundance from the Desert: Classical Arabic Poetry
Raymond Farrin

A Brave New Quest: 100 Modern Turkish Poems
Talat S. Halman, ed. and trans.

Contemporary Iraqi Fiction: An Anthology
Shakir Mustafa, ed. and trans.

Lebanon—Poems of Love and War, A Bilingual Anthology
Nadia Tuéni; Christophe Ippolito, ed.; Samuel Hazo and Paul B. Kelley, trans.

Martyrdom Street
Firoozeh Kashani-Sabet

My Bird
Fariba Vafi; Mahnaz Kousha and Nasrin Jewell, trans.

The Pistachio Seller
Reem Bassiouney; Osman Nusairi, trans.

Seasons of the Word: Selected Poems
Hilmi Yavuz; Walter G. Andrews, ed. and trans.

Sleeping in the Forest: Stories and Poems
Sait Faik; Talat S. Halman, ed.

A Time Between Ashes and Roses: Poems
Adonis; Shawkat M. Toorawa, trans.

A
MUSLIM
SUICIDE

BENSALEM
HIMMICH

Translated from the Arabic by Roger Allen

Syracuse University Press

English translation copyright © 2011 by Syracuse University Press
Syracuse, New York 13244-5290

All Rights Reserved

First Edition 2011

11 12 13 14 15 16   6 5 4 3 2 1

Originally published in Arabic as *Hadha Al-Andalusi* (Beirut: Dar al-Adab, 2007).

∞ The paper used in this publication meets the minimum requirements of the American National Standard for Information Sciences—Permanence of Paper for Printed Library Materials, ANSI Z39.48-1992.

For a listing of books published and distributed by Syracuse University Press, visit our Web site at SyracuseUniversityPress.syr.edu.

ISBN: 978-0-8156-0966-7

Library of Congress Cataloging-in-Publication Data
Himmich, Ben Salem, 1947–
    [Hadha al-Andalusi. English]
    A Muslim suicide / Bensalem Himmich ; translated from the Arabic by Roger Allen. — 1st ed.
        p. cm. — (Middle East literature in translation)
    ISBN 978-0-8156-0966-7 (pbk. : alk. paper) 1. Ibn Sab'in, 'Abd al-Haqq ibn Ibrahim, 1216 or 17–1270—Fiction. 2. Sufis—Spain—Murcia—Fiction. 3. Musilm pilgrims and pilgrimages—Fiction. 4. Islamic Empire—History—1258–1517—Fiction.
I. Allen, Roger. II. Title.
    PJ7832.I445H3313 2011
    892.7'36—dc23   2011040711

Manufactured in the United States of America

Bensalem Himmich has taught philosophy at Muhammad V University in Rabat, Morocco, and is currently the Moroccan minister of culture. He has published six novels, four collections of poetry, and books of essays and literary criticism. He was awarded the Riad El-Rayyes Prize for the Novel in 1989 for *Majnun al-Hukm (The Theocrat)* and the Great Atlas Prize in 2003 for his novel *Al-'Allama (The Polymath)*. More recently, Himmich received the 2009 Naguib Mahfouz Award from the Egyptian Writers Union.

Roger Allen is the Sascha Jane Patterson Harvie Professor Emeritus of Social Thought and Comparative Ethics in the School of Arts and Sciences at the University of Pennsylvania and Professor of Arabic and Comparative Literature Emeritus in the Department of Near Eastern Languages and Civilizations. In addition to numerous studies on the Arabic literary tradition, he has translated fictional works by, among others, Naguib Mahfouz *(God's World; Mirrors; Karnak Café; The Final Hour)*, Jabra Ibrahim Jabra *(In Search of Walid Masoud)*, Yusuf Idris *(In the Eye of the Beholder)*, 'Abd al-rahman Munif *(Endings)*, and Mayy Telmissany *(Dunyazad)*.

Part One

The Search for the Missing Manuscript

You have already heard about the beauteous maidens that this peninsula has produced, daughters of Greece, bedecked in pearls and coral, gowns embossed with eagles, boudoirs in palaces of crowned kings . . .
> —part of Tariq ibn Ziyad's*[1] oration to the conquering army in Al-Andalus

Habit erects a veil against God. Veils invoke a sense of remoteness and villainy. Habit is therefore the very source of remoteness and villainy. To break habit and cast it aside is thus the source of intimacy and happiness.
> —Ibn Sab'in, Commentary on Ibn Sab'in's "Testament to His Students"

The Opening

Woe is me!

Woe is me for what I have lost, leaving a huge void inside me.

I have been asked to explain the nature of this loss by a voice that I've grown used to hearing in my dreams.

"You herald of the unseen," I have shouted back at the top of my voice, "you ask me about it, and yet you know more about it than anyone else!"

---

1. Please note that items in the text indicated with an asterisk (*) are discussed in the glossary.

1

My shouts rose and echoed through the darkness of night, so much so that they shook me awake. The weather was cold and rainy, and yet springtime was to bring with it a magic of its own.

I got up at once and went outside, wandering through the alleys of my own quarter and neighboring quarters too. As I crisscrossed them, I was sometimes lost in my own thoughts, while at others I concentrated my entire attention on the dawn of the day to come and the stirrings of plants and creatures all around me.

Yet again, maybe for the thousand and first time, I performed my prayers, with no other plea than that the All-Knowing One would direct me to my manuscript, my missing essence and lost pillar of support.

Fragments, snippets of sentences, isolated words, that's all that remains of my manuscript. I have tried to follow its traces by jotting down various bits during hours of intermittent wakefulness, on the crest of an all-too-fleeting bout of clear thinking, or whenever scattered glimpses and fragments have flashed across my mind. Here now are just a few of them:

"You should espouse plenitude in existence, for that displays more purity and intelligence . . . and is . . .

"Knowledge is a token of sublimity . . .

"Love constitutes within its confines the fertilizer of the living and the means of well-being . . .

"As you proceed ever upward, may your progress be spiral . . . so faulty circles are broken; so you can implant your branch on the heights you have reached, not the place where you started; so you can await the onset of drowsiness and ever-turning habits . . .

"Many's the intellect if it is pure, your own portion will not elude you or disappear . . .

"The very obscurity of my discourse is my means of concealment. Whoever seeks to interpret me without understanding, that person is ignorant of my secrets and has become my foe . . .

" . . . I belong to You, O God. To You I will return and be gathered . . .

"In Your splendor and glory implant me in Your firmament now, now. Set me down so that I may scatter the clouds of plurality, so I may establish an element of certainty in true existence and unity.

" . . . My routine involves isolation and seclusion . . .

"Concerning the reason why I persist in this direction, . . . just watch me and do not ask.

"Reconciliation with your whole self is the correct path. . . . Traveler on the way, remove from your self all attachments and attributes. They are all blemishes and illusions.

"L O V E . By all women with their beautiful eyes, I am not a worshipper of the P N S nor am I a crazy presence in your midst."

■ ■ ■

My manuscript is my foundational location, my untouched flame. If I ever find it, I will rejoice and will find my endeavors invigorated. But if I am deprived of it and the loss lingers for some time, I will feel the fire of anguish and turn in on myself . . .

People may well be surprised that I am so intensely sad at the loss and that the mere memory of it brings a lump to my throat, as though I'd been robbed of someone very dear to me, or had lost a precious possession, something irreplaceable. Ah me! The comparison is exactly right and captures my feelings so well! The text of my manuscript is a unique example of its kind. In it discourse adopts an elevated plane, carefully and finely interwoven. I would not wish to claim that it constitutes the ultimate of revelations to me—heaven forfend, heaven forfend! If some form of imagery makes things easier, then let's say that it's like a set of blessed, luminescent tablets, tablets whose consonants are the purest flowing blood, while its vowel sounds are the result of the subtlest flashes of lightning; tablets of the kind that time never proffers twice, as evidence of which I can cite the fact that the majority of its ideas and contents have been completely erased from my memory, leaving behind nothing but a few notable traces and an alluring waft of scent.

If only you realized, the pages in my manuscript are just like vessels that I replenish during my hours of sleep and quests of the beyond, fueled by a desire for pearls concealed within my internal sun or else in my imagined rains. When I receive a God-granted state of harmony, I feel pure enough to compose my ideas. With that I rush to embrace the wind or to send kisses to the stars in the zenith of the firmament. At that very moment my sense of delight knows no peer, a yardstick for the sheer health and fertility of life that I feel, the guiding compass, the holy lamp guiding my path to the abodes of sublime felicity.

Were my delight to be measured in terms of its connections to people, then foes of my flashes of intoxication would deny it; every savant connoisseur would get his share of it, each in accordance with his rank and ability.

In the wake of this loss, I have started—if only you might realize!—undertaking the task of writing as though it were the twin brother of prayer itself. For that purpose I am equipping myself with every kind of spiritual and cognitive material that may be needed, all out of a strong desire to entice into its trap every kind of idea and proximate entity. My manuscript was replete with such things; its very odor perfumed both heart and mind in gleaming moments of illumination.

In order to lighten the heavy load of my loss, I have developed certain strategies. I make a point of performing preparatory rituals and concocting liquids of such a kind that, when they are drunk, the memory is sharpened and stimulated. Long periods of waiting, either continuous or intermittent, in the day's early hours, all in front of blank sheets of paper; at times this involved bouts of sleeping, at others staying awake, so much so that you might imagine I were drunk even though I was not. All these measures and others like them have had as a goal a quest for vision and inspirational thoughts, for a means of recreating my missing manuscript—if only bit by bit or segments in place of the whole thing. These strategies of mine may not have borne fruit as yet, but they have become a kind of drug that I can take in order to bring some relief, albeit a little, to my wounded heart, to let me utter some sighs of regret with the hope perhaps of taking a deep breath once in a while and feeling some sense of release.

After a good deal of effort and cogitation on my part, I have finally become convinced that the harvest it will produce will be scant. My endeavors may occasionally produce a flower, but as with Sisyphus will never fully bud. It will be exactly like what I have described above, namely something of a kind that, were I to write it down, the surface words could be understood but without all the hidden nuances that it contains. All of which means that there is no point in recording it and attracting feeble intellects to its contents.

True enough, before I was beset by this enormous disaster, it would occasionally happen to me, like any other human author, that my ideas would simply dry up. Even so, I felt too proud to use that as a pretext for doing nothing or for going into some kind of decline. At such times I would practice my other kind of activity, bringing to the forefront some older problems: I would pose some questions on theological issues and the hidden inner meanings of things, convoluted issues of extreme complexity such as one for which the only solution lies in a reliable and rigorous mode of analysis.

But as of today, even that mode of resolution is rare and unattainable. There is no power or might except in free Truth!

1

TO BE THE LIVING, breathing person, someone scored by despair and grief, the memory alive to a loss that lingers like a sharp knife under the skin, and yet at the same time to go out into the world fabricating a radiant Buddha's smile and all the symptoms of well-being and contentment;

To address people in a manner that suggests an assertive and rigid optimism, one that at times almost rises to a shriek;

To make resounding declarations of enthusiasm and present things as though surreal or else wrapped in ideals—

All such things involve sheer rhetoric; they may even be the acme of rhetoric. If not, then so be it. After all, rhetoric is no easy, uncomplicated function, nor is it within the powers of people whose dreams, tastes, and disposition are not up to the task.

In fact, ponder along with me, those of you who possess the requisite mind and spleen. Just imagine where we would now find ourselves were it not for various skills of dissimulation and concealment, imaginative powers and oil from empty bottles, psychological tricks and superabundant fantasy!

How can I avoid devoting particular love and affection to magic, alchemy, geomancy, and even the words of poets; after all, as the saying puts it, "The sweetest poetry is the most deceitful!"

On the same subject (and maybe in quest of some relief and consolation), I disguised myself and went to the desert area outside Murcia to consult a Jewish fortune-teller who was renowned for her ability to tell people's fortunes and offer advice. Along with a lot of other people I waited for quite a while. When my turn came, she stared straight into my eyes, then said something amazing: "The thing you've come to me for, Ibn Sab'in, that's something for which I have no cure.

Neither my implements nor my potions will be of any use. Go back whence you came and, to the extent possible, immerse yourself in your own past. Write down your efforts and whatever you see. Perhaps then you will remember, or forget."

I tried to say something, but she stopped me. When I wanted to pay her, she refused to accept anything. With that I got up reluctantly and followed her enormous servant to the exit door.

▪ ▪ ▪

Following the fortune-teller's suggestion, I proceeded to sequester myself for seven consecutive days, concentrating entirely and exclusively on those occasions and moments that immediately preceded the loss. The idea was that such a procedure might serve to relive my agony and guide me to what I had lost and needed so much. Among the things that emerged was a picture of the brash and impetuous youth that I myself had been. I had been brought up exactly like Imam Ibn Hazm,* nourished among women's thighs and passed from one lap to another. It was among women that I had memorized the Qur'an and poetry, the art of chanting religious texts, and correct diction, even handwriting and playing both lute and flute. When I think back, I find myself breathing in the scent of their mouths and breasts. It feels as though a gentle perfume is wafting through my very self.

For me, my sister, and my brother, my dear mother, Umama, was a paragon of tender, loving motherhood. Whenever my father got angry and piled abuse on me, it was my mother who provided refuge and protection. My father was actually a retainer for the ruling Banu Hud* family, a group of rulers who were forever playing musical chairs with executive positions and intriguing against each other. My father's plan was that I should be an exact duplicate of my elder brother, namely a carbon copy of himself, heir to his secrets, expert in the various ways of climbing the bureaucratic ladder of ranks and salaries, and of grabbing a portion of the prestige involved. However, my entire nature resisted such a notion; I wanted something entirely different, something more in line with my own inclinations.

From my teenage years into adulthood, the parts of Spain that were still in Muslim hands were shrinking from one decade to the next. Where prominent rulers and politicians were concerned, the situation showed a relentless slide toward fragmentation and a resort to the lowest common denominator. I myself followed the lead of the majority of such people and their offspring by indulging in all sorts of reckless luxury and pomp, seeking pleasures and delights of every kind. I became very adept at such activities. It was as if I were going to die the very next day, or else Izra'il, the Angel of Death, was allowing me some extra time, but only on condition that I concentrate entirely on sensory pleasures that would inevitably result in my demise.

Faced with what seemed like all-encompassing disaster and imminent terror, these rulers—fathers and sons alike—started devoting themselves to those pleasures that provided the greatest consolation and distraction: food and sex. For my part, I can vouch for the fact that I favored the latter over the former; indeed I can identify it as being the most successful and efficacious antidote to the occasional fits of depression that would come over me.

My father divorced his second wife and married another woman younger than both himself and my mother. With that he divided his daily routine between two separate households, and his activities and preoccupations multiplied. As a direct result I now found myself liberated from his violent moods and direct control. My mother was well aware of my current proclivities, but chose to ignore them as long as I concentrated on my education and studies. Even so, she was well aware of my dallyings with our female neighbors, both divorcees and virgins, and of the way I consorted with prostitutes who had to pay a tax for their professional activities to the amir's market-inspector; for that reason they were known as "poll-tax women," that being a label that was known far and wide in the Peninsula.

What am I supposed to say about these poll-tax women? Invoking the advice of the fortune-teller, I will now trawl my memory, but all I can remember about them is a few vague impressions that recall both the phony gaiety of their existence and its sheer vulnerability. By now I have completely forgotten their predominantly black color. I have no idea what their fate has been. I suspect that some of them may have died or suffered a premature old age; for others opportunities may have opened so they could either make their own way in the world or else gain manumission and seek repentance for their sins.

In spite of everything, I can still remember the brothel on the northern outskirts of my Spanish city that I used to frequent with some of my friends. The madam was a huge woman. Every time she welcomed us to the establishment, she would open the doors and pull back the curtains. Obviously drunk and chewing gum, she would yell at us with her coarse voice. "I'm forced to do this," she would shout; "I'm no hero!" Then she would go on, "Okay, boys, choose whom you want. As the Qur'an puts it in the chapter on women, 'marry women as pleases you and then be generous!'" In fact, the eldest among us would never "be generous" unless among the women he found one who, in his own words, would display a complete professionalism in her manner. The rest of us would turn that quotation into a joke.

People who regularly consort with prostitutes can come up with any number of excuses. The one most commonly invoked is that such entertainment provides a distraction from the hardships of life, even in the realm of the imagination, and is acceptable as long as you offer the women a fair reward. For my part and in addition to what I have just mentioned, there was the fact that I felt drawn to the women by my desire to experience with a neutral eye the sheer superficiality of our ephemeral existence here on earth, something that was manifested through the artificiality of their demeanor and their proclivity for idle chatter, finery, and perfumes.

Whatever else I may have forgotten, there was one girl in the very prime of her beauty whom I can never forget. It was not in any brothel that I got to know her—heaven forbid!!—but rather in the house of a devout pilgrim lady who had both prestige and influence. She used to take into her care young girls who were either orphans or else had fallen on bad times. They were all penniless, and so she took it upon herself to protect them from profiteers and pimps and to bring them up until such time as she could find them either husbands or means of escape or repentance. This pious woman, who was known by the name Umm al-Khayr, accepted me as a companion for her girls because, it would appear, she detected good intentions in my person and inclinations.

The sessions normally took place, once a week or more, in the house garden in the company of a troupe of musicians, each of whom was an expert singer of Andalusian poems, *zajals* and *muwashshahs*.* The result was a wonderfully joyous atmosphere that swept away all troubles and removed all concerns, if only for a while. The lady of the house gave the company such food and drink as was available and permitted. She made sure that the young men and women remained separated and only communicated with each other through gestures and glances. Those who were bolder and more daring found this particular mode of communication to be the entrée into some amorous escapades, all of which would occur outside the house and by arrangement with some of the female servants.

That was how I came to make the acquaintance of this girl. I managed to take her with me on my horse to a cave I knew that was close to a deserted stretch of beach. There it was that we lay together on a velvet rug and indulged in a superb sexual union, a routine that was a replication of the waves of the sea close by. Truth to tell, she was without peer and utterly unforgettable. Just before it was time for us to go back, she sat down beside me; deep in thought, she allowed her gaze to wander off to the horizon. I imagined that she was admiring the beauty of the sea that stretched away into the distance. I blessed what she was doing and encouraged her to continue. She was a person of few words, but what she had to say astonished me: that she used to consign the worst moments of her anguish to the sea, using the lapping sounds created by the movement of the breeze on the sea's surface. Once she had learned how to swim, she said, she wanted to do it properly. I promised to serve as her instructor in that and mouthed some amiable phrases in the hope of providing her with some comfort. With that I convinced her that it was time for her to return to her residence.

It was only a few days later that one of Umm al-Khayr's servants came with the news that the girl had drowned in the sea. She had informed her that her mistress was very angry with me and did not wish to see me ever again in her residence.

I can remember, oh yes, I remember well, how much I grieved over the death of that girl, but now I can't even remember her name or anything about her. For a while I stayed in my room, claiming that I was spending my time studying. However, there was no way that I could hide my anguish and distress from my mother and sister. I spent eleven whole days fasting and giving my food to the cats. Whether sleeping or awake, my sole preoccupation was with that poor girl who had had such a miserable life and died unknown. I recall that I composed an elegy in her honor that I later included in my missing manuscript; but now I cannot recall its meter, vowel rhyme, or text.

What brought this state of affairs to an end was when my sister, Zaynab, came in and told me that my mother's health had deteriorated badly. Immediately I rushed downstairs to reassure her that I was fine, thinking that the reason why she was not well was because of me. I would also be able to lessen the pain she was feeling because my father was still neglecting to visit her. But no sooner did I lean over her than she started raving and mentioning one name over and over again: Our Lord al-Khidr.* I felt her pulse and realized that fever had her in its grip. I asked Zaynab and the servant-girl to get some medicines and grasses. I then prepared a potion that I had learned from al-Razi's* book on medicine and gave it to my sick mother. I also put a band moistened with rosewater on her forehead. After an hour's wait there was no sign of improvement, and that made me panic. I was about to go and ask the doctor to come, but then another servant-girl came rushing in to tell me that Our Lord al-Khidr had arrived. I asked my sister if the man was a doctor. Her reply astonished me: "He's the only doctor who can help our mother!"

I tried to recall what I could remember about this forty-year-old bachelor, especially about his fine reputation and the great respect my father and other notables had for him. I put all my trust in his skills, and hoped and prayed for my mother's recovery at his hands.

When he came in and greeted us, he was looking neat and well turned out as usual. He had a regal bearing, and his face and features sparkled; his smiling visage and gentle looks and gestures all managed to give one comfort. I watched as he sat down beside my mother and leaned over to kiss her head. What happened next was, by God Almighty, totally amazing: she opened her eyes wide, removed the band from her forehead, and sat up. It was as though the mere image and scent of the person sitting beside her had been enough not only to arouse her senses for living after a period when they had seemed to atrophy and fade away, but also to restore her to health following a bout of illness that had sapped her energy. She kept whispering his name in sheer delight and clasped his hands so she could kiss them, staring at them sometimes and at his face at other times. It was as if she needed to be absolutely certain for herself. While she was in this trancelike state, she paid absolutely no attention to either myself or my sister; we had both withdrawn to a corner and were simply observing. She did not bother either with the two servant-girls who were vying with each other to keep the table loaded with food and drink. It seemed to me that it was only when Al-Khidr suggested that she eat something that she regained her bearings again and began to take note of what was going on around her. She seemed delighted to follow his advice and tucked into the food with relish. When her savior was on the point of leaving, he summoned the two servant-girls and instructed them to stay with their mistress through the night in case she needed anything. Looking in my direction, he told me with complete confidence that, God willing, my mother would be restored to complete health on the morrow.

And that is precisely what happened. My mother woke up and started washing and putting on makeup. Neatly dressed, elegant, and full of energy, she spent the entire day dealing with household matters. She was particularly concerned about me and my affairs. Just before I went to bed, I took my sister aside and asked her what she thought about this man Al-Khidr.

"'Abd al-Haqq," she replied in a tone full of confidence, "our dear mother adores Al-Khidr. This fine man nurtures her spiritual affection with considerable integrity and kindness. When her condition gets worse, he comes at once. What you witnessed yesterday has happened before without your even being aware of it."

"What about our father, Zaynab? Does he know about this?"

"Yes, he knows. He is absolutely convinced that the doctor is a decent person, and that stops him from feeling jealous or angry."

She rubbed her hands together, uttering a prayer that He protect my mother and her innocent adoration from any taint of sin or fall from grace.

At noon on the following day, I can recall paying a visit to Al-Khidr in a monastery he used to frequent in a suburb of Murcia. I was anxious to confirm that the man was indeed devout and pious. He greeted me warmly, but was immediately aware that I had something on my mind. As he invited me to sit down and talk, he asked me gently what I wished to discuss . . . and yet, as I revert to the days of my youth and turn things over in my memory, I can only recall a tiny fraction of the conversation I had with him. One thing I do remember is that I asked him about the people in Spain and the sorry state of affairs that had now beset them. All I can recall about his response was what he had to say by way of conclusion:

"My boy, I can say for sure that our presence in the Iberian Peninsula is heading, albeit gradually, for an unprecedented era of disintegration. One can see sign after sign that should serve as harbingers of the fissures developing within our domains; and they are working their relentless way into our own existential and intellectual fabric as well. You can start saying funeral prayers for our Muslim Spain, a society that is bound for destruction unless the mighty miracle occurs."

It was with my own mother's passionate devotions and her relationship with him in mind that I asked him about faith.

"My boy," he replied, "as far as I am concerned, there are three proofs—and how very rare and remarkable they are!—to bolster the nature of true belief:

"First: In my view, assemblies, weddings, and the joyous occasions during our life in this world for the most part all lack any sense of either fruition or warmth. So why should I not propose instead a different world for the spirit, one that is both more radiant and ideal, indeed something that no eye has seen, no ear heard, and no human heart even contemplated?

"Second: within the framework of ongoing delays and missed opportunities, I have destroyed all comparable records and reached the very summits. In the long run, I have become convinced—but then, who can know for sure?—that this may well be the means whereby I can wager this faulty world of ours against another one that is more beautiful, compact, and enduring.

"Third: after a good deal of thought and contemplation I have come to believe firmly in resurrection and the Day of Judgment. The reason is that everywhere in this world of ours I witness so much violence and cruelty. Crimes remain unpunished. That is something that I find completely intolerable and unbearable.

"By way of commentary on these three proofs, I secretly invoke the following entity: mankind. Man knows full well that his body will become food for worms. While still alive, all he can do is devote his entire attention to sympathy for himself. For that reason he provides another domain for it, one that is eternal and pure, something totally in keeping with his limitless arrogance and the precious qualities of his spirit.

"Beyond these three proofs, I can see no others, even if we include the wager of Al-Ma'arri,* the blind poet, whether it be less subjective or more evidentiary."

I asked my companion what exactly was Al-Ma'arri's wager, and he recited for me the poet's two verses:

> *The astrologer and the physician both have said:*
> *The body is not gathered on Judgment Day.*

> *If you are right, I replied, then I am no loser;*
> *But, if I am right, then the loss is yours.*

I can also recall asking this man so beloved of my mother about love and its characteristics, in the hope that he might gradually lead me toward my desired goal without his even being aware of it. He talked to me about it, but I was so young that I found it absolutely impossible to follow his train of thought. His wonderful phrases were all reasonable enough, but they did not make any sense. Then I forgot them completely.

Al-Khidr's words as a whole were characterized by their boldness and profundity, and I set about memorizing snippets by heart. It was those snippets that I had remembered and put down, along with some remarks of my own, that are in my missing manuscript.

It was barely a month after our meeting that news spread to the effect that he had completely disappeared. Stories abounded. One stated that he had been killed and his body had been buried, at the hands of men who were afraid for the honor of their wives and daughters. Another claimed that he had died a martyr, one of the last defenders of Cordoba. Still a third claimed that he had traveled to the East in order to fight the Franks and to seek help and support for the people of Spain. Two months after his disappearance, my mother died one dark night of a fever that caused her terrible agony. My father soon followed her into the next world. Verily it is to God that we belong and to Him do we return.

"Retrace your steps and immerse yourself in your past as much as you can." Those were the instructions of my Jewish fortune-teller. Well, in spite of the occasional pearl of information, the results of that process of immersion had provided scant nourishment, singularly useless and uninformative. Viewed in the mirror of my missing manuscript, it was all the mere embryo of something much larger, something separated by various phases and stations from what I had previously recorded with all due clarity and understanding regarding my early days (about which I knew neither my name nor my identity), regarding my mother who loved and Al-Khidr the object of her love, and regarding a variety of other things, the primary supervisor of which was God and man in the firmament of the unity of all existence and the ascent toward that which is the essential, the luminous, the sublime.

2

ONCE I HAD FINALLY DESPAIRED of ever recovering my missing manuscript, along with its unique basic content and its initial luminous framework, I decided that the best plan was to forget about it; that and nothing else. In other words, my plan was to become more involved in that phase of my life that had been part of my earlier experiences, a phase that I called my period of frivolity and discourses on love, one that I had indulged in during my teenage years. As I noted earlier, this was a time when erotic desires were my primary endeavor, duly followed by a number of verbal contributions, both perverted and elusive.

An endless text, that is woman!

In your quest for a copy of the perfect woman, was it not the case that each example was bound to lead you to another, either through a process of imitation or else in a gradual progression toward something yet more beautiful? Such was your quest—did you but know it—that no one lifetime would have been enough to fulfill it, even supposing that you focused entirely on research, observation, and a good deal of sighing, and converted your own bed into a haven for fascinating, buxom women of temporary residence.

As a way of both guarding against mental collapse and erasing my sense of loss after such a tragedy, I told myself that I needed to assume that genuine reality was actually different from the one on whose basis and within which I had been operating up until that point. I would need to collect images of the world that were contrary to the ones I had been perceiving with my five senses and to strengthen my personality through various kinds of exercise, all that before I could embark upon the process of spending time meeting people.

So, as a start, let me focus on women.

There were ten women in all, and they are still helping me bear the burdens of the journey and negotiate difficult traversals of narrows and straits. When my ability to endure the trials of our grimy existence and the passage of time was involved, they all had the better of me. For my part and in ways of which I may or may not have been conscious, I may have somehow managed to offer them some services just as they did for me.

My powers of seduction meanwhile remained at their strongest. When it came to "plowing the fields," those powers were full of vim and vigor, although once in a while they would flag and dry up. Without a doubt I was going to be pretty close (or even closer) to the sunset of the above-mentioned phase in my life.

Since at this point I am on the threshold of the project I am proposing to initiate (or to return to), this can be considered a kind of testament, something that I may already have recorded in a more effective and acceptable way in my missing manuscript. It has a token value, in that it traverses the different phases of life and every type of behavior: "He who seeks, wins; he who wins, profits; he who profits, can be kind; he who can be kind is zealous; he who is zealous increases his quest; he who increases his quest emerges with that which he neither intended nor anticipated; and that is his ultimate perfection . . ."

Any quest for beginnings is not like a return to them; the process of rotation only gains vivacity and strength through various phases and conditions—namely gain, profit, kindness, and energy. They are all aspirations aimed at plowing the realm of possibility and investigating the hidden aspects of the unseen.

So what exactly is my quest today?

I have none other than women.

If it were not for them, in the face of my current crisis and what happened to me earlier, I would already have surrendered myself to the fates in defeat and allowed the chips to fall where they may.

In their company I was the one who profited, gained sociability, and felt full of energy. They were the ones to call me by names normally used by disciples: Ibn Dara, magnet, master, to which they appended two others: comforter and curer. Even so, I never made the titles they gave me a point of pride or boast; instead I used them to comfort distressed women and provide services to lonely females who were either spinsters, widows, or divorcees—and how many of them there were in the region where I was living, between Murcia and the village of Raquta.* The same applied to other parts of Muslim Spain as it was being relentlessly torn apart.

Born innately softhearted and sensitive, I was endowed with all the handsome attributes one can imagine. So how could I possibly look at a woman who, deprived of strength and discretion, was suffering or languishing without extending to her a hand of mercy, all the while turning toward her Creator with frowning visage and asking bitterly, "Why, O Lord, why?"

Within a context such as this, I may forget a great deal, but there is one woman whom I can never forget. She had a Muslim father and a Byzantine mother. Before she committed suicide, I spent some time as her faithful lover, all in secret. My understanding was that her absolute and impetuous optimism was not merely a phase or a jest, but rather just one aspect of the skill she had in making light of her genuinely tragic feelings about existence; in other words, an antidote for the cursed portion of blows and disruptions that fate had decreed for her.

With regard to another of these women I will say, "A pox on hashish." And yet how beautiful she was, this Christian girl! I used to watch her during her waking hours as she spent time preparing her meals, then eating them in small bites or gulps, and all as part of some strange rituals that came from heaven knows where. She used to confront her critics with a series of rationales that, at least to my taste, were distinctly vaporous: hashish, she would say, helps me survey my altruistic relationships and erase the situation in which I find myself, even if it is only an illusion.

With that in mind, a friend we had in common commented sarcastically, "If hashish distributors in Badis,* purveyors, and members of the Hadawa Brotherhood* were made aware of this motivation for using their preferred drug, I'm sure they'd be glad to guarantee her a free supply for the rest of her life or what's left of it!"

If only I could recall the situation of other women, just a few brief snippets, I would have exactly the same things to say. Senses and comments all at the ready, I would invoke my nostalgia for all those women whom I loved, whether platonically or as part of an affair.

What I do know is that gossips and would-be legal experts who preferred superficial learning and tactics of suppression would regularly circulate intentionally false rumors about me during their gatherings. One of them, named Zayd Abu al-Hamlat, called me "seducer in chief," and then attributed to me words that I never uttered. The gist of it was that on my deathbed I would address this complaint to the bed: "Woe is me, forced to leave this world in which there are still so many women. Now my conquests will never win them. My only consolation lies in the prayer that on the day of my resurrection the angels will welcome me with all their feminine charms . . ."

On this matter I follow the lead of the Prophet: "In this world of yours perfume and women have been made beloved to me." If that is true of desert oases, then how much more should it be the case in the regions of Spain that remain in our hands and in this eastern city where I reside, a city with its river valley flowing downward from Shaqura,* bestowing lovely melodies amidst canals that are transported to the skies by water-wheels and accompanied by the tuneful songs of birds that make fruits and flowers glisten. A moist, scented breeze wafts perfumes across gardens and courtyards and distributes them as gifts and booty to promenaders and lovers.

It is from all these lovely examples of God's bountiful gifts and many others like them that the current invasion of Castilian, Leonian, and Aragonian Crusaders is striving to expel us. Meanwhile, our own sovereigns and their cliques, hearts rent asunder, have forgotten God, just as He has them. All they can do is strut around and take both excess and fear to bed with them, while with swords drawn they proceed to finish each other off.

My grief is two- or rather threefold, and my complaint is to God Almighty: first over my missing manuscript; second for Muslim Spain that Muslims are losing bit by bit; third and last for the loss of our spiritual nourishment, one limb at a time. When it comes to confronting these various aspects of my grief, discretion is becoming increasingly limited. By now it's become reduced to mere patience and the fortification of the soul with the good things in life.

So then, pleasures are the greatest resort.

"Save your energy and look for your manuscript among your former paramours. The thief may prove to be one of them. God knows best." This shout from the beyond coincided with the counsel I received from a female astrologer who appeared to me in a dream a few days ago. At first I did not take her seriously. "Ibn Sab'in," she told me, "the thief may be one of your former paramours, whether she's a Muslim like you, Christian or Jewish, or pagan. Who knows . . ."

3

IN THE COUNTRYSIDE northwest of Murcia there's a village on the side of a valley with verdant pastures, orchards, and abundant water. As has been noted earlier, it's called Raquta. A rider can get there in a few hours. It's there that I was born in the month of Rajab, 614 AH [1217 CE]. I owned an estate there that I inherited from my father—God have mercy on his soul! I had given part of it as a gift to Maymuna, the divorced wife of my elder brother, Abu Talib, and to my widowed sister, Zaynab. Every time I appeared in their midst, summer or winter, they used to pitch a tent for me, in accordance with my wishes. They would then compete with each other to make me happy and show me respect. From time to time they would remind me that the house was mine, to which I would respond that the house belonged to God alone and He could give it as an inheritance to whomsoever He wished. The two of them, I said, happened to be the ones He wished. Their principal goal was to leave me on my own so that I could devote myself to my studies. Whenever they were with me, they rarely spoke except when matters of great importance and moment were involved or else when I myself asked for information.

When Maymuna had just been divorced, she complained a good deal about my brother; she used to lean her head on my shoulder and share her gripes with me: "My name was never mentioned. I'm an unlucky woman. How often did I beg Abu Talib to accept the fact that I was barren and let me stay underneath him. He could have married another woman or as many as he wanted. But what he craved was the wealth his new wife brought with her, not to mention her father's prestige, so he went along with her wishes and agreed to all her conditions . . ."

I used to give her advice that, she assured me, she was prepared to accept with good grace. I never said a bad word about my brother, even though I was well aware that he belonged to a group of degenerates who aspired to high positions, in the process collecting both promotions and the salaries to go with them. As far as I was concerned (and my inquiries proved the point), they were all merely fancies of this ephemeral world of ours. That is why the only thing I could do was to let him play in the mud along with all the others.

My sister was still a beauty, even though it lay concealed behind the deep wound that remained after her husband was killed at the Battle of al-'Iqab* [Las Navas de Tolosa] in 1212, an event that was indeed "a punishment" ('iqab) for Muslims who had been relentlessly stabbing each other in the back and breaking up into separate fiefdoms. Still other calamities made the wound even deeper for her: in particular, she was devastated by the death of her only son as a result of an incurable disease. These days she was managing to overcome her permanent sense of loss and our brother's neglect of her by bestowing on the world a gentle, gleaming smile that never left her face. I still managed to provide her with some solace and consolation. Whenever we met, she would say, "God and yourself, that's all that's left for me."

Even though both women had been badly dealt with by fate and were post-menopausal, they still managed to spend their time on any number of household chores, on chat sessions that included a fair amount of joking and tall tales, and even on the occasional muted or raucous laughter—all depending on occasion and place. One of them complained to me once about a pain she had (which I realized was purely imaginary), so I gave her a potion that was actually a placebo, boiled in water and honey. She got better and thanked me profusely.

I always seek refuge at this estate whenever the number of pupils around me gets too much for me or politicians start to impinge upon my activities. This time, I have used the opportunity afforded by such isolation to read *The Pure Good* by Proclus* and parts of the *Theologia*★ attributed to Aristotle (although I tend to believe that it's actually by Plato). In the past I also used to pore over *The Beautiful Names of God* by Ibn al-Mar'a* from Malaga and the notes he transcribed from his *shaykh*, Abu 'Abdallah al-Shawdhi* from Seville; and over the compilations of linguists working on nouns and particles such as Al-Buni* and Al-Harrali*— God have mercy on the souls of all of them! During these periods of seclusion I also used to peruse books on medicine, chemistry, and natural magic. My attraction to these particular sciences may have been amplified by my ever-increasing interest in trauma care and also in the cracking of secrets and riddles, among them—indeed the most significant of them all—being the disappearance of my manuscript and my subsequent loss of inspiration.

■ ■ ■

"There are ninety-nine aspects of pleasure that make a woman superior to a man, but God has chosen to make them bashful." Those are the very words of the Lord and Seal of all the Prophets. However, in this Spain of ours that has forgotten all about God, just as He has about it, that bashful trait is no longer to be found among Jewish and Christian women nor even among Muslim women and others as well. Things have now reached a stage where, if a woman finds a man attractive, you'll see her adopting a number of strategies and expedients to achieve her goals, ones that she alone knows how to implement and carry through.

On the seventh day of my stay in Raquta, I was visited by a young man, one of many who, in spite of my own diffidence, wanted me to be their teacher and counselor. Many of them are under twenty years old, and I am only a few years older than they. This particular young man was clearly the most aristocratic of all the ones I had met and showed the greatest proclivity for learning. After greeting me, he sat down. He looked flustered and awkward and apologized for coming to see me without any prior notice.

"How did you find your way here, Abu al-'Ali?" I asked him.

He now looked even more worried. "Master," he replied, "how can anyone led by his heart and possessed of both sense and tongue possibly lose track of you?"

"What is it you need, my brother?"

"I need your counsel. I don't know if you remember Rachel. She became available to me after she converted to Islam and recited the statement of faith. She took the name Fatima, and we were married in accordance with the practice of God and His Prophet."

He stopped talking abruptly, and I seized the occasion to congratulate him on his marriage. However, I also noticed that he seemed distressed and unhappy.

"God should not bless this marriage. It took only three months for me to discover that my wife had become a Muslim only superficially; she was actually still Jewish. I have proof and evidence for what I am claiming. Master, I am in a complete quandary as to what to do. I have abandoned the marriage bed to avoid any suspicion of hypocrisy on my part, which would make my situation difficult, if not impossible . . ."

22 | Bensalem Himmich

A tricky situation indeed! What was I supposed to tell him? While I was preparing an answer, I asked him about Rachel's elder sister with whom I had had a relationship a while back. He told me that she was primarily responsible for the situation he found himself in; it was she who had incited his wife to go through the pretense.

"Put your trust in God," I told him. "He will suffice for you, and He is a good trustee. Allow your good intentions to control your bad ones. For the time being, stick with what is on the surface. However, if what lies beneath floats to the top and causes trouble, then marshal your intellectual forces and separate yourself at your own discretion. You possess such power and responsibility. As regards Sara, I hope to be talking to her fairly soon, God willing."

This follower of mine seemed pleased with what he had been told. Standing up, he said his farewells and left. He was trailed by my affectionate looks and the memory of a story connected with the girl who was in love with him. When I was living in my house in Murcia, she came to see me two or three times before her marriage to complain about how strict and prudish her husband was. Quite apart from the undeniable fact that the girl was extremely beautiful, she also spoke Arabic and had memorized poetry by the great Arab poets. No sooner had she come in and greeted me than she started describing the situation, using wonderful lines of poetry from the classical tradition, all beautifully rhymed and metered. I in turn recited some others and related to her tales of love and other similar topics, all in an attempt to offer her some comfort and consolation. There was one occasion—it was almost nightfall—when my house-servant informed me that this woman was at the door and her condition seemed serious. I allowed him to bring her in and stay with us. She was indeed a nervous wreck; her face was pale and her eyes were red from weeping.

"What's the matter, Rachel?" I asked after returning her salutation.

Sitting opposite me, she downed a full glass of water. After taking a deep breath as though to gather together all her strength before telling me something really serious, she seemed to calm down a little.

"I used to think that the reason why my husband kept avoiding me was because he was so fond of you," she told me. "But as of today I'm the one who's started avoiding him because it's you I'm in love with. That is how my first lover has handed me over to my true love. You are the reference point; everything else is a mere shadow of it. You represent everything I aspire to and hope for . . ."

As the old saying has it, "He who eats with the kids before the fast begins becomes one of them himself." So that this maxim would not apply in my case, I asked the girl to go back to her family, demanding of her that she remain true to her first love. I wrote a couple of lines by Abu Tammam on a piece of paper and gave it to her:

> In matters of love place your heart where'er you wish.
> Love is only for the first of all;
> How many dwellings does a man know and love,
> Yet he always yearns for the first.

"Take this piece of paper," I told her, giving Salman a meaningful look. "Read it at home and think about it, then hang it up somewhere so in the future it'll protect you from any illusions or missteps."

The servant came back after locking the door and sighed. "What an ugly era this is!" he said. "There no sense of shame or propriety any more."

4

SARA, RACHEL'S ELDER SISTER, is one of the women around whom my doubts concerning my missing manuscript revolve. I have my reasons for believing that, although they are both nebulous and complex.

So how did I get to know her?

My acquaintances with all the women I have either slept with or dallied with without bedding them came about as the result of a wide variety of brilliantly contrived preliminaries. Those unforgettable first delights—how lovely and amicable they were! One gloomy fall day I mounted my horse and headed for the seashore to the east of Murcia. I had every intention of making full use of wind and sea to counter the depression that would sometimes come over me. I was walking along the beach with my horse following behind me when I spotted a woman with a svelte figure and a mop of glistening hair walking a few paces behind me. I proceeded to ignore her and walked the remaining distance to a rocky area where it was difficult to walk. When I turned around to walk back, there was no sign of the woman. On the landward side I looked all over the place, then turned toward the sea. There she was, swimming as though in her own element, rising with the waves, then diving down as they crashed to the beach. Once in a while I could hear her clapping to her own singing and letting out whoops of joy. After first wondering if she might be a jinni or sorceress, I decided that she could be neither. Stopping my horse, I performed the afternoon prayer. No sooner had I finished the appropriate phrases than I heard a female voice behind me.

"So you're a Muslim," the voice said in an assured tone. "I'm one of Moses's people."

She had stopped where she was, and I stared at her in surprise. Her curly hair looked just like a dewy sash fluttering in the breeze and framing a beautiful face.

Praise be to the Creator! Her diaphanous dress was wet and showed every detail of her luxuriant body. How was I supposed to maintain her modesty by turning my eyes away when all I could think of was an even more wonderful pleasure. I wrapped her in my cloak, not so much because I was afraid she might catch cold but merely as a way of keeping my emotions under control and finding a way of talking to her.

"It's rainy," I said. "This weather's cold. Aren't you worried about getting sick?"

By now she had wrapped herself tightly in my cloak and showed as much of her face as she could. "No matter what the season," she replied, "I swim either in the Mediterranean or the Atlantic. My devotion to being at one with salt water is my way of salving my conscience for the Messiah's death. It's also my window on to the manifest abundance of the universe."

These were towering words emerging from the mouth of this strange woman; they made her luscious lips quiver. I paused for a moment before responding to her, trying to determine a better way of behaving toward her. Inside my head all kinds of sentences were clustering together, with both meat and substance. However before I could utter a single word, she walked over to my horse and whispered in its ear. Responding to her touch, the animal moved its head.

"This is an Arabian horse," she said, staring straight at me with her lustrous eyes. "It's purebred, headstrong, and assertive. It's a noble stallion, fully endowed with the spirit of generosity and power. A wonderful horse and a wonderful master!"

She paused for a moment, almost as though she were taking my pulse. "I hereby name him 'The Proud,' even if he has another name."

She asked me if she might ride him, and I agreed. She moved back a bit, then ran at "The Proud" from behind and leapt. Suddenly there she was astride him, just like a ring on a little finger. She took off, hands outstretched like wings ready for takeoff and flight. Framed between land and sea, my horse ran beautifully, something he had never done for me before. I got the impression he was concentrating his attention on the way his rider was clearly at one with him and wanted to respond as much as possible to her imperious demands. After she had ridden him for seven circuits, she brought him back to me and asked me to get on behind her and hold on to her belt. I did so, and the horse proceeded to take off again, but this time at a trot; it was as if he objected to the way I was adding my weight to hers. Just then, he decided to respond to my commands and took off at a fast gallop. I imagined heaven and earth as a dome, one in which this gorgeous rider and I were wandering and pasturing in its firmament, while between sea and land the wind was blessing us with its purifying wafts and dewy breezes. When the girl sensed that the horse was getting tired, she pulled on the reins and slowed it down to a walk, then leaned over to kiss its head and give it a snuggle. The horse was so content that it kept stamping its feet and neighing with pleasure. In this fashion we covered a certain distance. When we reached some heights with a few houses scattered around, she stopped the horse opposite a small house overlooking the sea.

"This is my little nest," she said.

I immediately dismounted, muttering some appropriate words to express my pleasure, and made ready to leave. However, she surprised me by saying, "I'm up higher than you are, so, if you like, grab me and carry me inside." I led the horse to an enclosure alongside the house with both grass and shade, then pulled its rider very gently toward me, carried her toward the door, and kicked it open. She invited me to complete the mission, while for my part I kept saying a silent prayer that I might keep my emotions under control as I struggled with her pulsating beauty on the one hand and my palpitating heart on the other.

"Put me down in front of that screen," she said, "and wait for me on that chair."

I did exactly that. She gave me back my overcoat with thanks and disappeared behind the screen. I got the impression she was washing herself so she could put on some perfume and change her clothes. My hunch proved to be correct, since, when she emerged, she was looking even more radiantly beautiful than before. Her hair was dry and combed; the kohl on her lovely, honey-colored eyes made them look even wider and brighter. Her body exuded the most delicate and subtle of perfumes. She offered me a plate of fruit and a cup of milk. She sat down, ate some of the food, and took sips from a glass of wine, which was probably permitted in her faith. I asked her what her name was. She gave me a smile.

"My name is Sara, daughter of Maymun," she replied, biting her finger. "I'm a descendant of Musa ibn Maymun. Have you heard of him?"

"You mean, 'Abdallah Musa ibn Ishaq ibn Maymun?* How could I not have heard of him? I've already been reading his *Proofs for the Perplexed,* and, God willing, I'll be doing some more."

"I too have read parts of that book, but I emerged from the process just the way I started: perplexed, indeed totally uncertain about anything. Do you think it's because I am one of those impatient people whom the author doesn't allow to read his text even with a tutor? But, in any case, let's forget about such aimless and useless matters. Tell me about yourself."

It occurred to me that I should probably inform this grumbler that her own ancestor and Ibn Rushd* were both of the same stripe, in that neither of them gives their readership the kind of detailed explanations that people really need, even specialists on dialectics and theology. However, I decided instead to answer her question.

"I'm a practicing Muslim, as you can see, a son of both East and West, and a permanent student of knowledge, though, as the prophetic tradition puts it, it be in China . . ."

"But what's your name, horse-rider?"

"'Abd al-Haqq ibn Dara."

She seemed to find my lineage somewhat strange and guessed that it was either Sufi or military. Even so she asked for no further explanation.

"I'm a Spanish Jew," she continued, "inheritor of the Torah, originator of the great covenant of monotheism, a faith that has been corrupted by rabbis and radical pseudo-interpreters of doctrine who have travestied the covenant of the Promised Land and God's chosen people. It's as though Abraham—God's blessing be upon him!—acted in their exclusive interest, wandering in the wilderness only in order to encounter their God, and not desiring to see the face of the god in all people. You should know, Ibn Dara, that I had a younger brother who dared to argue with them. They subjected him to all kinds of intrigue and insult. They put him in prison, whipped him, and cut off half his beard, so much so that he died of anger and sorrow."

She sighed and fell silent. I seized the opportunity to cheer her up a bit.

"I belong to the religion of Muhammad," I said, "the seal and scented closure of the great monotheistic tradition. We maintain a firm linkage to the Abrahamic tradition of prophets and messengers. In Spain we too have our share of jurists who manage to cause dissent and lead believers astray."

A white cat emerged from a room close by, leapt into my lap, and curled up with a few purrs of amiable contentment.

"That cat has decided it likes my house," my hostess informed me. "I feed it when I'm here, and it looks for its own food when I'm away. I've called it Najma."

"Najma looks very intelligent and astute, quite apart from the fact that she's a beautiful cat. Aren't I blessed to be with such a cat and her owner?"

As I mouthed those words, I stroked the cat's back. Sara's eyes gleamed to show that she fully understood that in using such words I was actually referring to her, just as I had taken her words about my horse as referring to me. One good turn deserves another, as the saying goes, and, as yet another has it, the person who makes the first move is offering the most.

So that was my first encounter with Sara ibn Maymun. As was my custom with overtures such as this one, I struck a jovial tone and kept my inclinations and desires in check with a display of discretion and innocent amusement. When I asked her permission to leave, she gave me a neutral kind of look, then accompanied me with some pleasantries to the place where my horse was tethered. She told me the times when she was to be found at this cottage of hers by the sea and when she was in Murcia itself.

This then was the first of many other clandestine rendezvous; some of them involved conversations, others sex. Both of us managed to pluck a good deal of fruit from the experience; together we concentrated body and mind on direct access to the essence of things rather than the external shell and on the reconciliation of opposites and differences. In the end she would witness to my Qur'an while I would point to the veracity of her Torah. Our only quest and ambition was the sheer pleasure of enlightenment and attraction.

One day the anticipatable happened: a separation that lasted for six months or more. Sara was married to a Jewish man, who then proceeded to divorce her for reasons I was disinclined to find out. Her relationship with her family and the rabbis favored by her father deteriorated. When she responded to my invitation and came to see me one morning disguised as a Muslim woman, I realized how such cruel circumstances had dealt with her. No sooner had she removed her billowing veil than her wan, unhappy face was revealed along with her sickly frame.

"See what they've done to me!" she said as she sat opposite me at a table full of milk and sweetmeats. "The reconquistadors are tightening the circles around the Jews and Muslims of Murcia, and yet my own people are doing their very best to throttle me as well. Day and night, Ibn Dara, I keep thinking of escaping to the Maghrib or even farther away!"

"Sara, do not despair of God's mercy," I replied. "Don't be too hasty. Hardships like these are always followed by release. 'Abd al-'Ali along with your sister, Rachel, is not too well, and, as you may have noticed, I'm not well myself. I'm feeling unhappy partly because we're losing our beloved Spain bit by bit, fortress by fortress, and partly because I've lost a manuscript that I wrote in a very special language, the language of enticement, dream, and luminosity. I'm presuming that it's been stolen . . ."

For a moment she looked down, then gave me a fixed stare. "'Ali can divorce my sister if he wants," she said, "but, if you've any doubts about me, then you're wrong . . ."

"No, no, heaven forfend! I've asked you to come to find out how you are and tell you about my own circumstances. It's your advice I want, that's all."

"So now all doubts about the Jewish woman have been removed for sure. You can continue your routine with your other girlfriends. And don't forget the polytheists among them either!"

She gave me that final piece of advice as she was standing up and adjusting her dress. Stretching out her hand, she touched my neck, then went ahead of me to the door and vanished, leaving me with the impression that I might never see her again.

5

"DON'T FORGET THE POLYTHEISTS AMONG THEM!" she had said.

I only got to know one of them; her name was Balqis. I lost track of her as well just before the manuscript went missing. Her house was on the southern outskirts of Murcia and was full of statues and icons. I visited her twice or more, and so did she to my residence. Then suddenly our relationship was broken off when she went away, I don't know where. Our contact never went beyond pithy, subtle conversation, a situation made necessary by the shortage of time, the need to be careful, and the avoidance of cocked ears and prying eyes. We spent most of our time talking about theological issues and major life questions.

I recall that on one occasion she invited me to attend the obsequies for the shaykh of a heretical sect known as "the earth-watchers," a group whom she served as amanuensis. First she vouched for me with the leaders of the sect, then I accepted the invitation on the premise that it is better to know things than to remain in ignorance, especially if the experience involves both listening and seeing. One of the most amazing things I saw and later confirmed through the medium of texts composed by my inviter was the following homily sent to the deceased caliph by his successor. Here are some of its most cogent paragraphs:

"Colleagues, if those of us taking part in this ceremony in which we are to say farewell to our revered master are few in number, that is because of the instructions in his last will and testament, namely that there should be not the slightest trace of either a cloak or religious beard during the rites of committal to his final resting place.

"It is no secret that the dearly departed—and may the earth welcome his remains into its bosom—was not in agreement with any of the existing religious systems. He was firmly convinced that it was the earth that was our mother, creator, and sustainer, and that for us humans that was all that was needed (and all that in spite of its insignificance in the system of galaxies). In the beginning there had been the great bang from which other celestial systems had emerged, duly ordained for new and remote times and eras.

"That was his firm belief, and in his view it was no less valid and reliable and no more rigid and ingrained that any other cryptic or religious faith system.

"Throughout his rich and fulfilling life he adamantly refused to exchange this belief of his for any promise of salvation involving some other world that was hypothetical or even imaginary or for any wager that was religiously opportunistic or ethically cowardly in the opinion of both himself and our careful sect.

"So let us affirm here that our late lamented master showed exemplary fidelity to his earthly belief, even though it did not provide him with as much as it took from him later in life in the form of the infirmities of old age and painful illness.

"The final words in his will to both us and those who follow our path are that we should take loving care of the rights of the earth and ensure that we stick to them, not polluting its waters and soil from which we all emerged into existence; nor should we chop down forests, which serve as the earth's lungs and symbols of its freshness. We must also make sure to maintain the purest level of air quality, otherwise we will all be poisoned and fade away.

"Everyone has their own private history with the heavens. However our dear departed master preferred to weave his own personal tale with the earth, it being the site of our coming to life, our maturity, and our one final resting place. Now may he return to its fold, safe and sound, and may we follow his lead along the clear path, confident, calm, and devoted to the earth."

It was only a month later, maybe less, that Balqis told me that she had left this sect, not in order to set up a rival one but rather to escape the rigidity and fanciful beliefs of the community. She was eager to discover her path to salvation as a result of her own efforts, by means of experience, study, contemplation, and insight. From the time of my first acquaintance with her, this highly cerebral woman never missed an opportunity to poke fun at the absolute and find fault with it. It was almost as though she regarded it as a quarrelsome neighbor or a thoroughly tedious person, someone who deserved to be ripped apart with her sharp and immaculately polished nails. But as she lived her life from one day to the next in a complete relativism, the absolute would sometimes infiltrate into her world and talk to her, as she readily admitted. "I'm falling," she would shout, asking for help; "I'm drowning. Somebody save me and lift me out!"

Balqis's sense of guilt would evaporate and disappear—God's truth!—behind the palpitations of her wounded being and the sheer eloquence of her deep-seated despair. Whether I accepted or rejected them, her questions and ideas generally had a sensitivity and a depth that required me to rouse myself and pay close attention, a feeling that was blended with a certain degree of amazement and even perplexity. She would often say things that I cannot recall exactly now, but what follows is an approximation:

"By the truth of the Lords of the universe, Ibn Dara, I will tell you that, were it not for your generous heart and clear intellect, I would not be opening my heart to you. I am Balqis, or what is left of her. Even though I am not yet thirty years old, I feel I'm at a low ebb. For me life consists merely of a clutch of fancies and confused dreams; no more. Since my personal crises first emerged, they have neither burst into the open nor have they in any way lessened. This countenance of mine that I turn toward you—and I have no other—wears me out since the processes of traveling and settling down so often have totally worn me out. I have no way of making it look better, even if I were to decide to start using creams and makeup.

"I was just twenty when my mother died. She was utterly distressed by the death of my father at the Battle of al-'Iqab. My elder brother had left the country and not returned; it felt as though the earth had swallowed him up or somehow squeezed him into the vacant third of it. Thereafter I married a drunkard. He used to drink alcohol neat, and never stopped until it killed him. I was left on my own, so I married another man, a stupid miser. He stipulated that there would be no wedding ceremony and no reception afterward, but even so I accepted. He went on to demand that there would no singing, drumming, or celebrations; this time I refused. He went away for a month to think about it and came back to announce that he would agree to marry me, and then I could sing and dance a bit with him playing the tambourine, but there would still be no band and no one else present. I reluctantly agreed because the rogue went on to yell, 'If you don't agree, I'll commit suicide.' My wedding night passed the way I wanted, but afterward he started playing tricks on me. 'Fula,' he would say in amazement (and that is what he called me), 'how puny and weak we are! Time keeps slipping away between our hands like quicksilver, crushing our senses and bodies. Stop the bleeding, Fula, stop the bleeding, or else I'll up and do something bad . . .'

"One spring day this imbecile put me on his donkey and told me we were going for a ride into the western desert. He had decided to leave me there, the pretext being that I was barren and stubborn as well. He suggested that I start counting pebbles while I waited for him to return riding Buraq,* the mighty horse who could touch the clouds and encircle the sky. With that he left, and I never set eyes on him again.

"What happened to me in the desert is amazing in itself. I was incredibly thirsty, but there was, of course, no water. As I wandered around, the sun was a series of red-hot brass bars burning my back. I kept mouthing some complex words that I can only remember because the camelteer who rescued me told me what they were. 'Lord of Lords,' I yelled as loudly as I could, 'why did You spread out the earth, and yet You did not roll it up into a ball? Why did You create the universe in six days and not in the flash of an eye? What do You gain, what goal do You have, in torturing me with such bad fortune, such ongoing evil, such continuing barrenness? I have high hopes of dying, and yet what is there between my burial and my resurrection, between my gathering on the last day and my being brought to account? How many lengthy ages and eras must pass while I wait?'

"I gave thanks to those deities who made sure that the Bedouin did not understand what I'd been saying. If he had, he would certainly have passed it on to others and denounced me. I praise them too for preserving at least part of my intellect—at least, that's how I saw it, even though my ordeal had made me terribly thin and bloated.

"So here I am today, doing my best to straighten things out for myself. Sometimes it works to my benefit, at least as far as I can tell; at others, to my disadvantage.

"But how am I supposed to evaluate my situation when this entire country seems to be utterly devoid of any notion of the Lord's spirit? Every part of it seems headed for collapse and destruction. Have I worn you out, Ibn Dara, with all this talk?"

"No, no," I replied, "heaven forbid!"

"If only you knew about the secret of my addiction to making complex statements! My body is an abyss of perdition. It causes me this tinnitus in my ears; it never stops whenever I speak or am spoken to. So please talk to me so that I can stop. You can talk about whatever you want."

It is never easy to hold a conversation with a woman such as she, one who has wounds of both body and spirit. The tongue may utter things that only manage to scrape the wounds, or the phrases may turn out to bear a variety of viewpoints and modes of interpretation. For that reason my tack with her involved concision and a resort to fleeting illusions. I can still recall what I told her:

"As you can see for yourself, Balqis, this is a period that brings tears to the eyes and agony to the heart. The catastrophes and disasters are enormous in both their impact and their dimensions, dragging everything down into their vortex. All of us are being tested, you included. Some of us can endure it and carry on, while others grow weak and fade away. You are in no way like the latter, rather much closer to the former. It is one struggle after another, until like discarded skin you find yourself gradually liberated from your former dishonor and able to move beyond your scandalous conduct through a whole series of subtle moves. True and enduring beauty is acquired and constructed on the basis of hard work and knowledge, especially when you have yet to reach the stage of total self-devotion to the loftier realms . . ."

I recall that at this point my interlocutor turned toward me. The look on her face suggested both severe doubts and considerable perplexity regarding what I had suggested to her. She described some of her statuary to me and then asked why I had not upbraided her for having them. I answered that, just as was the case with the great sage Ibn al-'Arabi,* my heart too was now open to every kind of image. "Even a house of idols?" she asked, to which I nodded a positive reply. She now talked about holy texts, to the effect that the God of the Gospels did not create such idols in his own image, while the God of the Qur'an did not release them from the state they were already in. I got the impression that this lonely woman only had minor deities to compensate for the fire that burned within her and the lack of relationship with the Most High. Those deities were visible and near, so that she was able to converse with them at close range, chide them, and even find fault with them occasionally. As a result, when her illusions vanished and she was granted a sudden clarity of vision, they would connect her, if only for a moment, to their Lord on high, genuflecting and uttering words of praise as they did so. For her part she would be in her own special prayer-room, candles lit and tongue mouthing paeans of praise.

Were a chaste level of shyness to be an actual person, then it might well fall victim to those people who fire themselves up in a competition to yell out in public—each one on his own terms: "I'm the unluckiest person alive!"

A Muslim Suicide | 35

I know people who have longed to have such a pronouncement recorded as a final confession ex post facto. Balqis was one of them. Before she disappeared, she left me the following note:

"Ibn Sab'in, my relationships with other people and the world in general can be likened to food that's hard to swallow. I am unloved and truly barren. You can say that I'm a purse of coins, a strait with no exit. Do you hear me? A strait with no exit! My individuality and yours no longer share warm, friendly greetings, as used to be the case in a wonderful period that has now passed. So I bid you a final farewell. Now I leave in order to disappear completely, intoxicated by oblivion, fumigated, shattered in spirit, fractured in body. By the truth of my Lord and yours, paradise will never really be paradise unless a time comes when those who enter its doors are like me."

Ah, such sterility, such despair!

Balqis, this polytheist in some compelling metaphorical sense, would not be one to steal my manuscript; she would have had neither control over it nor need of it. Any dream I might have of finding this lost love from the past—even supposing I had left my attachment to it extending behind me—was clearly useless. Any quest for Balqis would be a waste of time, a fading mirage.

6

Salman was by origin a Visigoth, but he converted to Islam and learned Arabic. He married a Muslim woman, then lost her, leaving him childless. Thereafter he chose a life of asceticism and self-denial and entered my own service.

He was a devout and charitable person, someone who kept me in touch with the poor and indigent population. He would tell me about their situation and choose the neediest among them to receive my help, going to enormous lengths to ensure that such help indeed reached them. Apart from times when he was either asleep or praying, you would see him going about his daily chores, whether routine or urgent. He used to focus his entire attention on such things, to such an extent that he gave the impression of trying to avoid thinking about those major issues that, as he could see for himself, were keeping me fully preoccupied. Another of his qualities consisted in his uncanny ability to make himself scarce whenever I chose to spend some time studying in seclusion. Whenever he came back after fetching what I needed from the city, you would see him making every effort to ensure that I would not be disturbed, only talking to me when I asked him for something or else when something else happened that made it impossible to remain silent.

Salman!

Tall and skinny, he looked just like a sprite residing in the walls.

"A group of students came to see you, Sir," he would say in his gruff voice. "They were asking after your health and sending you their greetings. I responded on your behalf and sent them away. I've heated the water for the ritual washing, and lunch is ready."

"God reward you! Bring me the water and a bowl. If the students come back tomorrow, let them in."

"Tomorrow, not before?"

"Yes, tomorrow. After lunch, get my horse ready."

I made my way through the city's alleyways and squares on foot, leading my horse behind me. The expressions on the faces of those Muslims who were fully aware of the current situation looked more and more gloomy and depressed; it was almost as though some kind of mourning process, one with no limit or end, were weighing them all down. It was the Muslim defeat at the Battle of al-'Iqab that had started it all, and the loss of Cordoba and Valencia had only made things that much worse. The Almohads* were weak and at odds with each other, and each year brought still more disasters and calamities.

In the alleys and streets people would make their way to taverns, mosques, or houses in quest of refuge. They were in a permanent state of panic, dizzy with fear, as though perched on the edge of a precipice and faced with the prospect of inevitable destruction. In order to plan for the worst and find some sort of relief, a number of stratagems had been developed, including regular indulgence in pleasures, both public and private, hoarding goods and being niggardly about sharing them, and lastly devotion to a life of seclusion and prayer.

Once I had traversed the inhabited parts of the city and reached the desert area that extended all the way to the mountains of the west, I prepared to mount my horse. Just then a group of young men came up and surrounded me. Some of them I already knew, including 'Abd al-'Ali and al-Sadiq. They greeted me with considerable emotion, and I returned their greeting, making it obvious at the same time how surprised I was that they had suddenly appeared. I invited them all to sit down with me by an aging oak tree. I asked them what was on their minds. It was the eldest among them, al-Sadiq al-Shatibi, who spoke up.

"This morning, Sir, we all came to your house," he said. "Salman sent us away. If the situation weren't so bad, we would not have come without an appointment."

"I am aware of it, al-Sadiq. Get to the point."

"Yesterday we were in the mosque, reading books that you had recommended that we study carefully. A jurist named 'Abd al-Qadir al-Qabri invited someone we know well to join his circle of students. No sooner had a group gathered around him than he pronounced the *bismillah** and *hawqala**; then he started ranting and raving, claiming that philosophers and mystics were not real Muslims, but were committing all kinds of heresy and blasphemy. He kept adducing all manner of Qur'anic verses and prophetic hadith in the process. He prayed to God to root them out of al-Andalus and purge the Islamic religion of their poison and filth. By way of proof of what he was claiming, the only name he cited was yours, Sir, although the text he quoted from was clearly a forgery. He told the group that the text was written in your own hand. He took the text out of his sleeve and read it out in ringing tones: 'Their leader, Ibn Sab'in, says, "In stating that there is no prophet after me, Ibn Amina, the Prophet Muhammad, has exaggerated." I ask God's forgiveness for citing such gross heresy. God have mercy, have mercy, have mercy.'

"He kept repeating the phrase 'God have mercy' over and over again," said 'Abd al-'Ali, continuing the account. "All the while his face was red, his neck muscles were bulging, and spit was flying everywhere. The naïve folk who were listening kept following his words, but we all stood up as one man. We pointed out to this gross provocateur that he should beware of God's wrath by indulging in such patent slander and falsehood. We told him that the quotation he had cited involved a deliberate reversal of the consonants in one of the words in the text recited by our revered master; nothing more and nothing less. We had all memorized the text in question; it reads 'In stating "there is no prophet after me," Ibn Amina, the Prophet Muhammad, was postulating [R-J-H], not exaggerating [H-J-R].'"

"With that," al-Sadiq now continued, "this jurist erupted with anger. He kept denying our version and uttering oaths, pointing to the text that he claimed to be in your handwriting. I snatched it from him so I could compare it with the handwriting on the copy that I had with me. Once it became clear that the handwriting was completely different, I showed it to some people standing around me and then proceeded to curse this deceitful and crooked jurist. His only way out was to claim that you could alter your handwriting because you were knowledgeable about alchemy, numerology, cryptography, and, he added, magic. With that, the entire mosque erupted in chaos, and people started pelting us with their sandals. We found ourselves expelled from God's own house. Heaven alone knows what might have happened if we hadn't decided to escape."

I gave them a friendly smile, hoping that I could calm their worries and make light of the whole thing.

"You did well," I told them. "God's houses are intended for His worship, not for spreading dissent and schism among believers. There is a total of seven copies of the text. On each one I write that it is a certified copy. Tell the followers of this jurist al-Qabri to compare the handwriting so they can tell the difference between the genuine ones and the fakes. If they change their tune, then that's what we really want. However, if they persist in their errors, then God is the only true guide. Decide what it is you truly wish, then be neither afraid nor sorrowful . . ."

"It's not ourselves we're worried about," said a sturdy and athletic young man, his eyes agleam, "it's you, Sir. What frightens us is the thought that stupid people who are intent on distorting our religious faith are going to tighten the noose around you and even do you actual harm. We've actually thought about setting up a roster to guard your house and accompany you wherever you need to go."

All the others in the group showed that they agreed with what the young man had said. I asked him what his name was and what job he had. He told me his name was 'Amr from Cordoba. When Valencia had fallen to the Christians and his father had been treacherously murdered, he had left the city. He added that he was now working in Murcia as an itinerant bookseller. He was studying Sufi ethics and some mathematics.

I welcomed him among his new colleagues and congratulated him on his job and his course of studies.

"Young men," I replied, "our fight is not with jurists; after all, they are part of our religious community. No, the real fight is against the Christians who are trying to reconquer the Peninsula by force of arms. They want to defeat us, then expel us from Spain altogether. Just consider Cordoba, the priceless pearl in the necklace, and other cities and fortresses, the way they have been wrested from us, not to mention other cities that have been handed over to the Christians through treaties signed by our utterly corrupt and feckless Muslim rulers. We ask God's protection from their evil intentions and deeds! Then there are Murcia, Seville, and other cities in the far south, all of them up for grabs. The only way that they can be saved is by amassing a huge armed force like the one the original Almohads used when they first came to Spain. Through constant prayers to God and remembrance of his divine unity they were granted victory. In this ongoing struggle each of you has a role to play. It is up to you to do whatever you can. Where jurists are concerned, confront them with even better arguments. Then, if they persist in their erroneous and heretical ways, move away and ignore them. They are the ones that the Prophet Muhammad is referring to in his noble hadith:

'Woe to my community when faced with evil scholars!' Beyond that, Abu Talib of Mecca* said things about such people that you have all memorized by heart."

At this point 'Abd al-'Ali and some of his companions chimed in as one voice: "'The scholars of this world are stalled in their progress toward the next. They have neither carved out a path forward, nor have they allowed believers to make their own way toward God.'"

"But I have to tell you all," I responded by way of instruction and warning, "that any of you who respond to violence with violence may have no affiliation with me, nor will I follow their path . . ."

'Amr looked a bit depressed. "So are we supposed to offer them the other cheek," he asked, "the way the Christians say you should?"

I looked down for a moment, thinking of a way to answer. "The Prophet of God was once asked, 'Wherein lies authority?' To which he replied, 'The mind.' On that basis, any resort to violence implies a weakening and breach of the role of the intellect. That is precisely the kind of outrage that the later Almoravids* and their pseudo-legists committed when they burned Imam al-Ghazali's* great work, *The Revival of the Religious Sciences*. The same applies to Ibn Tumart* as well when he declared the Almoravids heretics and regarded the struggle against them as being more urgent and important than that of the Byzantines. To the extent possible try to avoid the evils of excess and blind fanaticism that are so prevalent within your own Muslim community. As you proceed on your way, invoke the virtues of patience, resolution, and lofty aspiration in order to cope with the muddy terrain you have to traverse. Our next meeting will be as usual at the noon prayer on Friday. Now go and drink from the sources of your chosen subjects and don't forget books and texts that I've recommended to you. Among them I can recall the speeches and aphorisms of Imam 'Ali ibn Abi Talib,* *The Divine Signs* by al-Tawhidi,* al-Harawi's* *Stations of the Wayfarer,* and Ibn al-'Arif al-Sanhaji's* *Benefits of Sessions*. Now go in peace whence you came."

The group of young men went on their way silently, and with heavy tread. I got on my horse and went my own way. I cut across fields and meadows where the end-of-summer sun was decorating their soil with glimmering patches of light. Eventually I reached a forest whose lofty trees covered the hillside all the way to the top. The tree branches were swaying in the east wind, exuding the dampness of water-wheels and rivers and the sweet scents of plants and crops.

I reached the very top of the hill on foot, with my horse behind me, and headed at once for the hidden cave to which I would resort as a safe refuge whenever need demanded. Ever since I had discovered it, I had decided to use it as a good omen and blessing by naming it "my own Hira'."* Once I was there, even my horse enjoyed the lush vegetation and pure air. Inside the cave I prayed the afternoon prayer, then sat watching through the entrance as the sun's violet rays colored the distant mountains on the horizon and announced the imminent arrival of sunset.

Once again, when it came to inspiration and harvesting of ideas, there was just drought and more drought!

"If this blockage continues," I told myself, "then there's no hope left in life. It'll be better for me to throw myself off the top of this mountain. Even though there are obvious differences, didn't the same sentiment affect Muhammad, the Lord of Creation? That was the time when Gabriel left him and the sources of inspiration were cut off. But then, inspiration came back again when Surat al-Duha* was revealed, and Muhammad lived life anew, bolstered by hope and satisfaction."

I sat on the floor of the cave, overwhelmed by my own desperation. It was clear that I needed to rid my mind of everything, exclude all extraneous thoughts, and subject my head to a thorough process of cleansing, until I reached a point at which I wasn't thinking about anything at all. That nothingness I was craving resembled a uniform void, with no frame, limit, plot, or narrative.

However, no sooner had I embarked on this project than I was compelled to grab hold of my self once again because the state in which I found myself involved irresolvable contradictions. I was contemplating the process of not thinking about anything, but then I came to realize that my rash, foolhardy plan could only be achieved if I were able to surmount my own feelings and bodily frame, if I were to be substantiated in absolute knowledge and knowledge of the absolute. And that was something that I had as yet neither the ability nor the patience to achieve.

I imagined that a voice was ringing in my ears. "Your only way out," it kept telling me, "is by recovering your lost manuscript. It constitutes the foundation of your sublime aspirations and the very icon of your soul's curative quest."

With that I stood up and decided to return to my residence. I had been waiting patiently for so long that I was afraid I might fall asleep or else something bad might happen once night fell and the animals of the area came out.

7

ON THURSDAY MORNING I woke up early. My tongue still felt damp from a question that I had been asking myself while asleep: could Juanita, the Christian girl, possibly be the thief?

I had met this particular woman over a year ago, but two months earlier we had parted for reasons that I will disclose below. She was from a Christian family of Visigoth origins, but preferred to live among the Muslim community in Murcia, untroubled and unconcerned. I got to know her in a way that I was to know no other women either before or after.

It had happened through one of those amazing pieces of chance that time only offers very rarely. One morning I was heading for a copyist's shop on my way to the mosque when a svelte woman blocked my path. How gorgeous she was! She asked me the time in a singing, vulnerable voice. Taking my astrolabe out of my bag, I told her it was ten or thereabouts. She sighed, in the process revealing more of her bosom. She gave me a languid and frivolous look and then went on her way, but not before saying, "I was asking you about the final hour, not what time it is now!"

A few days went by, and I kept hoping that I would bump into this woman again, either on my way to the mosque or else in one of the alleyways or squares where I would habitually walk in a surreptitious search among Christian girls for one who resembled the one I was looking for—few though they might well be. When the search had worn me out, I decided to give up and concentrate instead on loftier and more profitable pursuits in the realms of knowledge and food for the heart. Even so I could not stop wondering to myself why this lovely woman had wanted to know about the final hour, almost as though in some way she were looking forward to it and wanted to make it come quicker. When it comes to contemplation on such matters, an irony of this kind is not easily resolved or forgotten.

Toward noon one morning I was returning to my house after a long session with my students in the small mosque. My eyes fell on a woman who looked like an exact copy of the Christian woman I had met earlier, except that there was a slight difference in hairstyle and in the way she walked. My mind entirely out of control, I walked over and asked her if she now knew when the final hour would come. My question alarmed her somewhat, so my next move was to ask her if she knew what time it was now. In reply she told me I could only get what I wanted if I followed her to her house. I nodded in agreement and followed a few yards behind her. I was entirely under the control of my animal instincts, and also motivated by a desire to discover the truth behind a nagging secret. The woman led me through alleys and quarters, some of them crammed with people on foot, others totally empty. Eventually she stopped in front of a house and signaled to me to follow her inside. Lowering my turban over my forehead and praying for a safe outcome, I did as she asked.

We were in a large room. She invited me to sit down on a comfortable couch while she adjusted her dress and attended to the needs of a dog that she treated with great fondness. The dog stared hard at me and barked a little. The entire house was a model of tidiness and elegance. The courtyard was attractively furnished and the floor was strewn with Persian rugs of matching colors and shapes. Alcoves were decorated with lamps that gave off a soft light, and the walls were covered with icons, paintings of the crucifixion of Christ, and saints with heads encircled by brilliant haloes.

The woman seemed anxious to avoid a long wait or else wanted to put my mind at ease, so she started talking at length. I gathered that she had divorced her husband, who was a corrupt drunkard, and had also rejected her debauched and unfaithful lover. At this point in her life her loyal and reliable dog was the only creature that kept her happy. I also understood that in matters of love she wanted to be the one in charge, a chooser rather than a follower; she preferred men who were handsome, reticent, and obedient. The only thing that in any way distracted me from her lengthy statement was the exquisite scents wafting up from the rosewater; maybe she bathed in it.

Once she had returned after perfuming herself and putting on costly jewelry and an expensive translucent dress, she looked even more gorgeous and amazing than she had before. She sat down beside me, obviously enjoying the glass of wine she was holding. She offered me a cup of mare's milk, then invited me to eat whatever I liked from a bowl filled with different kinds of fruit. Once that was done, she proceeded to upbraid me for trying to pick up women by asking them what the time was. Then she tried to make light of it in a way that astonished me.

"When someone like you is already promised eternity, how can you ask about the time?"

I expressed my thanks for her good opinion of me, but, without going into enormous detail to defend myself and my intentions, I proceeded to tell her briefly what had happened to me with the other woman who looked exactly like her. I explained that I had had no other motivation. It was clear that she believed my story, because she relaxed a bit. She swore by Mary and the Son of God that she was not the woman I had spoken about. Mentioning her own name and learning my own, she stated that fate had obviously decided to bring us together. I did not wish to appear rude or discourteous, so I agreed with her. As they say, never look a gift horse in the mouth!

Just then her necklace fell off her neck. I immediately picked it up and accepted her request that I clip it behind her neck once again. As I did so, she told me how scared she was that this necklace and the rest of her jewelry might be stolen by thieves with neither religious beliefs nor any sense of morality. She only wore such things, she told me, when she had time to relax and enjoy herself. She went on to say that this was one such occasion. With that she leaned over in my direction.

"I notice that you've perfumed yourself with incense," she said, "and are wearing essence of musk. So am I right in thinking that, like the Prophet of your own faith, you are partial to the delights of this world and women?"

I nodded in response. With regard to what happened next:

> What happened happened as I recall,
> So think nice thoughts and do not ask for details.

So that is how I came to know Juanita Arbos. Our relationship continued for some time, like the tide's ebb and flow. In that period I came to realize that her attitude toward life—and to her own life as an example—involved a crystalline, almost mechanical purity, whence stemmed her extraordinary concern with her own person and a parallel fear of anything that might muddy the waters or cause complications. The same posture also accounted for her view of illness as an impenetrable divide and process of emaciation. The time would come, she used to say, when her own body and soul would be so afflicted, in which case she would certainly commit hara-kiri. Asked about the meaning of that last phrase, she would make gestures to indicate that she was talking about suicide.

Juanita, who was by no means a religious person, did not go so far as to live and breathe her life as a complete lie, but she was well aware that life—her own life, at least—was a continuing complaint addressed to a stubborn and comprehensive weakness that she felt. For that reason, she would regularly indulge, according to her own relatives, in a bad habit, one that required of her that she convert all her ideas into utterly hyperbolic and opaque idealizations. She never spoke about the way things actually are, but rather the way it would be nice if they were. She followed this practice all the time as a way of making the world more tolerable for herself and people more acceptable company. However, and more's the pity, there were very few people indeed who appreciated the way she was performing these mental maneuvers and bearing her own existential burden.

Living among Muslims and Jews, Juanita the Christian was like a fish in the sea. Even so, she had nothing to say about the way her fellow Christians were waging war against the cities of Spain or about the various battles and disasters. It was as though she were standing outside the realms of history. If an echo of those events or a breath of wind reached her ears, she would merely arch her eyebrows in amazement or denial, then take refuge within her own internal domain like a suckling animal nestling in its mother's lap.

Juanita could babble on and on; in fact, she was a chatterer par excellence!

If you watched her talking, you would be convinced that, when it came to rolling up sentences and tossing them at people, she was a totally exceptional phenomenon. For her, talking preempted all her other daily needs. If she was interrupted or lost her train of thought, she looked as though she were perched on the edge of a precipice or confronting a potentially crushing danger. Whenever she was forced to be brief, she seemed to be having trouble breathing. In the context of her all-powerful tongue, my own utterances—and you can compare my own situation to that of others—consisted simply of periods, commas, and prepositions, recollection of which is directly connected to things she forgot, times when either she was asking me for a reference of some kind or else arguments were being summarized and collected. Topics discussed ranged from her dog (and what a dog it was!) to dress, jewelry, and powders, moving on to evidence of the existence of jinn, the evil eye, and other trifles, all of them issues that the primary speaker managed to raise to the status of the rarest pearls. When it came to her blatant opposition to male chauvinism, her tongue turned into an industrial torch. One might try to blow on it as hard as possible, throttle it with a sack, or spray it with a hose, but none of them was of the slightest use.

She told me once about a fierce argument she had had with one of her former lovers. "You blame me for talking too much," she had protested, "but you men have had a monopoly on talking for hundreds of years. You have exploited it to oppress and muzzle the rights of my wretched sex. So, if I expatiate now and choose to be more aggressive, that's not just for my own sake. I'm acting as spokesperson for all those compliant, silent women throughout history. I'm taking revenge for all of them."

She went on to tell me that her foe had stammered a reply. "I think you're exaggerating," he said. "But, even if you're right, am I to be punished now for the crimes committed by my ancestors in past generations?"

"Yes," she replied, "it's a terrible account that you have to settle; indeed a colossal debt you all owe. Men of the current generation like you must inevitably participate in the process of settling it."

With that the man lost his temper and declared that from now on he would dispense with her beauty. He preferred to leave her rather than to have to swallow sentence after sentence of her nonstop flow of verbiage. He justified his decision by saying that he had to take pity on his ears and hold firm to the vision he had of the complete, ideal woman.

When female company is involved, one has to keep a close watch on elements of similarity, even when there are obvious differences involved that do not actually cause any change in the basic resemblance. Juanita reminds me of a Muslim woman whose name I have forgotten, someone who was for ever bewailing the way she would eventually be joining herself to God on high—whether dying in bed or through suicide. She decided that the principal reason lay in the sheer paucity of lovers around her, all of which resulted in her tongue's shrinking away to nothing and a forced resort to a life of spinsterdom and isolation. In my now missing manuscript I recorded a passage to the effect that I continued my relationship with her specifically because I was the only person to realize that, where she was concerned, talking was her preferred way of diverting attention from a bitter sense of void that never left her. For her, words were like stones to be hurled at whatever stood in her way. When all the mirrors that enveloped her faded away except for my own, she chose to exempt me from the series of tasks that I could not undertake on my own. It was just a few months later that I received news of her death—may God have mercy on her! Eyewitnesses report that she surrendered her spirit with her mouth open, poised and ready to respond to any and all unexpected and emergency situations . . .

But back to Juanita. Perhaps I should not be surprised that her own demise closely resembled that of the Muslim woman I have just mentioned. We had been apart for a while, but then I heard that her health was rapidly declining. When I went to pay her a visit, she told me about a dire misfortune that had affected her so badly that she would not even name it for me. When I made inquiries, I discovered that what was involved was the death of her beloved dog, a very rare breed. In fact he was more of a puppy. There were pictures of him on the walls of his own special room, which gave ample evidence of the paeans of praise the dog had earned from cognoscenti of canine beauty.

So did I sympathize? To a certain extent, yes, but only by maintaining an untoward level of silence.

One day, while I was ferreting around in the drawers of my desk, I was amazed to come across some drawings I had made of the dead dog. I had preserved his memory in four different poses: the first—and funniest—showed him peeing or shitting under the tender supervision of his mistress; the other three were more varied and showed my beloved holding on to his leash and hurrying along behind him. While she was still mourning the loss of the dog, she obviously drew great consolation from my gift of these drawings, duly accompanied by a note with some sweet, ringing words.

Those drawings are now hanging here and there in the lady's house, along with many others.

On the day that the period of mourning she had designated came to an end, Juanita surprised me by immediately going out and buying two more dogs of the very same breed, and two others as well, all for a high price. She asked me to cover the total costs involved, including accessories and pedigrees. Showing a generosity worthy of Hatim,* I agreed, but only as a way of saying farewell to her and her dog-filled world, one in which for sure no angels ever trod.

The final hours I spent with this spoiled companion convinced me that I was like some kind of wormy excrescence in a universe where even talking about the money I had spent on the dogs was useless in the face of the hold they had on her. Once the four dogs sensed that I was their enemy and that their mistress no longer welcomed me the same way, they started scaring me off by lunging aggressively toward me and barking in chorus or individually. It felt as though they were forcing me to gather up my possessions and hasten my departure. And that is exactly what happened one night when I went on my way, treading lightly and erasing my traces and even the name "The True One" that Juanita had become accustomed to calling me. But, while I may have decided to stay away, I still could not forget her. Once I had withdrawn, I felt sure that a whole host of successors was waiting in the wings.

As part of my search for the missing manuscript, memory is, for sure, a precondition for discovering anything, although it is clearly not enough. But when it comes to more dubious bits of information, the only way that their probabilities can be weighed is by recalling each memory, one by one, and my own connection with them. Beyond that, the choices are either to cancel any residual obligations and say nice things, or else to have the doubts linger and grow stronger still.

In order to put an end to these doubts, I told myself that I had to meet Juanita again and raise the topic with her. I chose a safe and suitable occasion on which to do so. When I broached the topic, I listened as she upbraided me. It would be more appropriate, she said, to feel aggrieved over the loss of someone you loved, whether it be an animal or a human being, or over a valuable item that was irreplaceable; but not over a pile of papers that were utterly useless, neither making you rich nor staving off hunger. If she had come across such papers, she said, she would have fed them to the fire or put them out with the garbage if their owner had not claimed them within a reasonable period of time.

"True One," she went on, "when it comes to generosity, understanding, and lofty purpose, I have never encountered another man like yourself. I hereby swear to you on all the Gospels, indeed on your own Qur'an, that I've never seen your manuscript or stolen it. Believe me, or else cut off this hand of mine if you so wish!"

All my suspicions died in the light of her reddening eyes from which shone the clear indications of truth. And with that, any notion that she might be lying simply vanished.

8

ONCE AGAIN I'M LOST, heading in the wrong direction.

Despair, despair!

What I need to do now is to turn the page and stop looking. From today onward, no more desperate efforts, no more dogged insistence on chasing after a mirage that only leads to another one yet more difficult to grasp.

So, my soul, this is a specific prohibition, a command addressed to you. Sit up and take notice. Tomorrow—Friday—I intend to pray for you in God's house, in the hope that you will come up with an answer or at least some kind of initiative.

I left my house early on Friday and heard my group of seven students summoning each other as though they had been standing guard on my house all night. I glanced around at them; they were following me in a clump, assuming that I was not aware that they were there. I took full advantage of their presence and headed for the perfumers' market where I purchased my favorite vials, along with some toothpicks and incense. I then went to see a bookseller of my acquaintance and paid him what I owed; I also renewed my request for certain titles that I needed. With that I made my way through other markets and locations.

So great was the economic stagnation, lack of money, sense of impending doom, and paralysis that everyone looked utterly glum and disgruntled. I told myself that I might be able to find some relief from the general malaise by taking a walk through a nearby park. I headed for one that may well be the oldest in Murcia. Its courtyards and alcoves were a vivid indication of the general collapse all around: wherever you looked, weeds were overwhelming the plants, and dry rot was eating its way into the trunks and roots of trees. Whatever was left standing and alive was threatened with imminent decay. So, I told myself, here we are witnesses to infection as it transfers itself from the concerns of mankind to the world of plants and even animals. My own anxieties are part of the whole, and God is the only means of escape.

I calculated that it was almost time for the Friday prayer, so I made my way toward the communal mosque, with the seven young men still keeping a close eye on me. People were clustered by the entryway and on the thresholds. There were many male and female beggars as well. My students and other pupils, with some of whom I had become acquainted by now, came over, greeted me, and made a path for me. I meanwhile was doing my best to dispense alms to the poor and needy who stared hard at me as they uttered entreaties and pleas for sympathy. As I listened, I was reminded at times of my own situation, with me uttering pleas of my own for the return of my missing manuscript, and at others of other occasions when, in the very depths of despair, I would pray to my Lord to make me an example and prevent me from stumbling . . .

After we had performed the ritual ablution, we entered the main courtyard, and my companions gathered around me. I asked them to spread out a bit and not to guard me so closely. After all, this place was God's own house, where believers only gathered to worship and share brotherly sentiments. 'Abd al-'Ali, 'Amr, al-Sadiq, and some others all proceeded to remind me that the great legislator, 'Umar ibn al-Khattab,* the second caliph, had been murdered during prayers by someone called Lu'lu'a, not to mention several other pious and holy men who had suffered the same fate.

"Are things that bad now?" I asked.

"Yes," they all responded, "or even worse . . ."

And they were speaking the truth. From time to time, various men passed by the place where we had gathered and were giving me hateful looks.

When the time for the Friday sermon was announced, I went inside the mosque itself and sat in one of the back rows that my companions had reserved for me. They sat all around me. After just a few moments of throat-clearing and muttering, there appeared before us the imam of the mosque and his sermonizer, Abu al-Hamalat, the Maliki jurist, who was renowned for his narrow-mindedness and pedantic ideas. He proceeded to read out a sermon that was carefully framed and repetitive; the content had a good deal of bluster to it, but not much meat. He went to enormous lengths to expose the heresy of philosophers, people who, in his words, disguised themselves in the garb of mystics and spiritual guides. He declared that the danger they posed was even greater than that of the

A Muslim Suicide | 51

Christians. Fighting against such people demanded of Muslims an even more urgent effort. He had other things to say as well, based on outright error and sheer ignorance, the aim being to mislead people and to treat them like idiots. He closed his remarks with a ringing prayer on behalf of Rashid,* Commander of the Faithful; his father, Al-Ma'mun,* the late lamented ruler of Spain and Morocco; and the Muslim community.

We were then called to prayer, and I performed it surrounded by my protective force. I was concentrating my entire being on the One before whom all necks are bowed and who alone possesses life and death in His grasp; He has power over everything. When I had finished praying, 'Amr and his companions urged me to leave the mosque as quickly as possible, and I agreed. As I walked, I was surrounded by them like a sword in its scabbard. Eventually we reached the door, and a hail of stones and sandals rained down on us. With his enormous physique 'Amr picked them up and threw them back. Once we reached the exit door the crowd increased, and people started yelling curses and accusations of heresy and apostasy. I watched as hands were extended in my direction, bent on grabbing what was God's alone; one of them scratched my back with a sharp razor, but 'Amr was quick to grab its owner's hand and deprive him of it in a remarkable show of strength. With that he instructed his companions to take me to a safe location that he named. They proceeded to do so, while he and a group of poor folk kept on repelling their attackers with fisticuffs and a lot of pummeling.

'Abd al-'Ali led us all to a modest, dark shrine on a back street. The servant welcomed us and lit candles so that we could see where to place our feet and sit for a while. He did not ask any questions but made do with simply providing a box, noting that whatever generous gifts were offered would be spent on orphans, the needy, and travelers. I gave the man the very last purse of money I had, and he launched into a prayer for me and my companions, asking God to protect us against the Christian cavalry and infantry who were making their relentless way toward Murcia. If the poor man had realized that the people we were escaping from were not Christians, but Muslims from our own religious community, he would have been disgusted. He might not even have believed it.

For a few moments we sat there waiting in absolute silence; then we could hear echoes of yelling and fighting coming from the direction of the mosque. 'Amr arrived panting, his hands and face covered in blood. Everyone offered him some basic care; then I tended to his wounds, pouring a liquid from one of my vials, then rubbing in some cumin, and lastly wrapping them up in clean bandages. 'Amr rested for a while to recover his strength, then let out a chuckle for which he apologized to me. Some of the others present asked him why he was laughing.

"The servant of this shrine," he told them, "is the twin brother of my teacher when I was young. His name was Muhammad al-Habti. He would regularly ask the students in his Qur'an school the kind of question that contains its own answer: things like, 'Why must people save things for times of need and old age?' 'Why do people wear wool when winter comes and the temperature gets cold?' When I answered the question without any effort, he also used to tell me I'd done well!"

Everyone gave a token laugh, myself included. 'Amr now gestured to one of his companions (who by now numbered eleven) that he should give me his light cape. He then looked straight at me.

"Put that on, Master," he said, "and you'll be safe."

He then told them all to leave the shrine in twos and head for my house with me in the middle. He would guide us through some safe streets, far away from the river and crowded places. With that we left, while the servant anxiously rubbed his hands together, ruing the fact that we had been assaulted by criminals and that the sultan was totally unconcerned about it.

Once inside my house our group regathered. I invited them all to share my food, so Salman set about preparing some dishes that were easy to cook—strips of meat, eggs, cheese, and sweetmeats—all of which provided a particular blessing in that we were all able to eat our fill. Once we had finished, 'Abd al-'Ali introduced me to the ones I had not met before, and they all expressed their devotion in the name of God and their delight at meeting me. All of them were young, in the prime of their youth and fully open to the possibilities of give-and-take. Some of them were already married while others were still waiting. One of them, whose name was 'Adnan from Malaga, asked me for my opinions on what the preacher, Abu al-Hamalat, had said in his sermon where he had prayed for our own ruling dynasty that was busy mixing with the Franks and making them allies in their oppression and humiliation of their fellow Muslims.

"Unfortunately, my friend," I replied, "this preacher and his ilk are many in number. He is a veritable icon of ignorance. In fact he represents its essence; he doesn't even know his knee from his elbow. He keeps stumbling around as though blindfolded. He is indeed one of those 'evil jurists' and 'mini-minds' as described for us by both al-Ghazali and Abu al-Walid ibn Rushd. Our Prophet (peace be upon him!) has this to say: 'Religious scholars are the trustees of prophets, just as long as they do not mingle with rulers or involve themselves in secular matters. If they do so, then they are betraying their function vis-à-vis the prophets. In which case, beware of them!' Such stick-in-the-mud jurists are inimical to existence itself. Their knowledge of religion is exiguous in the extreme, and yet they will wave the little that they possess in your face and utter threats. However, their motivations are entirely different. They don't use debate in order to make their points, but instead resort to fault-finding, abuse, and sheer slander. When it comes to interpretation—assuming that they will even acknowledge the concept—they have absolutely nothing to offer. All they can insert into the process is their own faulty powers of perception, coupled with minimal intellectual abilities and mean-mindedness. They use violent methods as a way of imposing their own shortcomings as principles for discussion and treatment of other people. I wonder, am I repeating things I've told you before?"

From his seat 'Abd al-'Ali gestured that he wished to respond to my question. "Every time you have spoken, Master," he said, "you have given us the benefit of your broad knowledge and acute understanding. We are well aware that the things you tell us have to be taken very seriously and provide us with both contentment and grace. I was able to pass on some of what you have said to a mixed group in Seville. Everyone there, male and female, was in complete agreement, but there was one exception: a gloomy, cantankerous jurist, who started railing against me and protesting in his coarse voice. But just them a beautiful woman fired back at him . . ."

One the young men who had just joined the group interrupted him and asked with a smile, "You say a beautiful woman fired back at him, 'Abd al-'Ali. Tell us what she was like!"

"In the presence of our master," 'Abd al-'Ali went on, "I will simply state that she was extremely attractive; at the same time she possessed a degree of learning, self-assurance, and modesty that attracted our attention. She fired back at the jurist and criticized him severely. 'If you would only shut up,' she said, 'you would spare us your ignorance and give us a break . . .' Another woman continued along the same lines: 'People such as you, rude man that you undoubtedly are, fall flat on their face whenever they open their mouths. Any judgments you make are unfair and invalid.'"

The people present and myself all heartily approved of what the young man and the two women had said on that occasion in Seville. One of them seemed to be surprised: 'So here we're seeing cloistered women pronouncing sensible judgments!' while another commented that it was God who had put the words into their mouths.

"Be careful not to lay all the blame on jurists," I said. "If you do, you'll be just like the people who think that 'Do not approach the prayers' and 'Woe to all Muslims' are valid quotations. These jurists are all part of a larger whole. Within the sphere of rulership, there are obviously differences in the roles that people play, but these jurists are analogous to soldiers, bureaucrats, merchants, informers, and hirelings, to say nothing of fawning historians, astrologers, and panegyric poets. All these functionaries and others like them who operate within the framework of the state, they're all opportunistic chameleons, vainglorious racketeers, and aficionados of transitory offices and suspect deals. Their private slogan goes like this: 'We come first, then "après nous le déluge" and the destruction of Muslim Spain.' For professional spongers and hypocrites like them the decision made by the ruler to open the gates to conquerors is holy writ. They have neither knowledge nor experience. This regime manipulates the truth on the basis of diametrical opposites, and Abu al-Hamalat is one of its most typical products and appendages. Didn't you notice the way he praised the Almohad al-Ma'mun,* apparently blissfully unaware of the fact that this particular amir managed to annul and destroy the Almohad belief-system. He systematically eradicated its defenders and propagators in the thousands and hung their heads on the walls of Marrakesh until the winds blew away the foul stench they left. As if that were not enough, he set the Christians against his own Muslim people and let both them and their mercenaries take over the treasury and territory in our Muslim Spain. Among the places handed over was Valencia, that rich and fertile region! Then have you noticed the way this phony preacher went on to give special encomia to al-Rashid, al-Ma'mun's Almohad successor? He was the ruler who ascended the throne thanks to the support of Frankish troops. During his reign the Castilians used either sheer brute force or purchase to annex Algeciras, Cordoba, and many other regions as well. Then he crumpled, and our beloved city of Seville was left to be swallowed up as well. To God alone belongs the power and might."

I paused for a moment to catch my breath. "Most of these calamities," I went on, "are well known to anyone with insight, those who have heard the Words of

God: 'It is not the eyes that are blind, but rather the hearts inside their breasts' [Qur'an, Sura 22, v. 46]. For Abu al-Hamalat and his ilk, history is not worth a gnat's wing or even the proverbial grain of mustard seed. They can neither understand nor appreciate the significant events going on all around them. Abu Da'ud* reports a tradition passed on by Ibn 'Umar,* to the effect that the Prophet of God—on whom be the purest of blessings—said, 'Those who are ignorant of history ride blind and stumble around aimlessly. They attribute to recent times things from the ancient past and vice versa, without organizing their data in any way.' We seek God's protection from such idiocy."

The students were all outdoing each other as they recorded in writing everything that I was saying; all, that is, except for 'Abd al-'Ali and 'Amr, who were still listening intently; the former was staring off into space, while the latter lowered his gaze and tried to hide his injuries.

"Those Almohads," 'Adnan, the young man from Malaga, said to interrupt the silence, "rescued Spain when their power was at its zenith, but now they've split up into petty dynasties and become powerless. They've left us crushed between two opposing forces: the hammer of the oppressive Franks on one side and on the other the anvil of a cluster of kings best described by the poet al-Mutanabbi*:

> Rabbits they are, but actually kings;
> Their eyes may be open, but they are asleep.

"Those petty kings are the Banu Hud in Murcia where we are, and the Banu Who Knows What elsewhere. Muhammad ibn Sharaf* has a wonderfully trenchant and comprehensive description of them."

At this point everyone suddenly chimed in with the verses in question as though with one voice, some of them laughing, others making sarcastic gestures:

> In Spain's diverse regions I find myself missing
> glorious names such as Mu'tasim and Mu'tadid.
> All the names are in the wrong place;
> It's like a cat puffing itself up and pretending to be a lion.

Now it was 'Abd al-'Ali's turn to speak, almost as though he wanted to restore a sense of dignity and seriousness to our assembly. "Master," he said, "it is the extent of our concerns that makes us laugh. Previously you have advised us to poke fun at the received tradition regarding our true Prophet, but what are we supposed to be doing beyond that? Should we be declaring war against the Frankish enemy as a way of defending ourselves in this homeland of ours? If so, how should we proceed? Or should we instead be directing our anger at the sultan, aiming all our pent-up anger at his various machinations? Do we have the necessary power to do that? I may forget any number of things, but I'll never forget something you said to us previously, something I've memorized by heart: 'I enjoin you to consider the truths maintained in this era of yours as being heretical. Pronounce God's curse on them and all those who adhere to them. To call them "truths" is like saying that a snakebite is harmless.'"

"May your right hand never falter, 'Abd al-'Ali," I told myself at this point, "and may your mouth always speak the truth! I did indeed mouth those words, but I had forgotten exactly how I expressed the idea; I presume I was more precise and detailed in my missing manuscript. It may be that this young man has memorized some of my other statements. Maybe the spark they ignite will trigger a process that will refresh my memory."

'Amr's voice now resounded around the room. "If that's the way things are," he said, obviously trying to keep his worries in check, "then we must either aspire to the honorable life or else perish in the process. But how? Should we throw these petty rulers into faraway prisons as Emir Ibn Tashufin* did with al-Mu'tamid ibn 'Abbad,* the ruler of the city of Seville that is even now about to fall? My own dream is like al-Mutanabbi's, namely that we cut off the necks of these rulers so that we can restore Spain's power and instill fear into God's enemies and ours."

Voices were raised in support of his views. I realized that I needed to steer this young man's anger in the right direction and show him a better way.

"Heaven forbid that Muslims should fight a civil war against each other!" I said. "There's no need to kindle its flame. The allies of the Christians are already heavily involved in killing some of these rulers and subverting others; if politics so demand, they may even be willing to support still others. Apart from that, our rulers are forever fighting and killing each other. They think nothing of indulging in murder in order to hold on to their thrones. Haven't you heard the story about the Almohad ruler of Murcia, Abu Muhammad 'Abdallah,* known as 'Al-'Adil Bi-llah'? My father—may he rest in peace!—told me about him. When this craven coward of a ruler signed a treaty handing over fortresses and neighboring territories to Fernando, king of Castile,* people started cursing him in mosques and calling for his ouster. The guards in his palace revolted and gave him the choice of either relinquishing his throne or being killed. The reckless idiot decided to be stubborn, so they stuck his head into a lake until he drowned. Unfortunately there are many rulers like him—God alone is the protector."

'Amr and some of the other students asked me in alarm what should be done in the face of these calamities that were befalling the other parts of Spain. They kept addressing me with names I had asked them not to use. For a moment I lowered my head in thought.

"I'm going to say this again for the sake of those of you who haven't heard me say it already: do not call me Imam, Shaykh, or Sufi Master. I am simply a teacher who shares with you such knowledge as I have and gives you such opinions as seem right to me. Don't ask me for miracles or wondrous deeds, nor for things that are beyond my powers. How many times have I told you all that I do not seek leadership nor do I claim prophetic status? The very worst of disasters occurs when human beings, in their quest for perception and discernment, decide to revolt against their fellow humans. What is even worse still is when it happens among peoples who have been living together for generations, struggling, striving, chanting, and building. The sheer will to live and exist together and to create an Andalusian culture is an enlightened ideal—open, active, creative. However there are other forces, bristling with weapons and hatred, that are hell-bent on exposing our country to risks of fragmentation and destruction. Their tenets are all based on slogans derived from rigid, uncompromising ideas, ideas that involve fanatical devotion to particular ideologies, races, and cliques, not to mention a wide variety of other negative, obscurantist compromises. Our pathetic rulers are all too aware of the fact that there is nothing they can do for their own religious community. That is why you can see them leaving us for the duration in precisely the kind of situation in which we now find ourselves: dreaming thoughts of health and impregnability, aspiring to those loftier, transcendent spheres, or, at the very least, to being on the upward path toward them. However, while this particular sphere, our current stage of existence, may have experienced its own setbacks and ruptures, it is up to each and every one of you to investigate and explore it with all due energy and initiative, since it is the worthier of paths to follow. It is the key to firm understanding and appropriate action, your antidote against the illusions of those in power in this misguided and misguiding era of ours. That may well be the import of the words of mine that 'Abd al-'Ali has mentioned to you; or, at least, something like it.

"But now I wish to apply it in a more general frame of reference. Make sure that you neither ignore nor forget those brilliant flashes along the thorny paths of life or those moments of illumination during the darkest of nights. They are all like gleaming pearls, even if the necklace they are on is broken and in shreds. I charge you to study and remember some of the luminaries of the Umawi Caliphate in this Spain of ours, countenances of rare splendor, hearts open and wide: my personal favorites are 'Abd al-Rahman III* (the conqueror) and his successor, al-Hakam al-Mustansir.* Pay particular attention to the ways these two mighty caliphs involved themselves in matters of cultural education, in the establishment of well-grounded intellectual movements, and also in military defense. Study their deeds and internalize them, not so that you can show off and play games of one-upmanship, but rather to make yourselves fully cognizant of the lofty reaches of the mind that were possible such a short time ago and the training of both mind and body that needs to be recovered if we are to rediscover them in this age of ours. The only way that we will manage to convert all the accumulated negative features of our society into something positive, productive, and forward-looking is by embarking upon the program that I have just outlined and underscored as being the correct way forward."

"Enhancing capacities," a number of voices shouted at this point, "by discarding niceties, then removing all roadblocks on the way, so that it becomes possible to ascend the stairs that lead to the Creator."

"God willing," I said by way of closure, "I will continue discussing these ideas in the mosque."

"After today," 'Amr yelled by way of warning, then in a softer tone, "no more prayers in the mosque. The fanatics have turned God's house into a boxing ring. The wounds I've received should be testimony enough to what a thug and a policeman were able to do. You, Master, are very dear to us. It would be more than we could stand if you were to suffer any harm as a consequence of an attack aimed at you by a hired criminal or a deranged lunatic."

At this point I seized an opportunity to express my heartfelt thanks to 'Amr, who had managed to ward off an attack on my person. We were now interrupted by a loud knock on the door, followed by a noisy argument between Salman and the people knocking. When I got up to investigate the situation, I discovered two policemen at the door, demanding that I hand over 'Amr from Cordoba who was required to appear before the chief of police. I asked them why, and they informed me that on that very day he had attacked a policeman in front of several witnesses who had been at prayer. Was I now supposed to deny that 'Amr was present in this house, or rather should I refuse to hand him over on the pretext that he was under my protection? I had made up my mind to adopt the latter strategy, but 'Abd al-'Ali and his companions quickly surrounded the two policemen.

"We're prepared to testify," they said, "that it was the complainant who had struck the first blow."

"One evil begets another," I commented, "and it is the initiator who is more at fault."

The two policemen now demanded to search the house for the assailant, but I refused. I demanded that they bring me an official search warrant. The two policemen now had no choice but to leave, which they did under the threatening gaze of the students. They then told me that 'Amr had managed to get away over the roof of my house. They now insisted that I lock my door till they came back. Meanwhile they would try to find out more details.

Acting on their advice, I told Salman not to open the door to anyone whose voice he did not recognize. With that I asked him to uncover my back and dress my wounds.

9

SHOULD I SAY THAT, where my devotion to the quest for the very heights is involved, I entertain some peculiar, indeed twisted ideas? In my peers' opinion, it all comes down to a matter of courage. As the great Sufi writer al-Niffari* puts it, "In taking risks lies a portion of the path to salvation."

Whatever the case may be, I thought it best to continue my search for the missing manuscript and see the process through to its conclusion: either hope and relief, or else surrender and despair. How could I possibly not make one last effort when the sole initiative that I had left involved my Muslim lover, Qatr al-Nada?

This woman was slim, delicate, and svelte, so much so that she seemed—God be exalted!—as light as a feather. Even so she managed to exude a lofty spirituality whose music emerged from every single pore in her body, an effect that would induce in all those who sat with her refreshing effects that proved incredibly provocative.

Her husband was a financier and a total braggart, crude and cantankerous, debauched in his conduct and utterly undistinguished. When it came to sheer ignorance of things, he was a past master.

On their honeymoon he had mustered enough deception to tell her, "My beloved, for me you are guaranteed value, a winning throw of the dice. You represent profit and profitability."

However, no sooner was the honeymoon over than he showed himself in his true colors: a pathological rogue, sadistically violent. How else can you explain the conduct of a person whose married life only managed to provide any kind of validity or pleasure when he was eating and drinking to excess? All of which led him to emit gasses whose foul stench was accompanied by gross belching and farting and loud guffaws. The entire occasion would be replete with disgusting comments, such as "Shit and shit again on all Muslims in Spain. I shall convert to Christianity before they're all expelled . . ."

While this beast was sitting in the midst of his pals, he would talk about his wife. "One day I'll get to send this supposed woman off to the next world," he would note. "No doubt, I'll get to write on her coffin, 'Watch out for this one; she comes very cheap.'"

Qatr al-Nada's father was a copyist, well versed in reference works. A friendship developed between the two of us, one based on love and mutual respect since both of us loved books and manuscripts. He was a devout and virtuous man, magnanimous and fair-minded. The only things that disturbed the calm tenor of his life were the miserable state of the Muslims in Spain and the wretched married life that his only daughter had to endure. Whenever he spoke to me about these matters, tears always came to his eyes and dripped on to his white bushy beard. One day he astonished me by telling me that, when his son-in-law was deciding from among a list of names whom to choose to act as mediator between himself and his wife, he wanted only me. I had no idea why he had chosen me until Qatr al-Nada told me that he had made his decision by a toss of the dice, and that was it.

In any case I now spent an entire month making laudable efforts to reconcile the married couple with each other. The meetings involving the three of us were usually twice a week, but by exception there could also be other ones if tensions rose because the husband had lost his temper. He would often give his wife a terrible thrashing, then claim that he had summoned me to come but I had not done so. When my patience finally wore out, I suggested to him that he respond to the injured woman's wishes by agreeing to give her an amicable divorce. That made him furious, and he swore a terrible oath that he would never do that. Indeed he went even further and accused me of wanting to take Qatr al-Nada away from him. I decided to abandon the effort and withdraw. Soon afterward, the woman's father died in pain after suffering a heart attack—verily we are God's and to Him do we return.

It was just two months later that I heard that the husband had contracted syphilis; not much later I learned that he had died. When I went to see his widow to convey my condolences with a few sparse words, all she did was to stare back at me, her expression full of joy and affection. Once her waiting period was over, she came to visit me, after exchanging her mourning garb for something with much brighter colors. By now her body had been released from all the violence and suffering that it had gone through and revealed itself in all its beauty. As she sat down next to me and sipped from a cup of milk, her face looked fresh and bright.

"How is it possible, Ibn Dara," she asked me in her tuneful voice, "for two people, male and female, who are so diametrically opposite to each other in every way, to become man and wife? Tell me!"

For my own part, I too was invoking both memory and mind and setting them to work.

"That's a great mystery," I replied, "or rather you can say that it's one of those enormous and painful existential ironies in life. God knows best; the reason is that people cannot understand the truth and choose to ignore customary practice. The Greek philosophers noted that harmony undoubtedly exists within the system of the universe. However, when human beings are involved, there are so many terrible and unforeseeable coincidences. How often we hear about such tragic and violent unions!"

"That's one of those burning issues that I'll definitely be raising on the Day of Judgment, assuming that I am destined for such things . . ."

"Oh, you will be reborn as a virgin houri, your beauty forever renewed. God willing, I will be one of your lucky companions in the gardens of eternity."

What prevented me from keeping up my contact with Qatr al-Nada was the way people kept bad-mouthing me and raising a fuss. Even so, the way she arranged our meetings and shrouded them in absolute secrecy was a very model of its kind. Something else that bothered me were the doubts I had about the real reasons for my strong attachment to my missing manuscript. In fact, I even began to suspect that my decision to search for it among my suspect former girl-friends was simply an excuse for renewing my relationships with them. However I managed to ignore all such sentiments so that I could close the final gap in the circle, it being for me the last word on the fixed and sublime, the most precious of quests.

When I went to visit Qatr al-Nada, she welcomed me with great warmth and affection. She scolded me for staying away so long, then asked why I was visiting her now after such a long time.

"Dear lady," I replied, my tears betraying my sorrow and affection, "people are saying nasty things about me. Eyes are keeping permanent watch on me. But all the time you have been in my heart and secluded under my very eyelids."

"And you, dear Sir, were like a loyal son to my father—God have mercy on his soul! Now my relatives and friends have all gone to Granada or even farther, while I am stuck here, a pawn to two jailers: a house that is empty but for an aged and infirm mother, and a time that is a tissue of sorrows and disasters. I have no idea what the fates have in mind for me: will they leave me here to squat until I die or will they carry me away heaven knows where . . . ?"

"Dear sweet lady," I replied, "all of us who are living in our ancestors' land are now threatened with evacuation, unless some miracle happens or we receive reinforcements and supplies from some new Muslim power."

"My only dear friend," she said, "whether it's in bathhouses or elsewhere, I keep hearing women talking in crushed, tearful tones about their calamities and the loved ones they've lost. Some of them keep begging for an answer to their question: 'O Lord, what is my sin that You should vent Your anger in this way and abandon us? Have You created us just so that we can endure such torture?' And what about You? Isn't it the dreadful calamity that has struck us and the corrupt era we live in that has kept You apart from me?"

"Dear lady, that very calamity has kept me apart from my own self. What has made things worse is that I have lost my manuscript whose pages have been my major source of inspiration, an outpouring of spiritual ecstasy. Its exalted words, expressed in the loftiest of terms, were of a sort that mind and soul will only encounter once. No indeed, they come from a single, extraordinary moment."

Qatr al-Nada was intelligent enough to realize that she should not in any way belittle my sense of loss over the manuscript, even in the context of the prospective loss of the whole of Muslim Spain and the way it was being carved up into bleeding chunks before our weary, grief-stricken eyes. She did not say a single word or make any gesture, nor did she ask me about the contents of my manuscript, clearly aware that any question of that kind was liable to make things ever harder for me.

"There's one part of the manuscript," I told her in order to reassure her somewhat, "the content of which I can still recall, if not the format. It talked about our beloved Spain and the way it was bleeding to death and considered ways in which we might be able to escape the disasters that are afflicting us."

"If I had come across your manuscript," she said, "I would certainly have kept it safe and sound, close to my own heart and all those things that are dearest to me. Even so, your manuscript may have disappeared, but your inspirational mind remains in place, still developing and radiating its light. Be patient and forget, and you'll produce yet greater things."

Those precious words of hers fell on me like a cool breeze and a dose of tranquility. I used them as not merely a good omen but also as a prelude to a night of hugs and kisses, one of intense and happy intercourse till dawn broke and the cock crowed. Just then a loud knocking interrupted my pleasure. I arranged with my hostess a time when I would be at the graveyard where most of our beloved forebears were buried, then made my exit by a back way that I knew.

I went to the graveyard almost as soon as it opened. I gave the gatekeeper a large donation, and he thanked me profusely. I headed for the grave of Qatr al-Nada's father, read some intercessions for him, and prayed that he be granted forgiveness and mercy. No sooner had I finished than my companion was standing right behind me, her feminine perfume wafting over me. Without turning around I asked her who had been knocking on her door. Her response completely ruined my mood.

"It was the police chief with his team, coming to arrest you on a charge of fornication. I lost my temper and told them they could search my house inch by inch. They went away, duly chastened."

"God alone provides safety. Didn't I tell you, Qatr al-Nada, that now I'm surrounded by spies? Go home at once before some disaster strikes. Go home, and I'll try to work things out."

I turned around and looked at her, urging her to leave. Just at that moment a clown came over and grabbed the hem of her gown. She gave him some money and freed herself from his grip. Adjusting her veil, she gave me a sad look as though to say one final farewell, then rushed away.

I lowered the top of my burnous over my forehead, then made my way to the grave of my own father and others as well. I prayed over my relatives' graves and begged God to be merciful to them. Once that was done, I made my way out, taking all due care as I did so. Just as I was approaching the gate, a middle-aged woman who was both elegant and beautiful begged me to pray over two other graves that were close by. She told me they belonged to her husband and only son, both of whom had fallen victim to Castilian fire less than a month earlier. I responded to her request as best as I could given the circumstances. When I had finished, she offered me some money, but I told her to give it to someone else. Then I left.

10

TO ALLOW MYSELF TIME TO THINK, I decided to take a stroll. I walked along the banks of the River Segura, which was uncharacteristically full at the time, then made my way to the park, which was still in flower even though it had been sadly neglected for some time. On this particular morning I was especially eager to look at the palm, cypress, and pine trees that were still standing, even to hug them if I could. Other types of tree—walnuts, pomegranates, figs, and olives—had all shed their leaves and looked as though they were ready either to depart or to die.

All of a sudden I felt strangely petrified. Immediately cutting my walk short, I returned home. Nor was this merely a passing whim on my part, for no sooner did I approach my house than a group of my Muslim students surrounded me. They told me that my horse had been stolen; they had found Salman in the stable with his mouth gagged and his legs and arms trussed. They had untied him and put him to bed so he could recover his breath and get over the shock. I ask 'Abd al-'Ali about 'Amr, and he told me that he was still in custody at the police station. I gave him some money to buy me a mule, but he refused, pointing out that the very same thing might happen as had already occurred with my horse. There were now organized gangs specializing in the theft of riding animals; they would either sell them in other cities or else sell the meat to the indigent population. Even so I insisted that he buy me a mule. With that I sent him on his way along with his companions, enjoining them to delve into a set of books that I specified by both name and topic, to which I added some others as well. I then went in to see Salman and found him ashen-faced and downcast; he looked as though he had just lost a relative or been defeated in a fierce battle. Sitting down beside him, I told him not to bother recounting what had happened and to forget about the wonderful and reliable horse that had been as dear to him as it was to me.

Next evening 'Abd al-'Ali brought me a white mule, although some of its limbs were tinged with black just like my horse that had been stolen. It looked fit and healthy. He handed it over to Salman and gave me back the rest of the money. I thanked him and sat him down next to me.

"Things are going from bad to worse, 'Ali," I said, noting how distressed and anxious he looked. "Tell me about 'Amr."

"Well, Sir," he replied, doing his best to keep his anxiety under control, "yesterday he was transferred to a prison in an unknown location. His mother has gone on the pilgrimage and hasn't returned. His eldest brother has quit Murcia without leaving so much as a trace. For our part, my companions and I have no idea what to do to get him released. They've accused him of assaulting a police officer and inciting people to resist the Castilians, thus breaking the truce between them and our own Muslim leaders."

I lowered my head, realizing full well that what they were doing to 'Amr was in fact their way of getting back at me and forcing me to act. Once I started asking for his release, they would start haggling and specify their conditions and demands for compensation.

"Don't worry about it," I told him. "I will do my utmost to get him freed. How are you?"

"My parents have moved south to Granada. Once they had both despaired of convincing me to go with them, they left me enough to live on. I am in exactly the same position as everyone else who is resisting the thought of handing over the rest of Muslim lands to the Christians. I praise God who guided me to you, my master. It is your gatherings and your words that have restored my sense of resolve and purpose."

"And what about your marriage to Rachel (or is it Fatima)?"

"I forgot to tell you that I let her go. She became very angry. She's remained a Muslim, in the hope that either I'll take her back or she can work out some ruse. Just a few days ago the people around her were claiming that you were the one who turned me away from her. Don't pay any attention to this talk, Sir!"

I did not dwell on the topic so as not to force my interlocutor to reveal any secrets, by which I mean Rachel's pretexts by claiming that I had seduced her and wanted her for myself. It occurred to me to inquire after her elder sister too, but instead I decided to change the subject and discuss matters that seemed more broad-scaled and significant.

"Bring me details about your companions," I said. "I need their names, details of their professions, their talents, and their personal circumstances. Written documents are easier to memorize and refer to later on."

"I'll do the best I can," he replied, "even though the number of your devotees keeps on growing apace. By now they're calling themselves the 'Sab'inites.' They're longing to have another session with you."

"And I fully reciprocate the love they feel, my dear brother," I replied. "That goes without saying. But when it comes to providing them with some satisfaction and ideas about positive outcomes, I have no tricks up my sleeve. This is a much troubled, fractious era we're living in. Quite apart from schools, even God's own mosques have been shut in my face by the sultan. Those utterly corrupt pseudo-legists keep on launching scurrilous attacks against me. From now on, I'll have to meet my devotees in secret, either behind firmly locked doors or else outside the city."

"My master, those very circumstances only amplify their affection toward you. Your sayings reach them by way of auditors who are part of your coterie. Their hearts and minds are deeply affected by the transcendent light emanating from the very structure of those sayings and the eloquence of their sentiments. As they are compelled to confront the catastrophes and malfeasances of this dreadful era, they find themselves fortified."

Just then Salman appeared to announce in a coarse, broken voice that my eldest brother was at the door, requesting to speak to me on an urgent matter. No sooner had my visitor heard my permission to enter than he rushed in and greeted me with a hug. I returned his greeting, taking a sideways glance all the while at his expensive clothes. I asked him what brought him to my house on such a dark night. He paused for a while, looking warily at the third member of our company, 'Abd al-'Ali. The student immediately understood the situation, so he stood up, said farewell, and left.

I invited my brother to sit down so he could catch his breath. I asked how he and the family were. He thanked me and assured me that everyone was well.

"My dear brother, Abu Talib," I said, "don't beat about the bush. Tell me now what it is that has brought you here under cover of darkness. These walls do not have ears; God alone can see us at this point."

He adjusted his position and roused a smile in order to keep his embarrassment under control. "The first reason why I've come," he said, "is to renew our
filial acquaintance and bring you our greetings."

"After a gap of two years or more?" I asked. "What's the second reason?"

"By now the authorities have despaired of your ever joining their service,"
he said. "These days it's a far better and safer idea to come to terms with them."

"I refuse to acknowledge the authority of such people," I replied. "Between
them and me lies a steep slope, just like the one that the ascetic saint Uways
al-Qarni* saw when he said, 'Only a skinny man will ever climb up there.' Your
would-be authority figures have decided to stay on one side of this gap, indulging in all kinds of luxury and comfort, till they have lost all sight and insight.
They simply spend their time wallowing in frivolity and debauchery. Heaven
preserve us!"

My brother simply stared at me, his mouth agape, scarcely able to believe
what he was hearing.

"So let's make clear for you," I went on, "things that might otherwise be kept
under wraps. You will come to understand what I am saying and more. Frivolity,
that's the proper name for the scourge that rulers in Spain are totally incapable
of fighting or extirpating. It's spreading like a worm-borne microbe throughout
their organization. The symptoms are many, but the illness is one and the same:
favoritism, cronyism, and dissipation at the top; grand larceny and corruption
on the broadest conceivable scale, and lastly letting the culprits off scot-free, a
surefire sign of support for the ongoing series of disasters we are suffering. When
it comes to sheer shame, just take a look around you. You'll find politicians and
notables who personify the present crisis. In return for all this, they proceed to
hand over Muslim property and land to the enemy. Their own flesh and blood
have become eunuchs for the Christians. As the old saying has it, 'O woe for
Mu'tasim!'* All this is happening, and yet, my dear brother, you really expect
me to adjust my way of life and say nothing, simply to keep playing along and
remain silent?"

"My dear brother," he replied, doing his best to keep his alarm under control,
"in times such as ours, politics is the art of caution and circumspection, a quest
for something better. War is a contest; sometimes you win, sometimes you lose."

"When people in quest of something better are actually looking for something worse, then it's simply called debauchery and cowardice. Your companions

have corrupted political life by distorting it, transforming it into something cheap and nasty for barter. When it comes to warfare, any sensible person can tell that it's the populace that ends up suffering hardships. Don't you hear about the way the enemy keeps on disrupting life in their quarters and houses by launching raids and house searches? They take women away and orphan children. Men are forced either to convert to Christianity or else to refuse and leave . . ."

"But, my dear brother, the enemy is stronger than we are; there's no way that our weapons can blunt theirs. The only way we can behave toward the kings of Castile, Aragon, and Leon is to grin and bear it and adopt effective stratagems. Today we're in the process of negotiating with the most powerful and reliable of them, Alfonso of Castile.* But when it comes to fighting them, all we can hope for is that God Almighty will grant us victory by means of an army in His control."

"Are you seriously talking about our rulers, our puny set of kings, utterly discredited and dissipated as they are? Wineskins and songstresses, those are their gods. Their arrogance and squabbling have brought them so low that they now believe that their Christian enemies are the most powerful factor this side of God Himself. Whenever, if ever, they decide to confront that enemy, it is not with the benefit of a united front but rather a series of severed, fragmented ranks and a total lack of willpower. As a result, when they have to negotiate with the enemy, they come back to us with their faces slapped liked a buffoon. They get exactly what they deserve. God will never change the situation in which they find themselves until they themselves change their own posture."

All of a sudden my brother frowned and gave a deep sigh, as though he was about to tell me something really serious.

"Amir Baha' al-dawla Muhammad ibn Hud and his aides are displeased with you, my brother," he told me nervously. "They dislike you heartily. As far as they're concerned, you're inciting your colleagues and people in general against them and fomenting rebellion. If we were not both products of the same womb, I would not have agreed to try to mediate between you and them. That is what I've been doing here, all in an attempt to avoid their getting you involved in something that can only turn out very badly for you . . ."

"Go back and remind those tyrants that no human being owes allegiance to any ruler who disobeys the Creator Himself. Through my belief in God I'm not scared of blame directed at me by any scoundrel or of the trickery of blackguards . . ."

"So there's no way for us to reach some mutual understanding and be reconciled?"

"Only if your companions were to agree to move beyond the current impasse, rid themselves forever of their sinful, debauched ways, and purify themselves in the clear waters of glory and virtue, untrammeled truth, and the common good. But they're utterly incapable of doing such things."

"Some senior advisers of the amir want to see you and begin negotiations . . ."

"Not before they purge themselves. I find myself constrained by the command of my Lord: 'Address me not regarding those who have done wrong, for they shall be drowned' [Sura 11, v. 37]."

I have no idea why it happened that at this precise moment a wonderfully apposite phrase flashed into my mind, one that, no doubt, was part of my missing manuscript. It concerned those blind idiots whose description I was endeavoring to approximate by saying, "people in whose eyes the sun, stars, and natural and unnatural lights have grown dark, whether inside or outside their own minds; they operate within the wide-open spaces of their own folly; they purge all thoughts of surrounding conflict and suppress it completely, preferring to remain within the confines of their own insanity." The fact that I had remembered that phrase overjoyed me. I yelled to Salman to bring my brother, Abu Talib, some simple Sufi food or a tray of sweetmeats and fruit. My brother declined, claiming that he was not eating at night in an attempt to lose weight and restore his corpulent frame to a more reasonable size.

Truth to tell, my poor brother, my mirror image in appearance if not in essence, was only getting himself involved in politics because he wanted to rid himself of his bodily and sexual urges—as was the case with his colleagues and masters. Just like them, he was totally unwilling to contemplate the terrible state of his country and its people. Questions of fate and destiny failed to disturb him. He lived his life as though in a permanently drugged condition and was never going to pay any attention even though death might be just around the corner. Where he was concerned, I felt nothing but bitter contempt, although deep down I did also have some residual sympathy.

It was only when my guest gave another deep sigh that I emerged from my trance. He asked me one last time the question I had been anticipating about my response to the task he had been given. In response I told him that what I had already said was surely answer enough. With that, he stood up. It was as if he had suddenly woken up to the fact that he was actually a key member of the corridors of power and authority, someone who had undertaken an embassy on behalf of the Banu Hud to Pope Innocent, a role of which he was enormously proud.

"Very well then," he said in his new tone of authority, "the state authorities hereby order you to leave for the south or even farther. In exchange they will free 'Amr of Cordoba and stop harassing your disciples."

"Your bosses are relentlessly imposing a stranglehold on defenseless Muslims," I responded, controlling my feelings as best I could, "just like the Crusaders, or even worse. Go back and tell them that living in their shadow is demeaning and bitter. If I am now to be forced to leave my native city, then I have a model in Muhammad, the Lord of Prophets and Emigrants. Tell them to release 'Amr and stop harassing my colleagues first, then they can have whatever they want."

There was nothing more for my brother to say, other than to agree to pass on my comments and then bid me farewell.

With that I put out the lamp and curled up in bed, hoping to get some of the sleep that had been eluding me for some time. I allowed my mind to wander where it willed, and it headed toward a contemplation of this poor country of ours, wounded and bleeding, and its wretched inhabitants, panicked and suffering all kinds of abuse. I myself was still one of them, even though the people throwing me out were my own kith and kin (heaven help us all!).

It was so dark outside that I thought about taking a trip outside under cover of darkness so I could look at the River Segura and the gardens on its banks—a kind of farewell gesture. But a voice inside me told me not to do it, but to stay in bed. "We're living in dangerous times," it told me, "and people are harboring nasty ideas about you and slandering your name. Leave Murcia and head south. The Maghrib is your spiritual home; it can serve as a more useful base for your activities. Go to the Maghrib, and you'll be a winner."

11

SO IT CAME ABOUT that at noon on the first day of the month Rabi' al-Akhir I asked Salman to collect all my books and papers and put them in a box. I did not tell him I was intending to depart so as not to alarm him. I told him that I was leaving him in charge of the house for a few days while I went to Raquta. I mounted my mule and headed for my destination with a view to seeing my family and bidding them farewell in a spot that was less conspicuous. I used back streets to get there so as to avoid contact with the Christian soldiers in the suburbs of Murcia. The only people I encountered were Muslims heading out of town either alone or in groups. Between hills and vales I encountered beggars and itinerant clowns asking me for money, which I gave them to the extent possible. The weather was oppressive, almost as though it too felt the same degree of sorrow and fear as I did. Animals in their pens and fields looked lifeless and indolent, while even birds flying high or perched on tree branches seemed downcast and melancholy!

A pall with octopus-like tentacles hung over an entire people, one that its rulers wanted to remain despised and obedient.

Dear God, grant us all release or an end to this searing torture!

When I arrived, my sister, Zaynab, greeted me with a hug and made me feel very welcome. She asked me what had happened to my horse, and I made a gesture that implied that it had either died or gone away. I in turn asked her about Maymuna. She gave a sigh, then invited me to sit down and partake of some of the food and drink laid out on the table. Thanking her, I took a drink.

"She's well, I hope?" I asked.

"She's well in body, my dear brother," she replied, "but her heart . . . After your last stay here, she started visiting our Jewish neighbor, Rahil, and asking her for some medicine to cure her condition. Rahil easily diagnosed her condition and confided in me."

I asked her to explain, but she paused for a while. She then whispered to me that the problem was a hopeless love, or that's what the doctor called it. I asked her who the lucky beloved was.

"I'll say it," she told me after s brief exasperated pause, "and leave the rest to God. The beloved is you, my brother. If you could only see what change and illness have done to her, you would cry."

As I brushed my hands against one another, my expression was one of complete astonishment. Up till now I had supposed that Maymuna's love for me was related to a belief in God, but I found it hard to believe that she was in love with me to such an extent that she had become so ill. I asked my sister what I should do.

"According to Rahil," she replied, "the best thing, for the time being, is for you to visit the woman who is in love with you once or twice a month and make sure to treat her with love and affection. As to what happens after that, well, God alone is the sage dispenser . . ."

At this point I was thinking about telling Zaynab that I was under orders to leave Spain and that I had paid her a visit in order to make sure she had enough to live on and to arrange her affairs before bidding her farewell. However I balked at the idea for fear of making things even worse. Instead I asked her to heat some water so that I could perform the obligatory prayers and then take a well-deserved rest.

I slept heavily and reckon that I must have dreamed a lot of things. Next morning, however, all I could remember were a few snippets. I opened my eyes to see lights; there was Maymuna sitting by my knee, holding my right hand in hers and dropping hot tears on to them. As I sat up, I tried pulling my hand away, but failed.

Was this really Maymuna or simply a specter?

She was looking very pale and thin; her eyes were sunken and her lips looked dry and withered. Her hair was completely disheveled, and her clothes were torn and dirty. I used gentle words to chide her for what she was doing to herself. I asked her to go to the bathroom to wash and put herself to rights.

"Your wish is my command, my dear," she said in a weak, broken voice.

At this point Zaynab and Rahil arrived and greeted me. They helped Maymuna stand up and took her to the bathroom.

All this led me into a contemplation of love's strange ways. I recalled statements by poets and prose writers, so many of them, and pages from the *Kitab al-Zahra* by the jurisconsult Ibn Da'ud al-Zahiri from Isfahan,* and even more wonderful quotes from *Tawq al-Hamama* by the renowned scholar Ibn Hazm of Cordoba, the jewel of his era and pride of our Spanish domains—may God afford us the benefit of his knowledge and writings! I was amazed at the way in which hearts in the grip of love remain on fire and that there are so many and various doors to open into its domains, even in eras like our own when we are bombarded by so many convulsions and tribulations.

After two hours or more Maymuna returned with her two companions and sat facing me at a table full of food and drink. She looked a lot better now, and I could detect a musky perfume wafting from her direction. I noticed an eye-gesture from Rahil, from which I understood that I was supposed to encourage Maymuna to eat something. I responded by reminding the poor woman that she owed it to herself and told her to eat and drink before taking a rest. She gave me a loving glance, her face transformed by a radiant smile. I was as amazed as my sister when she began to tuck into the food with clear relish and obvious appetite. As for Rahil the doctor, her alert eyes and gestures made it clear that she was enjoying the experience of seeing her expertise and diagnosis proved correct. Once most of the food on the table had been eaten, Maymuna stood up without any help, came over to me, and kissed my hand. I kissed her hand in return and pointed to her bedroom. With an exquisitely delicate energy, she obeyed my command, followed by the two women, who looked both amazed and delighted.

I spent the rest of the day packing up my most valuable books into canvas sacks; then I went out to look for some of my friends from Raquta. The only ones I found were the elderly who were unable to leave. I chatted with them as best I could, sharing their utter despair at our rulers and hearing of their decision to remain on their lands even if it meant dying there. Before I said farewell, one of them stood up and addressed me.

"I and this other man are both Jews," he said, gesturing with his cane, "this other man is a Christian, and these are Muslims like you. Just ask them all how we've lived together in Raquta, not to mention many others in villages and other cities. By our One God, ask them, ask them!"

Many voices responded to this old man, with things like "Yes, just like the teeth on a comb!" "Like the fingers on one hand!" and "We used to give each other counsel and shared in the good and bad things that life offered!"

The old man went on, "Our roots in this land are widespread and intertwined, and they are irrigated by the waters of the One God. There's never been any question of separation or expulsion. My boy, tell that to the people in power in every religious community. Our country has been the ideal, the model, the enlightened community. Make sure they realize that!"

In the early evening I called Zaynab in and without the slightest dissimulation told her that I intended to leave first for Sabta and then for the Holy Territories in Arabia. Contrary to my expectations, she showed no signs of alarm; instead her response seemed quite controlled. I used a few terse phrases to explain that, wherever I went, I would make sure I was as safe as she could possibly wish. I then asked her if she wanted to go with me, but she declined, saying that she was attached to a village with which she was familiar and had no desire to reside anywhere else. That was all quite apart from the fact that she felt bound to stay with Maymuna. I doubted that she had any idea of the treatment that Muslims and Jews would be receiving at the hands of the Castilians and their allies—compulsory expulsion and exile—but all my doubts dissolved into nothing when she proceeded to tell me about the things she herself had witnessed in Raquta and its environs, and what she had heard from Rahil and many people about other regions as well.

"The fact that you're leaving, my dear brother," she said, "is something that's very hard for me to bear, but it'll be even harder for Maymuna. I feel in control of myself and can endure the consequences, but Maymuna certainly can't. My love for you is that of a sister for her brother, but she, poor creature, is passionately in love with you. As far as I can tell, her love has many aspects that are indivisible from each other . . ."

"Oh, Zaynab," I replied, "if only her love for me were in relationship to God! That's the way I understood it and enjoyed it. What do you advise me to do before I leave?"

"Ever since you came back, my dear brother," she replied, "Maymuna has only had one wish, that you take her for a ride, however short, on your mule."

"Good heavens! And after the ride, then what?"

"What Rahil says is that you need to leave some of your clothes behind, along with a lock of your hair. From time to time you should write her a letter with some kind words in it to cheer her up, assuming that you won't be able to visit her."

I gestured my agreement. "The ride first then," I said. "Tell her ahead of time so that she'll sleep well and have her ready tomorrow morning."

With that I left to give myself time to pack up the rest of my books and possessions. That done, I went to my house in the hope of getting some undisturbed slumber.

Immediately after breakfast and prayers next morning I left for our rendezvous. There I found Zaynab and Rahil, who had just finished putting Maymuna on the mule and loading it with a pannier full of various things. I greeted the trio with a warm smile, genuine enough to have a good effect on them all. For Maymuna on the mule I reserved a specially affectionate glance, at which her expression broke into a radiant smile.

I walked around to the front of the mule on foot and grabbed the reins. I walked with my head down so as to avoid looking at people and followed a path to a suburb that was far away from the Castilian army and its spies. That was how I came to traverse a number of grassy flats and dusty hills. Maymuna was perched on top of her mount; every time I looked round, she was breathing in the fresh air until her cheeks were rosy. She kept staring in amazed contentment at the gorgeous attractions that nature was displaying for her. I had no doubt in my mind that she was experiencing the most profound forms of inner serenity and happiness. What struck me forcibly was that our grassy, bowered path was completely empty of other living creatures, save for a few insects and worms wending their own way. Over them butterflies were fluttering, harbingers of spring with its own particular scents and perfumes.

For a while both of us remained in our own worlds. But, once we reached the top of a tree-lined hill with some shade, she signaled me to stop. I was not sure whether it was out of sympathy for my feet, or because she needed to excuse herself. I responded willingly, whereupon without even asking she simply threw her feather-light body on me. I hugged her in my arms, lay out a rug, sat her down on it, and brought over a bag whose contents I described to her. Looking straight at me, she invited me to sit beside her and share the food and chance to relax. I took the saddle and stirrup off the mule and let it meander in the field to taste the fruits of God's bounty. That done, I did as she requested and sat down beside her.

On that remarkable day I got back to my home just after noon; it was a day that I'll never forget as long as I live. I got down off the mule, lifted my happy, tearful companion down, and returned her to Zaynab, who was anxiously awaiting her return. I headed for my room with the intention of calming my own feelings and making arrangements for the two women once I had departed. At midnight I called my sister in. She brought me a light supper and sat down beside me. She was very happy and told me that Maymuna was sound asleep, something she had not been able to do for some considerable time.

"How's that?" I asked her.

"She's just like a suckling child," she replied, "one that's got everything she could possibly desire. And it's all thanks to you, my dear brother. You're now assured a good reward on Judgment Day!"

"No," I replied, "you should rather thank God who has taken her under His all-benevolent wing and provided her with what she needs, something I was unable to do. Now I need some rest. Tomorrow morning soon after dawn I'm going with God's aid first to Murcia, then to Sabta. My servant, Salman, is too old to accompany me; he prefers to stay where he was born and grew up. If he gets sick or needs anything, I am relying on you to give him sustenance. Here's some money that should last you and those with you for a while, or as long as God wills. My student 'Abd al-'Ali al-Nasir will serve as our intermediary. And now, my dear sister, go back to your bed."

12

ON MY WAY TO MURCIA, I thought about the people I was being forced to leave behind: my sister, teary-eyed at my departure; Maymuna, still asleep and clutching some of my hair and clothing; and Raquta, with all its sights, smells, and people. Today, all those particular moments from my youth seem like stars, shining even more brightly and luminously the farther away they are.

At the northwestern outskirts of the city I noticed Castilian soldiers setting up their billets and heading in groups toward the city itself. It was then that I realized that the surrender agreement was being implemented in accordance with the terms they had imposed on our debauched and defeatist rulers—God alone possesses power and might!

Close to the center of the city I witnessed a remarkable event. A vagrant clown came toward a group of soldiers who were stopping passers-by and searching them. With a gesture of his stick he insisted that they leave him alone and treat him like a warrior fighting for God's cause. They kept laughing at him and guffawing at his antics. Just then I watched as the man went up to two of them and plunged a dagger into them before running off. A hue and cry ensued, as voices announced that two soldiers had been stabbed to death. With that, the soldiers started beating up anyone wearing turbans or skullcaps. For my part I decided to get away as fast as I could so as to avoid this totally unexpected disaster. However, I had only gone a mile or so before another group of soldiers stopped me and searched my baggage. When they found nothing incriminating, their officer stared long and hard at me, then told me to move on. It usually happens that my eyes and general appearance get me out of sticky situations; maybe they are won over by the tokens of the spiritual traveler, one in quest of the realms of the absolute and essential. Whatever the case, many is the time I have managed to escape by the skin of my teeth and steer clear of the traps that this world presents to the unwary! These tokens that I seem to possess are a blend of innate talent and acquired skill. Without them I would certainly have found myself thrown into prison or madhouse, if not actually crushed and killed—that being the sorry fate of many of my peers.

Salman was waiting for me at the door of my house. He was overjoyed to see me and helped me get my things inside. He told me that the students had asked for me several times during my absence. I asked him if 'Amr had been one of them, and he told me that he had indeed. Before leaving to go about his own business, he handed me a sealed letter that my brother had sent. In it he notified me that the chief of police had released my disciple, 'Amr from Cordoba. Now I was obliged, he said, to leave Spain as I had promised. If I stayed with the Nasrids* in Granada, who were the sworn enemies of the Banu Hud and their amir, Baha' al-din the Mighty, then they would arrest all my followers and put them in prison.

What an utterly ridiculous threat! Having spent so long in the vicinity of the Banu Hud in Murcia, did they imagine that I would now exchange their regime for that of the Banu Ahmar* in Granada? That would be like leaping out of the frying pan into the fire!

I summoned Salman and asked him about Qatr al-nada, since I was thinking about sending her a letter. He told me he had heard that she had left for a town whose name he could not remember. I now told him that I myself was about to leave as well, and he received the news with a mixture of resignation and resolve, almost as though he already knew or expected it. I suggested to him that he might serve my sister, Zaynab, and keep her company in Raquta, to which he replied that he would certainly make sure to do that by visiting her and asking after her. However he also said that, provided that I gave my approval, he preferred to remain in this house until such time as either the Christians or death forced him to leave. I quickly assured him that such a plan met with my approval. I then asked him to get my bags ready for my journey tomorrow and to locate two guards to accompany me.

Next day Salman brought me my breakfast. He started complaining about the Castilians who had spent the night harassing the beggars and madmen of Murcia, throwing the whole lot of them—Jews and Muslims—into jail and torturing them until they either collapsed or died. That made me recall the incident of the day before.

"Blind revenge and group punishment is a widespread symptom of the Christians' insane policies," I told him. "God is the only victor!"

He then gave me three other bits of news: first, my baggage train was completely ready; my students were waiting by the door; and last, my mule had been killed and slaughtered. I had been planning to give the poor beast to my servant so that he would be able to carry out his functions more easily and have lesser burdens to bear. However, as I gave orders that it be buried, it was a clear sign that I needed to be on my way before my situation went from bad to worse.

I allowed the students to come in, but only 'Abd al-'Ali, 'Amr, and Al-Sadiq stood before me. They all greeted me warmly and sat down opposite me, although they declined to share my breakfast. I said some gentle, comforting words in the hope of mitigating their sorrow.

"My master," said 'Amr, "this is all too much for me. By leaving us you're bartering my own freedom. None of us who are devoted to you can tolerate the thought of your departure!"

"We will never be able to tolerate the idea," continued 'Abd al-'Ali, "even if you were to promise us another meeting in the near future!"

"Master," said Al-Sadiq, "most of us want to accompany you wherever you go and wherever you reside. Your learning enlightens us and your words give us strength in this gruesome era of terrifying collapse . . ."

"Our land is on a downhill slide," continued 'Amr, "with every part rolling down toward the bottom. Our rulers tyrannize their own folk just as much as they prostrate themselves before their enemies. The Banu Hud meekly pay them taxes, and Alfonso the Infanta, crown prince of the Castilian king, Fernando, struts around our city, doing just as he pleases to it and its people. They have now been forced either to convert and become Christians or else leave or be killed. By God, prison or death are both preferable to this life of humiliation and contempt."

I was afraid I would have to spend a good deal of precious time with this group of young men who now found their own land so unbearable that their only recourse was anger and rebellion.

"My dear colleagues," I told them in an attempt to calm them down and introduce a voice of reason, "life has great need of you, as does this land. Don't throw yourselves into perdition or think of leaving unless you are forced to do so. Just think of our Muslim kings. When the Christians started to invade their territories, our rulers yelled for help first to the Almoravids, then to the Almohads;

and when the Almohads turned against them, they turned to the Christians themselves. Now we have to lay our hopes on the Hafsids,* whose power is growing in Morocco; maybe they will be able to bring about change for the better. However, dear friends, you should not squander your lives on portents of despair. Rather you should remain steadfast, relying on the exalted heights of luminous learning; I wish you to follow the path of beneficial deeds. Before long Sabta will become the base from which I will be operating, my line of defense, and my refuge. It is there that I intend to investigate the state of affairs and appropriate spiritual postures and to engage with the bases of the protective enclosure. Now I want you all to embark upon actions that I will now outline for you. Make sure that, as you perform them, you do so in an upright and righteous fashion. Summon your colleagues to behave in a like manner."

As I had sensed, their companions were all gathered by the door, listening carefully to what I was saying. No sooner had I extended my invitation to them as well than they all rushed to join the circle of devotees, 'Adnan at their head, and greeted me with all due apologies. A chorus of voices begged me to give them a final homily. I instructed them all to be seated, said the bismillah and a prayer for the Prophet.

"Young men," I told them, "I can only tell you precisely what I tell myself and those students who are closest to me. How many times have I told myself, 'Rid yourself of all fanciful dependencies and attributes, and you will bolster your quest for the comforting shade of enveloping totality. Devote yourself entirely to your inevitable identity, and you will transcend your ephemeral one . . .'

"To the extent possible I always tell myself, 'Get to know God and only God, and you will know yourself. Through Him you will far outstrip your own self. Get to know God and only God, and you will be empowered against all evil. Mention His name, and by so doing you will render all other idols feeble; they will fall from your eyes like so many desiccated palm trunks.'

"This then tells you something about my personal state of mind. It affords me a capacity that continues to grow and aspires to touch the very heavens; it furnishes me with a delight that links my breathing to the pulses and footsteps of existence. Each one of you should only concern himself with his personal state, relying on the firmament of toil and creativity, and totally avoiding the pit of imitation and compliance. If you pursue the path that I am now recommending to you, you will emerge the winners and will prosper. You will possess both seeds and harvest.

"My children, you are the people of the word *Recite*. Each one of you should take on the words 'O John, take the book with power' [Qur'an, Sura 19, v. 12] as though they were being addressed specifically to you. You should also read the words of the prophets and sages as being epistles from them to you. Furthermore, each one of you needs to speak in the name of truth and supreme values as though emanating from the very fount of wisdom and the first of human speakers.

"The infinite universe is a book as wide as heaven and earth, so to the extent possible read it . . .

"The whole of creation is a book. Every era, old or new, is a book; every profound purpose is a book. If you focus your attention on all of this and let your endeavors set sail in its seas, it will fashion you anew and enrich you . . .

"In the past I have discovered, and still am discovering, that the only way to temper our consciousness and fructify it with the foibles of this world and the trials of existence is through acquaintance with the greatest products of human creativity and, to the extent feasible, by living in the lofty shadows of written works.

"'O how foul is the course of this world and all its goods!' Thus speaks the perennial pessimist. But the things that such a person recognizes as being the constituent elements of life: bitterness, disasters, misfortunes, and the like, are adopted by the sage researcher—duly bolstered by his own talents—as crude material to be transformed into an uplifting, brilliant poetic ode or a priceless work of enlightenment.

"So, here I am living yet another day! That expression of wonderment can serve to illustrate the different ways of interpreting tone and lifestyle. It depends on whether it is spoken by someone who is tired of life and dispirited, or by someone who is happy and full of enthusiasm and élan.

"By the reality of those strands stretching from heaven to earth, learn how to seek knowledge, though it be in China—as the saying puts it—and it will provide you with veritable banquets and festivals for your souls; it will be your tools and equipment. Unless you dwell in its welcoming courts, there can be no pleasure and no propagation. Apart from the one and only living, wise, and prudent God, it alone can provide you with power and strength.

"You all aspire to be part of the new generation, the alternative clay, do you not!"

The students all assumed that this expression of wonderment on my part was actually a question addressed to them. "Indeed we do!" they replied in unison.

"In that case make no copy of what I've just been saying," I told them, to indicate that the session was about to come to a close. "The message lies in direction and method, not in the actual contents or the text itself. Whoever finds himself in need of the latter, let him delve deeply into his own self and place it on the touchstone of higher things. He may then join those who are investigating the different aspects of my work, *The Epistle of Complete Comprehension*. As the Qur'an puts it, people 'who only encounter their own effort' [Qur'an, Sura 9, v. 79].

"Let me tell you all what happened to me on one occasion with one of God's itinerant saints. I sought to follow him and immerse myself in the river of his wisdom, but he astonished me by upbraiding me with these words: 'Make sure you never memorize what I'm telling you!' He thereby unleashed the reins for contrasts and the potential truths of contradiction, so much so that the pillars of place trembled at the sheer force of his modesty while the vessels of consciousness were almost smashed by the very power of his presence. So, all of you should bear that in mind and take note! . . ."

Now everyone stood up silently. I went out to make arrangements for Salman's livelihood. He put my cloak on me, then hugged me. I embraced him too, and noticed a tear in his eye. We all made for the door. I found that I could not help weeping as I made my way through the crowd of students and neighbors. One by one they embraced me; they were obviously deeply moved and invoked the most powerful prayers on my behalf. I mounted the horse that had been made ready for me, then proceeded on my way, with a guard on either side and the students following behind on foot. They kept waving farewell and shouting words of thanks and praise to God. As I reached the southwest edge of the city, their steps and voices gradually receded and then disappeared completely . . .

13

FAREWELL THEN, River Segura, you who have always spread brilliant verdant foliage on your banks!

Farewell, plants and crops growing in rich and plentiful gardens and meadows . . . !

Farewell, magical, time-honored Cartagena . . . !

Fields and valleys, hills and mountains covered with lush, interlacing trees of all kinds, I bid you all adieu!

I started taking in all the beauty and splendor of this land, but only in a secretive kind of way since I had no desire to exacerbate the pain of my enforced departure. There I was, now condemned to evacuate along with many others, wave after wave. As the procession slowly made its way southward, I must assume that I stayed in this frame of mind; indeed I remained distracted for the entire day. It made no difference whether the road allowed us to move at speed or forced us to slow down. With the first signs of nightfall I was forced to gather my thoughts and find somewhere to sleep in guest-houses and convents, of which I can only recall a convent in the town of Lorca and a guest-house in Wadi Ash.

It was close to sunset when we reached the eastern outskirts of Granada. I was met by a horseman who greeted me warmly and claimed to be acting on behalf of my elder brother, Abu Talib. He had been charged, he said, with taking care of me and guaranteeing my safe passage to Morocco. I made it clear to him that I was fully aware of the import of his task and preferred to be cooperative rather than obstructionist. He strongly suggested that I spend the night at a monastery close by that would suit my inclinations, so I agreed to go there. At the gate I and my companions were greeted by the shaykh. He had a special word for me: "You'll sleep especially well at the Al-'Iqab Monastery, my dear Sir . . ."

Once I was on my own in the room, I had some misgivings about this envoy from my brother and the Banu Hud, not to mention the very name of the monastery, one that inevitably brought to mind the terrible defeat the Muslims had suffered at the beginning of this cursed century in which we were living. In the middle of the night I felt beset by a series of worries that I recognized very well, since they were deeply ingrained in my soul. The only way I was able to overcome them was by reciting prayers and supplications. After that I slept lightly but peacefully.

Next morning I had some breakfast, then went up to the roof to take a look at Granada, with all its buildings, gardens, and palaces. I focused in particular on the magnificent Islamic monuments, although my admiration was tempered by worries about the city itself and the unseen dangers that it might still have to confront. While I was recalling the things I knew about Granada, past and present, a messenger arrived to convey greetings and inform me that my possessions had all been sent ahead by expedited service to Algeciras. He explained the process by saying that the idea was to save me any bother and hasten my arrival at my destination. I inquired about the two guards who had accompanied me this far, and he informed me that they had been paid the price of the horse that was now my property and had now returned whence they came. I paid him the amount due, mounted my horse, and continued on my journey. He stayed with me as we traversed the roads around Granada and started on the road toward Malaga. At that point he excused himself, saying that he had some personal business to attend to, and bade me farewell, expressing the hope that he might see me again on my next visit to Spain.

That is how I came to part company with the spy who had been sent to make sure that I did indeed leave, and with no palpable regrets. Behind me I left Granada, with its Nasrid* dynasty sporting themselves in its pools. I spent one night in Malaga and another in Estabona before finally reaching Algeciras at noon on a day in Rajab of the year 640 [1242 CE]. To my surprise I found the Banu Hud spy standing in front of me once again like some sprite springing up from nowhere. After greeting me, he grabbed hold of the reins of my horse and led me over to a sailing vessel at anchor. Showing me my baggage, he started putting it on my horse, then headed back to land—all the while wishing me a safe journey.

The ferryboat set off on its voyage. I sat myself down in an isolated corner; for a time I thought about the weather, but then I stole glances at the people all around me. Most of them looked exhausted and downcast. Once in a while a few of them did manage to muster a laugh, whether out of sheer anxiety or to make the time go quicker.

I was sitting by the stern. A beggar kept walking past with his thurible and prayers while another one kept uttering incantations. I gave them whatever alms I could afford.

Before the crossing came to an end, a middle-aged woman sat down beside me and started nursing her baby with her breast fully exposed. To my left was a man who looked like a merchant, snoring away in a deep slumber. I closed my eyes, hoping to find deep within me something to distract me from the breast on the one hand and the snoring on the other, but to my surprise the woman asked me to listen to the story she wanted to tell me and then to give her advice.

"My life has been full of calamities, dear Sir," she told me, "and I am beset with worries. After prayers to God I protest the way a man from Tarifa has behaved. The fates have clearly allowed him to overwhelm me. He pronounced the threefold divorce on me, then married me to another man, but only so that he could marry me again. But the second time the complaints he made against me were even worse. I told him to bring witnesses to confirm his accusations of fornication against me, but the only witnesses he had were the ones he saw in his dreams. A corrupt sorceress had told him that his dreams were true, but he would not tell me her name. He then converted to Christianity and refused to acknowledge that he was this child's father. Once that happened, I asked him to be rid of me, and he agreed, but only on condition that I cross the straits and never come back. So here I am, Sir, just as you see me, totally deprived and with no way of eking out a living or meeting my child's needs."

I took a sum of money out of my purse and gave it to her, mouthing some appropriately comforting words. She was amazed and delighted at my generosity. Imagine my surprise therefore when, just as the boat was anchoring, I saw my neighbor who had been snoring so loudly leap up and yell at the woman, "That lewd woman, my Lord, keeps going back and forth across the straits. With every voyage she manages to arouse people's sympathy by exposing her breast and her baby and cooking up a whole load of stories. By God, they're all a pack of lies!"

I took the man aside. "'Abdallah," I said, trying to calm him down.

"How do you know my name?" he asked in amazement.

"We're all 'Abdallahs, God's servants," I replied.

A Muslim Suicide | 87

"True enough. Just two weeks ago that woman told me a story too, and I gave her some money just as you have. Then last week she told me another one that made me forget the first! This time, the story was that her husband was laid up in bed because of a wound he'd suffered at the hands of the Castilians. He'd given her the task of collecting enough funds so that the two of them could escape with their baby as Muslims and cross over to Sabta. But this time I had no choice but to expose this trickster woman in full sight and hearing of all the passengers."

By now the woman herself had vanished into thin air and was not to be found among the disembarking passengers.

"You did wrong, my good man!" I said, turning back to him. "If you'd told me about this beggar woman when she was still with us, I would have given her even more. When this woman is forced to expose herself in public, it's poverty that's showing us the one weapon she possesses, her imagination. That is her only recourse, her means of livelihood, just as is the case with writers who compose poetry, stories, and books of *maqamat** and *zajal** poetry. She only told me one story. Had she told me many more, I would have given her yet more money. I am not bothered as to whether or not they are true. Our Lord is generous in both His rewards and forgiveness."

"Servant of God," the man replied, concealing his annoyance and amazement, "I don't think you can be either a merchant or a politician. And you can't be planning to stay in Sabta."

"You're correct on the first point, my brother," I replied, "but only circumstance and fate can tell whether you'll be right about the second."

He paused for a moment. "The people in Sabta," he said before saying farewell, "are either merchants like me or else merchants in politics. Among the rest of the elite you'll find legal specialists who play fast and loose with the Maliki school of law. Haven't you heard that Sharif Idrisi and even Judge 'Ayyad have both had to flee from this city of theirs? If you are of the Sufi persuasion, then your stay in this city—provided things work out well—will not be a long one. Just consider the case of God's saint, Abu al-'Abbas from Sabta.* He was forced to flee from Marrakesh. Once you've done that, you should bear the consequences in mind . . ."

After checking on my baggage, I mounted my horse and scanned the scene. Looking back, I could make out the woman with all the stories in the distance getting back on the ferryboat in preparation for the return trip to Algeciras. I made for an empty space close by and sat down on a tree stump in order to think about my situation and the next phase in my journey. However I was soon overcome by a powerful need for sleep and started having a very vivid dream. In it the ferryboat was being tossed around by a savage thunderstorm; the woman with all the stories was recounting the terrors of the sea, while the men on board kept trying in vain to shut her up. I watched as the merchant from Sabta picked up both her and her child and threw them overboard into the raging seas. Only a few moments later the winds snatched at the boat's sails, dragged it down, and rolled it completely over. Everyone, myself included, was tossed into the waters and began screaming for help in a total panic. At first I tried to help others, but then I was swimming for my own life. It was useless, and there I was staring death in the face. I handed things over to God Almighty and started sinking, sinking, sinking . . .

Part Two

Sabta, Haven of My Love and Monotheism

Knowledge is a mark of transcendence. Peace may bring security to an enemy. Serenity with your own self is the right path. Prayer with sincerity is a weapon. Beware of illusory hopes, of futile action, of things that corrupt the wisdom of custom and the principles of happiness.
　　　　　　　　　—Ibn Sab'in, Commentary on Ibn Sab'in's
　　　　　　　　　"Testament to His Students"

Genuine retreat involves the soul's escape from whatever is evil and destructive. It does not require a distancing of oneself from other people; nay rather, the astute adept is the one who is not governed by the destiny of categories; he is a category in his own right. He is from the people and one of the people.
　　　　　　　　　—Ibn Sab'in, *Epistle of Advice (or the Luminous)*

1

"SABTA, WITH ITS SEVEN HILLS, will become the base from which I will be operating, my line of defense, and my refuge. It is there that I intend to investigate the state of affairs and appropriate spiritual postures and to engage with the foundations of measures." That is what I had told my students on the day I left Murcia, and I expounded on it whenever they came to me, either as individuals or as groups from Granada and its environs where most of them had been forced to seek refuge.

By now almost two years have passed since my arrival in Sabta.

News kept on arriving about the way the cities of Spain were being swallowed up. More personal bits of information concerned the way my elder brother was involving himself in corrupt politics. I also kept hearing about people dying: men I had known, my servant Salman, and some of my students who had been killed. More recently, my sister, Zaynab, had died too. Shortly before her own death she had sent me news of Maymuna's passing.

"You'll remember, dearest of brothers," she had written to me, "the day when I told you that, when you had come back from your excursion together, she had slept better than ever before. You asked me how that could be, and I told you that she was just like a nursing baby that had got everything that it could want or desire. It was only one hour after your departure that I realized that she had closed her eyes forever. I didn't tell you about it at the time because I didn't want to add another source of pain to all your worries."

I learned that my two houses in Murcia and Raquta were now being used as refuges for crowds of indigents, sick people, and beggars. May God come to the aid of all of them!

I spent two years living in retreats and guest-houses, frequenting the shore-line, markets, the port, and other places such as baths and mosques. All the while I was meeting Sufis and other students, and convened a few learning circles as the occasion demanded. When I finally felt the need to spend time studying on my own, I moved to a *zawiya** on the east side of Sabta by Jabal Musa. The sultan's chamberlain, Muhammad ibn Abi 'Amir, had built a city on this spot with a view to moving the people of Sabta to it, but death had prevented him from doing so. Some two centuries or more later, all that was left of it were some walls and a few ruined buildings inside.

Near the zawiya was a wonderful, blessed spring that provided guests and passers-by with water for drinking and washing. Looking north from the mountain it was possible to gaze out over the straits, while to the south lay the restive Mediterranean and the port providing a refuge from the stormy winds. Wherever you looked, there were other small mountains, covered from top to bottom with various kinds of trees and plentiful plant life.

The zawiya devoted itself to closeted ascetics, travelers, and seasonal residents, people with a whole host of different demands and needs. There were both single rooms and shared ones, a wing reserved for observers of silence, and a courtyard open to the heavens for people who wished to talk. Its facilities included a bathhouse and a small mosque. About half a mile away was another house; people told me it was kept for the mentally ill and lunatics. The man in charge, whose name was 'Abd al-Barr al-Baradi'i, was a goodly person who made sure that money from the city-state of Sabta and contributions from donors were duly spent on every resident in accordance with his abilities and efforts. For my part I gave whatever I could.

I spent my time here in prayer, contemplation, study, and learning. Whenever I could, I wandered along the shore and up the hills. When the weather was nice, I longed for the Spain I'd lost. I looked over the straits at Algeciras and then at the Rock of Gibraltar right in front of me; in my mind I could envision myself climbing to the top of the mountain named after the great conqueror and leafing through the pages of glory and honor.

Over the course of the year I spent in my new abode, the circle of regulars who attached themselves to me as disciples expanded of its own accord. It felt like a plant in hibernation, even though some parts of it would disappear for cogent reasons that I did not understand. The core of the group consisted of a quartet, made up of 'Abd al-'Ali, 'Amr, 'Adnan, and Al-Sadiq. Every time they came to visit me and I questioned them about their personal circumstances, they were very reassuring, eager, no doubt, for me to remain assiduous in maintaining the sanctity of my own retreat and the fervor of my mission. I kept giving them details of my life inside the zawiya, in the hope that they would appreciate it and take it to heart.

Here now is something that I shared with them all on a sunny day in the mosque courtyard just before the noontime prayers:

"This dwelling, my dear friends, possesses an atmosphere that is replete with vision and nuance. Some of it comes to me when asleep, while other aspects occur in wakeful hours. What is not open to doubt is that they all descend from a lofty, innovative sphere, from a space that is both widespread and firmly established. In such a circumstance the only way I would have of preventing breaths from ascending or breaking arrows in their very bows is by leading people astray and acting unjustly, fomenting evil and ignominy—God forbid!

"As the days of my life proceed along their headlong path, my loftiest and brightest moments are the ones I spend here in this zawiya amid the mountains. I am liberated from all ties and obligations save those that link me to the untrammeled absolute that alone is suitable for me to be created and given essence in its names. Neither old age nor exhaustion has been the factor that has led me to strive in this direction, but rather a vintage maturity, a mystical gift that I have sought and struggled to attain."

With that, I started giving brief answers to the questions that some of them posed. Once they had finished, I asked them all to stand, and they did. The emotional expressions on their faces made it clear that they had comprehended my words and learned a lesson. In saying their farewells, they all embraced me one by one, then left. This time I did not allow anyone to stay behind, even those who were closest to me.

I can also recall another gathering with the same group in the zawiya's courtyard where talking was permitted. This time, however, there were more of them. I started the session by remaining silent for an hour or more. There followed another hour during which we watched a maniac pass by, talking to himself.

"Screeching silence," he was saying, "piercing optimism, passionate desire, although everything is roiled in misfortune and risk. I'm spending almost my entire life trying to cancel doubts with certainty . . ."

Still another ascetic walked past us, but this time he only communicated in gestures and signs. Having noted their implications, I proceeded to interpret the import of what I had been hearing.

"Just observe this holy man," I told them. "No sooner is he in the clutches of his linkage to the Most High than you can see him as he is now, reeling in utter joy, beating his chest, and ordering you busybodies to stay away from him and those things that you can neither see nor appreciate . . .

"The real tragedy, my friends," I went on, "is that we're all reluctant to learn about creation; either that or we're content with its outer shell as observed via mere fleeting images. Connections based on close bonds of love are eaten away by the passage of time till they rot and die away.

"Poor and indigent folk are scared and bloodied by the way we shun and despise them. We avert our gaze in order to banish them from our environment and consciousness, to such an extent that they grovel in dark caves of oblivion and neglect. Such behavior, if you would only think about it, is the very essence of error. It was Moses—peace upon Him!—who said, 'Lord, where should I seek you?' 'With those of broken hearts,' replied the Lord of Messengers and continued, 'and make sure you do not consort with the dead!' 'And who are the dead, O Prophet of God?' was the next question. 'The rich,' he replied.

"Lord God, grant us to be close to You, along with Your saints and the poor who are dear to You! Amen!"

The entire assembly devoutly chanted "Amen." Once I had answered a few of their questions, they all departed.

At another session in the courtyard open to the sky, I recall that my quartet of confidants informed me that the issue of absence was preoccupying their thoughts and causing them anxiety. Here is part of my response to the group:

"It's true that my mind spends its most profitable moments clashing with the willful elements that seek to oppose or deny it. Am I destined one day to become like Al-Hallaj,* Al-Tawhidi, al-Ma'arri, and al-Suhrawardi*—and before their time, Jesus Son of Mary and others—who all finished up in agony as they drew near to the absolute truth?

"What I do know is that every time I invert existence, I plunge deep into the labyrinths of meaning, far removed from well-trodden pathways and oft-repeated phrases. . . . Every profound researcher is honor-bound to eschew the pursuit of pleasure and the acquisition of fame.

"Since we all live in a milieu that is suffering from an acute intellectual sickness, with widespread and multifarious illiteracy, all the researcher who aspires to an untrammeled atmosphere can do is to choose to learn about the incredible, creative absence. In such a quest may lie his own private way of counteracting such rampant idiocy and working on high-level meetings between people whom I'll term 'absentees.'

"And who exactly are these 'absentees'? By that name I imply those who are attracted toward the Sublime, from among whom examples such as Ibn Bajja* from Saragossa and Ibn Tufayl* from Guadix come to mind, models made up of possible identities, representing the truth of time by means of emulation and enrichment.

"So do not heap blame on poets, philosophers, or Sufis if they decide to enclose themselves in ivory towers! Instead hold them to account; indeed, censure them if their isolation fails to produce something that is rare and valuable and if what emerges from their towers is not something to delight the soul and entice the observer.

"My dear friends, as I noted earlier, our era is indeed suffering from an obvious intellectual weakness, by which I mean the absence of any kind of investigation into the real meaning and import of our existence here on earth when confronted with the trials and tribulations of this world and time itself.

"In order to counteract such things, we need to start by observing points of focus and evidence, by gathering our share of Promethean fire, and by revealing our bid as a freshly formed indication of our own presence in history.

"It is a task that is as difficult as it is inevitable, way beyond the reach of intermediaries and totalitarians. What it requires is explorers and innovators.

"Those two groups, explorers and innovators, should be used by you as models; you should strive to imitate them. As you strive forever upward, they should be your contacts and companions. God alone is to be asked for help!"

Yet another of these sessions was held by a crumbling wall at the stables behind the zawiya. I can recall that I gave an address to the assembly that focused specifically on the correct way to behave. I restricted my remarks to my own self, since I didn't want to preach or impose any obligations on anyone. Here is part of what I said:

"My friends, we are living in an era of moral conformity and inflexibility. I cannot tell you all how often people have suggested to me that on all matters I need to conform and adapt and to stay dutifully in line with the dictates of time and place—neither conservatively backward nor ahead of myself and custom. I am constantly being told to wrap up my actions and gestures in a deceitful garb of fawning and flattery, all couched in honeyed and hypocritical discourse.

"However, like every free and intelligent individual, I am an iconoclast when it comes to customs. I have never made up my mind about anything without being keenly aware of the need to speak and witness to the truth. I regard myself as being continuously at war with the rampant triviality of our times, something that is only growing worse. My involvement in it has been and remains forthright and committed. I refuse to countenance the slightest degree of shirking or contempt. The reason is that the only genuine sense of release I feel involves resisting the corpse that stays crouched on top of the chest of the living person and combating those symmetries whose outmoded tyranny I can measure within the framework of ever-ascending and existential essentials of life. Beyond all that, my overriding task and indeed the very essence of my being involves turning my life into an incredible work of art, albeit incomplete—needless to say. Thus, my hope against all hopes is that those few dwindling petty dynasts will not manage to spoil my wedding day by curbing that spirit of defiance and resistance in me that perseveres against all odds. Cruel, dry winds and sands may blow their worst. They claim that they will indeed come, and no doubt they will, in the process obliterating my work of art and converting it to mere chaff . . ."

I said all this and more with great energy, but then suddenly fell silent, a silence that turned into a veil. Thereafter I addressed my own self, but found it hard to transfer the words to my throat. "You've spent a long time," I told myself, "more than necessary in fact, discovering that, in the long run and in the context of life and action, eternity is merely a conjecture, an original, dynamic, and lofty notion that can silence all the eloquent statements that are played on the strings of doubt and despair. It can postpone the tokens of decline till a time that remains unnamed or that may never come. To the extent possible, it manages to protect the researcher from the assaults of the Angel of Death and the erasures of forgetfulness and separation. In the light of such things and with due reliance on them, all success must aspire to a hope for either eternity or at least a degree of continuity, something that only has genuine validity when it is nourished and supported by an absolute desire for eternity . . ."

I muttered these unintelligible words to myself with my eyes closed. My close confidants must have carried me to my bed, either sound asleep or else in an extreme state of distraction and rapture. When I awoke next morning, I could still remember the session of the previous evening; not only that, but I could also recall the last comments I had muttered. Obviously I had been in some kind of trance, and the whole thing had simply overwhelmed me. Clearly it had to have had some sort of connection with my missing manuscript.

2

SIX MONTHS HAVE NOW PASSED with no news from my students. Perhaps our last session together made them feel that, since I was now in retreat, their visits were somehow bothering me and I preferred to do without them. Then again, maybe the trials and tribulations of life in our times have kept them away. Even so, I'm sure that my quartet of close confidants will be back, even if the time-lapse is a year or more.

Throughout the days and weeks I've gone back to reading books on Sufism and theology that I had brought with me as part of my baggage, and others in copied form that I got hold of through the good offices of the person in charge of the zawiya and a shaykh named Isma'il al-Tadili who was a vigorous proponent of the cloistered life. So, in addition to reading the *Risala* of al-Qushayri* and the *Ihya' 'ulum al-din* of al-Ghazali, I undertook a concentrated study of *Manazil al-sa'irin wa-zad al-'arifin* by 'Abdallah al-Ansari al-Harawi, *Dalalat al-ha'irin* by 'Abdallah Musa ibn Ishaq ibn Maymun [Maimonides], and *Fusus al-hikam* and selected chapters from *al-Futuhat al-Makkiyya* by Muhyi al-din ibn al-'Arabi. Truth to tell, the sheer perfume given off by the sublime fascinations of this treasure-trove of brilliant Islamic learning stayed with me even when I had to attend to my own personal needs. I might be asleep or taking a stroll, but I would still be able to smell and relish the scent.

So research took up most of my time, only interrupted by my modest attempts at prayer and other beneficial obligations. My own love of learning was undoubtedly my most cogent driving force, but the thing that gave it an even sharper edge was that, once in a while, snippets of my missing manuscript would come to me in a flash. I used to write them down at once in case I could use them to recall a larger segment of it.

At the end of each week I used to take walks, and that too helped sharpen my mind and enliven my spirits. The one I liked best led me to Jabal Musa ibn Nusayr⁴ to the west. I used to stroll around there, enjoying the gardens and orchards watered by fresh springs and full of sweet basil and fruit trees. There I joined other people picking the luscious fresh fruit. Occasionally I would come across an ascetic who was not actually picking but merely watching in amazement, or still another who simply stared in wonder at the gorgeous flowers and tree blossoms as they opened up. Among the most memorable occasions for me was one when I was able to watch a horse giving birth to a foal. "Praise be to the Living One, praise to the Living One!" I would shout repeatedly. At times I might ask a dervish what was the quickest way to get to a particular place I would name. Such a person would then ask me if I were on the road; if I replied yes, he would advise me to keep going and not worry . . .

I may forget some things, but I can never forget one particular ascetic, who might have been Jewish, who was facing a wall and addressing it in an audible voice. Among the words I was able to pick out were: "'O Lord, it is of no matter to me if the weather is bright or gloomy, nor do I have any objections to rainfall and the assaults of fate. No, the thing that I would ask You to do is to dispel my despair at the words of those who would distort the Torah and the equivocations of Ibn Maymun."

I felt no real sympathy for or leaning toward those ascetics, people who combined disorder with compulsion. It was just that, when things got bad for them, I understood and forgave them. Riding on the back of flashes of bogus inspiration, they were full of the wildest notions and gestures.

One day I was wandering my way through the Jamal Musa ibn Nusayr gardens with all their natural splendors. I was approaching a particularly beautiful, shady tree when all of a sudden a thought came to me, one that I had no doubt came from the inner core of my missing manuscript. I made use of the words at my disposal to write it down:

"I am not myself an ascetic, nor do I follow their path. The reason is that I am primarily concerned with order and harmony. To the extent possible I make use of image and idea in order to create. I seek to substantiate fantasies and worthy texts and make use of every sinew and resource to establish their significances. I demand all that and much else besides as I seek to traverse the wobbly bridge of life unharmed, without falling off or rolling downhill. Those people who go to great lengths to censure fanciful notions and analogical tropes clearly have no understanding of the synthetic forces and energy generators from which life derives its momentum and invigorating trends."

Early next morning I borrowed 'Abd al-Barr's horse and went to visit Tangier, intending primarily to look at the booksellers' shelves there. No sooner had I reached my destination than I started examining the city's squares and quarters and promising myself that I would come back several times more. I started exploring the city, up hill and down dale, visiting markets and stalls where professional craftsmen were trading their wares. I passed by the port where various ships and barges were anchored, a lot busier than the port in Sabta. From the highest point in the region I could look across the straits and see the Atlantic Ocean stretching away. I remembered the story that the geographer Al-Sharif al-Idrisi* and others told about Alexander's* ("the two-horned one") digging a trench in the straits between Tangier and Spain when it had previously been completely dry. Needless to say, the whole thing was a myth, something with no basis in either intelligent discourse or material possibility. The same kind of tale is told about Alexander's descending in a glass box to the bottom of the sea in order to confront the satanic beasts that, according to the story, had prevented him from building his city of Alexandria. He had made a number of facsimiles of these beasts, which had managed to overpower the actual beasts and expel them. We must seek refuge in God from such utter claptrap, stuff that is entirely the product of an overactive imagination.

Just as I had decided that it was almost time to make my way back to Sabta, I spotted a bookstore. Walking toward its owner, I gave my greetings and started perusing his stock, using both eyes and fingers. All I found were some titles dealing with topics in the Maliki legal system, along with some commentaries by recent scholars on *Al-Muwatta*,* the work by Malik ibn Anas,* the renowned Meccan legist. When the owner saw that I was disinclined to buy it, he told me that his book collection was very good. He assured me that Malik ibn Anas's book would be really useful to me, and the price was fixed. He went on to say that the other three booksellers in the city only sold frivolous materials, poorly copied at that. I asked him if he had any other books.

"The true believer's eye is never wrong," he said after staring hard at me. "I'm a believer, and I can tell that you're a keeper of secrets, someone who eschews the company of most people. I have in my possession a whole sack of books that a devout jurist advised me to burn. But I could not do such a thing, so I have hidden them from prying eyes; they're inside the box I'm sitting on. If you like, you can take them from me for a very cheap price. If you decide to do that, then take the bag with you and only open it in your own home, not here. So what do you think?"

I gave him double the price he asked. He was so delighted that he proceeded to put all the books in my saddlebags. I then went on my way, the man's prayers following me until I had disappeared from view.

After I had done some twenty-six miles, I decided to take the mountain route in the hope of shortening the remaining ten. I slaked my thirsty anticipation by fingering the precious cargo locked away inside my saddlebags, but a few miles farther on an unforeseen disaster struck. I was waylaid by three highwaymen who, with due threats, robbed me of my horse, everything it was carrying, and all the money I had left. I begged them to at least leave me the bag, whereupon the oldest of them split it open and checked what was inside. He decided to let me have the contents, which he described as a worthless pile of paper that was not worth the bother of carrying away. He told me to pick it up and leave as quickly as possible before he decided to change his mind. So that's exactly what I did.

My only recompense for what had happened was that I managed to get away and save myself. In return I had managed to acquire a load of new intellectual nourishment. I ate something, performed the obligatory prayers, and then sat down on my bed to take a look at what I had acquired, hoping, of course, that it would prove to be a rich set of pickings—all that, needless to say, before I had even broken one of the seals. The entire package consisted of eleven books; at least half of them were in reasonable condition, but the rest were in poor shape. In the first category were the *Categories, On Generation and Corruption,* and *Meteorology,* all by Aristotle;* the *Isagoge* of Porphyry;* an incomplete copy of Ibn Rushd's commentary on Aristotle's *Metaphysics;* al-Farabi's* *The Collection of Opinions of the Two Sages, Plato and Aristotle;* and Ibn Sina's* *Logic of the Orientals.* The second category included epistles and texts by the Brethren of Purity,* al-Mubashshir ibn Fatik,* and al-Suhrawardi. I had actually read most of them before, when I was in Murcia, while others were still kept in the boxes of my personal library. After thanking God for providing me with such a cache, I willingly surrendered myself to sleep.

Next morning when I awoke, I felt more than ever before the urge to immerse myself in the intricacies of Aristotle's writings. In studying the works of this divisive genius, my firm intention was not to allow myself to be taken in, something that was clearly the case with most of our peripatetic philosophers. My method would not involve blind, hand-in-glove imitation as was the case with Ibn Rushd [Averroes], nor would I follow Al-Ghazali's path, namely a method that involved cognitive shortcomings, disreputable emendations, and sectarian extremism. No, I would invoke both mind and critical acumen. When matters became tough and risky, I would seek the counsel of my own thinking, experimental self. Had I not told my students on several occasions, "Yes indeed, the person who decides to rely on his own self will find relief!"

That is how I came to spend several days in a virtually non-stop process of pouring over the works of the great Greek sage, coming to terms with their major principles and tracing the gradual processes whereby he reached his conclusions and summaries. It seemed to me that they all followed a fixed pattern and displayed particular logical qualities, whether the worlds that he investigated involved inanimate objects, flora and fauna, or human beings, even to a certain extent the heavens themselves. There was little to find fault with, except in matters of detail, of introduction, or other otiose, randomized, and only partially applicable suppositions. However, when it came to matters of theology, the ideas of the great sage began to go badly awry. Issues were confusingly treated, and both methods and goals were severely impaired. In that realm he went totally astray and led his readers down the same erroneous path.

I kept taking notes on things that I found interesting. However, when I found myself confronted with highly complex and obscure matters, I decided that the best plan was to take a walk outside in the hope of clearing my mind of their muddle. Once I had made my way through the door of my residence, I spotted the warden, 'Abd al-Barr; it was almost as though he were waiting for me to emerge. After we had greeted each other, I handed him a coin purse, explaining that it was in recompense for his horse that had been stolen from me. He swore a solemn oath to the effect that he would never take money from someone whom he considered a close friend and assured me that the horse was bound to come back unless, of course, the people who stole it decided to kill it for food. I uttered a prayer to God that things might turn out that way, then asked my companion how things were going with the zawiya and its facilities.

"Pinnacle of the Faith," he told me respectfully, "there's a fixed number of actual residents, but the number of itinerant visitors keeps growing. Ibn Khalas, the governor of Sabta, has doubled our assistance in funds and material goods and has instructed some of his aides to take charge of the insane asylum, which I can no longer manage. He's also told his aides to respond to any request concerning the facilities here."

"He's a genuinely good man!"

"Good and generous as well. But his one overriding quest is for us to rid the city of beggars, madmen, and wayfarers. He's strong-willed and rigorous and a fearless guardian of Muslim interests. His sole concern is to make sure that Sabta remains secure against any consequences of Christian victories in the many and various regions of al-Andalus. I've sat with him on more than one occasion and have had the opportunity to observe the probity of his actions and the genuineness of his intentions. I get the impression that news of your identity and presence here has already reached him, so don't be surprised if one day he asks you to come and debate with him, something he likes doing with men of learning and religion."

The warden suddenly fell silent, clearly aware that I was reluctant to get involved in a conversation about something that did not interest me.

"The governor has charged me with a task that I could not turn down. He wants me to give you a document that has reached him from the Almohad sultan, al-Rashid. It contains some dilemmas raised by Frederic,* the ruler of the Christians. He has previously dispatched it to Muslim sages in several regions of the East seeking responses, but to no avail. Then he sent it to Tunisia, but with the same negative result. Finally he sent it to Spain and Morocco. People gave him your name and whereabouts and told him about your high repute when it comes to matters such as those for which he is requesting a response. So, if only for the sake of myself and the livelihood of the people who live in these parts, would you please take a look at the document?"

I took the document from my dear friend and reassured him with a smile that I would do whatever I could, on condition that he himself would convey my response to the governor so that I would not be compelled to meet anyone in authority. I could not stop myself from taking a look at the questions that the king of the Christians had posed. I got the impression that, once I had managed to move beyond their confused jumble, I would have little difficulty in responding to them.

A Muslim Suicide | 105

"So, 'Abd al-Barr," I told him, as a way of reassuring him that the matter was easy, "the king asks me whether the world is ancient or more modern. How would you respond?"

"When it comes to proofs and analogies, I'm totally ignorant," he replied. "However I'm quite sure that only God is ancient, and that the worlds in general are all the consequence of His making and creation. That truth represents what our monotheistic faith tells us and calls us to believe."

A huge guard now came over to us, holding on to the arm of a blind youth; he clearly needed the warden for something. But the warden told him to wait while he listened to my own response:

"Your response, 'Abd al-Barr, is completely correct; all it needs is a little refinement that, with God's help, I can provide with my knowledge. The same applies to the other two questions concerning theology—its premises and goals: the nature of the soul and proofs of its continuing existence after death, and the issue of categories and Aristotle's subdivision of them into ten subdivisions. Given enough time for cogitation, you could respond to them as well."

The warden looked astonished. "Absolutely not! I have no such resources at my disposal. My dear master, you're charging me with something that is quite beyond my capacities . . ."

"To the contrary, think along with me for a moment. We both exist, and so do these two men. Everyone who shares their human essence with us possesses a self-identity—substance. That is the primary category, and it serves as the basis for other factors and additions. These are the other nine: You and I and these two other men possess quantity, quality, relation, collocation, and situation. We exist in time and place; we act and are acted upon. These categories have been termed predicates or accidents in view of the fact that they can change from one self to another; indeed they can be different within a single self. All this is apart from a few explanatory details and refinements that I can write down for the ruler of the Christians so he can learn and fully comprehend things. Have I made my point clearly enough, do you think?"

"Indeed you have, extremely well. And that even applies to someone like myself whose aspirations and abilities are minimal!"

"If you bring all these nine separate categories into a single unified whole, the number becomes ten. That's the way Aristotle organized it, no less, and certainly no more."

The blind young man let out a malicious laugh. "Anything more would come from the head of an idiot!" he yelled loudly.

"I shall also write to that effect to the Norman king, the Christian ruler," I went on, "in the hope that he'll take note and understand. 'Abd al-Barr, you can tell the governor that I'll be sending him my responses to the king's questions very soon—all with God's help, of course. For the time being, get the doctor to look at this poor young man, and ask him to treat him as best he can."

"Poor young man?" the guard yelled angrily. "Dangerous idiot, you mean! This blind youngster is causing mayhem among the insane inmates. He steals, hits people, and strips naked in front of everyone. He keeps threatening the residents with group extermination, swearing the foulest oaths to the effect that he intends to crown the exercise by killing himself either by hanging or a knife."

The young man echoed what his guard had said. "Madness is a blot on the forehead of man's intellect. Madmen are a nasty burden on society, roadblocks on the world's pathways. Killing them off is both a remedy for them and a release for mankind in general. Isn't that the truth, people?"

I told the guard that this young man had clearly reached a hallucinatory stage in which only close observation and patience would be of any use. Once I had turned my attention away from the young man, I was told that none of his companions wanted to die before the others.

"What if the plan doesn't work?" asked 'Abd al-Barr.

I paused for a moment's thought. "The major problem," I said, "is that this young man looks on his companions as mirrors that continually project the image of his own flaws and shortcomings. That's why you see him telling himself that the way to eradicate the image is by smashing those very mirrors. Just for the sake of experiment, let's try putting him in the wing with the contemplative folk and silent devotees. Maybe in the short term that will help him find some solace . . ."

After counseling patience and forgiveness, I said my farewells and withdrew.

■ ■ ■

The residents got to hear—I don't know how—that I was an expert on medicine and pharmacology. In emergency situations, 'Abd al-Barr, the warden, used to refer to me the cases of certain patients whose symptoms were not improving. Most of them involved people who were depriving themselves of their basic requirements in terms of cleanliness, food, and basic sanitation. I used to give them specific instructions on these matters, citing for them various Qur'anic verses and prophetic traditions on the topic. At the same time I used to give them food and liquids to consume, even if it meant forcing them to take them. I think that I managed to save most of them from yet worse situations, except, that is, for one old man and another who was middle-aged. The former insisted on following the pattern of the ascetic Bishr al-Hafi,* who only ever ate bread and imagined to himself that it was dipped in butter. The second man adhered to the practice of al-Bistami,* the mystic, who had this to say about himself: "I summoned her to perform a few pious acts, but she did not respond. Whereupon I deprived her of water for a year." These two men remained defiant till they died.

The kinds of sickness that used to affect residents and others passing through included colds, fever, measles, diarrhea, constipation, and the like. With God's help and the vegetal concoctions and drug compounds I put together, I managed to treat everyone. But, among all those residents, how can I possibly forget the person who preferred to suffer pain till death rather than allowing me to examine his hemorrhoid-infected anus? All of which calls to mind another story that concerns Imam Idris al-Shafi'i*—may God give us the benefit of his memory— and yet another situation of a different and particular kind. It involved a highly disturbed mental patient—how can I possibly forget it?

That morning 'Abd al-Barr came to see me. As he told me about the patient, he was clearly distressed.

"My dear Ibn Sab'in," he said as we shared breakfast, "this particular patient is really strange. He professes no religious faith and believes that his own creation is badly awry; he's convinced that he looks exactly like a monkey. His delusions are now so bad that he runs away from any park or forest where there are monkeys; in fact, it's the same even with pictures of those particular animals, which he describes as debauched and uninhibited. Oh dear, what can be done when these symptoms make themselves evident, intermittently at first but then with great insistence? The same thing is triggered by his dreams as well and by the way other people treat him, all of which makes it impossible for him to ignore what's happening to him. What aggravates the entire situation is that we have no idea what to do about the mirrors he insists on putting up so he can regularly check on his dreadful resemblance to monkeys. As time has gone by, his condition has become so chronic that I've been forced to call in fortune-tellers and mystics of various kinds. Their counsel to him has been to pray and seek the sweet scent of the divine. Thus far, they've decided to keep him away from people and mirrors so that his animal instincts can be obliterated through a concentrated focus on contacts with the spiritual realms. At this point he's been here at the zawiya for a year, following these regimes, but there has been no palpable improvement in his condition. It fluctuates between periods of relief and others of chronic intensity. I've even offered to teach him how to read so that he can use the enlightened learning of the major source-texts on matters heavenly and earthly as a means of protection, but all to no avail."

As the warden finished his account, he gave me a look of one seeking a solution or at least some help.

"A really peculiar situation!" I replied. "If the measures you've described have not worked, then God alone can provide a cure."

"God alone," he said, "and you as well."

I shuddered to hear him say such a thing.

"The patient tells me," the warden went on by way of explanation, "that the only time he feels any relief is when he is looking at your face. He wants to join your coterie of visitors and companions and promises that he won't be a bother or burden to you."

I welcomed the idea, although I was still not a little surprised. The warden looked relieved and clapped his hands twice. A middle-aged man now appeared and stood in front of us, eyes lowered in embarrassment. He looked like a human being, not a monkey, with a circular-shaped head and snub nose. He was short and narrow-shouldered, and his lips were chapped. I stood up to greet him and help him relax. I asked him his name and profession. With a sideways glance he told me his name was 'Isa al-Aftasi, and he had had a number of minor jobs.

"Do monkeys realize they look like you?" I asked. "Do they have any way of knowing?"

He shook his head.

"Even if we supposed that monkeys could know such a thing," I went on, "do you think they would be going through the kind of grief and trouble that you are? Do you think they would be trying to outdo each other, the way we are now?"

Again he shook his head.

"So, you're you," I went on, "and they're they. The only thing in common is an animal nature, and that can't possibly have any connection with the traits that

God has given you: an expressive soul, a mind, and thought, just like every other human being He has created and endowed."

The man's expressions changed, and he burst into a smile. He asked my permission to leave, followed by the warden, who was rubbing his hands together. "Good heavens!" he kept repeating.

3

IN MY CURRENT QUARTERS time passed pleasantly; the days were full of positives rather than negatives, of ups rather than downs. Even the birds, it seemed, headed our way in quest of their own share of their particular qualities and features. I used to go into Sabta once or twice a month to stroll around and get whatever I needed; I would frequent its Kasbah and mosque and make some purchases at the port: ointments, perfumes, fish, and bread.

The city itself had expanded outward because floods of people kept arriving from Spain, Muslims and some Jews as well, the elite and common people alike. Some were wealthy, others indigent, but they were all united in their sadness and grief. Fortunately they had no difficulty integrating themselves into the daily lives of the people of Sabta, where they could feel safe and respected.

One day I was meandering my way through the fishmongers' stalls at the port, looking for some shark, mullet, and carp, when I spotted a woman staring at me, her eyes gleaming behind a thin black veil. Completely oblivious to my surroundings, I began to take in her perfect beauty and to exchange deeply meaningful glances with her. I only came back to my senses when the fishmonger whose catch I was still holding addressed me: "God be praised! Do you like what you see?"

"Who?" I asked.

"Excellent choice! Good and succulent . . ."

"Who?" I said again.

"The fish you're holding!"

I paid the man for the fish and some others that were smaller, but declined the other fish he offered me. Once I left his stall, I noticed that the woman was still in sight, so I quickened my pace. But just then an annoying dervish stopped me and refused to get out of my way until I had explained to him how it was that beans and humus were called poor man's meat; and what wisdom was there in choosing fish over meat? While I was concocting a response that this idiot could understand, I realized that the object of my quest had by now disappeared without a trace. Rather than go on looking for her, I decided to trust in God and return to my residence.

It was almost evening by the time I got back to my room. I sat there, looking at the carp, with its eyes open, its thin nose and lips, its delicate features, and its wonderful shape and smell. So tempting and luscious was its body that it seemed to be enveloped in a gleaming white halo. I was so thrilled by its appearance and eager to consume it that I rushed to prepare it for grilling so that I would gain the greatest possible benefit from eating it. And so it was. Once I had finished, I gave thanks to God Almighty and lay down to concentrate on the concept of those gorgeous, bright, mascara-lined eyes I had seen. When I had first spotted her, she had lowered her gaze, and I got the impression that I was looking at a devout recluse. But then I had taken a longer look, and the sense of pleasure I felt was even stronger and more penetrating, the kind that, within the context of women and pleasure, will regularly strike the lover—all in accordance with the practice of the Prophet of Islam, who declared, "There is no monasticism in Islam." It was that stronger and more penetrating sense of delight that was affecting me now, as I lay there on my own recalling the face of that lovely, radiant woman.

How amazing that I should feel so passionate toward those who make up half of humanity!

How amazing that I've not forgotten those who are the companions of men, particularly in view of the fact that this period that I'm spending in seclusion in this zawiya imposes no barriers between myself and the supply of women!

No, I am no ascetic when it comes to women or my own portion of this life on earth. I'm neither an ascetic nor a monk, the kind of people who go to excessive lengths in displaying their poverty, harboring their frustrations, and renouncing all of life's demands on them.

While my memory, associations, and impressions were all at their height, I had the vision of a woman whose name and other particulars I had forgotten. All I could recall were her facial features and the fact that she loathed men. She used to spend precious time setting snares to trap her lovers, then cast them off and laugh at their indignity. No sooner had God seen fit to enlighten me about her behavior than I made good my escape.

There was another woman as well about whom the only thing I can remember is that I'd spoken to her as she emerged from a swim. "That water's dirty and unsafe," I said. "You're extremely beautiful and deserve much better. Shall I show you where such water can be found?"

"Haven't you anything better to do," she responded with a sarcastic laugh, "than hang around leering at me?"

I cannot remember how I replied. All I know is that the exchange marked the beginning of a profound relationship that was only broken by a rich merchant who managed to immerse her in a vast sea of money and gifts and kept her like a toy doll amid all his other possessions and property.

Had I kept on invoking memories like these, I could have come up with images of other women, scattered and fragmentary though they might well be. For that very reason I decided to think about nothing; yes indeed, nothing at all!

Come to ablution, then prayer! That done, I kept sleep at bay by finishing my reading of Ibn al-'Arabi's *Bezels of Wisdom*, actually the final section, "The Bezel of the Unique Wisdom in the Word of Muhammad." I contemplated the significance of several amazing paragraphs, among which were the following:

Concerning the category of love, which is the basis of existence, he said, "In your world three things were made objects of my love, in that the world contains a threefold aspect. He then mentions women and perfume, with prayer as the most desirable of all. Thus, the Prophet began with women and placed prayer at the end, in that woman is a part of man in the basic manifestation of her source and man's awareness of his own self antecedes that of God. Knowledge of God is a result of self-knowledge. For that reason the Prophet—peace be upon him!— said, 'He who knows himself, knows his Lord.'"

Here is another wonderful passage: "Muhammad—may God bless and preserve him!—is the clearest proof of his Lord. Every part of this world gives evidence of its source, namely the Lord; so take notice! Women were made beloved to Muhammad, so he longed for them since it is part of the longing that the whole feels for its individual parts."

And another one: "When a man loves a woman, he desires union; that is, the goal of union that exists through love. In the image of essential formation there exists no greater union than that of marriage."

And one last one, although by no means the last of all: "The witness of the Truth regarding women is the finest and most complete of all. Marriage is the finest union. It is akin to divine direction given to those whom He has created in His image in order to create him. Thus, in him He sees His own self. He molded him, adjusted him, and breathed into him His own spirit which is His own self. The outer surface of Him is creation; the inner part is Truth . . ."

No sooner had I finished reading this chapter and started contemplating its significance than I fell into a deeply contented slumber. When I woke again, it was to realize that the inevitable had indeed happened: a dream in which I was dancing with a carp that had been transformed into a mermaid, the most beautiful and gorgeous imaginable; and another dream involving pleasantries exchanged with virgin girls, followed by sex with exquisite houris, and a life of bliss. And all of it thanks to a dream culled from my reading of paradise as envisaged by Muhyi al-din Ibn al-ʿArabi, to whom I express my gratitude.

So come to purity and prayer, and then the ritual of union!

■ ■ ■

These reflections were interrupted by a series of gentle knocks on the door. I allowed Tariq to come in and found myself facing the quartet of my closest confidants. I stood up to embrace them all and asked them why they had stayed away for so long, hoping all the while that it was all to the good.

"Yes, everything's fine, praise God!" said ʿAdnan to reassure me. "The problems of daily life have kept us occupied, but you, beloved friend, reside permanently in our hearts."

"You asked that your seclusion be unsullied," ʿAmr went on. "For that reason we were anxious not to disturb you."

"Even so," Tariq added, "we found the long separation unbearable, so we've come to see you along with the ever-growing number of your admirers. We won't be staying any longer than necessary."

"You are all welcome," I told them joyfully. "Bring them all in."

There were about thirty people, so my room was far too small. I invited them all to take a walk on Jabal Musa so we could stroll around, fill our nostrils with the fresh air, contemplate the things we saw, and appreciate the miracles of divine creation. I began by introducing myself to each one of them, but then we made our way to Jabal Musa; sometimes I would be in the lead, but at others I preferred to stay in the middle. I said rather little, choosing instead to give free rein to gestures and the vistas before us.

We made our way through a shady forest with overhanging branches and leaves. It was inhabited by monkeys, gazelles, and other species of animals whose calls we could hear without actually seeing them. We then reached an open park area with rippling brooks and lush trees. At their tops birds of all kinds competed to sing the loveliest song as though to provide welcome and entertainment in celebration of our arrival.

For the benefit of the overwhelmed students I pointed out one of the ascetics, who was transferring his gaze from the heavens to the stone tablet on which he was drawing. But, when some of us drew near, he grabbed his tablet and ran away. I then went on to identify someone else who was watching in fascination as flowers and trees shed their blossoms; and still another one, whom I had never seen before, stark naked except for a loincloth, who was rolling around in the dust and water, repeating over and over again, "He is God . . . He is God!" I told them all not to go near him, or else he would vanish in the blink of an eye.

During the course of our walk we came across a lake that I had not known about before; a number of streams emptied into it. One of the young men asked my permission to have a swim.

"Water belongs to God," I said; "it belongs to anyone who enters it uttering praises in the name of the Living One."

They all stripped, adjusted their underwear, praised God, and then plunged into the lake one after another. Others did likewise, and soon there were a lot of people swimming, all diving and splashing each other. They were so happy that they started singing verses from zajals and muwashshahs. They sang with powerful voices, till one of them interrupted with a new key: "God, oh God!" to which they all replied, "Hu-li, hu-li!"

I noticed that my quartet of confidants was not joining in the fun. I was curious as to why not, so I asked them.

"Is having fun swimming in a lake appropriate behavior for people like us?" 'Amr said in response to my question. "You must be aware how desperate the situation of Muslims in enemy territory has become, and yet you give us very little instruction and advice and only have time for an occasional chat."

His colleagues indicated their agreement with what he was saying.

I told them to sit down under a blood-orange tree somewhat apart from the people who were swimming in the lake.

"'Amr," I said, anxious to clarify the obscure and simplify the complex, "it's perfectly fine for those young men to have some fun if it serves to prepare them to adopt a serious and committed attitude to life. As I've told you before, the human soul begins to feel overwhelmed when worries turn into a constant and recurring nightmare. The resolution of such feelings comes with initiative and enthusiasm.

"You talk about Spain, where at this point only a few unstable petty dynasties remain on the southern fringes of the Peninsula. However, I can tell you that, whenever you see me falling silent, it's precisely because that country is constantly on my mind. As far as I can see and surmise, the only way out of this crisis—and I've said this before—requires first and foremost that we ourselves bolster our spiritual armament and psychological stamina; in other words, we need to make sure that there's no weakening of our resolve or slackening of our personal pulse and resolution. We should also be relying on the political power of the Hafsids once they have established their control over the Maghrib territories, they being the heirs of the first generation of Almohads. Ah, hope, hope! Our Prophet Muhammad—peace be upon him!—said, 'Hope is a mercy from God to my community. Without hope, no mother would ever nurse a child, and no one would ever plant trees.' Hope and action, they are the means of escape for those in the know: action and hope.

"Have I made things clear enough? I'll say it again: I am neither imam nor missionary. Peruse the texts I've recommended to you, then you can bring me your questions and problems. By then the essence will have matured and the parameters will be visible. At that point we'll be able to study them all by means of effective insight and constructive dialogue. Convey this message of mine to your friends, those who have come with you and the others who have not. Don't come back unless you have taken my words to heart and carried them out to the full. So, 'Abd al-'Ali, why haven't you taken a swim?"

"In my pocket I'm carrying a piece of paper," he replied, "that I've kept with me all the way. It's a contract for the sale of your two houses in Murcia and Raquta. The offer comes from a Jew who claims he knows you. His name is Abu Zakariyya ibn Ezra."

"Yes, I do indeed know him. A while ago he sold me some rare books very cheap. But what about the indigents and vagrants who are living there? Where are they supposed to go?"

"All kinds of thieves and rogues have joined their number. They threw the poor folk out and turned the two houses into dens of vice. Ibn Ezra has promised in front of witnesses to take good care of the two houses, including the best interests of the people to whom you were committed, both Jews and Muslims."

"Fine then, bring over the contract for me to sign. Distribute the revenue from the sale among the poor and needy. Come on now, let's catch up with our friends; they seem to have had enough of the water too soon."

Now that the exercise and swimming had made them all feel hungry, a few of them approached me joyfully and asked my permission to eat some of the fruit off the trees. No sooner had I told them to go ahead and eat to their hearts' content than everyone started picking fruit, each one according to his own needs. When they had finished, I signaled to them all to sit down so they could rest for a while and contemplate their own souls.

Silence reigned, only broken by the swishing of the grass, the discourse of birds, and the rustle of leaves in the trees. After about an hour, I stood up and invited them all to think about what they had lived through and witnessed that day, in the hope that they might learn things from its particular lessons and indicators. Once I had said that, I bade them all farewell one by one, then went on my way to continue my stroll by myself.

Alone I walked up hill and down dale. According to doctors and sages, walking brings with it tremendous benefits and helps stave off stiffness and bodily shrinkage. So, my soul, put on your shoes and join me in exploring the world's different spaces! Travel with me and adopt a positive attitude!

It now felt as though all the elements, whether in succession or fragments, were not merely accompanying me, but also addressing themselves to my walking gait. Ideas—good heavens!—so, so many ideas kept coming to me, separately or all crowded together. Concentrating my attention on the most plausible and using them to guide my path, I proceeded to challenge myself on various issues and to act as my own interlocutor. I was considering contradictions and opposites, wresting from them whatever could be reckoned both constant and attribute. I was proclaiming the concord of their substantiality through the very extent of my own expansiveness and passion. When I was so engaged, I saw myself turning my back on all that was foolish and base. My longing, my desire for the truth, stretched forth like the coursing of blood through the veins, illuminating things for me through the atom and the very universe . . .

A Muslim Suicide | 117

So were these the lights of transcendent knowledge passing through me? Was this then the grindstone of the one existence that was making itself known to me?

By all that is true, I am not some buffoon trekking through the wilderness nor have I lost my mind. . . .

I had not brought a compass with me, so I was afraid that, if I kept on walking like this, I would get lost. I decided to go back the way I had come before it got dark and I would not be able to make out the way back to my residence. While I was walking through the mountain forest, I spotted an ascetic rolling in the mud and dust; it may have been the same one I had seen earlier with the group. I hurried over to him, but no sooner did I get close than he rushed off. I chased after him and watched as he shinned up a tall tree and lodged himself at the very top. I tried to climb up, but in vain. I only managed to get a grip on the huge trunk by making a pile of refuse and rocks, but the thick clusters of wet branches blocked my ascent. The effort wore me out, and I resorted to shouting out to him that he should come down and tell me who he was. When I shouted again, I heard a voice coming back to me like a whistling breeze:

"I am the one you espied craving to embrace the truth. By the very truth of that truth, you will never manage to comprehend me until you dispel all the encumbrances around you and lighten your load."

And with that, he simply vanished, almost as though he had borrowed some aerial pathways and transcended the treetops in leaps and bounds.

I continued on my way, pondering everything I had seen and heard. I do not know how it happened, but I managed to end up at the base of the mountain and then the port itself. It was only then that I became aware of an image, the quest for which had been guiding my way. I now decided it was better to go back to my residence rather than linger in a place where there was no commerce, whether buying or selling. When I reached the zawiya, all was quiet. Entering my room, I washed myself, did the ritual ablutions, then said my prayers. That done, I made straight for bed without eating anything or even reading a section from al-Muhasibi's* *Book of Contemplation,* which lay open in front of me. What I really wanted was to go to sleep, a calm and gentle slumber.

4

NEXT MORNING I was eating breakfast and arranging papers and pens with a view to working on some pages of my letters when I heard a gentle tap on the door. The warden told me that he was sorry to disturb me but it was something important. I opened the door and welcomed him.

"Forgive me, Sir," he said, looking unusually flustered. "'Isa al-Aftasi has packed up and gone back to his family in Granada. He did not dare wake you up, but he made me promise to convey his thanks to you and his enormous gratitude for the way you managed to cure him of his illness. He has now made peace with the image in the mirror and confirmed that man is indeed more capable and noble than the ape. He no longer addresses such creatures with 'hail to myself.' Things have reached such a point that he has now adopted a monkey and keeps telling it that he is himself, and the monkey is itself too. Cordiality and play are the only two things that bring both of them together."

"This comes," I commented, "as a result of God's grace and favor."

"There's a young man at the door," he went on, "who insists on seeing you. I haven't been able to keep him away. He claims that he's bringing you a message."

The young man stood in front of me and hesitated to say anything. The warden said his farewells and left. I invited my visitor to sit down and reveal his message. The tone of voice and gestures he used both failed to conceal his effeminate manner.

"My mistress has instructed me to convey her letters to you without comment," he said.

After handing me the sealed letter he disappeared like a flash of lightning. I broke the seal with eager anticipation. The letter was written on expensive paper

119

in an elegant Maghribi script. The writer began by expressing her praise and thanks to God, then went on as follows:

"My eyes fell on you, and yours on me. But I was the first to do so, and so my delight is double. By contrast yours is just one, but the second remains with me as a form of compensation. Whenever you desire it, my servant will guide you to me. If you so wish, be at the port either tomorrow or any morning. If a week goes by and you feel no desire to respond, then be prepared to acknowledge, you handsome and resolute man, that I have made contact."

I read the letter again, sentence by sentence and word by word, the way I always have done when reading the choicest aphorisms, prophetic accounts, and major source-texts. Once I understood the import of the message, I dropped everything else and gave free rein to thoughts about its potential implications. It felt as though I had just been taxed with a highly complicated juridical or mathematical problem. I proceeded to assess its precedents and parameters and exercised my mind in recreating a sequence according to the principles of both congruity and clarity. I was hoping thereby to reach some mental conclusions, in the light of which I could determine what should be my posture and course of action. However, truth to tell, after expending considerable energy contemplating the event from every angle and putting it through the grinder of my thought processes, I discovered that I was no further forward in deciding either what it all implied or what was the best solution to the issue. Once again I came to the firm conclusion that anything connected with humankind and questions of love and passion will always resist attempts to apply pure logic and similar approaches to its solution. Perhaps that is what God is saying in the Qur'an: "Humanity is the most disputatious of things" [Sura 18, v. 54].

I had no problem working out that the woman's messenger had trailed me from the port to Jabal Musa and had thus discovered my hiding place. It was equally easy to guess that my addresser was a woman, one with no male person to tend, guard, and interrogate her. But how was I supposed to know for sure that her goal was something other than getting me into trouble? To be sure, the fact that she had taken the initiative by looking at me and sending the letter was nothing unusual in the women of our region and era, and yet women with those characteristics fell into two categories: the first were free and high-minded, but the second were deceitful trollops. So to which of these two categories did this woman belong, who was now preoccupying my attention and distracting me from my primary goal in coming to this remote mountain spot?

I stood up to pray and perform my obligations. I tried to write something, but failed; when I tried to read, I found I could not concentrate. I told myself that I could overcome the mood I was in by taking a promenade around some of my favorite spots, in the hope that the gorgeous vistas they offered would provide me with some consolation and distraction. But, even though I implemented such a plan, the walk did me no good and the vistas totally failed to enchant me or put an end to my bewilderment. Retracing my path to the zawiya, I was fully intending to find some people to talk to so I could avail myself of some diversion and means of forgetting. But, although I searched in all the halls and corridors, I could only find a tiny portion of the residents. Avoiding the wing where the observers of silence were housed, I headed for the mosque to perform the evening prayer with the others. And so it happened, although this time I made a point of greeting many of the worshippers, but without finding any effective way of engaging them in a conversation. All of which confirmed what 'Abd al-Barr, the warden, had told me previously, namely that the majority of people were only staying in this lofty zawiya to put their own affairs in order, something that required them to separate themselves from the rest of humanity, squelch their desires, and refrain to the extent possible from both food and conversation.

As I was making my way back to my room, I noticed 'Abd al-Barr rushing in my direction. He told me that a Christian had arrived that day and was lodging in the transients' quarters. He had requested that, before he resumed his travels, he might seek the opinion of a Muslim sage concerning something that had happened to him in his own country. The warden gave me the kind of look that begged me to take on the task. But how was I supposed to take on such a charge, when what I really needed badly was to forget the past and find consolation elsewhere? Even so, I indicated that I would be waiting for his guest in my room and requested that he send over some food and drinks.

An hour later or less I heard someone knocking on the door. I stood up to welcome my visitor and invited him to sit down with me. Like me he was in his thirties, with a beard thicker than my own and somewhat threadbare Castilian dress. His remarkable eyes had a fiery sparkle to them, and his hoarse voice wavered between ebullience and softer tones. He told me that his name was Pedro

DelCastio. He was a discharged soldier, unmarried and with no children. Few of his original family in Toledo were still alive, and he had spent much time traveling between the domains of Christians and Muslims.

The servant brought us a pitcher of milk and a bowl of assorted fruit. I invited my guest to partake, but he declined. In order to give him the opportunity to talk, I kept my own mouth occupied by eating.

"Sir," he said, "I am wracked by diseases, ones that trouble my soul, not my body. I have been married three times and divorced. The Castilians dragooned me into their infantry, but I found that I was neither able to grant death to anyone nor did its own assaults manage to sweep me away either. One day when I was in a central church in Cordoba belonging to my sect, I encountered a counselor monk, Father Paulo, and explained the way my conscience was troubling me.

"'I will conceal nothing from you, Father,' I said. 'I'm not fit for anything. My life is one long chain of disasters and failures. I can show you lost opportunities and crucial mistakes in setting and meeting any sort of goals. Needless to say, I'm not proud of any of that, but it's the truth, and there's nothing I can do to make it either go away or change. I beg you therefore, Father, don't tell me that the Creator fashioned mankind in his own image and form. If that were true in my case, then the Creator who made me would need to be ashamed of what He had created and chew His fingers in sheer regret.'

"The monk was not the slightest bit upset by what I had said nor did he treat it as sacrilege. Instead he gave me a response that was consoling and reassuring. 'Every lost sheep thinks the way you do, my son,' he said. 'But, whenever the times seem to turn against you and other weak creatures like you, they make sure that you are returned to the fold because of your excessive concern about the minutiae of this ephemeral world of ours. That is the way it has been since the beginning of creation and for century after century. The ways of God are not for knowing or examination.'

"It was with firm step and resolution that I withdrew, my eyes riveted on the earth beneath my feet. Ever since that encounter, I have had this desire to meet God so that I can discuss with Him (in a short chat or a dream even) a variety of pressing and complex issues. I want it to be head to head, over a table, in a cave, or under a tree, with the wind blowing free. No ceremony, no intermediaries, and no translator.

"Eventually there came the night—perhaps after a hundred of them—when in a dream I saw a being crowned with light. Not for a single second did I hesitate before ascribing to Him the attributes of God. At first I was somewhat scared, but then I prepared myself to embark upon the conversation. But I had scarcely opened my mouth before I felt myself violently enveloped by a sharp, loud voice that simply repeated the precise words that Paulo the monk had used with me earlier. When in my panic I spotted that same Paulo drawing ever closer to me with a mocking, crafty look on his face and then withdrawing amid the ringing of chants and bells, I leapt out of bed, eyes bulging, tongue lolling, and body sagging. It only took a few days to complete the purgation of those things that tied me to this world and its people, after which I set out on my way. I have traversed my homeland and the straits, and now here I stand before you, Sir, all tatters and anxieties. By now I have despaired of the above-mentioned priest and my own God, and I ask for succor from your own God."

I immediately started communing with myself, asking God the Almighty, the Lofty and Powerful, God of all peoples, to offer forgiveness. What was I supposed to say to this vagrant, recusant Christian? Would he understand me, I wondered, if I spoke to him in a way that would normally require me to use gestures and symbols with my own students?

I decided to use uncomplicated language in the hope that some of it might manage to offer him some comfort and ease his situation.

"Brother in faith," I told him, "it is by observation and experience that I have now been drawn to the conclusion that anyone who fails to aspire to the loftiest of delights must inevitably find himself groveling in the lowest of pits. The elixir of perfection lies in the quest for it. God's pathways are treacherous, because they are tortuous and steep, and yet they are neither closed nor inaccessible to those who would tread the path of knowledge. Those who decide to pursue that path are given commands. 'O human,' they are told, 'strip yourself of your illusions and fancies. Make it your goal to rise upward, thus overcoming inertia. You are bound to encounter the luminescence of closeness to God. Make a point of regularly engaging in rigorous endeavor and forceful hypothesis, and you will find yourself blending with the corpus of phases and the comprehension of the Living One. Through knowledge and exploration you may well arrive at the very dominion of truth.'"

As I said this, I suddenly realized that it was almost certainly like a passage from my missing manuscript: "If God is either extremely obscure or extremely obvious, there can be no need for learning."

With that the man leapt to his feet, his eyes agleam with the spark of someone who has just become aware of God. He paused for a moment, as though contemplating or recalling something, and then addressed his soul in his own language. As far as I could understand, he was posing it a question.

"What are you asking about, thou guest of God?" I asked.

"The ascetics' forest! Am I anywhere near it?" he inquired.

"About two miles away," I replied.

"The words you have just spoken—may God reward you for them!—have made me long to be there. I will make my way to it and to its inhabitants."

"By all means do so," I told him, "but you need to realize that the people dwelling there will only warm to you if you discard all the superfluities of your existence the same way they themselves have. If you find them pondering the heavenly kingdom and praying submissively, do not try to talk to them. If you do happen to speak to them and they run away, you should be aware that it is the very smell of you that makes them distance themselves. At that point, Pedro, begin as they began. Don't hurry. Roll in the dust and purge yourself with water whenever you find any. Warm yourself by the lighted candle and breathe in the pure air. Wherever you alight, wherever you turn your gaze, there will be the face of God. Just speak His name, and you will see Him looking into your eager, monotheistic soul."

I stood up to say farewell to my guest. He hugged me joyfully and, with tears in his eyes, wished me well. With that he hurried out.

"O Lord," I prayed, "I have counseled your erring servant who needed to do things I have not done myself and have thus empowered him. So forgive and restore me, then move me toward those sublime goals and still loftier love."

I kept praying to my soul for elevation and purity of spirit, when all the while it was completely preoccupied with the woman who kept disturbing my waking and sleeping hours and penetrating my inner self and every line of text. . . . A woman about whom I was totally ignorant! The way she had looked at me at the port, her letter to me . . . Now here I found myself drawn toward her in a way I had never felt before. Was this a disaster that the fates had thrown in my path in order to test me? Or was it instead a form of relief and an opening? Or again a fall into the abyss? In the context of the present, that is the glaring question; indeed, more than that, the very foundation and principal core of those questions.

The rest of the day afforded me enough time to embark on some selective investigations. On the morrow however, it would be a matter—with God's strength—of more applied and focused energy.

5

NEXT DAY I WOKE UP full of energy, although my mind was still moistened by a dream whose particulars had dissipated, leaving behind some vague and contradictory shards. I performed my ablutions and prayed, then put on my clothes and some scent. I was planning to go down into the city again to replenish my provisions and check on the general situation of the people there. That is exactly what I did.

The first place to which my own two feet guided me was the port. Right by the entrance I spotted the woman's messenger, almost as though he were waiting for me to arrive. Using body movements and winks he gestured to me to follow him, but I decided not to do so in case people were keeping an eye on me and for fear of arousing suspicions. Instead I went into the fish market and bought several types, except for carp, that is. Then I went to the herb and perfume markets and purchased whatever supplies I needed. Every time I turned around, it was to find the same young man watching me and making the same lewd gestures. I headed for the vegetable market and filled the remaining space in my basket with fruit and vegetables.

Just then I felt someone touching my back very gently. Turning round, I discovered a pregnant beggar-woman with children. She was telling me that, because she was pregnant, she was perpetually hungry; she particular craved the fish whose smell was wafting out of my basket. I responded to her request by emptying the fish in my basket into her bag. At this point, one of the elderly residents of the zawiya, whom I knew by his thick white beard and with whom I may have exchanged a few words before in the mosque, stood in my way. We greeted each other, but then I listened as he bemoaned the corruption of his era and people and the bad times they were living through. Everyone was scowling and downcast. He then went on to describe anyone who could muster a laugh as being either totally preoccupied with worries or else stark raving mad. I asked the man to move beyond such thoughts and to pray to God his Maker that He might bring relief to the people of this city as well as others. While this man was enumerating for me the drawbacks of this world and the evils of mankind, the young man who had been trailing me came over and addressed the old man.

"My mistress adores the saints of God," he said sweetly. "It is her devout hope that you visit her in her house, both you and your friend, so that she may seek your blessing."

The old man agreed immediately. The young man snatched my basket from my hands and with a happy stride walked ahead of us.

We made our way along streets both wide and narrow, sometimes uphill, at others down. The old man was holding my arm as he breathlessly told me about the main features of his city of birth and upbringing, Meknes. He gave me an account of its delightful terrain, water, and air and named all its holy men one by one, recounting their miraculous and generous deeds. I wanted to give him a breather, so I started telling him about aspects of his native city that he had not mentioned, but he soon cut me off by suggesting that I ask him about the reason for his leaving Meknes and coming to Sabta when his native city was bursting with both charity and blessing.

"I ask God," he said, "to open for me opportunities wherever it may be. When He comes, I shall return to my birthplace and never leave it again. Would you like to hear why I left now, or when we are back on the mountain?"

I was on the point of suggesting that he postpone his account, but I saw that our guide was opening the door of a house in a side alley and inviting us to accompany him inside. We followed him as he led us down corridors and through halls until we reached an absolutely exquisite inner garden, topped by a green dome and surrounded by lofty decorated and painted doors that opened in turn on to beautifully furnished apartments. The young man invited us into one of them where we could await the arrival of his mistress. Then he disappeared.

Once we were seated, my companion started looking at the furniture, benches, and plush carpets.

"A woman who owns a *riyad** such as this," he said admiringly, "and who loves pious men is clearly a mystery, one that I will have to crack for myself."

I advised him to lower his voice, whereupon he leaned over and urged me to listen to the second reason. I was surprised until he reminded me that what he meant was the second reason for his leaving Meknes and coming to Sabta. I told him to keep the story for a more appropriate moment. By now the old man was emerging from his peculiar frame of mind and still seemed fascinated by his surroundings, as though he had never seen the like of them before and was anxious to talk about them or anything else.

We remained seated like this until the servant came back with two others carrying a table piled high with food and drink. They placed it in front of us and left. I refrained from grabbing anything off the table, but my companion launched into the food as though he were breaking a fast of some duration or using chewing and swallowing as a substitute for talk. The servant insisted that I have something as well, so I took a fig and a glass of milk. At this point the servant started plying between the two of us, whispering into the ear of each in turn. He did his dogged best, but eventually the old man let out a bellow.

"I'm only going to leave this riyad when my companion does," he yelled with his mouth full, "and that's it . . ."

The young man came over and spoke to me.

"I've been suggesting to the old man that he take as much food as he wants and leave, but you can see for yourself that he absolutely refuses to do so. I've tricked you into coming to the house without my mistress knowing about it, but this old gaffer is ruining the whole plan. My mistress is bathing and is anxious to see you by yourself. What do you advise me to do?"

What was I supposed to say? When I agreed to enter this house, this fellow from Meknes was serving as my chaperone. It would be quite wrong to throw him out or simply wash my hands of him. That is basically what I told the servant, and I went on to promise that I would come back to visit his mistress whenever it was convenient. He gave a deep sigh and went skipping away like a sprightly fawn.

"Young people today! They have no shame or sense of decency . . . Tell me, for heaven's sake, have you ever seen a cat scampering away from a bridal residence?"

The old man kept up his rant between bites of the food. I managed to calm him down and reassure him.

For a moment I was distracted from my surroundings. I let my consciousness float amid the various levels of memory and contemplation until I reached the firm conclusion that the anticipation I was sensing was something the like of which I had never experienced before: patience combined with relish and delight; a wakefulness full of visions and dreams; time flowing on its exuberant way, measured not by its usual subdivisions but in terms of heartbeats and bursts of emotion. I found myself beyond such ties, being drawn irrevocably toward an opening that brought me blessings and an ascent that I devoutly desired.

While I was thus endeavoring to assess my situation, I suddenly felt the Meknesi's hand touching my thigh.

"Dear holy man of God," he said, drawing my attention back to my surroundings, "do you see the things that I do? How can any human tongue convey the truth of it? Mere words are completely inadequate. Praise be to the Creator of all that is beautiful and perfect, the Lord of mankind! That is all I can say."

I took a look around me and shared the amazement that my companion was expressing; in fact, my own astonishment was even greater. Here was an extremely beautiful and graceful woman walking toward us in the garden, surrounded by servants, both men and women. When she drew close, I stood up, and so did my companion, wiping his mouth sheepishly on his sleeve as he did so. She greeted us both and invited us to sit with her.

Her ravishing beauty—O my God!—was yet another sign of the Creator's existence and a cue for paeans of praise to His beautiful names.

"I am so sorry for the delay," she said in a soft, melodious voice. "My home always relishes the sweet scents brought by holy men of God. I always greet such people with an inquisitive heart and uncovered visage. Does that bother you?"

The old man stepped on my foot under the table.

"No, no," I replied, "it doesn't bother us at all!"

He stepped on my foot again, urging me to go on talking.

"Dear lady," I said, "thanks to the particular situation, your wishes conform with God's desires."

She was quick to understand my meaning. "My late husband," she went on, "always went along with my wishes. No one has the right to stop me doing so. Sitting with virtuous men is a key to the acquisition of virtue; talking to paragons of piety is the best means of access to pious attributes."

"My lady, you are absolutely correct in your observations, even though there may be times when the quest falls short . . ."

"God has provided me with a special sense, one that guides me toward what is proper and away from what is wicked. It allows me to recognize virtue and piety through their very scent and qualities."

"May God grant you pleasure in what He has given you, and protect you in this world from all that is cheap and nasty."

With that the woman raised her hands in the air. "Dear God," she intoned, "accept the prayer of this holy man and do not frustrate his aspirations and hopes."

The old man sat there like someone who has swallowed his tongue. He was listening to my conversation with our hostess and sipping a glass of milk. Every so often he sent negative signals back to the servant who was still suggesting that he follow him outside the house. Once I noticed that the situation was getting bad, I asked the lady of the house's permission to depart. Astute as she undoubtedly was, she realized the situation and stood up to escort us to the door, having obtained our solemn promise to include her in our private prayers.

As we made our way through the halls and alcoves, I was walking alongside this stunning woman; we were both behind the old man from Meknes. He kept leaning heavily on the arm of the servant, who was constantly warning him to look straight ahead in case he stumbled. We meanwhile walked slowly, touching and moving toward each other. Out of the corner of my eye I could see her ample breasts pointing in my direction and could breathe in the scented breeze of her presence. My senses were completely bedazzled; they wanted nothing more than for this walk to go on forever. Once we reached the outside door, she placed her hand in mine to say farewell. "This house is your house, thou Lord of the people," she whispered in my ear.

"Tomorrow, dear Sir," she said, addressing my companion, "you will receive a gift from me."

He thanked her profusely and, looking straight at me, prayed that she would soon find an honorable husband. She smiled, and the servant chimed in with "Amen."

My companion now grabbed me by the sleeve in order to hurry me away. Once we were a distance from the house, I asked him why he had stayed so silent in the presence of the lady.

"This is a remarkable day," he said, pausing to catch his breath, "one that I'll never forget as long as I live. I'm normally a chatterbox, but that lady's beauty was enough to strike me dumb. God's truth, she put a clamp on my tongue. But, as far as you're concerned, the entire thing is crystal clear, as clear as the day is long. We Meknes folk know a good thing when we see it—as we say, when someone from Meknes treads on a raisin, he can smell how good it is. Even if I were blind, I would still be able to smell it and feel it."

"Smell and feel what precisely, O holy man of God?" I asked with a laugh.

"Even though not much was said," he went on, "I could get the gist of everything and more, even though that rogue of a servant kept trying to put me off. The devil treated me badly, and I'd like to give him a cuff or two at some point."

I smiled in delight.

"God knows, if only I were the same age as you are, I'd be in there with you, fighting for her with every means possible, come hell or high water. But since I'm old and decrepit, I simply say to you, 'May God bring it all to pass!'"

"But you were the one she promised a gift to, not me . . ."

"So now you're using your age superiority to mock me! She's going to give me a gift, but she's a gift for you, all of her! You lucky so-and-so! You must have been born in white togs, bringing your parents a great boon."

When we reached the city plain close to the shore, the sun was turning red on the sea surface as it prepared to set. The old man leaned over to me.

"The only way to purify yourself now," he whispered in my ear, "is to take a swim, then return to your beloved duly cleansed. You need to ask her for your basket, which you left at her place, or whatever you decide to do. From now on and with God's good graces, I'm going to return to my residence. Once there I can contemplate the delights of that remarkable session we had."

The old man was entirely correct: I certainly was dirty and needed a wash; and I had forgotten—or maybe pretended to forget—my basket. But when it came to his advice that I go straight back to the house of the lady who had so entranced me, it seemed like a good idea to postpone it until a day when my mind felt more stable and my emotions were better under control. In anticipation of such a day I had such feelings of delight and pleasure that they almost resembled what I would feel if I ran across my missing manuscript. The happiness I was feeling had taken wing and was flying free; no mystic divine or philosopher before me had ever experienced anything like it. Words fail me; metaphor, simile, and other devices all pale in its context. No poet, whether Spanish, Syrian, or Iraqi, came to my aid. If the Spaniards were to provide me with such feelings now, I would be able to use the sheer intensity of my feelings to reconstruct entire lost cities and fortresses; it would be greater than the deeds of Hercules himself and his defeat of the lion.

In my paeans of joy today my only rival is Archimedes on the day he discovered the law of floating bodies and yelled "Eureka! Eureka!" Mounted now on the steed of overwhelming love in heavenly flight, I too can tell myself, "I have found her, I have found her!"

Beside the sacred enclosure in Mecca itself she is my ultimate focus!

After God Almighty she is my sweetest and most attractive pole!

She is someone who makes you more beautiful and intelligent merely by consorting with her.

She is the very symbol of my felicity and my ongoing struggle, as I set my sights toward the One toward whom noble souls longingly strive, gather together, and return.

The sheer wonder of her name is such that I have neglected to ask it, but it surely shares in the qualities of God's beautiful names.

So come, let me swim in a sea where the liberated lover such as me faces no danger!

Come to the sea whose surface has now been warmed by the setting sun, extending through its dying rays both warmth and farewells.

I made my way to a deserted section of beach, took off my clothes, and used my turban as a loincloth. I waded in with cries of praise and thanksgiving and headed fearlessly into deeper water. Once there I sometimes swam on the top and at other times allowed the waters to embrace and cover me. I had the impression that the very fishes and underwater plants were all extending their particular greetings to me, and I responded fulsomely. I found myself dancing and clapping in the waves, and told myself and the waters all around me that the serenity of the sea here is so vast and wonderful, and the sheer intoxication of swimming in these waters has its own sense and piety attached to it.

My father—God have mercy on him!—had taught me how to swim, and he had done it very well. He told me that it was a very useful skill. "An islander who can't swim," he had told me, "is like an inhabitant of heaven who's never happy!" The very fact that I was swimming in the sea in a state of joyous harmony and sweet delirium was entirely due to the woman whom I termed my very blood when I opened up my heart to the wonders of existence. For the Divine Transcendent I became both attribute and sign.

So there I was using all my limbs and swimming in the name of the One who made every living thing from water. Once I was tired out, I lay on my back motionless and let the waves do with me what they willed, rocking me like a loving mother, swaying and tilting to and fro, spreading all round me a dreamlike atmosphere that was replete with a calm intensity. From time to time I closed my eyes. Every time I opened them, it was to find evening gradually lowering its curtain on the world and spreading everywhere. Then, all of a sudden and with no warning, a flood of water lifted me up high and then plunged me into the midst of a maelstrom, swamping me from all sides.

"Back to dry land," I told myself, "and quickly!"

My beloved loves me alive and well, I told myself, and then yelled, "No, no, I am not going to drown!" Just then I recalled my father's advice: "Don't tie your hands to your neck and don't stretch them far out. If you happen to find yourself in a riptide, just mention the name of God to yourself till you have recovered your breath and can thus recoup your strength and save yourself." After a good deal of effort and endurance, that is precisely what I did. Once I had landed on the beach once again, utterly exhausted, I came to realize that I had called the sea's bluff—heaven knows why—and gone out much too far. I got up to search for my clothes, but could not find a trace of them, as though the waves or the night had made off with them. I could feel the chill of cold penetrating my body and started shivering and sneezing. Under cover of darkness I decided to warm myself up by running around and doing some exercises, and did so. Once back at the zawiya, I slunk into my abode safe and sound. God had eased my return path, although some stray dogs had decided to accompany my passing with growls and barking.

6

SO HERE I WAS back in my room and breathing normally. I washed myself and performed the ritual ablutions, put on some wool clothing, took a potion and some hot liquids, then prayed before going to bed.

Next morning I woke up feeling unwell, but knowing the symptoms full well: a very bad cold. I called it "a love cold" as a way of accepting the inevitability of it and relieving the symptoms. Relishing my condition, I decided not to medicate myself. Lo and behold, I found myself totally congested, with a roaring headache and intermittent fevers and chills—all of which I dutifully ignored; or, better put, I allowed the lady who had so entranced me to distract my attention from my bodily aches and pains. This went on till I had turned into some kind of ethereal abstracted entity with neither substance nor shape, floating around in a firmament where the only existing thing was a single woman with no partner or equal. It was as though all the beautiful women in the world had decided to crown her victorious over them all or else that she had managed to gather to herself the sum total of their exquisite nectar.

There was a slight tapping on my door. I told whoever it was to come in, assuming that it would be the shaykh from Meknes, but it turned out to be the zawiya's warden. He greeted me as he entered and placed two baskets stuffed full of provisions alongside my bed. He told me that he had refused to allow the servant who had delivered them to give them to me in person, but had promised him that he would give them to me himself.

"Did he say anything else?" I asked in a croaking voice.

"I can't remember. He did suggest that you'd find some things in the baskets that would make you happy."

"Then what?"

"Nothing. Oh yes, a present came for Shaykh 'Abd al-Kamil from Meknes. I couldn't for the life of me understand him this morning. He refused to get out of bed and kept ranting and raving; I've never heard the like of it before. I gave him a physical examination, assuming that he was sick, but he seemed fine. On the other hand, you, Master, look very ill."

"Don't worry, dear friend. It's just a cold, nothing serious . . ."

He then told me that my fine reputation among the residents had led many of them to request to talk to me. The case of one of them, a sick old man, was urgent, in that he was spouting heresy, while another middle-aged resident was under observation because he was refusing to eat or drink anything and was contemplating suicide. I promised to visit both men after the afternoon prayer. Saying farewell, he left.

I pulled the two baskets close, anxious to find out what presents had been sent to me. There were a variety of costly foods that I took out, but in the very bottom there was a sealed letter. I opened it hurriedly and read what follows:

"From Fayha' of Sabta to the one who is beloved in everything:

"But for a cold I would have invited you back to see me at once. My great longing for you with all my heart is what is making me feel better, indeed invigorating and energizing me. Dear man of noble character and gleaming visage, I am praying for you and providing you with whatever I can in order that God may choose to preserve you for myself and for the things you love and cherish."

So this woman is to be my cure!

I took some of the bread she had sent, dipped it in honey, and ate it with relish. Then I tried some Indian dates, her delicious pot-pie with sugar and sauce, then some luscious, sweet-smelling fruit. I accompanied it all with thirst-quenching draughts of juices and nonalcoholic wine. I felt more sated than I had ever done before. I gave thanks to God for restoring my appetite and at the same time giving me back my health and vigor.

With my cold now breathing its last, I got up and bounded my way over to the warden's place. His welcome was accompanied by astonishment.

"Here's my own horse," he told me, "the one that was stolen from you. He's made his own way back here, God be thanked! Get on behind me, and we can shorten the distance to the asylum where the two men I spoke to you about are being housed. We'll start with the one who wants to kill himself, and then visit the aged heretic."

I was delighted that the horse had been restored to its owner and praised God for bringing it to pass. I was then happy to accede to my colleague's request. The horse took us up hill and down dale over muddy terrain until we eventually reached a bare hilly spot; it was almost as though the trees had all been stripped bare or had been killed off in a fire. We dismounted and made our way toward a wide, low building. The doorman greeted us both profusely, and I followed the warden across a wide courtyard. It was populated by an odd assortment of humanity wearing strange clothing and behaving in unusual ways. Every one of them and every gesture they made indicated that they were all operating within spaces that were far removed from the normal dictates of reason, spaces where religion held no sway. I had encountered such people before and observed from close quarters as the powerful forces of delusion and self-destruction wreaked havoc on their facial expressions and features.

"Have all these people lost their minds?" I asked my companion in amazement.

"Yes indeed," he replied, "every one of them has a particular tale to tell that has brought them here. Some of them have run into trouble or suffered some disaster, causing a loss of resolve and a descent into madness . . ."

"My experience with the insane has always involved a good deal of yelling and screaming—shouts and moans. But I don't hear any of that here!"

"And that's thanks to that hermit you see standing over there. All the lunatics here are afraid of him and try to avoid making him angry. You can see that he's holding an olive branch. That branch is a godsend for him, and what a godsend it is! Just one gesture or whack with that, and the most violent lunatic turns into an obedient dog, a veritable lamb, in fact. That's why he's been called the lunatics' overlord. The name has stuck and spread."

We walked over to the hermit, and I stopped to introduce myself. It was at this point that I realized that this man was the very same ascetic whom I had seen rolling in the dirt, the one who had run away from me a while ago and shinned up a tree so that I could not reach him. He spotted me approaching and realized that I wanted to talk to him.

"Climb it first of all," he said, "then perhaps and maybe . . ."

And with that he left his post and disappeared.

The wing for mental patients consisted of a row of cells watched over by six strong, surly guards. The warden greeted them all, and so did I. He led me toward a distant cell and invited me to go in while he waited outside. The man inside was tied to the bed; he looked very thin and scruffy, with knotted beard and hair. I sat down close by him and greeted him in a friendly fashion. He gave me a blank, disapproving stare, but it soon softened when I smiled at him and put my hand on his forehead to feel his temperature. He was undoubtedly not at all well. But, as 'Abd al-Barr had already told me from the superintendent, if I suggested that he eat something, he would refuse point-blank.

I leaned over him and asked what was the matter. Why had he asked for me to come? He in turn asked me to put my ear to his mouth. He proceeded to tell me a long story punctuated by sobs and sighs. I learned that his name was Hamdan al-Badisi; he was divorced and had no children. He had lost both parents in crossing the straits from Spain; through some miracle he himself had managed to make it across to Sabta. I now gathered that he had learned about me from the other person who thought that I had cured him of the illusion that he was actually a monkey. From all this information I drew some conclusions: he was obsessed by the notion that he was carrying the head of someone who had recently experienced terminal expulsion from the Garden of Eden or from setting foot in an enchanting, magic land. From the face that he presented to the world I could tell that the general impression he gave was of someone engaged in a nonstop, vicious war within himself, one that only afforded him sufficient respite to assess his grave spiritual wounds and staunch them as best he could. Another symptom was that for no identifiable reason he would suddenly turn gloomy and glower; it could happen even when nature was showing itself in all its fascinating splendor, radiant under never-ending skies of blue and offering all kinds of wonderful pearls of beauty. Once he had been restored to his normal state of mind, he would almost always stare at the planets and stars or else disturb the daytime insects, all with the goal of diverting himself and avoiding a sense of vertigo. After any number of stumbles and misfortunes, he began to hit rock-bottom, failing in both love and gambling, and losing that vital internal urge to dig himself out. All he could do was to get drunk on the most powerful wines made by Christians and Jews. As he himself told me, "Once I'd become a total drunk, I used to lean over to my closest drinking companion—someone I didn't even know—and tell him exactly what I'm telling you now: 'Listen, pal,' I'd say, 'every day I dig myself deeper into misery, while the mud keeps piling up.'"

What a cartload of complexes this man had, I thought to myself, pile upon pile of disaster! O God, how was I supposed to lighten his burdens?

A Muslim Suicide | 137

Where was I to locate the origin of his deep wound, the nub of his sorry tale, and the fulcrum of its intolerable burden?

How was I supposed to detect something that he himself did not know? The only one who knew was his Creator.

I asked him if he really wanted to be cured or not.

He responded that he certainly did want to be cured, but a real cure, not some illusory pseudo-cure. He had endured the latter several times, and the only consequence had been a terrible relapse and a desire to end his life.

"Then promise me," I told him, "that you'll respect your own right to life and think positively about a cure. Do that and leave the rest in my hands. They have God as a wise mentor."

He promised and swore an oath on it. I summoned the superintendent, and in the warden's presence had him remove the restraints from the patient and bring him some food. He dithered a while, but, once I had yelled, "So what do you think this place is supposed to be, a hospice or a death-trap?" he did as I asked and ate. After a while he straightened up and, with a smile on his face, started rubbing his hands and legs. He began to eat, slowly and carefully. I suggested that he take a walk in the courtyard in an hour and promised to pay him another visit the next day. He started raining kisses on my hand, but I withdrew it and leaned over to give him a hug. I signaled to the stupefied warden that he should take me to the second man's cell. Once he had escorted me there, he told me he had things to attend to concerning the hospice's facilities. I told him that, once I had finished with this second visit, I preferred to make my way back to the zawiya on foot. With that I said farewell.

I entered the old man's cell. He leapt up to greet me and invited me to sit on his floor-mat. He was really old, with no hair or teeth; he had a bushy white beard, and his deep-set eyes radiated vestiges of a spark in the midst of a face that was otherwise furrowed and worn. His body consisted of a set of bones that clung to his veiny skin. He told me the various names he had had, all in accordance with the different phases in his adherence to a particular faith that he had subsequently left. The most recent, he told me, was derived from the leader of the Greek skeptics, Pyrrho* the doubter. He insisted that he would only demand a little of my time. All he wanted was to hear my opinion on the position to which his own existentialist thinking had brought him. Contrary to what everyone else thought, he believed in such things. Not only that, but he had full enjoyment of his faculties and was in complete control of his mind.

"My son," he told me, "for a long time I've been promising myself and those around me to devote the final word to God Almighty, provided that a sudden demise does not prevent me from doing so. But before such a promise could be fulfilled, I've had to take on a number of other projects and a crucial and complex problem that I've wanted to solve. However—more's the pity—I've managed to achieve neither. Faced with a succession of failures, I've adopted the following as my oft-repeated slogan: 'You must turn the page.' In the final analysis my entire life consists of nothing more than a whole series of turned pages.

"As my life now draws to its close and I find myself chewing invisible grass, I can claim with considerable confidence that life consists of one long series of ruptures, or rather complete disjunctures, that manage to convert mishaps and failures into whole clusters of consequences and reckonings. For that very reason I choose to shout out to anyone who wishes to hear, and with a great deal of conviction and enthusiasm: 'Life is undeniably devoid of meaning. It is thus the duty of every individual to draw the necessary logical deductions from such a premise.'

"My personal beliefs are beset by doubt. Here I am, living a contemptible existence and—something that is both weird and rare—telling my enemies and counselors alike, 'On the day when, if only for a microsecond, I see a fresh corpse giving me a wink or else—if you prefer—using rude gestures, at that point I'm prepared to swear to you on my mother's grave or in the name of all the pious saints that I will take up my faith once again and without delay. Is there anyone out there to take up such a challenge?'

"As I lie in this place awaiting my death, here is what I am prepared to state with total conviction: 'Much as I despise people who make a big show of their religious beliefs and live it up even though they are old and decrepit, so do I admire people who manage to discover God for themselves and through their own endeavor while their life is still ahead of them. These latter people—and you are undoubtedly one of them—live their own life-stories with the Almighty as one enormous spiritual adventure, an experience that can be at turns boisterous or serene. On the other hand the former distort their relationship with Him, turning it into a personal set of concerns, a feeble penance, if you will, a kind of penitential gargle, the goal being to assure an interest-bearing deposit or insurance for the world to come."

By way of conclusion, the old man proceeded to pose me a direct question, with no long-winded prelude, noting as he did so that he did not expect any answer nor did he need any thanks.

"Isn't this lower world of ours, with its waters and clay, supposed to exist with the least amount of pain and grief, of vanity and hurt, that is feasible? A contemporary of Abu Hayyan al-Tawhidi once asked him with tears flowing down his cheeks, 'What wisdom can there be in the suffering of children or mindless animals?' Or perhaps now that you have seen the conditions inside this asylum, you yourself may wish to ask the question as to what is the point of torturing the demented and insane? That man, al-Badisi, whom you just saw, poor, wretched, and disturbed soul that he is! Did you but know it, there are many, many more people here just like him. If you investigated their stories inside this jail one by one, you would find yourself spending months, indeed years; you might not be able to avoid the contagion that is rife around here—but God prevent any such thing! So, my dear son, leave here with your mind still sound and do not burden yourself with any more questions than those you yourself have experienced and addressed. Go back and leave me to live out my life with my doubts, my black insects, vermin that will not leave me alone whether I plunge into water or explore matters in detail. If your Lord had wished to rid me of them, He would already have done so. Leave in hope then. You have no solution for me, nor does anyone else."

Without saying a word I kissed the old man's head.

"So, 'Abd al-Haqq," he asked me with a smile, "do you smell in me the foul stench of heresy?"

I gestured that I did not, then left the room after bidding him farewell. In the corridor one of the older residents stopped me. "So, dear sage," he said in a feeble, despairing tone, "even you will counsel me to remain steadfast in resisting evil. But what can a poor devil like me say when he has gone to extreme lengths in his indulgence in both evil and endurance?"

That said, he turned around and left without waiting for the benefit of my wisdom on the subject.

As I left the asylum, the things that I had witnessed were making my head spin, even though they were obviously just the tip of the iceberg. Equally disillusioning was the impotence I had experienced in the face of so many images of human misery.

I promised al-Badisi to go back and see him, but what was the point when it occurred to me that I should have been urging the man named Byron to question his own doubts but had decided not to do so out of modesty and respect for his avoidance of argument and preaching? How was I supposed to behave any other way, when in this regard the only difference between the two of us lay in the fact that the downturns and trials in his life had led him to believe that man was made from dust and returned to it, just as chemical compounds are reduced by dissolution. For my part I was and still am involved in my own emotional flights, my intellectual contemplations, and my mystical fantasies, seeing the spirit exempted from such an outcome and wagering its redemption and resurrection after death.

Once I reached the zawiya, I made my way to the cell of the Meknesi shaykh. I found him stretched out on his bed, so I sat down beside him and offered my greetings. I started telling him about the things I had witnessed at the asylum today, but he was far away and not paying any attention. Sometimes he kept his eyes closed, while at others he kept mumbling things I could not understand. I gave him a shake as though I were waking a sleeping man and made him aware I was there by asking him what was distracting him.

"What's distracting me, you ask?" he replied, staring vacantly at me. "This memorable day, dear man. Its light has made me aware of the sheer futility and uselessness of my life. That woman—may the One who created her and made her so beautiful be praised! If God has indeed willed her to be yours, then you are a really lucky man, really lucky!"

"And here I thought you despised this world," I said.

"No, it's not that. That's not enough to make people sad. How can you despise something you don't even possess? I've watched as the world has expended enormous efforts in shunning me. As a result I've adopted a policy of despising it as a way of laying the blame where it truly belongs and taking my own revenge. Tell me, by God, have those people who are to enter paradise been promised only ugly, deformed women? Or crude matting, patched garments, and bread dipped in lard and water? Or is it that they've been promised something much better and lovelier than that? When we visited that beautiful woman's riyad, I saw images of precisely those things. Today I'm not leaving my cell here. To the extent possible I'm going to fast and pray—my only prayer being that God may speed my journey to paradise and eternal life . . ."

"Are you going to leave me," I asked jokingly, "before you tell me the second reason?"

"Which second reason, Ibn Dara?" he asked with a frown.

"You only gave me one reason for leaving Meknes for Sabta," I said. "You promised you'd tell me the other one."

"Here I am talking to you about my desire to leave this world," he responded angrily, "and you're asking me about something I've completely forgotten. Are you making fun of me?"

"No, heaven forbid," I said. "And what about the lady's wonderful gift, 'Abd al-Kamil?"

"Clothes made of expensive materials whose names I don't even know. If I put them on, people would laugh at me or say I'd stolen them. Here they are, under my coverlet. When I die, put them inside my shroud. Then, when I wake up in paradise, I can put them on and strut about like a peacock. Yes indeed, a peacock. During my lifetime I've suffered enough deprivation and mockery and spent far too long pretending to be scared and poor. It's as though for some reason or other I needed to apologize for being alive and walking around in the midst of other people."

"Paradise is guaranteed to you," I said, trying to keep a chuckle suppressed, "that's for sure."

He clearly found my comment peculiar. "But paradise is reserved for people who are pious and poor," he said. "I'm both, so if I'm not among the very first to get in, then who's it intended for?"

I made a gesture to indicate that I thought he was probably right. Kissing his head, I made my way out, promising to come and see him again soon.

7

BACK IN MY ROOM I did some routine chores and recorded all the things I had seen and heard during my investigations that day. I read some pages from the anthology of Arabic love-poetry and ate a good deal of my beloved's food, resolving as I did so to visit her the next day.

My sleep was full indeed, being embellished by a dream that I could vividly recall when I woke up. At the very top of the oak tree that I had been unable to climb in my quest to talk to the lunatics' overlord, my beloved, the mistress of my very being, sat cross-legged. She was inviting me to come up and pick whatever I wished. I duly responded to her invitation, whereupon we embraced and clung to each other enough to cause the branches we were on to snap. Thus linked together we fell to the ground, which had prepared for us piles of soft grasses and straw. We rolled around together in the most delightful way, relishing the union of marital intercourse and indulging in its pleasure till dawn and the arrival of daylight.

This woman is lifting me up, entrancing me, and giving me new life!

Reluctant to interrupt such a vision, I nevertheless got out of bed, washed myself, and performed the prayer. I put on my best clothes and perfumed myself. After breakfasting on some of my beloved's food, I went out and headed for her dwelling, full of longing and passion. I soon reached the quarter in question. But no sooner did I arrive at the door of her house than I saw a huge black man standing there and watching as I anxiously paced to and fro. He told me to move on, and I had no alternative but to do what he said, not least because a lot of nosy men and women were now watching my movements with considerable curiosity.

I went into the center of the city, mingled with the city folk, and then sat down on a bench opposite a square teeming with people. I started practicing my secret hobby, desiring to make light of my doubts and feelings of nausea. Had I been in the desert, I would have stared fixedly at the flights of birds passing over my head or at the herds of cattle so I too could have felt myself turned into a bird or animal. But in an urban setting my strategy involves looking at people as they pass by and weaving a story around each of them, male or female, even though it may never have applied to them in particular nor would it. For example (one among many possibilities), this particular man looks like a criminal, a brutal murderer, or a vicious enforcer, while that one seems like someone condemned to death although the sentence has been commuted, or else someone with one foot already in the grave; still another one has a face beneath which is another countenance with a thousand and one secrets to it, a passionate lover perhaps who allows his imagination to fabricate an entire web of desire and longing and fashions his dreams on cords of wind and leaves of sand. Anyone who can do what I do, steering the ship of the imagination in better directions, will never be a professional historian, but rather a narrator of promises, a ploughman for the marginal and secluded.

As I made my way back up the hill, I decided the best plan was to proceed to the oak tree. As I approached it, evening was lowering its initial curtain, but I was not looking either to left or right or paying attention to things animal, vegetable, or mineral. When I reached it, I rolled up my sleeves and took some deep breaths. Flexing my limbs, I pronounced the phrase "God is Almighty" and invoked His aid before beginning to climb the tree. This time I managed to climb higher than I had on the previous occasion and took that as a good sign. Very slowly and cautiously I climbed higher and higher, one branch at a time, not daring to look down in case I felt dizzy. I kept looking upward toward the spot that was my goal, and eventually, after a good deal of effort and resolve, I managed to sit cross-legged at the very top of the tree, albeit with less splendor and confidence than my beloved had shown in my yesterday's dream. Even so it was definitely more splen-did by far than the way the petty rulers of Spain were sitting cross-legged on their tottering thrones. As I sat there, I came to regard my success, somewhat tardy though it might be, as a promising sign and symbol of good luck, something that might please both the hermit in the forest and the overlord of the lunatics.

For a few moments I just sat there, recovering my breath after all the exer-tion and enjoying the wonderful vista spread out before me, valleys, forests, and hills, all of them inhabited by a variety of God's creatures, whether visible to the eye or not, capable of speech or not. How many wondrous things there are in God's world: birds descending from the skies all around me and returning to their nests. Some of them hovered right above my head; I could hear their cries and the beating of their wings, as though they were perplexed by my being there and urging me to go back to my own nest. And how could I not respond to their urging when night was beginning to cast its dark cloak over the land, accompanied by the usual drop in humidity and temperature.

A night like no other!

Sitting cross-legged on my bed, I started rereading the things my beloved had said in her two letters. My goal was to use those words as a means of dispelling my doubts and the suspicions that the accursed devil was prompting, to make use of the phrases and images to cast things in an optimistic light. By so doing, I could bolster my arguments by recalling the tangible gifts that I was still holding and cherishing dearly.

I told myself that etiquette and politesse demanded of me—indeed repaying one good deed with another, the initiator being the more favored—that I send the beautiful and noble lady a letter in which I would declare my love and my heart's devotion to her alone.

I composed the basic elements of this letter in my head. First, all the wonderful and gorgeous women in the world would feel toward my beloved a sense of natural love and affinity. Second, my infatuation with her would ensure that, after my own death, my name would never be forgotten since generation after generation would recall my devotion in the eternal, time-honored arcade of love and in the anthologies of great lovers. Third . . . Third? Eek! I would describe to her the things I am imagining now: a winged horse prancing proud and gleaming white—I don't mean like Buraq, the horse that conveyed Muhammad on his night-journey into the heavens, no, no, heaven forbid that I should indulge in such blasphemy!! No, no, what I mean is a horse with no saddle or bridle, taking me to the roof of my beloved's house. She climbs on behind me, clinging closely, and the horse takes off at a moderate height in accordance with my instructions, thus avoiding both the prying eyes of people on the ground below and the eddies and disturbances of the upper air. With the morning agleam, we now embark on a journey across climes and weather patterns, exchanging fervent greetings with the birds who pass us in flocks and alone. My beloved still clings tightly to me; if she removes her right hand from my waist, it is only to greet the clouds and pluck

pearls and wafts, or else in sheer delight to give name to the land or sea beneath—
it could be the ocean or else the straits.

Then I have an idea. I ask our "pilot" to fly across the straits and take us on
a tour of as much of our gravely wounded Spain as possible. I want to give my
beloved an overhead view of Murcia, where I was born and spent my youth, as well
as my village of Raquta, the River Segura, the spectacular gardens extending all the
way to Cartagena and the slopes of the snowy mountains, and the skies above . . .

I have another idea as well, but my mind will not allow it, the pretext being
a fear of catching cold and the changeable weather patterns, not to mention
the highly skilled and murderous Christian archers and their carefully aimed
arrows. With that in mind I order the horse to take us back safe and sound to our
base, although my heart and soul are joining the poet in singing:

> Whenever the zephyrs do blow,
> I cry out "O my yearning for Andalus!"

As we begin our descent, I change my position so that I am facing my beloved,
who has little to say but is much affected and multifaceted. Circumstances bring
us gradually closer together in embrace, followed by a plunge into the deep waters
of pleasure and passion. We only emerge and take note of our surroundings when
the horse neighs twice as a way of indicating that the airborne journey is at an
end and we have arrived back safely.

I composed these three elements in my head, then secured them firmly in my
heart. I hoped thereby to convert them all into the foundations of a wonderfully
structured dream, a dream without parallel, to which, if and when it happened, I
proposed to append my letter.

I performed the obligatory prayers and embellished them with some additional intercessions and meditations, before going to bed with an empty stomach
but a mind brimming with expectation.

I have no idea how long I slept, but it was interrupted in the morning by the
occasional neighing of a horse close to my house. Without bothering about the
neighing, I got up in the usual way and started eating my breakfast. I started leafing through my memory, trying to work out what, if anything, I had seen while
asleep, but nothing came to me, or else the devil had made me forget. There was
nothing, no images or even threads of them, no fragments, not even a single trace.

Very well, I told myself, I will compensate for my loss by composing the letter. However, my mind simply closed down, and the words refused to come; or rather what did come totally lacked the necessary loftiness of purpose for such a noble goal. The entire situation was made that much worse and the neighing outside intensified. I found myself going outside to see what was happening. When I opened the door, I had the surprise of my life: right in front of me was a splendid white stallion, wonderfully caparisoned. As soon as it saw me, it quieted down. Right next to the horse stood a huge black man, the very one I had run into by the door of my beloved's residence. He hurried over to me, gestured a greeting, and handed me a sealed letter. I immediately guessed who it was from and opened it with shaking hands and a palpitating heart:

To my master, 'Abd al-Haqq:

"Lord of my heart and soul, gentle overlord of my every move and of every quarter, you who reside in my dreams day and night, you! So did you grace my house with your presence? I have a request to make of you, but in person if you would be so kind."

How could I possibly not accept this request on such a splendid morning! Needless to say, I accepted her request out of love and respect, it being my major priority and aspiration.

I told her servant to wait long enough for me to wash myself, put myself to rights, and dab on some perfume. Within the hour I was fully prepared to respond to the invitation and proceed to her house. As I approached the horse, it started making a big fuss and pawed the ground with its hooves as a sign of welcome and acceptance. I mounted it, happy and proud, while the servant grabbed hold of the bridle and led it on foot. He never looked behind him, neither to left nor right. The entire area around the zawiya was free of residents or passers-by; it almost felt as though they had decided to let me enjoy and relish what was happening to me on my own.

Going down the mountain was easy and untroubled, just like plunging into delights I had never encountered before. The horse proceeded on its way slowly and obediently, while the servant said not a single word, as though he were either dumb, had been told not to speak, or else was praying silently. The path toward the one who had so infatuated me, my own path, was embellished with springtime's gleaming raiment, whose various components were bursting into flower and arraying themselves all around. As I took it all in, my very consciousness was totally overwhelmed with the kind of happiness that is only rivaled by that of a bridegroom on his wedding night.

I dismounted by the door of my beloved's house and was given a warm greeting by a young eunuch, who accompanied me to a hall illuminated by lanterns. There I found the lady of the house looking absolutely radiant. She was waiting for me in the company of two servant-girls, one of whom was holding a tray of dates while the other had a tray with cups of milk on it. As I approached, I gave my hostess a greeting, and she responded with words of welcome. The way she was looking at me was even more fervent than my own glances. She pointed to the dates, and I took one; then to the milk, which we both drank from a single cup, looking at each other all the while. She then took me across the interior garden and through two passageways to a reception room even bigger and more lush than the one I had seen on my first visit with the Meknesi shaykh. She sat me down opposite her, close to a table that had all kinds of food and drink laid out on it.

Her expression made it clear that she was feeling both shy and deeply affected. When I tried to initiate a conversation with her, all she could manage was a few stuttered words of welcome. She clapped her hands, and the young man behind the screen called out, "Abla, bring in the scent, and you, Hafsah, bring in the tray." With that the first maid put some more aromatic wood into the enormous brazier and sprinkled rosewater around, then the second one came in with a tray so I could wash my hands, which I did.

Then I was left alone with the lady of the house.

"I'm not sure I deserve such a lavish and wonderful welcome," I said.

She responded with a few broken phrases, the significance of which—if I read her correctly—was that I fully deserved it. She invited me to eat, and I took a little while informing her that I was normally satisfied with the small amount of food that Sufis normally eat. She now asked me about the holy man from Meknes, and I replied that he was alive and well, but spending the remaining days of his life in prayer and sleep. His one remaining and abiding hope, I told her, was to meet his Lord in a purified state and gain entry to paradise as soon as possible. I added that in his devotions he was constantly praying for her. She let out a loud sigh and lowered her gaze, as though she were either afraid of stuttering again or else waiting for me to initiate further conversation.

For a moment I thought about talking to her about the various components that would make up the letter that I was proposing to send to her once I had actually written it, but I was afraid that that might make her even more emotional, so I decided not to do so.

Then I thought of drawing attention to the letter that she had recently sent to me, which might lead her to explain the request that she had said she wanted to make of me, but I was afraid that that might only distress her and make her even more tongue-tied than she already was.

Dear Lord, what am I supposed to do?

Here's a woman who holds the trump card when it comes to things that delight me and lift me up, things that can transform me and raise me to higher planes. Her initial invitation to me, her wonderful figurative words, her first letter brimming with love and passion, her second letter in which she proclaims her love and urges me to hurry to her, these latest gestures on her part, not to mention one boon after another, all these things inevitably demand of me that I seal and bless them with kisses planted on the mouth of the one who has fostered and provided them.

As I envisioned things, the benefit of such kisses would be twofold, and so would the rewards: in the first place I would be able to establish without any doubt that in this adventure in love my suit had a distinct chance of succeeding; and second—and this was more important by far—I would be able to untie the knot that was restraining my beloved's tongue. Once that was done, the words would flow freely between us, replicating the purest ether or the coursing streams of paradise. With regard to this latter category, I can actually recall a previous occasion, one that I can summarize briefly, following the principle of one thing reminding you of something else:

During my frivolous youth in Murcia one of my love-escapades led me to know a beautiful woman with a stutter that made it impossible for her to communicate with other people and hold conversations. She asked me for a cure, and my response was to recommend that, whenever she felt tense and unable to express herself, she start taking rapid breaths, stop thinking about the words she wanted to use, and instead make use of synonyms, invoke metaphors and images and hand gestures. My suggestion only helped a little. What was far more effective was showing her affection and giving her a kiss every time she found it difficult to speak. The process whereby I used to drink the sweet nectar from her mouth turned out to be the best way of resolving the problem and opening up the paths to conversation.

By now I have forgotten what that particular woman looked like; it's only by chance and on this particular occasion that I have remembered the way I solved the problem. So by analogy should I now be applying the very same cure in the case of this lady Fayha'?

I was still considering the wisdom of this course of action when the lady in question broke her silence by clapping her hands, in response to which two servant-girls appeared. One of them held a bowl as I washed my mouth and hands, and cleared the table, while the second one told her mistress that the private quarters were now ready, as she had requested.

Her mistress and mine—yes, by God, my mistress—now invited me to follow her, and I did so with the greatest pleasure.

The private quarters consisted of a small room, neatly furnished with elegant cushions and wall-hangings. Subdued candlelight illuminated the space. In the middle was a table loaded with drinks of all types and colors. It was a warm and intimate space, and the songs from the birds, both indigenous and migrant, outside in the garden were a perfect accompaniment to it. In the midst of such music Fayha' handed me a glass, and I did likewise to her. We both drank with discreet relish, savoring the attractions of the moment, while from a neighboring room the sounds of the oud wafted to our ears. I asked her who was playing, and she stuttered a reply: "It's Ghaz . . . zzz . . . zzz . . . lan. Do you like it?"

I nodded that I did. How could I possibly not like such melodies and bird-songs? Not to mention the intoxicating delights of other things as well, and they were legitimate at that! The whole thing was a boon from God on high, a time-honored spiritual treasure.

And here was I, member of a religious community with no monastic traditions! I was indulging in my own share of the world and giving whatever talents I have in return.

In the midst of such delights any kind of reserve is pointless. It is, in fact, inappropriate to keep one's instincts on a leash; it is far more suitable to unleash pent-up emotions and give them a golden opportunity to take the initiative. In that way I could return to my beloved's tongue its normal eloquence. Trusting in the One to whom one can consign such faith, I drew her toward me and embraced her; so close was she that I felt the irresistible urge to kiss her gently on both cheeks. When I felt her relax and ask for more, I turned to her lovely mouth, tasted its sweet nectar, and massaged her tongue for as long as passion and longing allowed me. All of a sudden, the birdsong and lute-playing came to a stop, and silence fell, only interrupted by the pounding of our heartbeats. If I had not been scared of possible evil consequences and transcending the bounds of appropriate behavior, I would almost certainly have plunged ahead and indulged myself in the sweetest pleasure of them all. Instead I decided to see what effect my behavior thus far had had on the lady in question.

"Tell me, my beloved," I said. "In your letter you mentioned something you wanted me to do? Tell me what it is, and I'll do it for you."

"The way I'm feeling now," she replied somewhat less diffidently than before, "I certainly can't put it into words."

"Well then, tell me with signs and gestures."

My companion now used her thumb to point to her bosom and then to me. She then used her middle finger to expose both her breasts before my very eyes. When she saw that I was flummoxed (actually "dumbfounded" would be more appropriate), she took hold of my right hand and intertwined her fingers in mine. At this point my only course was to ask her point-blank if she wanted to be married to me, and, without further ado, she responded that she did.

"Our hearts have a language of their own," I went on. "The mind has no control over it. What I said has come straight from my very soul, so I am innocent of any charge against me. In my particular form of language my love for you stems from complete free will."

It was amazing to see how her own language now proceeded to flow in joyous, sweet sequence. Either my cure had worked, or else her previous stammerings had been a façade. Whatever the case, the suggestion she had made lifted me up to yet higher planes of delight, and I was certainly going to accept it with the very greatest of pleasure and joy. Even though she had not been the one to take the initiative by talking about it, she had certainly now made her intentions very plain.

"My dear lady," I told her, "I'm honored by your suggestion." But then, by way of clarification, I went on, "I feel exalted, but . . ."

"But what, my dear 'Abduh?"

I had never been called by that abbreviation before. From now on, it would certainly be appended to my other names; in fact, because it came from the

A Muslim Suicide | 151

mouth of the one who had managed to capture my heart and love, it would now occupy primary position.

"My beloved," I replied, "I am a man for whom knowledge and learning are cherished entities. My life has been fated to be one of seclusion and devotion to scholarship."

Biting her fingertips in sheer bashfulness and longing, she blushed becomingly. "For you, my dear," she said, "I will be able to provide what is far more restful and sweet than mere seclusion. If you wish, I will have a special cloister built for you inside my house where no one will bother you and I will never venture. What I desire with all my heart is simply to be close to you."

Oh my, what wonderful, sweet, and unforgettable words those were! Oh my, how they penetrated my inner being and lodged happily inside my soul! I decided to check just one thing before finally acceding to her wishes:

"Did you say, my lady, that you would build me a cloister?"

"If you wish, I'll even build a tower where you can seclude yourself."

"But, my sweet lady, Sabta will not be my final resort. I may well be forced to leave here, just as I did my hometown of Murcia."

"Dear 'Abduh, devout shaykh who loves all pious folk, no harm can come to you here. My late father was a much respected man whose deeds will never be forgotten, and my late husband was director and supervisor of his council."

I accepted this response of hers with a smile and asked for no further details regarding the specific aspects of the marriage contract. I did not wish to reconsider my feelings and complicate matters, nor did I wish to look as though I were haggling over things. I decided to exploit the joy of the moment and savor its exalted purpose. Even so, the highly astute lady in question seemed to anticipate some of my concerns.

"My dear 'Abduh," she went on, "if you wished to make the acquaintance of the governor of Sabta at your convenience, it can certainly be arranged. As far as our own union is concerned, that can be arranged in short order if you so desire. No relatives on my side are going to make any fuss about things, since there's nothing standing in the way of either yourself or a widow like me."

All of a sudden the sounds of the lute once again wafted into our little hideaway, almost inevitably rekindling the passions I felt for the lovely woman who had put her head with its silky hair on my chest. Without looking up, she started to say something softly, but it only came out as a stammer: "Dear 'Abduh, would you k . . . k . . . k . . ."

I took this as an indication that she wanted more of my cure-method, so I turned her face toward me and started covering her with kisses even more passionate than the first time. I took the advantage in all it offered, but she responded in kind, albeit with a bit more modesty. Once again it managed to loose her tongue from its chains.

"Do you love me, 'Abduh?" she asked.

My response came not with words, but in very explicit actions that found their inspiration in my very soul and body. I hugged and kissed her over and over again. Once more I was afraid that our mutual passion would lead us down a slippery slope into illicit territory. She may have detected my malaise, because at this point she slipped gently out of my arms. No sooner did the lute-playing stop than we heard the muted sound of gazelles heralding the arrival of Umm Haniyya, who was waiting in the reception hall.

I leapt up. "Make the necessary arrangements for our wedding," I whispered in my beloved's ear. "Choose whomever you like to help you and also the messenger who will ply between us. God alone will bring success, and in Him do we put our trust."

She signaled her agreement by kissing me softly. As she withdrew happily, the lute player, who now appeared from nowhere, accompanied me via a back door to a corridor that led to a capacious stable.

"My mistress gives you this fine horse," he said, the expression in his eyes conveying a host of meanings, "with her very best wishes and fond farewells. You luckiest of men, please be so good as to mount the horse that you have blessed by allowing it to bring you here."

I asked the boy to convey my deepest thanks and appreciation to his mistress, mounted the horse, and rode away.

This blessed horse made no attempt to hide how happy it was to have me as its rider; it was neighing and snorting with pleasure, almost as though his owner had instructed it to treat me well. It conveyed me across the city of its own accord and at a modest pace, but, once we reached the part of the city by the mountain, it started cantering in order to show me how powerful and well endowed it really was. As I turned my face toward the gentle breezes, how often did I embellish

the space with luscious kisses and affection! I felt as if my mount were transporting me on wings, as though I myself were flying as I recalled the passionate
moments I had spent with my beloved. No words had ever tried to describe the
feeling before, and indeed none of the famous love-poets of the Arabic tradition
would be able to do so even if they were to combine their efforts. The elemental
footfalls and profound spiritual heartbeats that accompanied such joyous emotions of love were beyond the scope of mere words. Muhammad al-Niffari,* Abu
Hayyan al-Tawhidi, and other major intellectual figures had all spoken about the
impossibility of using words to encompass larger concepts. Were my friend the
Meknesi shaykh to have experienced moments such as these, he would willingly
have surrendered his soul out of sheer emotion . . .

I reached my own quarters in record time and sought out ʿAbd al-Barr. I
asked him to find someone to take care of my horse, and he assured me that he
would do so. He then informed me sadly that Shaykh ʿAbd al-Kamil from Meknes
had actually died that very afternoon. On his deathbed he had been continually
invoking the names of God, his Prophet, and my own name as well. From time to
time he would say peculiar things, like "Here's a chicken with cumin, Ibn Dara;
God has given it to you . . . and here's the really good deal . . ." I had to suppress
the urge to laugh, and promised the warden that I would meet him at the funeral
the next day. With that I headed for the dead man's room, recited some verses
over him, and then bade him a final farewell.

Before noon prayer the next day (which was a Saturday), I conducted a
funeral rite for the dead man, and then he was buried amid a flood of prayers,
including the ones that were dearest to him while he was still alive—namely that
God would accord him a place in His paradise and pour on him the abundance
of His blessings without interruption or recompense. . . .

Immediately after the noon prayer in the mosque, ʿAbd al-Barr invited me
to have lunch with him in his house, and I duly accepted. Part of our conversation revolved around death and the next world, while other parts concerned
people's lives and the troubles they faced in this world. I got the impression that
my host had something he wanted to tell me but was hesitating. With a broad
smile on my face I asked him directly what was troubling him. He frowned, gave
a deep sigh, then explained to me how bad the situation was with the facilities
at the zawiya, especially the quarters for travelers; worst of all were the conditions in the lunatic asylum. In the latter facility there were only five orderlies

and assistants left, who persevered patiently in spite of the paltry salaries they received for their pains. The thing he feared most was that the overlord of the lunatics would die, and then the place would fall apart and descend into complete chaos. The number of regular donors was going down, he told me. But for the financial help he had received from the governor, Ibn Khalas, whom he praised profusely, the entire zawiya and its facilities would long since have been swept away like so much dust.

Since this was the second time he had alluded to the governor in complimentary terms, I decided to exploit the opportunity.

"My dear 'Abd al-Barr," I said, "these days governors are all of the same ilk, vicious, domineering, and tyrannical. Morning and evening they all sing the same tune: me first, and my own interest, and 'après moi le déluge . . .' If any of them shows a modicum of mercy and kindness, then it is for a very specific purpose that they have in mind. So is this Ibn Khalas different from all the others? Is he a bird that sings a different song?"

"For my part, dear Sir," he responded in all innocence and sincerity, "I can only go on what I can see. Whatever lingers inside men's hearts I entrust to the One who is all-knowing about the unseen. I have previously described the governor to you just as I have come to know him. As regards the running of the city's affairs, he is fully on top of things, and makes every possible effort to be fair and reasonable. If he were like many other governors who run government affairs these days, he would have apprehended you as soon as you arrived in Sabta and compelled you to follow his line. But, as he has told me many times, he has decided not to harass people who incline toward mystical ideas and seclusion, those believers who tread the delicate path toward God. This posture of his is totally at variance with that of the sultans of the region, Al-Rashid, who rules as sultan in this particular era, being prime among them."

I made no comment on my companion's remarks but preferred to ponder my own thoughts in silence. It was as though there was something I needed but was reluctant to bring to mind. Seeing my mood, he asked me gently what I was thinking about.

"Do you know the lady Fayha' from Sabta?" I asked him.

"I've not met her thus far. However I do know that she's from an illustrious and much respected family. Both her father and husband—may God have mercy on them both!—worked in Ibn Khalas's department. They were both devoted to excellence and admirers of genuine learning. They always were glad to offer assistance to migrants arriving from Spain."

"Tell me frankly, 'Abd al-Barr," I asked, "can you see her as my wife?"

"Anyone who manages to have her as a wife is a lucky man indeed. Put your trust in God and show the best of intentions toward the one whose hand you seek. Aha! So now I can understand what our late friend, 'Abd al-Kamil from Meknes, was talking about on his deathbed. She must have been the really good deal he kept talking about. What a wonderful person that happy devotee was! Now he has left us, and you are about to do so as well. Who knows what's going to happen to all the other good folk living in our midst?"

I noticed the sad expression in his eyes and made a point of assuring him that I fully intended to keep my connection with both him and the zawiya. He heaved himself to his feet and departed, offering me his prayers as he did so.

8

SO NOW I'VE MADE UP MY MIND.

When both this devout man and the shaykh from Meknes share the same opinion, it cannot be wrong.

I'm waiting for you, Fayha'. So give me a sign, and I'll obey. Issue your instructions, and I'll respond at once. While you are making everything ready for us, I will inevitably have to take some dives, albeit briefly, into a well-defined quadrangle within the broader sea of religious and secular learning.

For that particular day and others that would follow it, I made a selection of books, some of which had long been awaiting my attention. They each issued an invitation, tempting me to read them for the first time or to reread them. I put them either on my table or under my pillow, all with the goal of perusing them whenever possible as a way of compensating for my lack of concentration in recent times. As is my usual practice when it comes to making the most effective use of my learning time, I examined the various genres of writing laid out before me from the perspective of those areas of knowledge and preoccupations that were my particular concern at that point. It seemed inevitable to me that I would have to reread the section from al-Ghazali's great work, *Revival of the Religious Sciences*, devoted to "marriage customs," in which the great sage manages to give a superb presentation with regard to both its analytical presentation and its clear exposition. In this section (and also in another section devoted to the proper practice of seclusion), he elucidates for the reader his rationale for basing the discussion of differences in people on different life circumstances and personalities, although he goes on to point out that humans in general have a tendency to find a happy medium—to the extent feasible—between devotion to God and marriage and between seclusion and congregation with others. However, anyone who adheres to one of these pairs rather than both is responsible for his own decision and can justify himself on those grounds with no call for censure or blame. As the text itself notes, Malik ibn Dinar* was asked, "Why haven't you married?" to which he replied, "Given my druthers, I would divorce my own self." Then there's the quotation from Ibn Adham*: "Nothing good has ever come from someone who is used to women's thighs." That comment needs much more precision and specificity, and can be interpreted in a whole host of ways.

With regard to my personal circumstances and corporeal existence, it is obvious that I am going to have to close the book on my bachelorhood and all talk of youthful passions. Only then will I be able to use marriage as a way of guiding my desires and passionate urges in the right direction so as to earn the approval of the Prophet. In this matter as in others, my model the Prophet (whom I have seen in dreams on more than one occasion) tells me, "Marriage is my custom. Whoever admires my modes of conduct, let him follow my custom." So, once I have fulfilled to the maximum extent the obligation of investigating my beloved, let my marriage be with God's blessing and in accordance with the Prophet's custom. It is Al-A'mash* who transmits the saying "Any wedding undertaken without preliminary investigation will end in pain and grief." I also followed the advice given by the most exalted of prophets to lovers when he says, "Let none of you have sex with his wife like some animal. Instead let there be a messenger between the couple." The Prophet was asked what he meant by the word *messenger*. "A kiss," he replied, "and sweet, tender words." My model and example, what wonderful words those are! May it all happen as you recommend. In treating the woman who lifts me up and entrances me have I behaved in a way that is any different from what you suggest, my most reliable source-text?

Permissible actions are intended to be modes of both diversion and recreation: what a wonderfully foundational principle that is in my own faith community, one that shies away from tedium and encourages enjoyment and good company! With that in mind, the prospect of marriage and its alleged pitfalls cannot scare me, particularly when God has guided me to an honorable woman who is possessed of both beauty and determination, someone who deserves a partner who is sound in both body and mind.

I happened to notice the book *The Attractions of Assemblies,* by the Spanish writer Ibn al-'Arif al-Sanhaji, but soon came to realize that his chapters devoted to ultimate abstraction and total asceticism no longer suited my personal situation;

either that, or else they were more appropriate for an age group other than my own. I glanced at another book, Ibn Qasi's* *The Removal of Sandals,* and took another close look at the linkage of this Portuguese Sufi with Ibn al-'Arif and the influence that the latter had on him, something that led him to rebel against the Almoravids along with a group of his devotees. Assuming that God will grant me enough time and prepare the proper circumstances, I will question the Sufis and engage with their writings in order to distill to the extent possible the ideas of their great mentor, Ibn Masarra.* He was born in Cordoba and lived in the mountains nearby; a renowned Mu'tazili Batini Platonist Sufi, his two major works, *The Book of Forebearance* and *The Book of Letters,* are both lost (all we have of them is a number of short extracts cited in works on annalistic history and biography).

These thoughts and impressions emerged as a product of my reading, and I duly recorded them at the time, with the idea of returning to them at some point in the future and reorganizing them with a view to further study and publication.

I recalled that my copy of *The Removal of Sandals* was one that 'Amr of Cordoba had given me, but in a very poor edition. That brought to mind the question as to what would happen to him and my other students in Spain. Even though I had long since attributed the complete lack of news about them to their many preoccupations and the disasters of this era of ours, I still felt strangely depressed. At the same time I forced myself to suppress the notion that, with my forthcoming marriage, my own fortunes were on the rise while his were continually beset by misfortune.

I spent the remainder of the evening washing and praying without eating any dinner, then lay down on my bed and warded off sleep by reading selected parts of *The Great Book of Songs* by Abu al-Faraj al-Isfahani.* I must have read a great deal, because, when I woke up the next morning, I found the page open at "the story of 'Umar with the girls who were staring at him through a hole in the tent."

I found myself wanting to visit the baths more than ever before, so I made my way there early to avoid the crush and noise. The masseur welcomed me and, as was his habit, selected a medium-warm spot, brought over a bucket of hot water and other things I would need, and started rubbing and pounding my joints with his usual skill. Once the sweat had poured off me and my muscles and tendons felt duly refreshed, he left me to relax on my back and wished me health and well-being.

It is amazing how tiny moths of drowsiness start fluttering over my eyelids just a few moments after such a massage. The way I keep them at bay is by pouring water over my face so as to keep myself awake and alert. Between one round of water and another, I get the anxious feeling of someone who needs to keep his mind concentrating and not let his body relax too much so that he'll doze off and fall asleep. In this case, however, no such problem arose; I had something much better in mind. I made use of my wakefulness to recall absent friends and loved ones, after which I put my dreams in order, categorized them, and filed away my musings and findings. It became completely obvious to me that the person whose presence towered over the top of all these elements was none other than the lady with whom, with God's will and help, I would soon be living. Once enfolded in her companionship and tender care I would be able to forget the ordeal that the loss of my valuable manuscript had caused me.

I allowed my mind to wander into contemplation of having her close as my life companion and spending time together, all of which seemed to augur well for our future. I came to see my marriage to her, and indeed to her alone with no other wives, as being a symbol and pledge of a deep-rooted commitment on my part to enter the phase of all-comprehensive monotheism. This marriage would bring together the aspirations of my flesh and body by providing a release from the excessive variety of ways I had used to fumble my way around the thighs and embraces of various women. Fed jointly by Fayha' and knowledge, I would inevitably be destined to substitute profundity for superficiality and grain for chaff. The partial can only be known through the totality, the branch only through contact with the root. The sheer validity of what is possible in creation lies in its attainment of the Necessary Existent, which draws all existing things toward the one who is God alone . . .

My daydreams or sleep were interrupted by a noise from outside. I was aware of the masseur leaning over in my direction and asking my permission in his Maghribi dialect to wash me down. Pointing to my back, I sat down and asked him what all the fuss was about. He told me that the owner of the baths had refused to allow three lunatics to enter the baths, his idea being to prevent any trouble or disturbance. With that, he left me and went out in a hurry. I did not set eyes on him again until I had taken my spot in the lounge room, where I was able to pay him his fee and listen in on the heated conversation between the bath owner and the lunatics. They were claiming that, like everyone else, they had a right to bathe themselves with hot water, while the owner kept telling them that entry to the bath was restricted to people who were sane. The entire amazing conversation revolved around definitions of who was sane and who was a lunatic, and what the differences between the two might be. When things reached the point of threatening gestures with sandals and clenched fists, the masseur came over to me and asked my opinion on the subject of the argument. I was presented to the assembled company as being someone who was able to make authoritative decisions, besides my being a person of piety and devotion. They all accepted my arbitration in the matter.

"Esteemed holy man," the senior member of the lunatics demanded, "before any further chit-chat, please define sanity for us all."

First I dried my hair and put on my turban, all the while thinking of the simplest way of making the masseur, the lunatics, and the bath owner understand the definition involved.

"Sanity, my friends—may God provide you all with it," I said, "consists of a balance of light whereby mankind can distinguish truth from falsehood, good from bad, and beautiful from ugly. Some people claim it is centered on the head, others on the heart, and still others on a combination of the two."

The bath owner now addressed me in a tone that blended high esteem and complaint. "Dear Sir," he said, "these men possess no intelligence in any part of their bodies. They insist on using this bath without payment and playing havoc as though they were devils or troublesome teenagers. Once or twice I've overlooked their behavior, but this time the answer is no!"

"If God had provided us with some money," said a second lunatic, "we would certainly be willing to pay. And if someone were willing to heat some water for us in our residence, then we would wash ourselves there . . ."

"Here's what our minds tell us," said a third. "This bath belongs to God, so any of His servants may enter it . . ."

"Dear holy man of God," begged the bath owner, "rescue me from these accursed people! Use your logic to keep them away . . ."

"Let me handle these poor wretches," I replied, using the tone of a sage who never speaks on a whim. "They'll go into the bath one by one. Everyone will have his turn. That way, everyone can be satisfied, with no cause for distress or harm."

I got to my feet and paid generously for the entrance fee. Since the men's silence seemed to imply that they were satisfied, I said my farewells and departed, leaving it to everyone else to put my fatwa into practice. All the while people kept flocking into the bathhouse.

As soon as I got back to my house, I found a sealed letter under the door. I opened it eagerly and read my beloved's message in her clear handwriting. She sent me her greetings, in so doing addressing me as her dearest darling, and went on to let me know that, God willing, our engagement would take place on the evening of the first Friday in the current month of Rabiʻ al-Awwal; all the necessary arrangements were in place. She closed the letter with expressions of love and desire.

There were just three days or fewer left before the appointed day. Even if it had been less time, I was feeling so utterly thrilled and in love that I would have accepted it in any case. The sheer rapture I was experiencing afforded me an inner sense of the true meaning of life in all its wonder. I swiftly went about my daily tasks, then lay down on my bed to relax and think for a while, all in the hope of crafting a safe haven for my present life and a course of action for my anticipatable future. Right from the start, I realized that every limb in my body was pulsating with desire for the one whom I longed to hold as she did me. That desire was a reality, with no ifs, ands, or buts; it was a reality that now had total control over me, so much so that it was pointless to fake its impact by referring to the writings of ascetics and hermits—neither that nor indulging in negative thoughts about possible outcomes and the games that fate plays with human beings.

So then, my beloved is my other focus after the *qibla* in Mecca and my ultimate resort! So be it! By the Lord of the Kaʻba, she is not to be a mere plaything so I can pass the time of day in frivolities and indulge in an excess of passion.

She is the one with the sweet face to die for, with its subtle expressions and abundant coquetry, one that I would take in my hands, a devoted reader who would contemplate its beauty forever and make my way around its grace and elegance, finding within it a light to shine on my conduct toward humanity, as I praised the one God and sought to enhance my standing in the eyes of the Almighty.

That is the way things are, and there is nothing else to revive and invigorate me in Sabta, the place where I now reside, my secondary base and exile abode. Anyone who claims otherwise is trying to defame me and is totally mistaken.

I manage to control the inner turmoil I'm feeling by staying in my house and keeping as calm as possible. I'm afraid of losing my self-control, so I don't go out anywhere where I might show people how overjoyed I am. Over time that very joy has only increased; in so doing it has eliminated any number of dogged problems that have beset me. If I were to go outside, I am sure that idiots would say, "Aha, he's just like us in every way, and we don't care whether he agrees or not." On the other hand, poor people who are intelligent and devout would probably put it differently and say, "Dear holy man of God, your joy is increasing in intensity; it is at odds with the spirit of this era that saddens us and makes us bleed. So take your personal joy and move it far away from our broken spirits and never-ending grief. Away, far away . . ."

Such talk is incoherent, in that it lacks subtlety and precision, seeking instead to downplay the role of listening and understanding. I have never claimed total absolute control for my feelings of joy, nor do I seek to absolve it of a sense of grief over the fall of Al-Andalus or, for that matter, of any anxiety over current or future situations.

No, I regarded it as a sign, something to revive and embolden me in the face of so many trials and tribulations, a flag fluttering in the breeze to indicate my endurance, courage, initiative, and resolve. With lofty ambition and firm resolve I would be able to embellish my defiance and determination with a stolid sense of happiness in order to be able to confront any notion of defeat or perdition. A voice whispered in my ear, "Have you not read in the text of the Qur'an: 'Rejoice not, for God does not love those who do so?'" [Sura 28, v. 76], to which I replied, "Yes, but I have read it in its context, not separated and in isolation. It refers to the people of Moses addressing their leader, Aaron, and involves someone who is joyous to the point of wonder and pride in their mighty treasures. My joy on the other hand comes from an entirely different source and motivation. So try to understand."

9

I WAS JOLTED OUT OF MY REVERIE by a gentle tap on my door, followed by a soft neigh. Opening the door I found myself face to face with my horse, almost as though he had come to inquire about my health and check up on me. I held his head close and nuzzled him, whispering words of affection and good cheer to the effect that he would soon be conveying me to my mistress and his. After indicating that he understood and concurred, he turned around and happily retraced his steps. It occurred to me that I might follow him to make sure he went back to his stable or pasture and then take the opportunity to meet and talk to some of the folk residing in the wing for those who could talk, but instead I decided to remain in isolation and allow my daydreams completely free rein.

I settled myself down to read chapters in the books I had used to frame my bed. Whenever an idea or an inspiration occurred to me, I would write it down in my notes before it disappeared and Satan erased it from my memory. I kept this up for a while, not bothering whenever my stomach demanded food or the muezzin called people to prayer, only interrupting things in order to contemplate what I was reading and writing for a while. When it was early morning, I again opened Al-Harith al-Muhasibi's* *Book of Contemplation,* specifically at the section that had originally worried me and made me reject the ideas of this Sunni mystic who was so well known for his piety and virtue. He is talking about the believer who is promised an afterlife in paradise, within it "houris with soft-skinned bodies, virgin and sweet," residing there for evermore, lovely companions who will provide glasses of wine and cups of honey, milk, and water.

> *Just imagine the sweetness of her body as she embraces you in her arms, so soft*
> *and gentle that your two bodies almost blend with each other. Then imagine*
> *her beautiful breasts touching your chest and the sheer delight in fondling*

them. Smell the perfume of her cheeks, so enticing that your heart will forget
everything else as it wallows in the sheer pleasure of it, filled with an unspeak-
able delight emanating from the exquisite touch and sweetly perfumed rap-
ture that she has conveyed to your soul.

Thus far I found myself relishing the ideas, since up to this point things were
limited to embracing, blending one with each other, and mutual touching, all of
it followed by two beloveds sharing feelings of pleasure and rapture. But where I
found myself opposing his visions and heartily disapproving of the sheer obscen-
ity of his ideas was with regard to the following passage:

While you find yourself in this position, they will flirt with you. They will lean
over and keep on hugging and kissing you as they cover your chest with their
breasts. They will envelop you in their gorgeous faces, cover your body, and coat
it with their fluids. Your nostrils will be filled with the sweet scent of their cheeks.

Such talk as this finds an analogy among the ancient Greeks under the name
"orgy," the kind of thing that the god of wine and communal mayhem, Diony-
sus, would call for (duly imitated by the Romans with their god, Bacchus). Those
peoples had the customs that they did, and we monotheists have adopted some
of that heritage of wisdom as part of our own quest, along with certain aspects of
its polytheism and legend. But it makes no sense to see even a merely superficial
and unintentional influence in this parallel depiction of the Muslim paradise. My
personal opinion is that, in this particular chapter—on revelry and debauchery—
Al-Harith al-Muhasibi has done a poor job of cultivating imagination's fertile
fields, failing completely to appreciate either meaning or intention. With that
in mind I have questioned my own soul about paradise, assuming that it takes a
form such as Al-Muhasibi describes it. I have determined that it is only against
my will that I will ever be dragged to such a place. Instead I much prefer the other
version, a place the like of which no eye has ever seen, no ear ever heard, and
no human heart ever conceived. We might perhaps excuse Al-Muhasibi on the
grounds that he is addressing the general populace and people with few dreams.
His audience is the many deprived and oppressed people in the world, so he
writes in accordance with their very limited imagination, people who perceive
everything without the benefit of investigation and metaphor. May God never
involve us in such delusions and anxieties. Amen!

Invoking this reasoning, I put Al-Muhasibi's book aside. Instead I started contemplating the refreshing bliss that would soon be my good fortune. On the day of our engagement and marriage night, I would be in my beloved's arms. Putting out the light and extinguishing the candles, I closed my eyes and addressed my own soul:

"Imagine, my soul, that you have just woken up on the promised day, carefree and happy, mouthing words both sweet and scintillating. Then you have done your ablutions prior to performing the obligatory prayers and eaten just enough to keep your hunger at bay. At the bathhouse you have scrubbed and washed yourself with hot water to freshen body and soul, and trimmed your beard and hair. Donning your most elegant clothes, you have daubed yourself with perfume and straightened your general appearance. During the noontime prayers everyone has been staring at you in admiration, wondering what kind of special occasion you are going to as you sit astride your faithful and blessed steed.

"Next imagine that, before you leave, you have decided to take a walk up the mountain that has served as your protector, not to say farewell but rather to look around. You have headed for the summit, passing by the asylum and hearing vague noises and shouts emerging from it. You have then headed back down again via the hermits' forest where you have caught just a few isolated glimpses of them. You have made your way through the shady, fertile valley with its abundant crops and reached the lake where men and boys used to swim, splashing each other with water. After that you have whispered instructions in your horse's ear to convey you slowly to his and your mistress's house. He has neighed in agreement and followed various winding back-gullies till he has eventually reached the main path. Once there the earth has revealed itself to you in all its wonderful color and forms: trees decked in their finest garb and subtlest hues, birds singing and chirping sweetly, and a gentle breeze wafting through the elements of nature so as to bring them into a state of harmony and concord.

"Next imagine that these scenes of beauty all form a pathway that has been laid out for you toward the city where you have passed through squares and alleyways. People have stared at you reverently, assuming that you must be a personage of high rank. Now imagine that you have arrived at the door of your beloved's house surrounded by a retinue of servants, then entered the house with all due honor and respect. There you have been met by young maidens who have greeted you with as many songs and ululations as possible. Once they have settled you in the guest quarters, surrounded by tables of delicious food, your beloved has shown you her lovely visage by peeping out from behind a curtain. 'Very soon,' she has told you in her sweet, melodious voice, 'the men and witnesses will be arriving. Then, my dear beloved, our engagement will be concluded in a way that accords with your wishes and is pleasing to Almighty God.' That said, she has disappeared. Just a few moments later, a group of august, pious-looking men have arrived. I have stood up to greet each of them in turn. The eldest has informed me that he is serving as the bride's representative; two others seem to be his companions, while a further two are people whom you may have met at some point but don't recall.

"Next imagine that you are exchanging expressions of affection and compliments with this group of men. An official witness now brings out the text of the marriage document with all its habitual terminology and ritual. Someone else has asked you for your name and profession, and whether you agree to marry the duly cloistered lady, Fayha', the daughter of the late lamented Hajj Al-'Arabi from Sabta and his late wife, 'A'isha al-Sinhaji. When a request is made to specify the dowry price, you declare that it is too little and quadruple the amount. Now just imagine your overwhelming delight when the document is signed and the official legal certification is completed, followed by a communal recitation of the Fatiha of the Qur'an and their prayers that you and your wife may reside together in all blessing and well-being. You have then joined them in some food and drink, accompanied by conversation appropriate to the seriousness of the occasion. Once in a while you can all hear the sounds of the women in the house, praising God and chanting peals of joy. With the official ceremony over, the two witnesses have offered me their congratulations, stood up to leave, and hurried away with the excuse that they have a large number of Qur'anic duties to attend to. The bride's representative has leaned over and asked you if it suits you to have the actual wedding night in the middle of the current month, Rabi' al-Awwal, and you have agreed, noting that, as the saying goes, the best charity is that which comes soonest. You have been about to ask him for his permission to return to your hostelry, but you have listened as he summons the entire assembly to pray the afternoon prayer with him as imam; and you have done so. Once the prayer is concluded, he has talked to you and his companions about a variety of issues, both religious and secular. In response you have given all kinds of responses and have thereby earned their approval and assent. Like you they have expressed the urgent need for a concerted effort to be made with regard to Spain so that the dangers implicit in the new Christian alliance will not become so severe as to threaten Sabta itself, the other Maghribi cities, and the ports on either side of the straits. The conversation has continued in this serious vein until dinner is concluded, at which point the group has headed for the central mosque where you have prayed in their company. With that you have said farewell and mounted your horse to return to your residence.

"Next imagine your wedding night, along with all the festivities connected with it that remind you of similar occasions in Murcia during your childhood—food, dancing, and singing. How wonderful, oh how wonderful; the women have all been at organizing the rituals involved and keeping the fires burning in their own quarters, sounds of which have wafted all the way to the men's section. All the men have put on their finest clothes, and they have been eating, drinking, and sharing anecdotes and jokes, wishing you well and a life of happiness. The very thought of that future has wreathed your face in smiles of joy and gratitude. Once the hour has come for you to be alone with your bride, a group of sturdy young men has heaved you up on to a raised platform and carried you on their shoulders. Singing and praising God, they have paraded you in triumph around the men's quarters to the accompaniment of drumbeats. After that a group of old women has accompanied you with peals of joy to the private quarters of your beloved. The door has been locked behind you and the blinds have been lowered. However, when it has come to describing your wife's beauty and the delights of that particular night, you have commanded your soul to remain silent and discreet in order to keep such things secret and in accordance with proper decorum. The phase of life that you have now entered is no longer one of reckless behavior and idle talk. Now it is a matter of a concentration on monotheistic faith and marriage to a single woman."

When I woke up next morning, my mind was still preoccupied with the sweet memories of these musings of mine. They may have already been speaking to me before I actually fell asleep and when I was dreaming, so the strands became tangled. Daydreams and nighttime visions commingled till the dividing lines became blurred and then disappeared. So how could I not assume that life's succession of days was not itself merely an aggregation of dreams?

I got out of bed to purge myself of ritual impurities and conduct the necessary ablutions before performing the obligatory prayers. That done, I ate a modicum of food. Going outside to check on my horse, I found the warden hurrying toward me as though he either had something urgent to tell me or wanted me to do something for him. After greeting him, I asked him what was the matter. He was panting so hard that he could not initially reply, so I took him for a stroll till he could recover his breath.

"Yesterday," I told him, "I didn't leave my house. It felt so good to remain in seclusion!"

"That's why I didn't want to disturb you," he replied once he could talk again.

"Is anything wrong?" I asked.

"No, no," he replied, "I just wanted to give you back the deposit you left with me. You may need to spend some money on your forthcoming marriage."

"You're right, my dear 'Abd al-Barr," I said. "Let me have half of it, but keep the rest in trust. Is there something else?"

He paused for a moment, then shook his head in a way that was almost invisible. It seemed that he preferred not to comment, so I did not push him. I thought about inviting him to the wedding, but decided to leave that to a more appropriate moment. I asked him how things were going at the zawiya and its facilities, and he told me everything was fine, albeit in very curt terms.

Just as he was about to ask my permission to leave so he could continue with his duties, the bath attendant came over.

"God bless you and your famous fatwa, my fine master!" he yelled in a gruff tone. "Let the lunatics enter the bath one by one,' you said. You seem to have forgotten that a single madman is still utterly confused. How come you didn't think about that, O learned sage?"

"Shut your mouth, you rogue," said the warden in a harsh rebuke. "Do you know who you're talking to?"

"I'm talking to the person who's made a bad situation even worse, who apparently can't even see straight . . ."

"Keep your mouth shut, or else I'm going to complain to your boss!"

"He's the one who's annulled the fatwa by refusing to allow lunatics to enter the baths, even if it means using fists and canes."

That said, he went off guffawing. I then told 'Abd al-Barr the whole story about the baths and the lunatics.

"Many, O how many, are the weird and amazing things I've witnessed on this mountain," he said, rubbing his hands together. "If I told you even one of the

A Muslim Suicide | 169

least complicated tales, it would soon make you forget all about this particular problem. O God, I ask for your forgiveness and protection!"

Saying farewell, he promised to return soon. With that he departed.

When the time for the engagement and wedding finally arrived, almost everything went according to plan, just as I had imagined it. There were only a few changes and refinements as demanded by the actual situation. The most significant differences were that her representative was her own uncle on her mother's side, Hajj Hamza al-Sarraj, a wealthy merchant from Tangier; the two witnesses were 'Abd al-Barr al-Baradi'i, my friend the warden, and 'Ukasha al-Khalti, the supervisor of the lunatics! The guest of honor at the wedding banquet was the governor of Sabta, Al-Husayn ibn Khalas, but the person who really got the party swinging was Al-Ghulam Ghazlan; neither of them had featured in my imaginings. The governor offered me his congratulations and gave me his warmest good wishes, so I exchanged compliments and affectionate greetings with him. As for the second, his mellifluous voice could be heard singing in the women's quarters and sometimes in the men's as well. He was egged on in his performance by the accompaniment provided by a group of Sudanese musicians. As he danced, he would say, "OK, you men, warm up the ambiance for me! Here we are at the wedding of Lalla Fayha' and Master 'Abd al-Haqq. So sing along with me:

> Bring her in, O bring her in; do not let her get away!
> Bring him too, bring him; and do not leave him behind!
> He deserves her, O God, he is fit for her;
> Likewise she deserves him, O God, and is fit for him.
>
> What a lady, O my, what a lady!
> Cut off the hand of any who fails to keep her safe!

This risqué young man only interrupted his song when he wanted the troupe to join with him, as they accompanied him in a muwashshah poem (by Abu al-Hasan al-Shushtari,* I think):

> Sweet night, be there dew or not,
> To stay awake with you is an obligation.
> Were my own moon to linger with me,
> I would not need to attend to yours.

10

SO NOW HERE I AM living with my bride under a single roof, like butter and honey. We have been spending many wonderful hours in each other's company, chatting and sharing the sweet delights of married life. As a way of adjusting to life in my new home with all its facilities, I take the trouble to talk to the house staff. I often go up to a room on the roof where on one side I can look out at the sea and on the other at the mountain with its meadows and forests. I have also been taking a look at the archive of my late father-in-law, its shelves loaded with works on accounting, commentary, and law. The roof room and the archive are connected by a staircase that leads to the prayer-cell that my beloved promised to provide for me. The whole thing was built in short order, and, in spite of its small size (as I had requested), it nevertheless provides its occupant with an ideal space for seclusion and profound cogitation, the very acme of serenity and peace: no more furniture than necessary, windows open to the sky, and luxuriant gardens from which, night and day, it receives just enough light.

In leisure moments I took to searching the archive's library for useful works that I had not read before and organizing in my mind sections of a new book whose purposes and contents I had been carrying around in my head ever since my period in Spain had come to an end. I decided to put it into written form and polish it, all under a title that meant a great deal to me: *Escape of the Gnostic*. For me the word *escape [budd]* implies a number of notions: a line of poetry, the fulcrum of a millstone, a firm principle, or you might even say that it and its synonyms all blend together to produce a single meaning, namely the loftiest ideal, with no equal, the first and last, the perceived and hidden; the only path toward it involves uncovering its signs and secrets in the persona of an ever-striving humanity. Whoever knows himself knows his Lord, as the prophetic hadith puts it. The "gnostic" of my title is one who realizes that adjuncts and additions are mere coincidentals, or rather fantasies. Time consists of periods and moments; place mere sectors and partialities; and all of them collapse into something inferior to both unity and genuine cognizance. The gnostic person is someone who realizes all this and has experienced it, as a consequence of which he has demolished the normal icons of habit and instead adopted a posture whereby he strives for the essence of essences, the quality of qualities, and the perfection of perfections. That is all made possible by virtue of a lofty and cogent motivational force that such a gnostic can foster and strengthen by dint of his own efforts and abilities. By my own life, here resides the true significance of the struggle, one aimed at achieving a conception of divine abundance, an experience of the ever-present opaque eternity, a conjunction of the possible and Necessary Existent, one that results in a transcendent state through a permanent residence beneath its glory and beauty. Is it not God Himself who has said, "To Him shall you be gathered"; "Verily to your Lord is the return"; "Verily with your Lord is the final resort." If you are able to comprehend this clear divine discourse, then my commentary will be of help to you; if I become too complex, then it will make things easier.

O God, within the welcoming folds of my beloved's house, let me focus my mind on You, and with all willingness and delight!

O God, aid me and my beloved so that I can turn my self, my nature, and my situation entirely toward You!

O God, give me a glimpse of the heavenly light of Your face in the beauty of my wife, she who is the means of my elevation and proximity to Your presence and Your kingdom. Amen!

As the second month of my marriage began, I asked my wife's permission to go up the mountain to the zawiya to collect my books and bring them back to my new prayer-cell. Thus it was that Bilal al-Sikkit accompanied me on the trip along with two mules. Putting the boxes of my library on their backs, he secured them with an unrivaled skill. When I went to greet the warden, I decided to leave him my clothes and some money to dispose of as he saw fit. It was very hard for 'Abd al-Barr to say farewell, even though I promised to come and visit him whenever the occasion allowed. I felt a genuine nostalgia for the period I had spent residing on the mountain. Amid all the emotions at parting, he told me that, just before my marriage ceremony, he had learned some disturbing news from a passing traveler whom he trusted. However, he had decided not to tell me about it for fear of spoiling my happiness. When I pressed him, he told me that one of my students, 'Amr from Cordoba, had been killed in the suburbs of Granada after an armed engagement with a column of Castilian troops. The news came as a shock to me, and I could feel my expression pale in sorrow. Even so, I made do with a request for mercy on his soul and prayers to God. I asked the warden to direct any of my Spanish friends who asked after me to my new address, then told my companion to go on ahead of me since I wanted to ride on my own for a while as a way of lessening the overwhelming anxiety I was feeling.

Here then was the incident that I had anticipated happening in conjunction with the sheer happiness of my marriage, like some foul dissonance! How else could I respond to it other than by repeating the usual expressions: "Every soul will taste death, and verily we belong to God and to Him do we return!"

No indeed, since I had trained myself to strive toward the absolute and the lofty heights of truth, there could be no other way. If I failed to achieve substantiation in the ultimate, it could not be held against me. What does seem relatively certain is that I will never be able to achieve that felicitous state so long as I remain alive and am continually put to the test by feuds, trials, and petty jealousies; or, put another way, by an existence that is bound and foreordained. The real lesson to be learned lies in desire and means of focusing it and in longing and means of kindling it, to such an extent that I can repeat the words of Abu Yazid al-Bistami:

> I have drunk love cup after cup,
> Never did it run dry, nor did I quaff enough.

But, no matter how much time I may spend trying to rid myself of my own materiality and corporeal form, I will never be able to match the words "Praise be to me, praise be to me, for I am the truth. . . . in heaven there is God alone," those being the words that poured from the mouth of Abu Mansur al-Hallaj—may God sanctify his spirit and forgive him his willful provocation.

When it comes to famous mystics like Al-Hallaj, to Rabi'a al-'Adawiyya* before him, and Al-Suhrawardi after him, not to mention others who chose to confront people and rulers with the truth, I find myself hardly differing from any of them when it comes to adopting controversial positions. Indeed there remain spheres and dimensions that I would never be able to traverse even if I were to live two lives or more. From my perspective the foundation of all thought is always there to watch over my contemplations, offering advice and direction every time my passions and enthusiasms are aroused and my mind tends to wander off into realms of temptation. Today more than ever before, that consistency stays with me. To the controls imposed by my own self I have now added those of my household, although I have to note that, with regard to the latter, I will never play the tyrant. Rather I will only adopt whatever is readily available, since I fully intend to entrust both keys and rituals to the lady of the house, she being the decision-maker and organizer.

Ah my sweet lady and beloved! Whenever I find myself needing distraction and good company, I call her or send someone to fetch her. She appears with a smile and kisses my hand; I do likewise to hers. She washes my feet, and I do hers. Then we may eat and pray together, after which I may share some ideas about the principles of faith or teach her how to play chess. After a while I let her win, but, when she realizes that I am faking it, she starts pounding my chest. "You phony," she yells, "you absolute phony!" With that, she lies back on my knees, or else I use her lap as a soft pillow. Depending on how much time there is, we then share sad stories with each other. She tells me about her family in Sabta and Tangier, and what its various members, chief amongst whom is her uncle, are doing to assist the impoverished families who keep arriving at the two cities from Spain; and about how much she loves songs, muwashshah poetry, and playing the flute. For my part I give her a few concise details about my past life in Murcia, about my students who now constitute my own family, and about the death of 'Amr from Cordoba at the hands of the Castilian forces. However I decide not to say anything about my Sufi philosophical preoccupations, leaving it to my wife's intelligence to indulge in surmise about that particular topic. With regard to other matters, they reside in the bowers of intimate conjugal life about which no details should leave the private domain.

Several months went by like this, with me thoroughly enjoying life in the care of my beloved wife, praying, studying, and writing in my own prayer-cell. I was also able to relish some moments of intense emotional rapture and crystalline ideational radiance, blessed glimpses perhaps of promised eternity.

One day I was finding it impossible to finish a chapter of my book, *Escape of the Gnostic,* so I went for a stroll around the quarters where the house was located—something I regularly did when I found myself in such a fix. It was evening, and I started hearing some music and singing. I rushed over to its source and peered through a crack in the door, only to see Fayha' playing the flute, accompanied by Ghazlan on the lute and Hafsa on the drum while 'Abla danced and sang a lovely muwashshah poem that I did not recognize. It turned out that I was to secretly observe such a scene on several occasions until there arrived one final occasion about which I cannot remain silent. I happened to look at my wife and noticed that she was taking turns with Ghazlan eating an apple and then playing her flute while the boy rested his head on her thigh and sang a sentimental song. I could not control myself. Throwing the door open, I yelled, "What's going on here?" The boy leapt up looking alarmed and ran away. For her part, Fayha' stared at me, then burst into a peal of laughter the like of which I have never heard before. I asked her why she was laughing so hard. She calmed down, looked straight at me, and spoke so calmly that it gave me the shivers. "'Abduh," she said, "Ghazlan is like a son or daughter to me. Can't you see that he's a boy who looks just like a girl? Why all this jealousy and anger?" With that she burst into tears, interrupted by expressions of regret because she was barren and words of gratitude at her lot and praises to God who had enabled her to adopt Ghazlan as an orphan and let him provide her with some degree of consolation.

I immediately apologized. Once we were in bed, I asked her again to forgive me, cursing the Devil who had thrust suspicions into my mind. I whispered that I too intended to adopt the boy. I'm going to name him Muhammad, but you can keep calling him by his usual name. Fayha' agreed to the idea. "So be it, Abu Muhammad!" she said, finally relaxing a little. Next morning I told the young man what would happen. After a moment's thought he kissed my hand, clearly much affected by my decision. "My lord," he said, "name me Hamada instead!"

There came another day when the angel of all evil whispered in my ear yet again. "Your lady wife leaves the house on Mondays and Thursdays, and once or twice a month she travels to Tangier, while you stay here ignoring the whole thing!"

My wife had already told me that she was still in close touch with her family in both Sabta and Tangier; she needed to maintain her family ties and offer help to the aged and infirm. But, in spite of all that, I decided that I needed to squelch once and for all the needlings of the accursed Devil and to resolve any remaining doubts by establishing the facts for certain. Every time she was compelled to go out without telling me—her excuse being that she did not want to disturb me, I started following her in disguise. In Sabta my detective work showed that she went either to see her elderly aunt, Umm Haniyya, or to visit various charities like the infirmary, orphanage, and home for indigent émigrés from Spain. From various sources in those facilities I also learned that the generous lady used to bring as many anonymous gifts in money and kind as she could. With regard to her trips to Tangier, she told me how long they would take and where she was going. She used to travel with the servant Bilal, the young boy Hamada, and other travelers. I trailed them on horseback and through my secret observations was able to reassure myself that my wife was well protected at the residence of her uncle, Hajj Hamza al-Sarraj. That settled, I headed for the city mosque at sunset, performed the prayers along with the congregation, and then performed the supplementary intercessions. My only prayer was that God would forgive me for my suspicions and place a firm barrier between me and such evil thoughts. I then made my way back to Sabta, taking a back road with few travelers on it.

11

BACK AT THE HOUSE, the only person I found there was 'Abla, the servant-girl. She took my gear from me and accompanied me to my prayer-cell. Without paying any attention to my annoyance at this situation, she asked my permission to wash and massage my feet. My response was neither positive nor negative; I simply sat down and surrendered my feet willingly to her ministrations and the hot water soaked in sweet basil. While she was doing it, I was either staring up at the ceiling or closing my eyes to the seductive delights of this gorgeous white-skinned girl. When I signaled to her to stop, she dried my feet with a towel. Picking up her equipment, she asked me if I wanted dinner now; if so, she would bring it. I pretended to be full and sent her away with wishes that she sleep well. But just as she was leaving, she tripped, fell down, and let out a cry of pain, claiming that she had twisted her ankle. I hurried over to help her, and she let me massage her where she was pointing. Once she was able to stand up again, she departed, with modest expressions of thanks.

No sooner had she departed than I rushed to the bathroom to rid myself of the impurities of this contact with another woman. Hoping to wake up and rid myself of the exhaustion caused by my travels, I washed myself, then performed the ritual ablutions. I found that I could not avoid feeling guilty toward the woman who had opened her bosom and home to me and saved me from sinful distractions. In the hope of overcoming my guilty conscience and asking God for forgiveness, I performed my prayers, then fell asleep.

Sometime during the night I opened my eyes in the darkness with the sense that there was someone beside me in the bed. "Fayha'," I asked, "when did you get back?"

"It's 'Abla!" replied the voice of someone spread out at my feet.

I lit a candle and sat there, desperately thinking of a way to keep the girl at a distance and to find a better solution to the problem.

"What you're doing is wrong, my girl!" I told her, doing my best to control myself and trying to be as cordial as possible.

"We're the only people here," she replied in a soft, tender voice.

"Not true," I said. "God is the third, so fear Him!"

"Do you realize, Sir, that I'm a virgin? No man has ever touched me before!"

I decided that I could not ask her to explain why that was so and what was the problem, in case my tongue got things wrong and made it all worse.

"I will never be that man!" I replied in a terse and harsh tone that surprised even me. "I'm a married man and I fear God!"

"But just a while ago I washed and massaged your feet," she pleaded. "I only want you to do for me what I did for you."

I made it clear that I was still going to say no. I ordered her to go back to her own bed. No sooner had she got up off the bed and headed for the door than I stretched out and extinguished the candle. But now she turned around and pounced on me like a famished hyena, scratching my neck and chest with her sharp nails. I did nothing to resist her onslaught, but still kept telling her to stop behaving this way and live in fear of her Creator. Suddenly she let go of me and sat on the edge of the bed, crying and sobbing uncontrollably.

"Prayers from a devout man of God such as yourself are much to be desired," she said. "Pray to your Lord that I may be married to an honorable man. Pray to him also that He may relieve me of the tyranny of the man who has power over me . . ."

Lighting a candle again, I asked her to tell me more about this person and what precisely he had done. For a moment she said nothing, but then she told me that she had sworn on the Holy Qur'an not to reveal either his name or what he had done. I explained to her that, if he had made her swear anything under compulsion, then the force of the oath was annulled. With that she stood up and went over to a corner by the door. Sitting on a bench, she paused for a moment to calm down and recover her breath.

"My lord," she said, "forget the things I've just told you. Instead please focus on praying for me."

"Dear 'Abla," I replied, "I'll make a point of praying for you all the time."

"All in anticipation of our Lord responding to your petitions. Meanwhile, let's agree that, to the extent possible, I'll continue to wash your feet and you'll do the same for me. That is, as long as you don't want me to say anything . . ."

"Saying anything about what?"

"The scratches on your body are sign enough of the way I tried to resist your advances."

"That's sheer falsehood!"

"My story is much more plausible; by contrast yours seems implausible. And then, I'm only asking you for a fairly light touch; no need for greater involvement or whisperings. Just imagine that I'm your obedient servant-girl, and you're my wonderful doctor. That can be the pact between us until God chooses to set me free. What do you say?"

"I'll think about it when I can and let you know."

"Oh no, dear holy man of God! This pact is an act of kindness. As the old saying goes, the best kindness is rendered the quickest."

I had the bitter feeling that this young girl in my presence who was successfully confronting my faith and probity with her lures had been empowered by Satan himself in order to prevent me from embarking upon a deeper sense of God's unity through my marriage to a single person and to push me right back into my earlier phase of sheer frivolity and unfocused talk. I yelled at her to get out of my sight, but she paid absolutely no attention.

"No, no," she replied in a threatening tone. "If you give me a massage, then I'll say nothing about you and you can say nothing about me. But, if you refuse, I'm going to yell and scream out loud. And then it'll be the neighbors and police!"

It was obviously preferable to do what this flagrant girl demanded—if only to an extent—rather than risk a wholesale scandal.

So I went over and sat down beside her outstretched legs. She grabbed my hands and kissed them. Daubing my hands with a clammy cream, I took a deep breath. She meanwhile kept sighing as she watched what I was doing. I started rubbing the cream on her feet one by one all the way up to her ankles. When I tried to move my hands to her legs, she sighed again and stopped me. Just then I saw her insert one of her fingers between her thighs and start moving it. I turned away, wondering what she was doing as I heard her let out a series of moans, but then I realized. Stopping my massage, I was about to scold her for her scandalous behavior when she suddenly let out a shriek and ran to hide behind the door like a shot from a bow.

Purification and ablution, that's what I needed, and then reading the Sura of Joseph from the Qur'an before performing the morning prayers. Once that was done, I would be locking my doors and windows in the hope of getting my due of sleep.

However, when morning finally arrived and I opened my eyes, there was 'Abla standing in front of me with a smile. I was amazed as she greeted me with a "good morning."

"How did you get in here," I asked, "when I shut the door and window?"

"When it's the heart that is your guide," she replied, "you can't go wrong. The true lover has no problems finding the key to the locked door. While I was waiting for you to wake up, I've planted some gentle kisses on your face and prepared some food for you, all of it prepared and cooked by myself."

I looked at my table and saw that it was full of dishes for lunch. I realized that I had slept the entire morning. I thanked her for making my lunch and asked her to go back to her own quarters. She told me that her mistress would be coming back soon, news that made me smile in relief. I asked her when that would be.

"Not before noon tomorrow," she replied. "So, my beloved, we have the rest of today, tonight, and tomorrow morning entirely to ourselves."

"Listen, girl," I said as firmly as I could, "show some faith in God, or else I shall inform your mistress about your behavior."

"If you do that," she replied, "then the old saying will apply to you: 'He beat me and cried, then went ahead of me and complained.' The scars on your body will be testimony against you on my behalf. There's no way out. You have to stick to our agreement."

I lowered my head in thought as I tried yet again to devise some means of escaping from this stubborn and crafty girl's nasty trap. I watched as she came toward me with her ewer and basin and sat down on the rug beside my bed.

"Do you deny me something that God has not forbidden?" she asked me gently when she saw how reluctant I was to go along with her plans. "How can you be so cold when I love you?"

"Enough of this nonsense, girl! You've lost all sense of reality."

"What am I supposed to do when, as you can tell, God has created me this way? My heart is what controls me; it is my sole guide."

Dear God, there is absolutely no point in arguing with this buxom virgin. So please come to my aid by controlling my passion so I can resist the girl whose illogical screams are her primary weapon. O Merciful and Compassionate One, should I respond to her suggestions and do things that are not part of my intention but are rather done under compulsion, then do not hold me to account!

I stretched my legs out to reach her basin and told her she could wash me as far as my ankles but no further. She undertook her task with consummate skill and obvious dedication, rubbing me with oil first and then massaging and washing. Once in a while she would reach up to my legs, but I would distract myself by letting my mind wander into the verdant pastures of memory or particularly thorny theoretical questions. What brought me back to the situation in which I found myself was the sound of her voice as she chanted parts of a muwashshah poem, the one, as I recall, by Ibn Baqi* from Spain:

> Love has dallied with my heart, so I complain
> Of the pangs of passion, and my tears linger.
> O people, my heart is on fire with love,
> Passion's tyranny rules out all fairness.
> How hard I try to conceal it, while my tears
> Trickle downward.

She kept on finding appropriate lines to quote that reflected her own situation, this next set coming from a muwashshah by Ibn Zuhr*:

> My heart is on fire and tears trickle down my cheeks,
> It is acquainted with sin, yet will not confess.
> You who turn away from what I depict,
> For me love of you has grown and thrived,
> Say not that in matters of love I am feigning.

In my little garden with its plants and myrtle trees, even birds accompany my moments of pleasure with unwonted chirps and songs. It was only when I realized that I was taking a headlong plunge toward grave sin that I withdrew my feet and dried them with a towel. I then asked 'Abla to stand up and leave.

Looking at her face, I noticed that she had been crying so hard that her eyes were red.

"I've washed your feet with water and tears," she said as she stood up and headed for the door. "Wait for me tonight. Then it's my turn. If you refuse me, then so much the worse!"

Once again I leapt to my feet in order to rid myself of this enforced impurity and performed my ablutions in preparation for prayers and a plea for forgiveness. With that I kept myself to myself.

12

I NOW MADE A HUGE EFFORT to concentrate on the most valuable portions of the learning of the ancients, but it was all in vain. My mind was completely disoriented, and I found it impossible to focus on the texts, whether generalities or particulars. My entire consciousness was focused on this crafty female devil who was robbing me of my sanity and powers of concentration. I decided to spend the next night either in the mosque or else in a hotel. After that I would make my way to the city in the hope that my wife, Fayha', would return. Then I would have her protection and could live in peace and quiet.

Toward evening I slunk out of my prayer-cell and made for the door. It was closed and locked, so I went up to the roof door and found the same situation. I therefore had no option but to go back to my little room. Once there I started making preparations by locking the door and window and then barricading them both with furniture and other stuff. For a while I just sat there, waiting fearfully and using my weight to reinforce my bed, my boxes of books, and my papers. As night began to descend, I recited as many intercessions as I could. Then I heard 'Abla's voice, begging me to honor our pact and allow her to enter. I stood firm and remained silent. She now threatened to raise a hue and cry and vowed a dreadful outcome, but I still said nothing and stayed where I was. Indeed she did start letting out cries that sounded like moans, puny and feeble, coming from a wounded animal. All of a sudden she stopped, and there was a total silence, as before a violent storm. And that is exactly what happened. A few seconds went by, feeling as oppressive as a load of lead, seconds that I spent in almost total panic, and then the girl started yelling and screaming all over again. Using an axe or something like it, she started digging a hole in my front wall; it was soon large enough that you could see and reach through it. I ordered her to stop, and for a moment she paused to recover her breath, all the while staring at me with tearful, distracted eyes. With both her status and mine in mind, I begged her to show that she feared God. She retorted with the very same thought and went on to demand that I explain why her Creator was choosing to deprive her of her right to meet the one she loved; why was He depriving her of the joys of love and intercourse. I told her that her love of love was an empty qibla that could only ever be inhabited by a champion with neither beloved nor spouse, someone who longed to find a partner who could love and take care of him. 'Abla now seemed to come to her senses, but not for long. Taking up the axe again, she started enlarging the hole till she was exhausted.

"Now, my lord," she said, "I can see your gleaming face in its entirety. Tell me about this bachelor champion. When will he come knocking on my door and become engaged to me? Will it be happening soon, or only after I've grown old and grey-haired?"

"The answer to that question, 'Abla, lies with God alone. Keep praying to Him, and never despair. Keep yourself busy with other things. Your release may come when you least expect it."

"It's your prayers that are answered, not mine. Pray to my God for me that He will remove from me the damage caused by the one who oppresses me. Pray to Him that he will hasten my encounter with the man who will marry me and treat me well."

"I shall do that morning and evening. But now go back to your own quarters."

Before I knew it, my hand was in hers and she was pulling it toward her, kissing it on both sides and bathing it in her hot, coursing tears. She started licking and sucking every one of my fingers, concentrating on the thumbs, emitting groans of pleasure as she did so. I tried to pull my hand back through the hole, but her hold was strong. I only managed to release myself when I heard her making a noise that suggested she had had her fill and achieved her purpose. With that she rushed off into the night, leaving my personal universe far behind.

I left my room the way it was, fully prepared for personal defense and ready for any contingency. Lighting some candles, I set about repairing the wall as best I could. When I had finished, I performed my ablutions, prayed, and focused on the girl who was eager to be married to an honorable man.

That night my sleep was much disturbed, interrupted as it was by fleeting nightmarish visions, terrifying enough in their sheer impact, let along their content. I stayed there in bed until sunlight was flooding my room. At about noon I heard a soft tap on the door.

"I'm fasting today, 'Abla," I said gruffly.

To which the person knocking replied, "It's Fayha', 'Abduh. I'm Fayha'!"

I rushed to put my bed back where it belonged and hid my scratched neck underneath the tail-ends of my turban. Opening the door to my beloved wife and savior, I hugged and kissed her for all I was worth, and she returned my gestures of love and longing. When she seemed surprised that my room was in such a mess, I claimed that I was in the process of cleaning and rearranging things.

"That's a woman's job," she said.

"And a man's too," I replied. "There are various tasks where men and women have equal responsibilities!"

I sat my wife down next to me and asked her about her family in Tangier and what she had been doing, hoping that, by so doing, I could change the conversation topic and divert her attention. She told me that everyone was fine; they all sent me their greetings and hoped to see me soon. She went on to tell me about various projects she had completed in the city, including ordering household items and clothes, some of which were for me. But she had nothing to say about her charity work on behalf of the indigent and orphans similar to what she was doing in Sabta . . .

I spent some lovely intimate moments with her. I drew her head to my chest so she would not notice the scars on my neck. For a while I spoke to her about my own work and my worries concerning my students, about whom I had not heard anything for some time. She whispered some soothing words in my ear, then stood up to leave.

"When it's time to break your fast, 'Abduh," she said, "'Abla can come and clean your room and rearrange things. Then we can rest and relax a little."

If my wife had not reminded me that I had earlier pretended to be fasting, purely as a means of self-protection, I would have taken her away to do the kind of things that God and his Messenger have permitted a passionate and hungry husband to do with his wife. Instead, only a short while after she had withdrawn 'Abla appeared, eyes downcast and showing signs of modesty and bashfulness. Without uttering a word she started sweeping and cleaning the room. Suddenly, however, another servant-woman, Hafsa, appeared, gestured to 'Abla to leave, and threw her out. She took over from the poor girl, and started rearranging the furniture with commendable skill. The only times she looked in my direction were to throw arrogant, brazen glances at me. Once finished, she departed without a word and slammed the door.

Never before had I set eyes on a servant like this Hafsa. She looked sturdy and strong, flat-chested, with short hair and a tawny complexion. She scowled and squinted a lot. Had she been given free rein to do what she wanted with me, she could easily have either lifted me up to the ceiling or stomped me on the ground. Now more than ever before I came to realize the incredibly offhand and rude way in which this giantess was treating me. I praised God that at least she was not in love with me and that He had provided me with such a woman as protection against 'Abla's brash provocations. It would be Hafsa whom I would ask to serve me if my wife had to travel again.

As the muezzin called the sunset prayer, I heard Fayha' calling me to "break my fast." I could do nothing but respond. The table of food that awaited my arrival in the private quarters was piled high with every kind of dish that the human soul could desire. I broke my would-be fast with the customary prayer, asking God to forgive me for such deception, then urged my wife, who was sitting by my side, to join me in eating. She did so, but only a little. I asked her about Hamada, and she told me that he would be coming back soon when he had completed certain tasks she had asked him to do.

Hafsa was acting as our servant, and she used the occasion to show her many virtues, not least the management of household affairs. My wife asked me if I agreed with her high opinion of Hafsa, and I told her that I did. She had the opposite to say about 'Abla because she was still very inexperienced and had not learned how to behave prudently. As an excuse she pointed out that 'Abla was very young and went on to tell me that the girl had only acquired a family when her late father took charge of her; till the age of eleven she had lived in an orphanage. By contrast, Hafsa was in her forties. My wife told me that she was experienced in the ways of the world, very strong and not a little stubborn. With her quick temper in mind, it was no wonder that she was still unmarried. Her late father had wanted her to be well cared for, so he had bequeathed her to Fayha'. My wife also told me that Bilal had also come to her household as part of the same bequest; her late father had manumitted him from a cruel previous owner who had cut out his tongue, claiming that Bilal kept talking without permission or need. I was already noticing that this poor giant of a man took the greatest pleasure in serving his mistress and her entire household with a truly rare sense of devotion. On Fridays and festival days he also valued the opportunity to pay an early morning visit to the grave of Rayhan the African in Hajar al-Sudan, after which he would return to the alley where the house was and show his organizational skills by making needy invalids stand in line while he helped distribute as many alms as we could afford.

With my beloved's return I recovered my emotional equilibrium and, along with it, my ability to focus on the religious and secular sciences that I found most valuable. I spent days and weeks, not only studying but also writing essays and composing new sections for my book, *Escape of the Gnostic,* as well as doing some useful editing of the parts I had already written.

13

FROM THE FOURTH YEAR of my stay in Sabta onward, events and news about them started to speed up. The governor of Sabta, Ibn Khalas, wrote to me that Frederic, the Christian king, had liked my responses to his questions and sent another valuable gift, even though I had turned down the first one. The governor suggested that, if I so wished, I was entitled to receive the gift from the governor's residence. I sent my reply straight back to the governor, to the effect that I continued to reject all gifts from kings. My justification, already dispatched to the ruler of the Christians, had not changed, based as it was on God's own words in the Qur'an: "Say: I shall not ask for any reward for it, save for love of those near and dear" [Sura 42, v. 23]. If the king pretends not to understand, I pointed out, then tell him—as I have already done—that "those near and dear" refers to the Muslims in Spain, while the hoped-for "love" implies coming to their aid in resisting the armed conflict and hatred aimed at them by the Castilians and their allies. I informed the governor that I would be composing a letter to the king in which I would outline the kinds of support that would be requested of him. In God alone is success.

The second wonderful event that caused me great delight was the arrival of a group of my students at noontime on Sunday. After asking 'Abla to show them in, I kissed them one by one, spoke to each of the seniors among them, and introduced myself to the new ones. I asked them all to sit with me in my prayer-cell, using various prayer rugs and mats. The young girl made her way among them in her diaphanous veil, flitting around like a little bird, smiling all the while as she offered them all some sustenance from trays full of drinks, sweets, and loaves of bread. 'Abd al-'Ali, Al-Sadiq, and 'Adnan all whispered their congratulations on my marriage and my new abode. Then all of a sudden Hafsa appeared at the door and ordered 'Abla to leave the room at once and follow her. All the poor girl could do was to obey and leave.

'Abd al-'Ali, who had not been paying any attention to what was going on, leaned over and told me that the purpose of the group's visit was to revive the old disciple relationship and check on my well-being. He went on to say that the students present were all people whom he knew to be polite and courteous. Just like the old trio, they were all inhabitants of Granada; they had crossed the straits specifically so that they could study with me for a while before returning to their jobs in their own cities. Al-Sadiq told me that other students from Sabta were patiently waiting outside the quarter until such time as I would be willing to arrange a time for a meeting in the city mosque. From people close to me I learned that my sayings had been circulating among people and were so popular that everyone wanted more.

When I noticed that they had all finished eating and drinking, I extended my greetings and compliments to everyone present and urged on them all the virtues of useful learning and honest work. I went on to pray that they would all be successful in whatever they undertook in the cause of God and the community of Muslims. They were delighted to hear my words. Standing up to say their farewells, they prepared to leave, while I promised to meet them all in the afternoon of the following day, Monday, in the great mosque of the city.

I asked the trio to stay behind, and they in turn asked if a young man named Khalid from Tangier could stay with them, he being a convert of Gothic origin. They took turns in extolling his virtues, his politeness and integrity. Among his qualities was his competence in both Castilian Spanish and Latin. The only thing they held against him, at least in my presence, was his distaste for marriage and his great passion for travel. The young man, who was sturdily built, brown-skinned, and handsome, justified his love of travel by saying that he could only stay in one particular place for a month before he felt the urge to move somewhere else. He told us that he found it relaxing to keep moving house, clarifying his views by stating that he would continue doing so until he had completed his wanderings by settling by the Ka'ba in Mecca. That last statement was one that I found very pleasing, and it served as a prelude to my decision to adopt this child of Tangier as one of my close associates.

The first thing I asked for was details of how 'Amr from Cordoba had died. They confirmed what I had already heard and went on to say that they had duly performed all the necessary rituals at his graveside in the one remaining Muslim cemetery in the Murcia region, which in any case was no longer big enough to hold the ever-increasing number of people who were dying. Hearing all this, I expressed my deepest regret over the death of this young martyr and prayed for his soul.

I then asked them for news about their own lives. They told me that, apart from Khalid from Tangier—stubborn bachelor that he was, they were all married and had children. 'Adnan, who had a reputation for witticisms, pointed out that, in Granada, every single young man of twenty or so had to have a girl with whom he could share the task of increasing the pomegranate crop on both banks of the River Genil or else somewhere in the copses, orchards, and gorgeous meadows of the region—all of it, of course, on the path to a legitimate union!

I was sure that 'Adnan was right, but avoided any exploration of the topic with 'Abd al-'Ali because I did not wish to disturb him by mentioning his first marriage to the Jewish girl, Rachel, and her pseudo-conversion to Islam. Instead I asked them all about people and politics in Granada. I gave them a brief summary of what I knew: The Banu Ahmar were now in control of the city and of Almeria as well, but people were scared and felt insecure. The only thing that was keeping the Christians from further attacks was that they were all fighting among themselves. But that would not last very long, and, once things were more settled, they would once again be attacking the Muslims and their strongholds in southern Spain. I asked them whether Amir Ibn al-Ahmar was not in fact allying himself with the Castilian tyrant king, Ferdinand.

"Yes, indeed he is," 'Abd al-'Ali replied. "He pays him taxes and keeps sending him all kinds of gifts. The whole point is to give him enough power to oppose his own family and community."

"The only reason why he is known as 'the Conqueror,'" Al-Sadiq went on, "is because he has beaten his fellow Muslim amirs. But, when it comes to King Ferdinand, he's all subservience and fealty."

They then took turns in providing me with snippets of information about people in Granada. I found myself having to adjust to the images presented by their accounts of extreme shortages and their loss of hope for this chaotic world, a world in which they were being forced to eke out a living, each one of them doing his best to work things out, either expecting something major to happen at any moment or else seriously thinking about exile.

For my part I told them about Sabta and the Maghrib. I pointed out that, while it was certainly true that—if only for a while—the current position of the Nasrids in Granada could be explained by infighting among the Christian rulers, the weakness of the Almohad sultan and his predecessors such as ʿAbd al-Wahid al-Rashid,* who had drowned in one of the pools in his palace, and ʿAli al-Saʿid, who had taken his place, was equally to blame. I reminded them all that, quite apart from the urgent need to supervise the implementation of God's injunctions, any vestige of hope seemed at that point to reside with the Hafsid rulers in Tunis, who seemed eager to revive the former power and authority of the Almohads in the countries of the Maghrib. After a pause I also alluded to another source of hope, namely the fact that Frederic, king of Sicily, seemed to be favorably inclined toward the Muslim peoples and certainly admired their learning in opposition to the power of the pope in Rome and the arrogant attitudes of the Crusaders. I gave them all a brief summary of my correspondence with this Christian ruler and the circumstances in which it had come about. I then explained that I had only responded to his subversive questions in order to get him to lend his support to a Muslim victory in Spain and the Maghrib that would be achieved by dint of preparedness and experience first of all but also by force of arms if needed, all based on the assumption that both he and his people would accommodate themselves to Islam and be guided by its illumination. I went on to inform my students that during the process I had turned down all his gifts and generous donations.

The students were amazed and delighted by what I had told them and asked for further details about the conclusion of this felicitous correspondence. I told them that the king had yet to respond to my suggestion. If he were to meet me and offer measures that would benefit our countries and God's servants who were living in them, then I would be among his most fervent supporters.

"Dear teacher," said ʿAbd al-ʿAli, "by the right of the worshipped God, I assure you that, during these long months past, the only thing that has kept us away from your presence has been our own petty concerns and the new circumstances in which we find ourselves in Granada, not to mention our fervent desire that you be allowed to retreat to Jabal Musa and devote yourself to learning and devotion."

"And don't forget, ʿAli," ʿAdnan went on, "that we've been neglecting our studies, the kind of thing that makes our master happy. I think we should all emigrate to Sabta so we can be close to our master and benefit still further from his erudition."

"No, no, 'Adnan!" I replied immediately. "You and your companions should stay where you are. Don't even think of leaving unless, as was the case with me, some emergency situation or urgent need demands that you do so. You can travel the distance between us fairly easily whenever possible. If it weren't for the fact that I'm not allowed to cross back into Spain, I would make the journey myself."

'Ali and his companions all signaled that they understood. "No, master," he said, "we will make the journey. Spies and intriguers of all kinds keep on collecting bits of information about you, Sir. For your sake and ours, it's much better for you to stay here where you can be safe with your family."

At that point Khalid was looking at the floor, as though something important was on his mind. When I asked him what was bothering him, he asked me to tell him about my responses to the Christian king. I gave him a copy of them, and he looked at them carefully, first at the summaries, then at the seals. He then read the following out loud:

> These topics about which Alexander differed with Aristotle are ones that I have raised in an artificial manner, something you can tell from reading the works of other people. Once I had realized that the matter was already well known per se, I decided not to refer to it or go into any detail, even though you yourself only wish to know what is generally accepted on the topic. For that reason, I have only discussed with you those aspects about which you had asked me. When we meet, we will be able to discuss these matters face-to-face, and that is much more satisfactory. So please be aware of all this— and God grants success through His beneficence, generosity, and grace. Here ends the discussion concerning the Sicilian questions.

From this section of my response Khalid concluded that I was encouraging the king to meet me so that he could profit from my learning face-to-face and be looking at me as I spoke. He asked me when the text had been sent, and I told him almost a year ago. He then asked me if I was sure that the text had in fact reached its addressee, to which I replied in the positive, noting that I had received a short sealed message accompanied by a set of gifts that I had asked the governor of Tangier to return to the king.

Khalid rubbed his hands together in disbelief. "Is it conceivable, you people," he asked in amazement, "that the king should admire Muslim scholars so much and receive from a senior representative of that group a request to hold a meeting with him, and yet not reply?"

"Maybe political issues have distracted his attention," I replied, "or else there have been problems with religious authorities or even emergencies that we know nothing about."

"Will you allow me, master, to give you my own reading of these circumstances—and God knows best?"

"Feel free to do so, Khalid."

"I have no doubt whatsoever that your response to King Frederic was abridged and altered by whoever it was to whom you entrusted its delivery. I suspect that the governor of Sabta and his aides made sure to remove your request to meet the Sicilian king."

"But Governor Ibn Khalas is a man of high reputation," I objected. "I cannot imagine his doing anything such as you have suggested. I say that even though I have yet to meet him."

'Ali looked at me in amazement. "Master," he said, "you have a good opinion of this governor even though you've never met him or checked on the validity of his reputation?"

"That's true enough, master," Al-Sadiq interrupted assertively to underline what his colleagues had already said. "Are you really willing to trust someone, when others in a similar position and with even more power and authority have already done you considerable harm?"

"By God," said 'Adnan by way of comment, "politicians are all of one stripe on both sides . . ."

I remained silent for a moment while I contemplated the opinions of the group regarding my letter to the Sicilian king and the possibility that malicious hands had distorted its contents. I decided that the best thing to do was to give my students a copy of the original document so that they could make copies and distribute them to their colleagues and anyone else who was interested. They all thought that was a good idea and promised me to circulate the document in Granada, Almeria, and their environs as well. Khalid went even further, and volunteered to travel to Sicily whenever he could with a view to finding out what had actually happened and maybe even asking for a meeting with the king and questioning him in his own language. I welcomed my colleagues' suggestions, even though some of them gave me pause.

There was a gentle knock on the door that I assumed was a woman's. "Who is it?" I asked, and in response I heard Fayha''s sweet, gentle voice. I allowed her to come in and introduced her to my students, who had all stood up. From beneath her diaphanous veil she offered them her welcome and greetings while they looked at her briefly with expressions of thanks and congratulations on our blessed marriage.

"'Abduh," she said, "these then are the young men about whom you have been talking and longing to see so much. God be praised now that you have met them again under this blessed roof!"

She asked them all to stay until dinner-time and to spend the night in the guest quarters, but they refused the kind offer with all due apologies, said their farewells, and departed. I accompanied them to the door, where I spotted 'Abla standing close by watching them all. When we came closer to the door and her eyes met those of the young men, Hafsa grabbed her by the arm and marched her off, scolding her as she did so. I bade my students farewell, in the hope and expectation of meeting them again at a session in the great mosque. With that I retraced my steps, with the intention of sitting with my wife and discussing with her a number of issues of varying degrees of importance.

14

FOLLOWING THE NOON PRAYER on Monday I headed for my rendezvous and found a huge crowd awaiting my arrival. My quartet of closest confidants welcomed me and sat me down on a small pulpit. I had no idea what to focus on during the lesson or what the people present expected me to say. I leaned over and asked 'Abd al-'Ali what he thought, and he replied that he only knew a few of the students who had come. In his opinion the best thing was to treat them all as virtual novices. They would thus prefer clear presentations and relatively simple content; that way any diffidence they might have about understanding and learning about complicated matters would be gradually overcome.

I signaled everyone to quiet down, whereupon they all stretched their necks and stared straight at me, notebooks and pens at the ready to take notes on what I had to say. I intoned the phrases "In the name of God" [Bismillah] and "God alone possesses the power . . ." [Hawqalah], greeted them all and spoke as follows:

"In Surat al-Zumar (Companies [Sura 39]) God Almighty says in the ninth verse, 'Say: Are those people who know to be the equal of those who do not know? Only possessors of intellect remember'—God Almighty has spoken the truth. In this context 'Those who do not know' refers to the common people, and they come in two categories: those who realize their ignorance and try to rid themselves of its trammels; and others who fail to realize their ignorance and thus fall victim to the clutches of indifference and sheer folly—and may God and His light protect us all from that. Those who know also fall into two categories: those who make a big show of how much they have learned, however little it may turn out to be; and those whose learning is rich and blessed, people who make due acknowledgement to God and to the extent possible use their knowledge to people's benefit.

195

"In this fractious and broken era the domains of theology and law are utterly gutless. Every so-called expert is satisfied with the knowledge that he has, applying whatever he knows and peddling it as part of his assessment of the status quo, his own static ideas, and his long-buried sense of initiative. Stultifying debates and inane disputes occur, where incidentals regularly win over essentials, branches supersede roots, and froth overwhelms substance. The word of truth is lost in the process of plowing fields consisting of stones and sand. Existence itself is peeled off its edifice and sense of unity, causing splinters to fly and bounce off in scattered fragments.

"So avoid this kind of religious learning, turn your backs on such people, and avert your gaze. Instead you should sit on different riverbanks and undertake research into other spheres and enlightening values, spheres that will take you away from mere quantities and divisions and lead you toward the framework of true understanding, something that will produce a profound sense of well-being and complete bliss. However, without genuine passion and a quest for the circles of proximity and fulfillment you will never manage to achieve such a state.

"Take as your example the inventive researcher who wishes to create something—in other words, a process of arousing his quest for learning, of honing his talents and his own confidence in them. In the course of carrying out this obligation with all due enthusiasm and seriousness, he enables you to embark upon a path that equips you to perform at your optimum level, all the while existing in a state of somnolence.

"I want you to act just like this inventive investigator. Train your memory and encourage it to memorize passages of prose and poetry, all of them chosen for their inimitable style and rhetorical and intellectual acumen. That way you will acquire the gift of language that serves as the very air of your ever-developing identity and its dynamic base.

"But language with no ideas behind it is an empty vessel, a skeleton with no flesh and bones. It is only through the power of ideas that language enables you to understand the All-knowing and His words.

"The intellect is a creative force through which truths are sought. It may manifest itself in a form that is either logically organized or else scattered and fragmentary. The process involves particular methods that my assistant, 'Abd al-'Ali, will now explain to you."

With that 'Abd al-'Ali stood up. "The first of those methods," he told his audience, "involves ways of framing and posing questions. The gateway to probing and lively thought and the primary mode of its instigation lies in the question itself. Among its worthy attributes are authenticity, creativity, and profundity. In that way the question itself raises issues and topics that require the activation of the mind, since it is able to distinguish between what is essential and what is coincidental, the mind that is in quest of the source, the totality, and the comprehensible.

"Second, the construction of hypotheses, a mental activity that focuses on knowledge and a reasonable inclination to invigorate what is static and keep the imagination at work.

"Third, an intellectual approach that makes use of logical, recognized methods: careful examination and inference, juxtaposing one problem with another once you have analyzed both, followed by a process whereby the two are combined into a single issue that manages to surmount the difficulties they present by preserving the essential qualities of each one of them. While still at the learning and experimental phase such practices are unavoidable, but, once a certain stage of achievement and maturity has been reached, then the 'escape of the gnostic' can be realized through impulse, discovery, and invention in a realm beyond the logic of opposites and the various rationales of adaptation, invention, and rotation . . ."

All of a sudden he fell silent. I was in the process of trying to come up with some vivid, tangible examples that I could use with the students to explain certain obscurities in my statements. But once I became aware of what was going on around me, I noticed that a stern old man was heading in my direction, accompanied by two other people like him. He leaned over and addressed me in a chiding tone.

"I am the supervisor of this mosque," he said, "and I'm responsible for what goes on here. Esteemed shaykh, teaching in this spot without a proper license is not permitted."

"But the mosque is God's own house," I replied. "Teaching the next generation is a solemn obligation enjoined upon those with knowledge."

"True enough, shaykh, but not without due permission from the local authorities. His Excellency the Governor commands that order be kept and forbids all kinds of sedition and dissent."

When my quartet of students heard what he was saying, they rose to their feet in disgust.

"My good man," said Al-Sadiq in a harsh tone that was clearly audible, "haven't you read in the text of the Qur'an those verses that encourage people to study and learn? Can it be that the words of the Lord of all messengers have not reached you, where he says, 'Knowledge is a cache of treasure whose key is questioning? So ask questions, may God have mercy on you all! There are four people whom He will esteem: the questioner, the teacher, the listener, and the one who loves them all.'"

"Yes, and that's a report recorded by Abu Nu'aym al-Isfahani* from 'Ali* himself," 'Adnan continued in support of his colleague. "We are gathered here to acquire knowledge in accordance with the ordinance of God and His apostle. We have no need of a license from any governor or sultan."

The entire assembly now stood up and chanted the words that 'Adnan had uttered. The entire situation was in danger of getting out of hand and moving to other quarters as well. Through the hubbub I heard the supervisor issuing threats.

"You're inciting young people to commit rebellion, shaykh," he said. "Either you break it up, or else I'm going to call the police and guards."

With that I too stood up and indicated to the group that they should calm down and make their way to the ablutions section. That is precisely what they did.

I sat down on the mat with my quartet of students around me, all of us coming to terms with what had just happened.

"It won't be difficult for me to obtain a license to teach," I told them. "If I make the request, Ibn Khalas the governor will be only too glad to give me one. But I'm afraid that such a move is bound to involve some kind of trap."

Khalid's eyes were gleaming. "The request to Ibn Khalas for a license won't be coming from you," he said in the tone of someone who has just made a discovery. "It'll come from us, in the form of a petition signed only by the students from Sabta, not others. They'll take it to the governor. That at least is my suggestion, although I'm not sure what the outcome will be."

"It would be better for the three of us not to be involved in the application," said Al-Sadiq to underline what Khalid had just said. "Then we can't be accused of sedition and incitement, something that would get us expelled. That's something we couldn't tolerate."

We all agreed to Khalid's plan and his generous offer to implement it. That settled, we all made ready to perform our ablutions before praying the sunset prayer. That completed, my companions all suggested that my best plan was to return home. They escorted me as far as the door. I offered them some dinner, but they declined, said farewell, and went their own way.

When I went inside, I had fully intended to keep what had transpired in the mosque a secret from my wife, but Hafsa informed me with a habitual frown that her mistress was going to spend the night with her aunt, who had suddenly been taken ill. I asked her about 'Abla, and it was obvious that my question surprised and offended her.

"Did she go with your mistress?" I asked in order to clarify my intentions.

"Oh, 'Abla's sound asleep!" she replied mockingly. "Shall I wake her up and have her bring you your meal?"

I shook my head and hurried away to my prayer-room.

15

MY SLEEP PATTERNS that night were much disturbed, and I spent several hours wide awake or else dozing off for a while. Whichever of the two states I was in, I kept on dreaming of spoken confrontations with different faces: Khalid and 'Abla, King Frederic, Ibn Khalas the governor, 'Abd al-Barr al-Baradi'i, 'Ukasha al-Khalti, the warden of the insane, Fayha' and her aunt and uncle. While I could remember snippets of the conversations I had with them, they dissipated as soon as I woke up or became aware of my surroundings.

Very early in the morning I decided to put a definitive end to my tossings and turnings. I got out of bed and proceeded to perform my ablutions and prayers before reading some texts of the ancients. I decided to resort to a walk around the house garden, in the hope that the earliness of the hour might refresh my senses and whet my distracted mind. Then I might feel more relaxed and be able to go back to the process of writing and revising my book, *Escape of the Gnostic*. As I was walking along a hallway leading to my destination, I happened to hear some groans coming from the room of Hafsa, the maid. If it were not for the sighs of pleasure and delight I would have assumed that someone had been wounded. For a while I stayed rooted to the spot, but, when it was a little lighter, I took a peep through the aperture. What a horrendous sight did I behold!! There was Hafsa, stark naked and behaving like some wild animal; beneath her lay 'Abla, spread-eagled like some piece of prey. Without the slightest doubt, they were engaging in lesbian sex, thrashing around and grabbing each other for all they were worth, not to mention the snorts, grunts, and gasps they kept making. The whole thing appalled me, but I decided not to stop them and reprimand them both severely for fear of consequences that I could not even envisage. No, I told myself, better to wait; definitely better to wait. With that I hurried back to my closet in order to think things over. I had heard before about lesbianism, but had never actually witnessed the kind of thing I had just seen. I now recalled that 'Abla had alluded to the fact that someone else was keeping her constrained, but she had kept it a secret. Now this very morning I had discovered it for myself. Obviously Hafsa hated men, but 'Abla was clearly being forced to do something she did not like. If not, then why had she asked me on several occasions to get her married? So now things were a lot clearer, and my earlier intuitions had proved to be correct. From now on I would have to sever this bond between the wild female beast and the young gazelle, indeed to save the gazelle from the wild beast's clutches. The entire operation would require a good deal of secrecy, skill, and careful management. As the saying has it, success comes only from God!

I spent at least half the day trying to overcome my lack of sleep, sometimes by writing and at others by walking around my quarters. All the while I kept praying to God that he would find 'Abla a good husband. At noontime I summoned her and told her to go to her mistress and help her take care of her aunt; she should not return unless it was with her mistress. 'Abla did what I told her, but Hafsa was there in the blink of an eye, her expression a tissue of anger as she glared in fury at both of us. Once 'Abla had left, this squint-eyed harpy came over and gave me a blank stare as if to make it clear that she was fully aware of what I had found out. Then all of a sudden she let out a laugh, and her attitude softened. She asked me if I needed her for anything, and I asked her nicely to bring me some food to the misriyya.* I decided that, from now on, I would not eat anything she had prepared and cooked, even if I was starving.

Late in the afternoon I left the house to perform the prayers in the Zaghlu Mosque close by the place where the legal counselors used to sit. There I found all my friends except Khalid waiting for me. As I performed my ablutions, I found myself surrounded by an ever-increasing number of young men. 'Ali told me that the petition requesting permission for me to teach was being prepared. When I asked him about Khalid, he replied that he had gone off to do something that he had not described any further.

After evening prayers, I spent a few moments in silent contemplation while all around me gathered a large crowd of young people, obviously eager to hear what I would have to say.

"May I request your opinion, Sir," Al-Sadiq asked, "regarding a young man who right up to yesterday was cursing marriage in all its aspects, but purely on the basis of choice and thought rather than experience. In the briefest time imaginable he's become just like someone who's fallen in love at the very first glance. He shows all the signs of love as described by Ibn Hazm of Cordoba—what a truly wonderful scholar!—so much so that the words of the poet can apply to him in every way:

> Ye people, when love strikes a young man in the heart
> And continues to develop,
> Then it will demolish some of his resolve,
> And down he will fall."

I did my best to look neither nonplussed nor amazed by this question. "Tell me," I said, "did this young man of yours fall in love with his beloved while dreaming, or did he actually set eyes on her?"

"He has seen her in flesh and blood. He has learned that she lives in a household endowed with honor and prestige, but, I assure you by God, he has never spoken to her or even made the slightest gesture in her direction."

By this point I had begun to develop a certain intuition. "This lover," I asked, "what exactly are his intentions and desires?"

"As he has lain on his bed in an agony of frustrated passion, I have heard him express a unique desire: to pronounce the threefold terminal divorce on his bachelorhood and marry his beloved without delay."

"Well then, Al-Sadiq, my legal opinion is that your friend should seek the beloved's hand from her family. If they accept, then he should trust in God and bind his life to hers."

Just by looking I could tell that the trio was utterly delighted with my opinion. I now decided to generalize my statement about the obligation of marriage.

"You young men of good will," I told them, "none of you should reach the age of twenty or so without searching for a wife to marry according to the law. That way you can steer clear of all kinds of censorious conduct and harmful indiscretions that inevitably accompany young people's unruly behavior—and how very many of those there are in this era of ours! Like prayer itself, marriage precludes fornication and evil conduct."

With a finger raised, a student now started reciting such Qur'anic verses and hadith reports as came to his mind on the subject. I thanked him for doing so and proceeded to comment on the passages he had cited, and in terms of both language and usage, going into detailed explanation whenever required.

At this point a voice was raised, inquiring as to whether it was better and more observant for a man to marry more than one wife or to have just one.

"'There is a noble verse in the Sura of Women," I replied, "that should be cited in full in order to understand what it is saying: 'Should you fear that you are not dealing fairly with orphans, then marry women in twos, threes, or fours. If you are afraid that you may not treat them all equally, then marry only one or whatever your right hand may own. That makes it more likely that you will not be partial' [Sura 4, v. 3]. So, if you all think about the matter carefully, you will conclude that this justification of polygamy is neither an obligation nor a command, but rather a kind of license dictated by temporary conditions and requirements. To be more specific, it is referring to the earliest conquests of Islam and the shortage of married men and bachelors that they inevitably caused. When it comes to a clearly fixed principle, the clinching arguments are based on the unequivocally clear verse that says, 'even if you desire it, you will never be able to be fair to all your women' [Sura 4, v. 129]. In this instance justice is not merely a matter of expenditure, but involves matters of the heart and emotional attachment. In this latter sense justice—being clearly the more worthy and positive—was something that Muhammad, Lord of all Prophets, found to be a challenge. So what can we say about those who are not endowed with the same morals and virtues as he?"

Someone now inquired about the permissibility of a husband's striking his wife, based on the verses in the Sura of Women that are devoted to the topic. I explained that with this particular subject we are confronted with a case involving ultimate sanctions, namely disobedience, estrangement, or desertion. They may involve any number of shameful and extraordinary situations that can mar the laudable principles and goals of married life, something that is established in more than one Qur'anic verse. I pointed out that the application of the traditional injunction "to command what is good," to marriage as well as to divorce is "the most hateful to God among what is legitimate." To the people that believe in the unity of God and its monotheistic faith, this principle is the chief cornerstone and the clearest possible injunction, as it says in the verse from the Sura of the Cow: "You may divorce twice; then keep them in charity or else let them depart in kindness" [Sura 2, v. 229]. With regard to the question of the permissibility of beating your wife as found in the relevant Qur'anic verse, we need to bear in mind something that zealots and pedants overlook and fail to give its required importance, namely that the topic of beating is placed in a position following other measures that are considered preferable and anterior: counseling and separation. If beating should take place, then it has to be lightly administered, nothing excessive—with the sleeve perhaps or a silk strap. That is what is enjoined in those exact terms as part of the sermon delivered by the Prophet during the pilgrimage of farewell—that being the final statement of the noblest of prophets and an obligatory core of Muslim law. Even so, the fact of the matter is that, as I have insisted before, the Prophet of Islam, who is our model and guide, never beat any of his wives even in the most trying and tense of circumstances such as the famous incident in which 'A'ishah, mother of the believers, was falsely accused.

I hesitated to recount this story and explain it, but I heard 'Abd al-'Ali continuing the discussion.

"Concerning the ideal woman, we children of this generation need to give maximum weight to what the truest of messengers had to say on the subject: 'Take fully half of your religious faith from this Himyari woman,' by which he meant 'A'ishah, the pure and noble. In another hadith he says, 'If I had to make a choice, I would prefer women to men,' and in still another, 'That which does honor to women is noble; that which belittles them is vile.'"

A student in the very back row spoke up. "My name is Zayd al-Masmudi," he said in an angry tone, "and I'm almost thirty. Everything the master has told us about the obligations found in the Qur'an has helped me a lot, but my problem is one that also affects others like me. It's not a case of whether one wife is better than more than one, but simply the fact that I can't find even half a wife. As the saying puts it, master, 'the eye may be able to see, but the hand is weak.' There is no way for someone like me who has exhausted all his resources and is trapped in the vice of unemployment to fulfill the obligations of marriage."

"Dear brother," I said in response not only to this anxious student with all his problems, but also to others like him, "unemployment is indeed a genuine curse on the nobility of mankind, a dagger-thrust aimed at the innate desire for knowledge and learning. Its harmful effects are felt in both present and future. But we're a group of people who try to ward off its harmful effects by helping each other and making an effort to find a decent job. When it comes to making a good-faith effort to get married, no one will fail if we are willing to offer our help. God's hand is with the community. So get to work and cooperate with each other so that you can grow in God's eyes."

Another student had a question. "What does our teacher advise," he asked, "when someone needs to get married or do something else, but he can't find anyone to offer him assistance or make him a loan without interest? Is he supposed to remain deprived till he grows old and decrepit, or should he bow to necessity even though it involves usury?"

I said nothing for a while since I wanted the students to listen carefully to what I was going to say.

"The Qur'anic verse dealing with usury is a late one," I went on. "'Umar ibn al-Khattab regretted the fact that the Prophet did not have enough time to clarify and explain it. My personal view on the subject is that it all depends on the price situation, living costs, and the value of money. If the total amount involved between the time of taking the loan and repayment remains constant, then the profits involved are indeed usury as defined by the text. If on the other hand the funds involved suffer change or loss, then the value added to the loan is considered compensation for the loss and any damage that might have been incurred. Just imagine, my brother, that you loaned someone else a large amount of money and reclaimed it after a number of years. You then find that the amount no longer covers the expenses that would have been incurred before. What are you supposed to do in such a case?"

The student remained silent and stared pensively at the ground. Another student now asked me about the ultimate sanction of cutting off the hand of a robber, male or female, and the requirements involved in carrying out such a sentence, whatever the case and time period involved.

"There is only a single verse on that subject, and it comes in the Sura of the Table. Its purpose was a general one, to scare people. As a result, when it comes to specifics and consideration of particular circumstances, two principles have to be taken into consideration: the first involves the need to avoid resorting to these ultimate sanctions on the basis of doubts concerning the case itself. As Muhammad himself—peace and blessings upon him!—says, 'As far as possible, avoid applying the sanctions on Muslims. If you can find a means of avoiding them, then allow them to go free. It is far better for an imam to make a mistake by forgiving someone than to do so in his punishment.' The identification of that avoidance mechanism—following the pattern of conduct of 'Umar, the caliph known as the 'arbiter' (God be pleased with him!)—is an obligation on all judges who exercise their discretion in legal matters and rulers in difficult times such as those in which we ourselves are now living. The most significant of those difficulties are hunger, need, and poverty. As the proverb puts it, 'Poverty is akin to disbelief.' 'What amazes me about someone with no food in his house,' says Abu Dharr al-Ghifari,* 'is that he doesn't go out in public with his sword drawn.' The second of these principles requires that the facts concerning the crime of theft be contextualized in terms of removal of the conditions that cause the thief to steal in the first place. Cutting off the limbs of thieves and making them an example to others is not the answer. Even when this ultimate sanction is applied, it is still not a sufficient deterrent when it comes to putting a stop to theft. In summary then, the proper thing to do is to find a way of dealing with the root causes of this severe problem and determining what are the appropriate reformatory or incarceration penalties in accordance with circumstances and possibilities. God alone can guide us to the correct answer!"

Another student now asked if it were required to apply Shari'a law to a recusant, whether it involve repentance or killing such a person.

"My brothers," I responded, "during the early conquests of Islam, recanting your conversion to Islam was a case of hypocrisy, indeed an enormous act of betrayal that threatened the very fabric of the young Islamic mission. For that reason the well-known rule in Shari'a law finds full justification. But, now that the blessed mission has grown strong, so that its pillars are firmly planted and its light has spread to many regions, there is no longer any need to worry about isolated acts of apostasy. In any case they occur most of the time in the context of Christian-imposed compulsion and in situations that involve sheer self-preservation. That is precisely what is happening in our beloved Andalus, which is being wrenched from our hands. Whatever the case may be, the moral here is to be found in God's own words in the Sura of the Darkening: 'Remind them all; you are only a reminder, and have no authority over them' [Sura 88. v. 21], and in the Sura of Jonah: 'If your Lord willed it so, everyone on earth together would believe. Would you compel people until they become believers?'" [Sura 10, v. 99].

At this point 'Adnan made an announcement: "Young men," he said, "that is enough for this session. You have heard a good deal of our master's pearls of wisdom and interpretations. If the general sense is clear, there is no need for repetition. Also I notice that it is time for the sunset prayers."

Everyone looked very satisfied, and I allowed them all to depart. I walked ahead of them all as we made our way with a subtle assurance toward the central mosque. It was drizzling. I could not help asking Al-Sadiq who was the friend of his who was so in love. He told me it was Khalid and then paused for a second before revealing to me that the girl he was in love with was the maid who had served them all in my own personal closet. "So then," I whispered to myself, "'Abla is about to pluck the fruit of his desires and my prayers!"

"So," I asked, with 'Ali's and 'Adnan's ears trained straight in my direction, "when does Khalid want to marry 'Abla?"

"If you asked Khalid himself," 'Ali responded immediately, "he would say tomorrow! We're desperately hoping that he'll get better soon. We're concerned about the petition to the governor of Sabta concerning your teaching and the transmittal of your letter to the king of the Christians . . ."

"I'll consult the girl in question," I said. "Assuming she agrees, the engagement will be on Wednesday next immediately after the afternoon prayer, God willing."

16

WHEN I RETURNED HOME AT NIGHT, I found my wife waiting for me. I asked her how her aunt was.

"She's not at all well, 'Abduh," she told me with a heavy sigh. "I've brought her here so I can take proper care of her and be near you."

"Let's go to see her now," I said. "Has Ghazlan, I mean Hamada, returned yet?"

"He's with her now. He never leaves her bedside."

"What about 'Abla?"

"She's helping serve my aunt."

"And Hafsa?"

"She's in her room. She's ill, or pretending to be."

When I went into her aunt's room, Hamada stood up to greet me, as did 'Abla. Her aunt looked very pale and weak; she was very thin, her eyes looked glazed over, and she was having trouble breathing. When she opened her eyes, it was only to utter some incomprehensible words and not recognize anyone. The young man whispered in my ear that her doctor had given up hope of making her better, and everything was now in the hands of the One who can grant life and death. With that he burst into tears, and my wife and 'Abla both joined in. I could see no point in examining a body wracked by old age and marked by premonitions of life's demise. I read some Qur'anic verses over her, then went to my bedroom without eating anything, fully intending to look into the feasibility of Khalid's being engaged to 'Abla before the aunt died. When my wife joined me late at night, I broached the subject with her, and she was clearly delighted at the idea. She confirmed my notion that, as the saying has it, "the best charity comes quickest."

Next morning Hamada and 'Abla brought me my breakfast. Without bothering about preliminaries I broached the subject of the engagement.

"If it weren't for the fact that your wife's aunt is so ill," said Hamada, "I would be singing, dancing, and ululating for sheer joy."

'Abla seized my hand, putting it over her heart and then kissing it and bathing it in tears of uncontrollable joy. She raised her hands up high in supplication and gratification: "Master," she said, "your prayers have been answered. You have made me so happy. Now all I ask God is to give you his blessings and bounty!"

And with that she launched into a whole series of other prayers on my behalf. Eventually I asked her when she would like to see the student who had asked for her hand before the engagement was formalized.

"You are my only representative in this matter," she said. "I leave it all in your hands."

"But should we go ahead with the marriage when Fayha''s aunt is close to death?"

"Good heavens, no!" she replied. "All I want is for the young man to be married to me and then take me away with him with no celebration or banquet."

I had not expected such a response, but I proceeded to urge her to be ready for a ceremony the day after next. She accepted with the greatest delight. I now told Hamada where Khalid from Tangier lived and sent him there with a message to the same effect, telling him at the same time not to say a word to anyone. As soon as Hamada had left, 'Abla frowned and looked grim. She handed me a bottle she was carrying round her neck.

"Take this," she said, "and use it to daub your bedposts. That way, you can keep the poisonous scorpions away."

"My dear girl," I chuckled, "which scorpions are you talking about?"

"If Hafsa finds out that you're the one who's arranged for me to get married," she went on, "she'll go crazy and try to use her poisonous insects to do you harm. Be very careful, master. She's a nasty witch!"

"So, poor girl, it's Hafsa who's been holding you back, is it?"

She nodded her head. With that I let her go, but not before I had calmed her fears and assured her that both she and I would soon be free of this menace.

On the first Wednesday in the current month of Rajab, I informed my wife of what I had decided to do. Close to sunset, I brought Khalid and three confidants to my closet. I made Khalid swear an oath to treat the woman he wished to marry with all due kindness, then allowed him to meet his bride-to-be and spend some time alone talking to her. After that, two legal witnesses arrived

A Muslim Suicide | 209

with Hamada, and the wedding contract was settled in accordance with the practice enjoined by God and His messenger. Throughout the ceremonies and the small reception afterward, the groom looked absolutely delighted. He leaned over and thanked me for bringing it all about, and received the congratulations of his three companions, duly leavened, of course, by a certain amount of joking and banter.

Once the two witnesses had departed, Khalid immediately started talking. "Thanks to this blessed marriage," he said, "my health and well-being are fully restored. Now I want to remind my master, who is entirely responsible for my happiness, that I made him a promise."

I had not forgotten that he had promised to take my letter to the king of Sicily, but I still wanted to find out why he was so keen to undertake the task when he was only just married.

"During my brief meeting with ʿAbla," he told me, "we agreed that our wedding night would be next Friday. Two days later, we plan to travel to Sicily so I can complete this task for my master. Then we plan to visit many other countries. ʿAbla is even more eager than I to tour around God's broad and wonderful domains."

His three friends started joking with each other, some of which I could hear. "So Khalid's eager to make attractive nature scenes a partner in his marriage! He needs them as witnesses and to have them dance for him!"

For my part, I was keen to support the groom's decision, and so I asked ʿAbd al-ʿAli to record what I said in a neat, clear hand. Here is what I said:

"Praise be to God, the one, the unique!

"From ʿAbd al-Haqq ibn Muhammad ibn Sabʿin to the ruler of the Christians in this age:

"Peace be to the one who emphasized the oneness of God Almighty!

"I have responded earlier to your questions concerning specific philosophical issues. In my reply I used some rather severe expressions, not out of a desire to show contempt but rather as a way of directing your interest toward independent inquiry and research and of provoking deeper levels of questioning and investigation. Any genuinely educated person who is either reluctant or negligent will inevitably go astray and fail to achieve the desired goal.

"In this short letter of mine I shall focus on a single topic, one that I would not be bringing to your attention were it not for the admirable qualities with which God has clearly endowed you: chivalry, generosity, courage, and bravery—traits that are similarly prized by Muslims. All that is over and above the other qualities for which you are already well known to Muslims, the love and estimation that you have already shown for their sciences and your announced inclination toward their cultural values, and that in spite of the opprobrium you have earned from those of your race and religion. With all that background in mind, learn a verse of the noble Qur'an—may God grant you success!—as addressed by Muhammad, the faithful Prophet of Islam, to Heraclius, ruler of the Byzantines at the very outset of his blessed and luminous mission: 'You people of the Book, draw close to a word that is common between us and you: that we should worship none but God alone, that we do not associate anything with Him, and that some of us do not adopt others as gods apart from God Himself. If they turn away, then proclaim that we are Muslims.' (The Lord of Mankind has spoken the truth [Sura 3, v. 64].) As it stands, this utterance serves to bring together beneath a single covering firmament of monotheism all those people who aspire to Islam or other faiths and who hope for peace as both a modality and a goal. It is this very statement that Muslims and those People of the Book who support their views have tried to establish, foster, and protect as a basic principle. In so doing they have resorted to creative ideas, sharing of gifts, and development of movements and monuments—all that in the land of Andalus, the ideal society where communities work together and share their learning.

"But in this era of ours we have witnessed an assault launched by those bearing swords and crosses, with the Castilians at their head. Their only goal has been to demolish this creative monotheistic fabric and destroy all dreams of civilization and peace. They have combined forces in order to attack Muslims and bring them low, spreading decay through homes, farmlands, and buildings. Anyone who has resisted them has been crushed and banished, forcing entire families and communities into exile. Since there is neither a religiously based factor to restrain them nor sacred texts from prophets and messengers of the past to give them pause, treaties and pacts have been systematically broken.

"Your Majesty, if you would only acquaint yourself with the current situation in the Iberian Peninsula, you would learn about the extreme levels of injustice and cruelty that people are suffering—something to make your heart bleed, the kind of images that the Castilians are at some pains to embellish as far as possible due to their own blind fanaticism and the sheer power of their weaponry and its fiery destructive capabilities. Just consider the matter for a moment and look at it from every point of view, invoking the aid of both intellect and a sense of justice. Once the truth has shed its light in your heart, you will be able to deploy troops of men firm in their faith and supply them with the siege-engines, ballistas, and flame-throwers that they will need, equipment that you have in plenty. So, please hasten to respond to this urgent request—may God tend you with his care! You will then be entitled to the bounteous reward that comes to those who support the true words of faith. Your name will forever be mentioned in the records of those who work to make Spain a land where adherents of all monotheistic faiths may live in brotherhood—a model for emulation by others and a beacon light.

"I shall await your written response, which you can give to the person who has brought this letter of mine to you. The end.

"And greetings to you and to all those who take note and allow themselves to be properly guided. The direct morphological linkage between the words 'Salam' and 'Islam' is one that only idiots and people with malicious intent would choose to ignore."

As I placed my seal on the letter, my companions tried to outdo each other in lauding its logic and complimenting me. I asked 'Abd al-'Ali to make me a copy and to give the original to Khalid. We now heard the call to sunset prayers, so we all stood up and performed them in place. Once that was done, we celebrated Khalid's marriage to 'Abla by feasting ourselves from a set of bowls that Hamada had brought in.

"Come on there, 'Antar the bold!" he told the groom as he praised the food to the very skies, "eat some of the food cooked by your lady, 'Abla . . . !"

Once we had finished eating, we started to chat. The major topic was the role that King Frederic was playing in the Crusader wars extending all the way to the Muslim East in spite of the fact that Salah al-din's victories had made the conflict that much more vicious and harmful. By contrast the king's attitude eschewed the fanaticism of the European monarchs and the heads of their church and showed a distinct sympathy toward the Muslims who had lost lands and entire territories. I pointed out two things to my colleagues: first, the support that King Frederic had provided to the Mamluk* Al-Malik al-Kamil against his brother, Al-Malik al-Mu'azzam, who was conspiring against him, in return for which the Mamluk sultan gave him virtual authority over Jerusalem and some Ayyubid* cities in Palestine, with the proviso that the holy places and actual administrative power remain in Muslim hands (rather like being anointed from an empty bottle); and second, the threat posed by the Castilians and their allies had been greatly increased by the defeat of the Christian Crusaders who were now returning in droves from the east and eager to take revenge on Muslims in the west, even in Spain itself. We were all unanimous in our view that the immediate threat presented by the Christians in Spain could only be effectively repelled by the Almohads and the growing power of the Tunisian Hafsids, all with the help of the Sicilian king—in addition, needless to say, to assistance from God, the One, the All-powerful.

Immediately after the evening prayers we all went our own ways, hoping that everything would turn out as we had planned. However, the death of Fayha"'s aunt early on Friday morning prevented that from happening. The funeral and burial took up a lot of time, but beyond all that the flood of people expressing their condolences, both during the ceremonies and after, kept us preoccupied for the whole day. The task of looking after all the visitors fell to Hamada and Bilal, ably assisted by our neighbors. My wife was extremely upset, but was surrounded by clusters of women offering her their condolences. For my part, I and her uncle, Hajj Hamza al-Sarraj, welcomed mourners singly and in groups. Among them were my quartet of students, many other students, and a group of grandees from Sabta, led by their governor, Ibn Khalas, who only stayed for a short while.

Before the governor left, he leaned over in my direction. "Saint of God," he said affectionately, "you have been depriving me of your company. I only have the very highest regard and affection for you. Next Friday afternoon, can I send someone to bring you to my residence?" I told him that I would come and wished him farewell.

Once the crowd of people had finally departed, I spoke to my wife for a while, then hurried to my closet. I moved the bed to the center of the room and turned it over to check things. Out crawled a vicious cat; it may well have been responsible for there being no traces of any poisonous insects. I did one or two usual chores, then looked forward to a bit of peace and quiet, but no sooner had night descended than I heard intermittent sounds of a woman moaning that made it impossible for me to get to sleep. I summoned 'Abla and Hamada to ask them what the problem was, and they both told me that it was Hafsa, who was upset because Fayha"'s aunt had died. However, 'Abla surprised me by suggesting another cause.

"Ever since Hafsa heard that I was getting married," she told me, "she's gone crazy. She stays in bed all the time. She doesn't eat or drink anything and spends all her time weeping and moaning. Like you, Sir, my mistress, Fayha', thinks that she is mourning her aunt's illness and death, but the truth of the matter is what I have just told you."

I rubbed my hands together in despair and sought refuge in God Almighty.

"You, Sir, are the only one who can deal with her," said Hamada, his soft voice conveying considerable distress. "You know the things that can possess people's hearts and how to handle them."

I told 'Abla and Hamada not to talk about the matter until I had been able to look into things for myself and reach a decision. With that I allowed them both to leave.

Next morning after a very poor night's sleep I called my wife in and asked for her advice about Hafsa. From her response I gathered that she had been unable to stop Hafsa from weeping over the death of her aunt; in her opinion, the only cure lay in patience and endurance. I found it difficult to confront her with the truth of the matter, so I decided to let things go their own way while I waited for some God-inspired solution.

Later that day I and my companions accompanied our bridegroom, Khalid, to the neighborhood baths so we could make sure he was cleansed and prepared for the wedding night. Everything went according to plan in the stimulating, hot atmosphere, it being a place that had yet to be spoiled by too many bathers. Even so, the masseur who rubbed my feet had some nasty things to tell me about Sufi philosopher-types coming over from Spain and even mentioned me by name as one of their leaders and operators in Sabta. He proceeded to tell us how dangerous such people were and to be on the alert for them. Khalid rounded on him: "The person you've just referred to, you bumbling imbecile," he yelled, "is the one whose feet you're washing at this very moment. He is indeed our teacher and leader." With that the man leapt to his feet in amazement and hurried for the exit. My companions wanted to chase after him and teach him a good lesson, but I stopped them and told them not to even think of it.

On Monday night 'Abla made her way to the newly married couple's house, accompanied by her belongings and a set of gifts that my wife wanted to be both precious and light. It was very hard to see the bride leave, and even harder the following day when we all said our farewells to 'Abla and her husband, including the trio of his companions and the group of other students. There were powerful emotions, red eyes, and tears, along with promises to meet again whenever

God permitted. While Khalid was preparing a mule and putting his new wife on it, he surprised me by saying that he had sent a copy of my letter to the king of the Christians with someone he trusted to the Marinid* amir 'Abd al-Haqq and asked him to be in touch with me about it. At the time I paid no attention to the matter, or rather I had no opportunity to look into it because the young man had already mounted his horse. He was holding on to the mule's rein and seemed eager to catch up with the caravan in the eastern part of Sabta. As he and his wife left, they took with them our fond farewells and best wishes.

When I got back to the house just before noon, I found Fayha' clearly distressed. She told me that Hafsa's health was very bad and went on to suggest that the real cause had nothing to do with her aunt's death. I comforted her by saying that things would soon return to normal. She told me that she had hired two middle-aged women to help run the house, and I told her to go and take care of her guests.

I remained in my closet, wondering how I could solve this problem of Hafsa so that the situation would improve. My hope was that she would get over her distress and return to a state of normalcy. I looked in my bed and various parts of the room for scorpions or poisonous insects, but was relieved not to find any traces of them. I now performed some menial tasks before praying and then eating lunch. Following that, I took a nap in the hope of recovering some of my peace of mind and clearing my brain, but to no avail.

Only a few moments passed before once again I heard the woman moaning and crying, loud enough that it sounded like screams. I made my way stealthily to her room and closed the door behind me. The combination of closed space and sunshine made the atmosphere damp and fetid. The woman paid no attention to the fact that I had come in; she may not even have noticed. Her lanky body was laid out on the bed, and she looked very frail and emaciated. Her face was pallid and sickly, and her eyes were glazed as they stared vacantly at the ceiling. She kept sighing, but even so she seemed in a permanent stupor. I sat down on the bed beside her and touched her left hand with a view to feeling her pulse. With that she opened her eyes with a start, and let out a piercing screech. I seized the opportunity to beseech her to take some pity on herself and give herself back to God with a humble and willing heart. For my part I promised that I would apply all my knowledge of medicine and law to restore her to health and common sense. Instead she turned toward me and fixed me with a vicious stare.

A Muslim Suicide | 215

"You claim to be able to cure me," she said, "when you are the cause of my disease?"

I asked her to explain.

"You've been digging my grave ever since you arrived at this house," she told me. "You've completely ruined my relationship with my mistress, and you've turned 'Abla away from me. As you have come to realize, 'Abla is my entire life and spirit. Here you are, wanting to make me better, when you're the one who's brought this calamity on me!"

The words of a desperate, perverted woman. So how was I supposed to deal with her? What legal or logical yardsticks was I to apply in this case?

"Listen, woman!" I told her, "you're not being serious. Only God alone can determine what is to be your lot. However you had absolutely no right to exert compulsion and pressure on a young, unmarried girl like 'Abla. Your behavior has no justification in either law or logic!"

With that she stood up, albeit with some difficulty.

"So," she railed at me, "you want me to justify my behavior, is that it?"

"Yes, I do."

"The only way for me to be cured is for 'Abla to come back. Will you bring her back?"

"Listen, woman," I said, "'Abla is married to a young man whom she loves and who loves her."

"That's utter nonsense! You're the one who made her think marriage was wonderful, and then married her off. You want to make me better? Fine, then release her from her marriage to your companion and bring her back to me."

"Hafsa, that is utterly out of the question."

"May God have mercy and offer His forgiveness. You insist on doing me ill. Get out of my sight, you agent of the devil in person. Get out, or else I'll kill you and myself as well."

There was nothing more I could do to calm her down, particularly since she started hurling all the furniture and appliances she could lay her hands on at me, wailing and shouting for help as she did so. I rushed to the door and opened it, only to discover Bilal and two servants facing me, with my wife standing right behind them with a worried look on her face. Hamada was standing by her side, shivering and weeping.

"Shut this woman up," I told them all, "but don't hit her."

With that I left the house and wandered around the alleys and squares of the city. Sometimes I paused to consider what on earth I had allowed myself to get involved with, and at others I simply stared at the groups of houses, walls, and human bodies, whether stationary or passing by, each one of which undoubtedly harbored secrets and riddles whose sheer numbers were known to God alone.

I meandered mindlessly along the shore, and only came to myself again when I approached the city itself and noticed how unusually blustery and miserable the spring season was: strong winds; dark, cloudy sky; turbulent, grayish waves, all of them enough to make you feel depressed and resentful. But even though nature itself may have been showing itself in entirely new garb, I had to admit to myself that my soul was feeling crushed by a nasty mix of humors. What made things even worse was that I was probably incapable of finding an effective way of rooting them out and repairing the damage they were doing.

In the dead of night I headed for the mosque, performed my ablutions, then prayed the sunset and evening prayers by myself in a darkened corner of the building; I then proceeded to perform supplementary prayers, one after the other, and muttered some verses from the Qur'an. In so doing, I was concentrating my entire attention on God the Eternal, the One, the only One, who knows all secrets and what is beyond our knowing, in whose hands is all authority and to whom we shall return. When I turned around, I noticed that three of my closest confidants were standing to my right, waiting for me to finish. I invited them to join me, and they did so, offering their greetings. I guessed that they had something to tell me, so I asked them what it was. Al-Sadiq told me that they would have to leave to return to Granada early the next day, offering as a pretext the fact that they had to attend to their families and children. I asked them what they had been doing the day before and today, and they told me about the goods and books they had purchased and the young people of Sabta whom they had met.

'Abd al-'Ali went on to tell me something that the others seemed reluctant to mention: in the main mosque they had attended a lesson taught by the jurist Idris al-Tadili, and had come to realize that the man knew absolutely nothing and had no particular method to his teaching. He merely prattled away about things he knew nothing about, made slanderous comments about learned scholars—accusing them of heterodoxy and apostasy. In so doing, he was setting himself as the great defender of the precious egg of religion, when he was not even equipped to look after a chicken's egg. They told me that, when they had addressed questions to him, whether on matters of tradition or interpretation, he had been unable to respond, except to rant and rail. He had then called them various rude names and had crowned his angry retort by calling them members of the "Sab'inid" party, something which, as he himself put it, was the very acme of heresy and disbelief. Here was this man, he said, residing in the Sunni Maliki city of Sabta, corrupting its innocent youth and denouncing its most prominent jurists and religious figures, not to mention its governing authorities. They finished by telling me that he had then said some particularly foul things that they preferred not to repeat.

I asked God for forgiveness and sought His protection against the wrongs perpetrated by charlatans and the lies of the envious and vengeful, He being the one responsible for them and the arbiter between myself and them in this ephemeral world and the next. I thought this was a good time to let them know that Ibn Khalas had expressed a desire to meet me.

"My friends," I said, "these nasty extremist jurists keep on making things difficult for me and convincing rulers to throw me out wherever I choose to reside and travel. Now the governor of Sabta is asking me to meet him and have a talk. I'm still doubtful about it."

"No, no, Sir," Al-Sadiq replied in a very serious tone. "Such diffidence on your part is entirely out of place. If the jurists of Sabta are conspiring against you, you definitely need to respond to the governor's invitation. If you find that he is an intelligent man, a faithful believer, and a judicious ruler, then so much the better for you. But if he seems to be the opposite, then you can use your own sagacity and experience to arrange matters as you see fit."

Both 'Abd al-'Ali and 'Adnan made it clear that they agreed with what he was saying, and I did likewise. I stood up to say farewell, and wished them a safe journey and a felicitous return to their families and loved ones. They in turn embraced me and promised to come back when circumstances permitted.

I felt sad that they too were leaving, not to mention Khalid and 'Abla; I was sad too because Hafsa was so sick; and sad because the jurists and their agents were conspiring against me. In alleviating so much sadness my only resort would be you, Fayha', you who have enabled me to show such "beautiful patience" (as Jacob declares in the Qur'an) and to seek sustenance for both soul and mind.

When I reached the door of the house, I was greeted by Bilal with a broad smile on his face of a kind I had never seen before. It was accompanied by gestures that intimated that Hafsa had gone out of control and been transferred to the asylum. As I hugged my wife, she confirmed what I had understood from Bilal and consoled me with the news that she had asked the officials there to take good care of her.

Inside the house rooms and courtyards were considerably less full of visitors, and the general atmosphere was much quieter and more relaxed. While we were eating dinner, Fayha' told me that she was delighted with the two new servants and had good things to say about their manners and general poise. I told her that that was thanks to God's good grace and the help of Rudwan. I alluded as subtlely as I could to Hafsa's odd behavior in the hope of getting her to talk about what she knew and was keeping to herself, but all I succeeded in getting were some censorious comments regarding the woman that comprised far less than what I knew and chose to keep to myself.

I fell into a deep sleep on our marriage bed just as soon as I lay down and wrapped myself in warm blankets. During my slumber I had a series of dreams of which I could only remember the smallest segments when I woke up.

17

NEXT DAY I STAYED IN MY CLOSET, concentrating on reading books and posing myself questions in the hope of doing some more editing of my book, *Escape
of the Gnostic*. I also had to write some letters, the contents of which I had been
carrying around in my head for a while. When it came to sleep, I was anxious to
keep it to a bare minimum and make do with only what was strictly needed, all
with the aim of avoiding the risk of terrifying visions and obsessions. I arranged
my prayers by combining them all in the middle of the night, as part of which I
performed a whole flood of devotions and channeled my mind and spirit toward
loftier truths.

I spent the entire morning in this fashion. It was just after noon when my
contemplations were disturbed by Fayha', who came to inform me that a horseman was at the door waiting to escort me to the governor's residence. I had completely forgotten about the appointment I had made with Ibn Khalas for this
Friday. With some reluctance I now had no choice but to change my clothes and
put myself to rights. I left the house, greeted the governor's messenger, and followed him on my horse. While we were on our way, I noticed that my escort was
taking me into the center of the city by the eastern shore. He dismounted, and so
did I. We were standing in front of an isolated house that looked out over the sea.
The governor welcomed me profusely at the door and led me into his reception
room, where he introduced me to his blind companion. He told me his name was
Al-A'ma the Sicilian and described him as his most reliable source of counsel. I
thought to myself that the designation was somewhat odd, but even so I sat down
alongside the two men. Staring up at the ceiling, the blind man now started to say
some complimentary things about me. A servant-girl of 'Abla's age came forward
and offered me some food and drink from the table; she then did the same for

her master, who, like me, took only a little. He then signaled to her to leave. With that, the blind man stood up to say farewell and followed her out, putting one hand on her back while the other clung to his walking-stick. The governor wiped his mouth and beard and then looked affectionately in my direction.

"Pinnacle of the faith," he said, "this is the first time you've honored my council with your presence, even though you've been in Sabta for quite a few years. I'm not going to upbraid you for that—heaven forbid! After all, saints of God concentrate on worship and learning, and no one has the right to disturb them in that task. As you can see for yourself, I'm welcoming you in a modest house where I can find some peace and quiet. Were it not for the burdens of my office, I would stay here all the time by myself."

He had called me "Pinnacle of the Faith," a phrase only used by my own students and a few other acquaintances, and had portrayed me in a fashion that was partially correct, but not entirely. I decided to adjust the portrait somewhat.

"My lord," I responded, "meetings with people of goodwill are a boon without price! Only those with pure intentions and sound mind can truly appreciate their value. The problem is that the bulk of rulers in this broken and contentious age of ours—and I don't think you are among them—prefer to seek the counsel of crooked jurists and sycophants. They much prefer such people to those who are genuinely in quest of the truth and proclaim its virtues by stirring their consciences and stoking their aspirations. When it comes to matters of devotion and retreat, I choose to adopt the middle path of moderation, working on the basis of the words of the Lord of all Prophets: 'Do not go to excess in your religion.'"

"I'm well aware that you have students and groups of followers. Your reputation as a stolid defender of pure Islam preceded you to this city of ours, and in spite of all the current troubles and adverse winds that are now blowing."

"Our era is certainly not without its share of trials and difficulties. When people in authority have found themselves tested by such events, some of them have used the power of faith and action to overcome them and achieve victory: the first Muslims, for example, and in more recent times, the two amirs Zanki and Salah al-din* and the first wave of Almohads. Others, however, are the exact opposite: their powers have flagged (God preserve us!), so they have become feeble and submissive. They include the current Muslim rulers in Spain, including the Banu Hud who expelled me from Murcia before their own collapse and the Nasrids in Granada. All they are concerned about is holding on to their thrones for dear life, even if only for a short while. They are entirely unconcerned about the cities and property that have been lost. If anyone dares to remind them about the obligation to defend the cause of Islam, they either ignore him or else banish him from the Peninsula."

Ibn Khalas looked at me sympathetically. "Pinnacle of the Faith," he said, "the city of Sabta welcomed me, and I'm from Valencia. So I have in turn welcomed to my city, my court, and my coterie both religious scholars and writers, like Ibn 'Umayra,* Ibn al-Ramimi,* and others. Today our city is honored and bedecked by your presence, and you are most welcome here."

I decided not to mention the fact that he had excluded from his list two poets, the notorious homosexual poet Ibn Sahl* from Spain and the shameless anarchist Ibn Talha.

"Lord of Sabta, the city protected by God," I replied, "may God give you a worthy reward! Since my arrival here in Sabta, I have gained three tremendous boons: first, a blessed and successful marriage; second, a stimulus to undertake research and do some writing; and third, a proximity to Spain that allows my friends there to come and visit and hold meetings with me. For me, Sabta has become a site for my spiritual rebirth and my intellectual development. That is what I term it, and that is how I regard it in my heart of hearts."

My host now stood up and invited me to continue our conversation on the upper balcony overlooking the sea. Once there, I continued what I had been saying, spurred on by both the lapping of the waves and my nostalgia for the land that I could see but had now left.

"Such wonderful boons they are! They have inspired me to show, in Jacob's words, 'a beautiful patience' [Sura 12, v. 18] and have reinforced my hope that release will be forthcoming from God and from those people who love the common word and monotheism and who wish to see its flag fluttering over the Muslims and People of the Book in Spain."

Ibn Khalas gave a gentle smile, then sighed as he invoked the Rock of Gibraltar: "God is my witness that, just like you, I mourn for a beloved land that has been forever lost to us. There are times, especially while I am secluded here, when I imagine myself crossing the straits at the head of a huge and powerful army and engaging in one battle after another in order to recover all the lost fortresses, cities, and regions. I see myself restoring a sense of security and welfare to every quarter and thus enabling everyone to turn around and go back to their homes and trades. But then my imagination grinds to a halt, and I find myself reverting humbly to the everyday concerns of residents and émigrés here, concerns that grow more urgent and difficult as day follows day. Pinnacle of the faith, the eye may see things, as the proverb puts it, but the hand remains ineffective. God alone has the power and might!"

I could not make up my mind whether to accept the sincerity of what the governor was saying or whether I should treat it as a trial balloon to get me to expound what I really thought deep down. I decided to assume the former.

"But what about the Almohad ruler 'Ali al-Sa'id?*" I asked. "Where is his eye looking, and what about his hand?"

He paused for a moment, stroking his beard and rubbing his chin.

"There are no eyes or ears spying on us here," he replied. "God alone is watching over us, and He is the witness to what I am saying. Ever since the amir al-Ma'mun* did what he did to the Almohad dynasty, his successors have only been worried about one thing, namely clinging to their thrones for dear life. Their posture toward the disasters in Spain has been that of someone whose eyes have never seen a thing and whose heart has never felt pangs of sorrow. If news of events in Spain happens to filter its way to Marrakesh, they simply block their ears and beg God to bring down on the Franks the same punishments as He did on 'Ad and Thamud and on the Egyptian pharaoh when he behaved tyrannically. In the times of Al-Rashid and his brother, Al-Sa'id, it was my lot to listen to sermons stuffed full of prayers of this type in the palace mosque and elsewhere. Along with hosts of other people I myself had to participate in all kinds of prayers, litanies, and supplications. Since that time I've come to realize that our current state of weakness is chronic and ongoing; in fact, things are getting even worse and yet more complex. If you asked the amir and his coterie to act and declare a jihad,* emulating thereby the first generation of Almohads and the Almoravids before them, they would despise you and turn their backs on you with a glower. Not only that, but if you held a position of some importance they would dismiss you and send you away. That's exactly what happened to some of my predecessors as governor of Sabta. As you well know, this city sits at the very mouth of the volcano, and yet my function here is clearly determined and limited. I cannot move beyond it, nor can I go against the amir's own instructions or those of his spies who operate all around me. Otherwise my career would be at an end. My role involves maintaining security and, to the extent possible, offering help to émigrés. God alone provides success, and it is to Him that I turn for support."

My good opinion of the governor was now greatly enhanced. I applauded his frank admission and went on to add my own comments.

"In these times of corruption and crisis," I said, "politicians maintain a stranglehold on all the normal traditions of power. When they're confronted with problems, whether obvious to the eye or beneath the surface, you'll find them seeking diversions and pretending not to notice. If anyone should actually aspire to bring about change or arouse the somnolent, the only choice that these politicians give them is to gird themselves in their paltry armor and wander their way around the same fetid pastures of illusion and supplication. As the Qur'an says, 'It is not eyes that are blind, but rather hearts within their breasts' [Sura 22, v. 46]. And God has spoken the truth."

My companion now brought out a rosary. Head lowered, he started counting off the beads.

"My dear righteous governor," I said, continuing the conversation as I felt I had to do, "I beg you to tell me, is Amir al-Sa'id really blind when it comes to appreciating the dangers posed by the Castilians and their allies in Spain, which is being relentlessly swallowed up? Isn't he aware that they're now biding their time over Granada? Are they really willing to let it go? Isn't he aware that, if the Castilians decide to extend their campaign, they will inevitably cross the straits and reach the shores of North Africa and beyond?"

A powerful mixture of resentful amazement and urgent questions was crowding my brain, but at this point I decided to stop expressing my opinions, if only for a short while, in order not to overburden my colleague.

He gave me a piercing stare that made me realize that I should tone down my comments a bit.

"'Abd al-Haqq," he said, "it's a symbol of how highly I value your worth that I'm now going to reveal to you something that, by God, I've never told anyone else before. At this point in time the Almohad dynasty exists only in name. The current rulers are playing around, trading on the heritage and prestige of their forebears. Amir al-Sa'id is just like his brother, al-Rashid, and his father, al-Ma'mun. When it comes to life and politics, he's only interested in the present moment. For him it is he himself and his coterie that matter the most. As far as he's concerned, 'après moi le déluge'! So how can you expect him to be paying any attention to Spain or considering the future?"

"Then, my brother," I said, "you should give him advice and open his eyes to the ever-growing dangers that are blindingly obvious to anyone with sense and foresight."

"As you well know, counselors who are both pious and honest are a very rare commodity. Those that remain are either bound and gagged or else keeping themselves out of harm's way. They are due, as the saying has it, 'the benediction of strangers.'"

"But the situation is drastic," I replied, "and things are only getting worse. Even so, we still have to identify people who are prepared to knock on the doors of hope and salvation."

"But, pinnacle of the faith, tell me how that can be?" the governor asked. "For heaven's sake, tell me how?"

"In Sufi houses and retreats and among brotherhoods you will find sources of faith and reserves of initiative and commitment. On both sides of the straits people are fully prepared to defend the faith. Saints of God can form a living army; all they lack is organization, munitions, and equipment. Ever since I've arrived in Sabta with its seven hills, I've regarded it as my rear headquarters, my line of defense, and my haven. I've vowed to myself that, while I'm here, I'll use it as a base for transforming the situation and seek to find a solid mode of resistance. On both shores of the straits there are many people such as myself to be found in mountain passes, fortress towns, big cities, and outlands."

"But, my dear brother," the governor replied, his expression one of frowning incredulity, "brotherhoods and Sufis are not fighting men, nor can they undertake defensive actions and preemptive strikes. How on earth can they confront the Christian legions with their enormous numbers and superior weaponry?"

"With that aid of God's power and might, we'll be following the tracks of the Almoravids and Almohads who strove till they achieved huge victories at the battles of al-Zallaqa [in 1086] and Ucles [1108]."

"My dear 'Abd al-Haqq, the era of Yusuf ibn Tashufin and Ya'qub al-Mansur* is long past. Today the entire dynasty is in terrible shape. Its major figures have their hands in the devil's own sleeve. To say it again, I swear to God that I've never said anything like this to anyone else before."

"The hearts of honest men are where secrets can be buried. You can trust me, my brother, and not be alarmed."

The governor let out a huge sigh. "However I look at things," he said, "our situation is dire and out of our hands. All we can do is hope that God will enable us to escape . . ."

"Whatever the case may be, we are enjoined to act. In our situation action is a form of worship, something that will enable us to come closer to God. Has Al-Saʿid forgotten that, as Commander of the Faithful, he is required to display good intentions and effective management in striving toward God Almighty? The only way to compensate for the weakness of the Maghribi armies is to rely on committed believers on both shores. Imposing a system of justice and putting political affairs on a more just and useful course is the only way for him to bolster his position. Asking Frederic, the king of the Christians, for assistance is certainly a laudable gesture, most especially since he has severed his fealty to the church in Rome and made known his admiration for Islamic science and arts. In fact, the head of his religious community has excommunicated him on the pretext that he's virtually a Muslim and denies the authority of the Crusader religion."

I decided not to allude to the relationship between King Frederic and Al-Malik al-Kamil, the Ayyubid ruler in Egypt, not only because there was not enough time but also because the governor might not be able to appreciate the complexities involved. My companion remained silent for a while.

"Is your response to the king's letter the reason for your requesting this meeting?" he asked with obvious concern.

"Yes, it is," I replied. "I was anxious to get him to offer help to the people in Spain and also to expand on my responses to his questions."

"But what happens if he doesn't respond to your request, even if it is authorized by Amir al-Saʿid?"

"At all events," I replied, summoning every ounce of courage, "one has to place one's reliance on God Almighty. The ever-growing power of the Hafsids may also provide us with a way out."

The governor seemed delighted by my reply, which he clearly took to heart.

"The Marinids are just a bunch of vagrant nomads," he said. "You can't possibly rely on them. Their brains are in their swords; they have neither knowledge nor belief system. Their leader, ʿAbd al-Haqq, claims to have performed miracles. The one that causes the most ribaldry is that pregnant women who kiss his headcap and trousers find themselves set free in favor of someone even more beautiful!"

I decided not to comment on my companion's opinion. Instead I invited him to pray the evening prayer with me, and he agreed. No sooner had we finished than I hurriedly said my farewells and thanked him for the way he had welcomed me. As he embraced me, he made every effort to keep his angst-ridden expression hidden from view.

18

ALL THE WAY BACK to my house my mind was churning with clashing sensations: had I followed the right tack in my conversation with Ibn Khalas, or had I strayed too far off course? Had I showed sufficient caution in my assessment of the situation or had I unknowingly been duped? But no sooner had I reached my house than I put the whole thing behind me and decided not to worry about any God-inspired disapproval. I took my horse to its stables, where I found Bilal preparing some fodder and buckets of water. He greeted me warmly, whereupon I apologized for having treated him inadequately on a personal level. After that I headed for the kitchen, attracted by the delicious aromas emerging from it, and checked on the two new servant women working there. I ate some of their cooking standing up, then, after offering them my plaudits, made my way to my wife's quarters.

In our bedroom I found Fayha' seated on the bed looking very glum. When I asked her what was troubling her, she told me that Hafsa's condition in the asylum was very bad indeed. I promised to investigate the situation very soon and leaned over to console her and offer her some comfort. She asked me about my meeting with the governor, and I gave her a short version in which I covered the essentials. She in turn warned me about his coterie and aides, the majority of whom, according to reports, were spies and intriguers. I told her to ignore all that, after which she joined me in some moments of duly sanctioned marital bliss and relaxation.

At noon on the following day the warden of the asylum asked me to come immediately. Once I was standing in his presence, he gave me his condolences on the death of Hafsa; he told me that some two hours earlier she had hanged herself. He took me to the place where her body was laid out and uncovered her

228

face so that I could identify her. There was absolutely no point in asking how she had managed to commit suicide when she was in such a terrible state and palpably incapable of planning and carrying out such a thing. He tried to explain the whole thing as being some kind of terminal gesture and all sorts of other pretexts at which he was clearly a professional. I in turn asked him to prepare a shroud for the dead woman and to make preparations for her burial in the city cemetery.

"My Lord!" he exclaimed in horror, eyebrows raised, "you're a man of the law. You're surely aware of what it has to say about suicides: they may not be prayed over or buried with other Muslims."

"That is a general principle, I agree," I replied. "People who are incompetent, insane, or handicapped are exempt. As you could see for yourself, this woman was clearly mad. There's no reason why you should not respond to my request."

"Were I to do that, Sir," he told me, "I would have all the jurists in the city against me and would immediately lose my job."

I decided there was no point in trying to persuade this man to accept my own posture toward suicide, when he would never be able to comprehend it fully. After several moments' thought, I glared hard at him and asked him what was to be done. His response seemed to be one he had prepared way in advance: "There's a cemetery in the open land between Sabta and Tangier. It belongs to a member of the elite. With the permission from the authorities, perverted people may be buried there. Otherwise all visits are categorically forbidden."

"See to it then!" I told him.

For a moment he said nothing, as though trying to persuade me to understand his position. I asked him how much it would cost, and he gave me an amount. I paid him on the spot, even though I thought it was excessive. He beamed with pleasure and assured me that everything would be done as well as possible, just before sunset on that very day. Taking one last look at Hafsa, I left. Close by the animal stall, a man stopped me and asked for a sum of money in return for revealing secret information that would be important to me. After I had responded to his request, he let me know that this so-called cemetery in the open land was simply the sea, into which they dumped the bodies weighed down with stones. God alone would know where they ended up.

I needed some fresh air!

To find it I rode on horseback alongside the seashore, then into the foothills. My mind was still overflowing with all the events that had happened in the months of Rajab and Sha'ban (which was about to end), some of which had been of major import, affecting the way of life I was currently experiencing: my letter to King Frederic, my truncated lesson in the mosque, 'Abla's marriage and the end of my enforced misdeeds, the meeting with Ibn Khalas in his retreat house, and Hafsa's illness and eventual death. It's time to bring your soul to account, I told myself, and seek some seclusion. What better month could there possibly be than Ramadan, which was about to make its appearance in the sky above?

I turned off toward the mosque in order to spend some time thinking and then perform the evening prayer. No sooner had I completed my ablutions than I found myself surrounded by a group of men, both middle-aged and young, who asked me to hold a session before the call to prayer in the private part of the building so they could be enlightened and enhance their feelings of love toward me.

"There's not much time," I said after thanking them for their sentiments. "All I can do is to rehearse for you the various statements about fasting in the marvelous month that is upon us."

"Esteemed teacher," replied one of them, fully supported by those around him, "we all know by heart the statements about fasting, as well as the different views on ablutions and preparing the dead for burial. We would prefer to hear about the opinions you are supposed to have, that philosophy can serve as a solid base for thought and that Sufism provides a clear sense of direction, both of them uniting as they blend and vanish into the waters of monotheistic belief."

"Is everything that exists known?" asked a second. "If there is a clear contradiction between reason and tradition, which of the two do you choose? Does everything that is known exist, even though it is not referred to in scriptures?"

"Can you confirm or deny the rumor," asked a third, "that you agree with Ibn Hazm of Cordoba in his opposition to Imam Malik ibn Anas and his assertion that the decision of the people of Medina to adhere to the Malikite tradition is a mere case of fanaticism, or, to cite his own words, stupidity?"

"God Himself speaks through the voice of the Queen of Sheba," a fourth of them now said. "She said, 'When kings enter a city, they corrupt it and debase its senior citizens. That is what they do.' Do you apply the import of the verse to the rulers of this era of ours, Al-Sa'id, Commander of the Faithful, among them?"

"And what about this hadith," asked a fifth, "'After me will be thirty years of the caliphate, and then it will turn into a nasty monarchy'?"

The majority of these questions had me smelling a rat. "Even if we were to sit down," I said in order to put a stop to the apparent flow, "there would be no point in giving short answers to your questions. The only way of dealing with this is for the warden of the mosque to bring permission in writing from the governor. If that happens, I will schedule a series of sessions with you. After each question has been duly assessed, it will deserve a separate session that will be held between sunset and evening prayers. God alone shows us the proper path."

These questioners and others insisted that I give them answers, even if it was after the prayer. The whole thing turned into a noisy debate. The warden came rushing over and asked what was going on. After listening to what the questioners had to say and then to my request for written permission, he gave a reply that strongly suggested collusion. "No, no, master," he said, "a major scholar such as yourself doesn't need any kind of license. So give them the benefit of your wisdom and do not stint in responding to your questioners."

Once he had had his say and gone away, I soon realized that the whole thing was a trap. While I was still making up my mind about what to do, I found myself surrounded by a group of young men, one of whom whispered in my ear that they were friends of my Andalusian students. He then shouted to the gathered assembly that they should wait till the prayer was concluded and then something would happen. When the call to prayer came, everyone entered the mosque, but my rescuers lagged behind. They confirmed that my suspicions were correct, in that a group of practicing jurists had hatched a plot against me and were inciting fundamentalist people against me. They accompanied me to where my horse was tethered and strongly suggested I go home. That is exactly what I did.

When Fayha' came to greet me, I was still looking very worried. She asked me if anything bad had happened to Hafsa, and I told her what I had found out about her and what I had done. I made a particular point of the fact that it was absolutely forbidden to visit her grave. She burst into tears and prayed that God would grant her repentance and thereafter forgiveness.

19

AS RAMADAN BEGAN, I confided in my wife that I intended to spend most of the blessed month in my retreat on Jabal Musa. She acceded to my wishes, pointing out, as she put it, that she wanted me to feel happy and serene. Next day at dawn my baggage was packed on my horse, and every member of the household was there to say farewell. I hugged Fayha'. "Just remember," I whispered in her ear, "that you are what has replenished my eye and my soul!" With that I entrusted her to the two servant-women and Hamada, then got on my horse and rode away.

When I reached the mountain zawiya, the warden, 'Abd al-Barr, gave me a warm welcome. He allowed me to choose between two rooms in the wing dedicated to silence, and I selected the one that was better lit and quieter. I explained to him the principal purpose of my month-long stay and asked him to take on whatever necessary chores I had. He understood me completely, but postponed answering my questions about the general state of the zawiya and its facilities and went on his way.

In my baggage I was carrying books that would suit the time and place, the most apposite of which was probably Al-Tawhidi's *Divine Signs and Spiritual Breaths*. The sessions that I had previously devoted to a perusal of this masterpiece and his other work had served as my own introduction to the rainbowlike beauty of their contents. The sense of harmony that they offered had broadened more and more, crystallizing in their author's statement that "worship of God as one is the very life of the soul," and in his supplication where he says, "O Thou within whom everything is one and existent in everything."

This mode of access that you have provided, Abu Hayyan, is no matter of "incoherence" or illusion, nor does it result from a conscious fatigue. To the contrary, it comes from experience and experiment, involving the need to write in the very hardest of circumstances, just like the poet al-Mutanabbi, only more so. You suffered through an era of great turbulence, enough to bring tears to the eyes. You made your living by being a copyist, dismal trade that it is, and as a guard at the 'Adud al-dawla asylum. Scoundrels robbed your house, and the authorities and pseudojurists of the time declared you a heretic, evicted you, and showed you their contempt. When your despair was at its very height, you decided to burn all your works in case you and they fell victim to the corrupt times in which you were living or came into the clutches of frivolous fools and phony scholars. Your justification for doing such a thing provides me with a spark of initiative, a cogent argument, namely that you are that "strange person," one who "when he recalls the truth, he is abandoned; when he is called to the truth, he is upbraided; when he holds firm, he is called a liar; and when he manifests himself, he is tortured." If only the people who drove you out and tortured you had any knowledge of the true nature of knowledge and appreciated your genuine worth, they would have rolled in the dirt at your feet and covered their faces in dust, begging your pardon and forgiveness.

The purest water of sincerity courses over your truth. You are someone who lived with no family or friends save those righteous and reverent souls who were already dead. So I beg you, dear friend, to accept me as a loyal successor, separated by neither time nor space, as is the case in the gardens of Eden where I will be searching for you next after the Lord of the Prophets himself. Accept me as a true and loyal devotee. From the pages of your works that have survived you pour out your own spirit, which hovers on the air. Thus you are able to provide me with words that are the best and most effective, duly released from the trammels of tradition and attribution, and allow me to compose my own sentences and associations that are profound and rich. They are all illuminated by your always dynamic fragments of thought and your brilliant rhetorical flair, far removed, oh how far removed, from the obscurities and barbarisms committed by Arab pseudo-Aristotelians.

Your greatest weapon is your courageous, forthright pen, which you use to probe the inner workings of the soul and the loftiest reaches of the truth. With it you scoff at the foibles of ministers and notables, resist poverty, screen your purpose, and brazenly, almost flippantly, flirt with death. The fact of the matter is that you made use of your pen to compile a mass of pleas and complaints, pouring out the flaming oil of your own story with God, to such a degree that at one point you went right over the top and blasphemed by saying, "O God, to You I complain about what You have brought down upon me; by Your truth, you have strengthened the bonds, tightened the noose, and waged war . . ."

How can I possibly not take pity on you and ask the Creator to grant you forgiveness?

After all this how can I not call upon you to give me your help?

I am in need of something to relieve me of your never-ending tensions and your permanent state of anxiety as you function amid the gaze of other people and the illusions of adjuncts. So protect my back!

Now I aspire to surpass you in ridding myself of yearnings, struggles, rancor, and enmity, anything in fact that would impair my exposure to wafts that emanate from the surging flood of truth. So protect my back!

I am now on my path toward the single totality, investigating both essence and meaning, aspiring to rise to other heights of perfection among the gradations of profundity and comprehension. So protect my back!

I have immersed myself in some of your writing: in *Divine Signs,* that lofty text; in *Treasures in Insights;* and in whatever *Epistles* I have managed to acquire. I have then proceeded to look at Al-Niffari's *Book of Stations,* the *Lamiyya* of Ibn Sina, and the *Nazm al-Suluk* by Ibn al-Farid* as well as his famous *Khamriyya* poem. In addition I've looked at the collection *Litanies* by al-Shadhili al-Ghumari* and similar works, all of which quenched my thirst for more knowledge and sharpened my mind with a rush of inspiration. After all that, I perused some literary works in both prose and verse. They all managed to bolster my initiative by using styles that adhered to both sense and fingers and have become an essential part of my inner self. After all, refined and lofty literature is the conduit that provides life with its value and purpose. How else could we appreciate the contents of sacred texts and establish the bases of the Qur'an's miraculous nature and the divine oath: "*Nun,* and the pen, and what they write" [Sura 68, v. 1].

In the same way I have spent days and nights exploring the insides of books and the contents of their pages, only stopping in order to keep body and soul together with a little breakfast, taking short naps and performing prayers. When the holy month was two-thirds gone, I started to get sick, easily recognizing the annoying symptoms; that forced me to stop writing and adjust my work pattern.

No, no, I'm not one of those authors who can just make up their minds to sit down and write, showing certain symptoms of arrogance and a far from simple ability to fabricate in both vision and gesture. By God, that kind of posture disgusts me and occasionally makes me laugh.

No, no, for me writing is an unexpected jarring sensation, a sudden flare of inspiration; it can also be a tense and tricky process of fermentation, a painfully slow internal course of fruition.

I started having dreams about my wife. I would call for her because I urgently wanted her to come; and she would respond, "Here I am!" I would show her how things were going and what a flood of divine inspiration had reached me. I would tell her to untie my belt, open up my gates, and respond to my expectations. Then I would summon her again and ask her to bare her breasts. She would hear me and reply, "My bosom is your own possession, and all my senses cry out for you!" I then imagine myself telling her, "So here I am today, Fayha', conveying to you some awesome words, so remember them. . . . No, instead I'm going to tell you some things that, if I compose them all in succession, will bring me contentment and ascendancy." And thus did I set down "The Ascetic's Epistle," "A Book Containing Aphorisms and Homilies," "The Epistle of God's Discourse through the Medium of His Own Light," and "The Epistle of the Blessed Tablets." And all praise be to the True One for the signs of His generosity and beneficence.

Those were all epistles in which my ideas and inspiration were fully formed. There were others from the same period where, because of a lack of time, I merely planned the basic format. They were all either additions to or modifications of the text of *Escape of the Gnostic,* or else refinements and epigraphs, all of them lightly footnoted and easily comprehensible. I think that they enabled me to come closer to the definition of the essence of the unity of existence and complete perfection, all part of the ongoing struggle to link the potential existent with the Necessary Existent; in other words, to be transformed by the beautiful names of God that are its very essence and to be found worthy of the divine succession.

On the twenty-seventh day of the noble month of Ramadan, Hamada and Bilal came to visit me, escorted by 'Abd al-Barr, the warden. The young man reassured me that everything was fine at home and that his mistress was longing to see me. Then 'Abd al-Barr informed me with due gratitude that he had received some sacks of food that Bilal had brought with him, which were to be distributed to the poor on the day after the festival. I invited them all to take a stroll on the hillside, and they willingly joined me. We left the zawiya behind us and headed for the forest where the hermits lived. I noticed how amazed and scared Hamada looked as he observed the weird appearance of the figures that kept appearing and disappearing before his very eyes. While 'Abd al-Barr and I were chatting, we heard the young man behind us yelling and asking for help. Looking behind me, I could see an arm stretching out from the limb of a tree and grabbing him by the hand. With my companions I rushed to help him, but we could not wrestle him free of the person in the tree who had grabbed him—and he looked just like the wild and uncontrollable hermit I had met before. I used soothing words to get the hermit to let him go, and he promised to do so just as soon as he had had his fill of the handsome, beardless young man's face. At this point I recalled that looking at beardless youths, just like losing one's senses, public exposure, fantasizing, dancing, and tearing one's clothes are all reckoned among the faults characteristic of hermits. God alone knows whether that is true or not and what mankind conceals inside his breast. In any case it was only moments later that the hermit fulfilled his promise by releasing the youth. I was thus able to rescue him and calm him down somewhat. Sobbing loudly, he begged me to let him go back to his home.

"Not before you join us in a visit to the lunatics' asylum," said 'Abd al-Barr with a smile.

It had not even occurred to 'Abd al-Barr that the young man was in such a panic, but then Bilal started slapping his cheeks and clawing his chest. "Woe is me!" Hamada yelled. "Lunatics? God protect me!"

I signaled to Bilal that he could leave at once, so 'Abd al-Barr went over to the scared young man, calmed him down, then carried him in his arms back to the place where we had left the horses.

As we made our way slowly back to the zawiya, 'Abd al-Barr asked me if the enormous black man had swallowed his tongue. I recounted to him the man's disturbing history and resorted frequently to mention of God's all-powerful presence. I in turn asked him about the resident in the asylum whom I had come to know. He told me sadly that Al-Tamimi had committed suicide, and Byron the old man and 'Ukasha al-Khalti, the asylum manager, had also died. He was sorry that the manager had passed away, and also that his replacement was a steward with a temperament just like Bilal's. The only way he could control the lunatics was by clapping them in irons, beating them with canes, and threatening them with the rack. The mention of this last device raised an issue that I knew nothing about, and my companion explained that the new steward and his brutal staff regularly showed it to any of the inmates who were particularly disruptive and noisy. Either he stopped doing whatever he was doing and calmed down, or else they would rip off his balls or pierce his skull. The entire thing utterly appalled me. I begged the warden to inform the governor about the situation and to ask him to appoint people who were doctors, not sadists.

Once he had indicated his agreement, we proceeded on our way till we reached the edge of the forest. From the top of a lofty palm we heard a voice. "Here I am," it shouted, "watching the Day of Judgment happen. Did not the Prophet himself counsel, 'If matters are entrusted to incompetents, then wait for the final hour!'" 'Abd al-Barr told me that this man had been behaving this way for some time, maintaining his vigil and eating figs from the palm tree and whatever else generous folk happened to send up to him by means of a length of rope. The steward at the asylum and his assistants were quite willing to disregard his behavior as long as he did not hurt anyone or start hurling stones at people. He advised me not to bother myself with either his condition or his words.

As we made our way back to the zawiya, I kept rubbing my hands together disconsolately and acknowledging God's almighty power both silently and aloud. By this time it was noon, so we prayed the prayer with the gathered assembly. Once that was over, I said farewell to my friend, in the hope of meeting him later in the evening to celebrate the Night of Power along with other believers.

And that is what happened. No sooner was the evening prayer over than the tiny mosque was filled with people. They all wanted to listen to readings of surahs from the Qur'an, while 'Abd al-Barr and his assistants went around hanging up lamps and lighting them, filling censers with incense, and sprinkling rosewater over the attendees. When they all turned their attention to other litanies and devotions, my very breathing and memory joined in lifting them heavenward and kindling their flame. Truth to tell, bonds of brotherhood and holy fragrances began to spread among the assembly, duly accompanied by the scents of purest incense. Afterward hands were raised in supplication to the heavens, ready to be inspired by prayers like so many pearls on this blessed Ramadan night, the Night of Power, which, as the Qur'an says, is "better than a thousand months." Once their voices had turned hoarse and their throats were dry, the warden and his companions suggested that I be asked to conclude the prayer session. Standing up, I launched into a series of prayers in which I included peoples on both shores of the Mediterranean, the community leaders, and humanity in general. I made a special point of mentioning our poor, suffering Spain, but avoided mentioning any political figures. I did my best to be as eloquent as possible. All around me people were listening, necks outstretched as they chanted "Amen" in unison. My final prayer was "Praise be to God, the Lord of the Humanity."

Everyone stood up, and I moved to leave, making my way through the throng and embracing everyone I met. Once I had left the mosque, I headed for my room to get some sleep and rest.

Next morning, I went back to my writings so that I could look them over and make corrections. Things went particularly well with the one entitled *The Complete Understanding*. Later in the afternoon, I washed, changed my clothes, and prayed. I then gathered up all my papers and put them in my pack in preparation for the trip back to my beloved's house. When I went out to go to the horse stables, I found a man waiting for me.

"Shaykh," he asked, after I had responded to his greeting, "do you believe your prayers are proper?"

"It is my sincere hope," I replied, "that God who hears everything regards them as such."

"Like any Muslim you are enjoined to obey God, His prophet, and the ruling authorities. So why did you not mention the authorities during your prayers on the Night of Power?"

The warden came rushing over at this point, panting all the way, and I greeted him. I told him that I was going back to my family, God willing.

"You can go back safe and sound," my interlocutor said, "but not until you explain why you did not offer prayers for Amir al-Sa'id yesterday. Did you just forget, or was it on purpose?"

"It was simply an oversight," 'Abd al-Barr hurriedly replied. "He simply forgot. Don't you remember what the poet has to say? 'Humanity [*insan*] is only named for its forgetfulness [*nisyan*].' That's the first half of the line, but I've forgotten the rest of it. By God's mercy, tell me what the rest of it says."

The man was confused for a moment and said nothing.

"The rest of the line," I told them, "is: 'And the heart's only facet is to be transformed.'"

The warden smiled in triumph. "So, my good man," he said, "I forgot half the verse and our master here remembered it. But you had no idea about either part. So go away and seek knowledge to the extent that you can."

The man stumbled away. As 'Abd al-Barr led me and my horse toward the gate, he told me that this ignoramus was actually one of governor Ibn Khalas's spies who had been coming to the zawiya for some time to pick up bits of information. After he had helped me put my bags on the horse and before I rode off, I embraced him warmly, but decided not to tell him that I had refrained from mentioning the ruler's name in my prayers quite deliberately and with forethought; it was no mere slip or case of forgetting. I told myself that it was quite enough that I had managed to avoid listening to any more abuse from this nasty informer.

20

NOW THAT I HAD RETURNED to my own home with my wife and had celebrated the Great Feast according to custom and tradition, events started to pile up and conditions grew steadily more difficult. The jurists of the town intensified their hue and cry against me and tried to do me ill. Followers gathered all around me, and several of them were clearly inclined to my points of view. The deputy governor made a point of preventing me from holding meetings with them inside the mosque and of not allowing my students from Spain to enter the city of Sabta. Ibn Khalas, the governor, sidled his way out of correcting the situation by claiming that he was too preoccupied with other matters.

This is all with regard to the country where I was residing. As for Spain itself, things were going from bad to worse for the Muslim residents: the Christian alliance had made a peace pact and was gradually closing up the cracks in its fabric. Meanwhile refugees were either descending on Granada and whatever was left of its possessions in hordes or else directly crossing the straits and heading for the Maghrib coast or the interior.

Amid this hubbub of events, I snatched as many moments of seclusion in my closet as I could in order to complete the process of editing and correcting my epistles. To them I added an essay made up of my testament to my pupils and companions. I was delighted that a group of them undertook to make copies of it and distribute them to those of my followers who were interested and equally happy when one of them undertook to send it to three of my closest confidants in Granada. One month later, he came back with news that they were all safe and sound, and with a commentary on my covenant to them and other people whom I loved as they loved me; not only that, but others as well who had never met me or been close to me. When I perused this commentary, I discovered that it was exhaustive, enlightening, and extremely useful; where I had merely alluded to things and fallen short, it provided explanation; where I had waxed too cerebral and opaque, it made things clearer—may God grant them all a just reward!

Amid this hubbub, I also did my level best to keep my tribulations and concerns from my wife, for fear of somehow diminishing her lively spirit and radiant self. But such was her innate sensitivity and intelligence that she sometimes noticed the frowns and anxious expressions on my face. She would then ask me what was the matter.

"Were I to tell you what is the matter, my darling, and go into detail, you'd only feel sad and burst into tears. There's been a consistent darkening of the atmosphere between myself and both political and juridical authorities, the latter of whom are bent, wherever I happen to settle, on tightening the noose around me so as to force me to give up and move somewhere else. I've been prevented from teaching or meeting my students in legitimate public spaces. All that and more. My dear Fayha', how can I possibly talk to you about all of it when I cannot bear to see signs of anxiety and concern on your lovely face! That's why I am going to make do with giving you just a few short details as a way of distracting your attention from matters that are much more serious and below the surface.

"My dear beloved, I belong to the group that aspires to discover things about present and future circumstances. Every time I learn something, my consciousness expands. Every time I become more aware, I feel miserable about the corruption and sorrow that mar this lower world of ours. But I thank God who has led me to you and made of you a warm refuge and gleaming beacon."

My wife smiled at me in gratitude and pleasure. "I have discovered, 'Abduh," she said, "that the governor is sick in bed and very ill. Haven't you gone to see him and check on his condition?"

"I'll certainly do that, my lady," I replied, "if it'll please you."

"At all events it'll please both me and God, my dear."

Next day at noon, I headed for Ibn Khalas's house opposite the governor's residence. Passing through the rows of guards and servants, I reached the waiting room, where I was met by an enormous man with broad shoulders. He introduced himself as the deputy governor. The way he said my name made it obvious that he had heard all sorts of malicious nonsense about me and my followers. In an utterly uncouth fashion he asked me what I thought of the jurists of Sabta and their mighty overlord, Sultan al-Sa'id. I replied that his question was entirely irrelevant to the purpose of my visit; I had come to see the governor and find out how he was. The man's expression showed that he was extremely reluctant to delay hearing my response to his question, but he did allow me to go in to see the governor. He cautioned me not to disturb him with unnecessary chatter.

The invalid was laid out on his back in bed; only his pale face, hollow eyes, and scruffy beard were visible. Watched by maidservants and retainers, I made my way over to his bed and leaned over to greet him. No sooner did he realize who I was than he drew me to him and asked me to sit down beside his bed. In a feeble, croaking voice he asked me if I knew what was wrong with him, and I replied that I did not. He asked me to examine him. In doing so, I examined his mouth, his eyes, his deadened tongue, his temples, and his neck. I pressed on his stomach several times and checked his pulse. I asked him to breathe in deeply as I pounded his chest and back. I asked him if he had vomited, coughed, or had fits of shivering or fever during the daytime, and he replied that he had not.

"Your symptoms, Sir," I told him, "point to a psychological rather than a physical problem. Take some days off and rest, and make sure you eat well. To the extent possible go for long walks. With God's help, that will lead to your swift recovery."

The governor now sat up and ordered everyone else to leave.

"My dear Pinnacle of the Faith," he told me with an affectionate look, "I had no idea that God had endowed you with the gift of medical knowledge as well. Through your profound diagnosis of the hidden bases of my illness, you have zeroed in on the true cause, but . . ."

At this point he paused for breath and heaved a deep sigh through his nose. It was as though he were making ready to deliver some momentous statement.

"Dear brother," he went on, "if only you knew how totally overwhelmed and oppressed I feel, you would have sought some remedy that would be more effective than the one you have suggested. A short while ago, I received a letter from Sultan al-Sa'id in which he upbraids me for not doing enough to oppose the Hafsid cause in Sabta. Just last week I received yet another letter, in which he insists that I prevent the populace from paying any attention to Sufis and preachers of heretical opinions; you are mentioned by name as being the principal instigator of heretical opinions and inciter of the populace against both jurists and political authorities. Recently the sultan has promoted 'Abbu al-Zughbi, the person who met you at the door, to serve as my deputy, with authority over both me and the people of the city. He has the authority needed to influence the jurists and senior figures in the city and can tell them exactly what he wants. He can pass on whatever he likes or tell whatever lies he chooses to tell. The Arabs may have their particular faults, and the Berbers as well, but this particular clod combines them all in one; he's the foulest and meanest type imaginable."

With that the governor paused to recover his breath. "So that's the way things are with me," he said, "and that's what's new. I'm exhausted and sick. So tell me, what's the best cure?"

The things he had told me were certainly enough to demand a fair share of sympathy and pity. My response was intended to give him encouragement to hold fast and bolster his resolve.

"In view of the situation as it is now," I replied, "the only solution requires you to fortify yourself with God's help and rule justly and truthfully. You need to show people how reasonable your actions really are . . ."

"My dear man," he interrupted angrily, "are you forgetting that I'm now under orders myself? I'm not in control any more. I'm supposed to be the sultan's deputy, not his foe. Do you really expect me to cajole the people of Sabta into rejecting their allegiance to Marrakesh? Ibn Sab'in, I'm already being accused of supporting your views. The only way I am going to be cured is if you leave Sabta. If not, so much the worse for both you and me! If I order you to leave, then Sultan al-Sa'id will be convinced that I am loyal to him and will not accuse me of being a Hafsid sympathizer. So tell your family and followers that you're planning to go on the lesser pilgrimage, and then the Hajj. Once the storm has settled down and things are looking better, you'll be able to come back safe and sound. That is a promise I can make to you as a token of my affection. Understand me clearly: leave now, make your arrangements with as little fuss as possible, then let me know. Now that I've told you this, I feel better."

I left the governor's presence without saying a word. He accompanied me to the door. As I made my way down the riyad's corridors toward the exit, I passed by a number of servants and guards, but saw no sign of the deputy governor.

■ ■ ■

So here we are, Fayha', facing another trial; I think this one is certainly the worst of all!

By God, I'm certainly not going to enter your quarters and sit with you when my expression is so utterly miserable and gloomy. How could it be otherwise, bearing in mind what has befallen me, let alone what awaits me?

A Muslim Suicide | 243

If there was one fixed point in my exploration of the upper spheres, then it was always through extravagant, untrammeled imagination. But now I find myself buffeted and sorely wounded. Even if I could somehow mount the fabled steed of my passions and inner tensions, the only consequence would be a yet more bitter pill to swallow; I would find myself weaving a set of tales whose endings would consist of convulsions, maimings, and death.

Maybe the only recourse I have in dealing with this chronic sense of disruption is to sit by the seashore and let the lapping of the waves and the breezes waft over me. I turned in that direction and headed for a spot between two large rocks. As I sat down by the sea, my only concern was to seek refuge in its vast expanse and cast all my troubles and worries on its waters, although I did allow myself to gaze off toward the horizon shrouded in a variety of colors and differently hued clouds and to stare at the clashing waves that beat on the shore. While I sat there weary and totally distracted from everything going on around me, I heard someone yell, "You there, the sea never provides comfort or offers advice, so turn your face toward the Creator of seas and worlds, the One who enables and levels. To Him is the resource and the return."

Whoever it was who yelled brought me back to reality and restored my sense of peace and security. I took the opportunity to return home, fully intending to keep the bad situation in which I now found myself from my wife. Once I made my way into our bedroom, it was already nighttime, so I did my prayers by the dim light of a candle and added some other prayers in a soft voice so as not to wake my wife. But, no sooner had I finished than I heard Fayha''s voice under the bedcovers asking me how I was and how the governor was faring. I told her that, thanks be to God, we were both well. She then asked me to come to her, at which point I hurried over to her as my haven and source of comfort.

Next morning at breakfast, I told my wife about my earnest desire to perform the lesser pilgrimage and then the full pilgrimage afterward. She in turn told me that she too would like to accompany me to the holy places, but went on to say that she could not do it during the coming season because her uncle in Tangier was so ill and she had to look after him. She told me that she was leaving for that city next morning and our servant-boy would be following a day later. I stared at her lovely face for just a moment, and then agreed to her plan.

I spent the entire day in the company of the lady who was my chief source of joy and mistress of my heart. The night was spent in fierce passion as we indulged ourselves in that magic that marriage permits. Our feelings were, needless to say, mixed, as we both realized full well that we were about to part. However, I tried to overcome such feelings by concentrating on kisses, warm embraces, and complete fusion of our two bodies. It was as though I were putting a very precious commodity into storage in anticipation of meager times.

Next morning, I had hardly had the chance to say farewell to my beloved wife—holding back the tears as I did so—when Hamada came over with a note that Bilal had taken in from a young man who had immediately taken off. Here is what it said:

"My master, I am one of your Sabta students. Yesterday we all went to the governor's residence to ask that you be given permission to teach us, either in the mosque or wherever they decided. The police and their aides met us with canes and truncheons and laid into us in a totally barbaric fashion. They arrested some of us, but the rest managed to get away, albeit bruised and battered. This is what I need to report to my master—and we can only lodge our complaints with God Almighty, He who is the only granter of victory."

Next day I received yet another note from the same source, informing me that a number of my followers had been imprisoned, and my trio of confidants had been expelled from the Sabta plain. This ongoing succession of bad news sent me into a deep depression. Soon afterward, Bilal came to see me in order to bid me farewell; he was carrying his lute and flute with him. I asked him to stay a little while and to play a flute piece that he did particularly well. Somewhat taken aback, he sat down in front of me and started performing the piece I had requested. The sighs and plaints of the tune conformed exactly to my own sense of deep sorrow, and the invisible bloodletting implicit in the soulful tune exactly matched my own spiritual bleeding. All of a sudden he stopped playing and told me that his caravan would soon be leaving. I stood up and clutched him to me, entrusting Fayha' to his care and wishing him a pleasant journey. He gave me a tearful look, kissed my hand and shoulder with more fervor than he had ever shown before, then went out.

Early next morning I could hear a hubbub at the door of the house. When I went to see what was happening, I found myself facing two policemen who were cursing and swearing at Bilal. They kept telling him to summon his master immediately. All the while passers-by kept stopping to watch and children were making a din. I informed the two policemen that I was the one they were asking for. They then came over to me and told me to accompany them immediately to the deputy governor's residence where there was a matter that concerned me specifically. I asked them to give me a document signed by the deputy governor in person, but they refused. Instead they grabbed me by the arms, clearly intending to take me away against my will. With that, Bilal came over and rescued me from their clutches with an ease that I found remarkable. All that he needed to do to get them to let go of me was to bang their heads together, then crush their heads under his armpits. All the while the onlookers were guffawing their heads off. The policemen only managed to escape his clutches when I told him to go back to work and lock the front door of the house. Once that was done, I made my way to the kitchen, where I calmed down the two maidservants, who were really scared. I then went to my closet to consider my situation and decide what I needed to do next.

I spent half the night thinking about a variety of things, with the idea of going to the holy places to perform the minor pilgrimage and hajj at the top of the list. I came to see the idea as a pious deed that would restore a feeling of serenity to my battered soul and refresh and strengthen my spiritual energy. The best charity, as the saying has it, is that which comes quickest, something that would inevitably involve visits to holy sites and various rituals that I had often performed in my imagination as part of both night dreams and daydreams.

When I woke up, it was well nigh midday. As I went to check on things inside the house, I was full of misgivings, suspecting that this day too would bring its own share of misfortunes. My instincts proved correct because I could find no trace of Bilal either in his room, in the stable, or by the door. I asked the two servant-women, but they knew nothing. But then some of my neighbors told me that they had watched earlier as a column of soldiers had led my servant away bound and in chains. I made ready to go out and headed for the governor's residence on foot, my idea being to come up with a plan while on the way that would get Bilal released and confront the urgency of this situation. I was greeted by a whole group of the governor's or deputy governor's aides; they accompanied me to a narrow, dank room where they asked me to sit down and wait. As they stood disapprovingly by the door, I felt the time passing as slow as lead. Eventually I lost patience, went over to the men, and expressed my extreme displeasure at the way I was being treated. I demanded that they arrange for me to meet the governor as soon as possible. When I realized that they were not going to respond to my request, I asked to be taken to see Bilal. They immediately escorted me across an overgrown garden to a rickety, moss-covered set of steps that went down into a basement with cells on either side, each with a tiny amount of light and iron bars on the door. I could just make out the figures of prisoners inside, all of whom seemed downtrodden and eerily silent. Some of them started calling out my name as soon as they saw me and, praying for me in unison, they chanted, "God alone! God the living! In good times and bad. God alone has the power and might!"

The two guards brought me to a cell apart from the others, opened the iron-barred door, and then locked it behind me before leaving. I found Bilal lying there in a pile without moving. When I said his name, he staggered to his feet, staring at me with teary, bloodshot eyes. He had bruises and welts all over his body. As I embraced him, I made it clear that I fully intended to get him out of this prison. He grabbed my hands and started kissing them, while I kept on trying to get him to sit down and get some rest. I sat down next to him. He made some gestures to ask how his mistress was and how things were going in the house, and I reassured him on that score. I asked him to stretch out on the mat and try to get some sleep, which he did. For my part, I allowed myself the time to contemplate and pray, to which I added some extra prayers and requests to God for aid. I then embarked on a period of mystical reflection that went on with variations until the latter part of the night. After that I must have fallen into a deep sleep, because the first thing I knew I was being awakened by the jailer, who informed me that his master was on his way. With that I stood up and adjusted my clothing as best I could. But suddenly there was the deputy governor coming into the cell, accompanied by another man who looked like a jurist of some kind.

"I hope you slept well, esteemed shaykh," he said in a gruff voice. "You're forcing us to stop you right in your tracks. This man is Sharif al-Hihi, the primary religious authority and mufti for this particular region. He is empowered to examine your beliefs and test the degree of your faith."

By now the shaykh had sat down on my rug. "To put it another way," he went on, giving me a sneaky look, "I am really seeking your guidance so that your followers may emulate your example. That way the country can avoid schism, something that is worse than murder itself."

There was a general air of lethargic propriety about this so-called jurist, not to mention the obvious fact that he was up to his neck in craven service to the authorities. I told myself audibly that I was still in the company of divine presence and needed to focus entirely on mention of God Himself so as to rid my responses of all irrelevancies and impure ideas. God is the companion of those who recall his name. "There is no god but God—Ha-Mim; only one is the Necessary Existent—Alif-lam-mim*; only the eternal is an existent—Kaf-ha-ya-'ayn-sad.*"

The deputy governor started showing signs of restlessness and squatted on the floor in the expectation that his companion would make some kind of gesture. However the jurist put on a big show of being calm and intelligent.

"I've not come here to listen to your rituals, 'Abd al-Haqq," he told me. "You're accused of things that, if I confirm them now, will earn you just punishment."

"Who has given you the authority to examine me? Under what regulation are you deputized to do this?"

"God and the authorities here, not to mention the general injunction to command what is right and put an end to what is abhorrent."

"The authorities here have strayed from the correct path. They have fallen out with one another so that in our poor tortured land of Spain they have totally failed. Their only concern and means of exerting power now consist of harassing and terrifying the servants of God through insults and tyranny. The very fact that you submit to their will is an act of rebellion against God our Creator, thereby rendering yourself unqualified to make judgments concerning His holy law."

This provoked a new set of shouts of support, albeit weak and intermittent, from the prisoners, echoing throughout their cells. Once again the deputy governor lost his temper. The look he gave his companion seemed to represent permission to start hitting me. From time to time, Bilal lying in his corner would utter sighs and groans of protest; he may have been intending to make it clear that he was well aware of how tense this situation was and that he was fully prepared to respond to whatever bad things might happen to me.

"I'm being patient with you, Ibn Sab'in," the jurist replied in a tone full of menace and phony sorrow, "because I want you to repent. I'm prepared to wait till you recant your grievous sin. That sin lies in the following outrageous statement: 'When Muhammad son of Amina declared that there would be no prophet after him, he was issuing a broad-scaled interdiction.' Do you now wish to crave God's refuge from such drivel?"

"Listen, you so-called designee," I replied. "You seem eager to cite my words from a series of falsifiers and calumniators. What I actually said does not talk in terms of 'interdiction,' but rather of 'surmise'."

"Here's another example of your heretical statements, or is it also an example of false attribution: 'Peace be upon both denier and believer, scholar and pseudo-scholar, errant and misled'?"

"Here you are again," I replied, giving him a pitiful, derisory smile, "examining me on a matter that would need a great deal of time to explain to you. In any case it's much too complex for a mind like yours to comprehend. It is true that I said precisely that at the conclusion of my 'Essay on the Poor,' but what you have done is to remove it completely from its context and rip it away from its lofty humanistic frame of reference. Is there, I wonder, any use in pointing you in the right direction by citing a verse from the Sura of the Cattle [6]: 'Your Lord has ascribed mercy unto Himself'; and from the Sura of the Cow [2]: 'God singles out whomever he wishes for His mercy, and God is the possessor of enormous bounty.' So seek for yourself a share of God's wide mercy. Peace be upon you, even though you obviously number among those deviant would-be scholars who are in the most grievous error."

That disconcerted the jurist and made him furious. "Calm down!" he shouted. "Let me make it clear that you're not going to get out of this prison until you repent of your calumnies and false claims. Your followers continue to spread your words of incitement, all of them aimed at breaching customs and annulling religious injunctions on matters such as usury, theft, polygamy, and wife-beating whenever the woman is recalcitrant and refuses her husband's demands. And there's lots more . . ."

"You keep on citing my statements in distorted and falsified forms. Do you really expect me to tell you what I really said when both time and place are completely inappropriate? I won't engage in such a thing unless it is in front of a whole group of people and with witnesses present, by which I mean people of integrity—and that doesn't include you. I've nothing more to say to either you or your superior."

I was surprised and astonished when the deputy governor kicked me viciously in my side. I sprang to my feet, ignoring the pain. "So, you uncouth boor," I yelled at him, "now it's kicking, is it?" I aimed a good punch at his face, and he lost his balance and fell to the ground in a faint. The jurist ran away, begging for mercy, and the prison guard came rushing over to help the deputy governor. However, Bilal pounced on him, threw him to the ground as well, and grabbed his keys. He locked the door and buttressed it with as much furniture and trappings as he could find inside the cell. I sat down on the rug to recover my breath and watched as my servant directed threatening remarks at the two men spread-eagled on the floor. He had his foot firmly implanted on the prison guard's chest. Opening the deputy governor's mouth and pulling his tongue out, he spat into it several times; he also yelled loudly into their ears. He kept pacing nervously around the cell, counting with his fingers and banging his forehead as he assessed the situation. For my part, I tried to guess what was going on inside his head and came to the conclusion—but then God knows best—that he was listening to two conflicting voices: one of them kept urging him to take action, saying something like, "Listen, you! This deputy governor is one of those petty tyrants who would cut out your tongue without a second thought and do you harm. So kill him and have revenge"; the second voice kept telling him not to give in to such ideas in case they involved his master in things that would not turn out well.

There was a knock on the door and a demand that it be opened immediately. Bilal refused and started making a big fuss; then he rushed over to the door to make sure it was locked and leaned his entire weight on it. Efforts to break it down from the outside failed completely. I could hear them making a din outside and arguing over what to do next. But then a sudden silence fell, the kind that augurs ill and precedes the arrival of a big storm. The deputy governor and guard started whimpering, and Bilal screamed at them both to shut up. I got the impression that the guards outside were getting ready to break the door down or else inject smoke into the cell. I could only imagine how they would then set upon both Bilal and myself, giving us a severe beating. After a heroic resistance Bilal would be left on the floor in a pool of blood, while I would be punched and kicked before being led away blindfolded to some secret dungeon . . .

These musings were suddenly interrupted when I heard the voice of the governor himself, Ibn Khalas, who was begging me to open the door so he could make sure I was safe and apologize for the way the idiotic and boorish deputy governor had behaved. I said nothing for a while as I thought about it all, but a voice outside swore a solemn binding oath that he would indeed keep the promise he had made. I told him that this promise had to include Bilal and all my imprisoned followers. "Pinnacle of the Faith," Ibn Khalas assured me, "I hereby swear by God that that will be done; indeed now, before you leave this place."

What else could I do but believe what the governor had said and accept his word? I gestured to Bilal to open the door and go ahead of me. He obeyed my instructions and moved cautiously outside. Ibn Khalas appeared in the doorway, looking both fit and determined. He came over to me and embraced me, apologizing and sympathizing as he did so. He told the deputy governor, who was still splayed out on the floor, that he was immediately stripped of his post and would remain in prison exactly where he was. Ibn Khalas then instructed me to follow him, ordering the prison guard to leave with him and lock the door behind him. I walked along that dismal corridor accompanied by his aides and noticed on the way that every cell was empty and there was no sign of the people who had been imprisoned there. My entire face was beaming with joy. At the entrance to the governor's mansion my rescuer urged me to go home so I could clean myself up and get some rest. He fixed the following day after supper as the time for us to meet at my home, then commanded his muleteer to accompany me home.

21

WHEN I GOT HOME, I found that things were relatively quiet. I looked in on Bilal and found him contentedly receiving the ministrations of the two servant-women. I went to my closet to clean myself up and perform the necessary prayers. When that was done, I decided the best thing I could do so as to allow myself room to recover and ponder what had happened was to stretch out on my bed. What preoccupied my thoughts was the question as to what the governor would be requesting of me the next day; he would certainly want me to quit Sabta at the earliest available opportunity. I could feel that I too was gradually leaning in that direction as well. By so doing all the current complications might well be resolved and clouds would disperse. Once that was settled, I would be able to return to my family and those who had inspired my best ideas. I would come back enveloped in the halo of the holy places and invigorated by the exalted wafts of divine presence. Returning from such a visit to Mecca might well serve as a wholly new impetus, a yet more effective path to the benefit of people.

Next evening the governor arrived at the appointed time. I welcomed him with all due ceremony, and we sat in the salon on either side of a table loaded with drinks and sweetmeats. He asked me how my family was, and I told him that my wife was in Tangier looking after her sick uncle. The governor extolled her moral qualities and expressed his hopes that her uncle would recover his good health. I in turn thanked him for what he had done the day before.

"Pinnacle of the Faith," he said, "you are a blessed man of religion. After our last meeting, I managed to regain my health—thanks be to God!—and recouped my energy. Sultan al-Sa'id has now turned his attention away from Tangier so that he can concentrate on the intrigues and conspiracies inside his own palace. If it were not for that fact, I certainly would not have been able to dismiss

Al-Zughbi, the deputy governor, turn his own troops against him, and throw him in jail. But who knows how long this particular interim will last? I don't need to tell you that nothing in politics stays the same for very long. One day you're up, the next you're down. And too bad for anyone who goes too far or slacks off!"

I got the impression that my companion was working his way round to telling me what he wanted me to do, indeed broaching the subject first and specifying the timeline for it. Even so, I decided to say nothing and wait till he had said everything he wished to, at which point I could consider the situation in more detail.

"I have performed the obligation of the hajj on seven occasions," he said, "and I can't even count the number of times I've done the minor pilgrimage. Every year when the season approaches, my very soul longs to go to Mecca and Medina. If things here were more stable, I'd certainly be girding my steed and heading in that holy direction. So tell me, 'Abd al-Haqq, have you decided to go on the hajj as I advised? We're half way through the month of Shawal. God willing, the hajj caravan plans to set out early tomorrow morning."

There was no way to avoid telling him what I thought. "How can I go on the pilgrimage when my wife is away and my preparations are not made? What's the point of rushing things when it would be better to wait till next year?"

"My dear brother," the governor told me, "your wife is like a little sister to me. I will make every effort to see that she manages to survive until you return. What's the point of going on the hajj now, you ask me? There's not just one reason, there are many: first, you'll be removed from all your followers, so their hue and cry will die down and I can relax a bit. By being out of sight for a while you'll be able to stay out of the way of people in both Sabta and Marrakesh who are trying to fence you in. They're just like beetles, conspiring against you and me nonstop. You sent two letters, one to the Norman king in Sicily and the second to the Marinid amir, 'Abd al-Haqq. My aides collected them both from your disciple, Khalid from Tangier. I'll tell you, by God, if the second one had fallen into the hands of your enemies and reached Sultan al-Sa'id, both you and I would have perished. Is all this enough for you, or are you still hesitating about making your decision?"

Even though the governor was obviously telling the truth, I still had my doubts. How was I to know what he had in mind and if his plan made any sense? The overall goal seemed to be to be rid of me and banish me from his domains for good.

"I shall entrust what I do not know to God," I told him. "My hesitation is only because of my family. How can I go on the hajj like this without even notifying my life partner?"

"There's very little time left, Saint of God," the governor said. "It'll be fine for you to return to Sabta once things settle down in Marrakesh and affairs resume their normal course. Make your arrangements now; there are only a few hours left. If you decide to go, then all well and good. But if my guards come to your house on Friday and you tell them you're not going, then on your own head be it! My men will go with you as far as the outskirts of Bijaya; then most of them will come back. If it seems like a good idea, you can use that city as a way station on your journey; that's up to you. But let me warn you in the strongest terms: before you get there, make sure you don't decide to take refuge in the Marinid Zanata* territory between Tafilalet and Tadla. The sultan's spies will certainly chase you down and kill you. The Almohad regime—or what's left of it—is certainly not going to allow itself to come to an end because of you, even if it's only a minor factor. Don't imagine yourself as being the Ibn Qasi of this regime, Ibn Sab'in!"

Ibn Khalas stood up and handed me a medium-sized sack. He informed me that it contained purses of gold that were a gift to me from the Norman king. I reminded him that I had originally asked that they be returned to their sender, but he replied that that would have been difficult, in fact impossible. He told me I could either take them as a legitimate gift or else leave them to tarnish in the governorate's coffers. He then pointed to a steed in my stable and informed me that it too was a gift from the king. Without even waiting to hear my reaction, he gave me a warm hug and wished me a blessed hajj and well-rewarded activities. Accompanying him to the place where his horse was tethered, I bade him farewell as night was falling. With that he departed, escorted by a squad of his guards and aides.

Part Three

Death in Mecca

Ah me! Total comprehension is virtually magnetic; existents are like iron. What binds them together is the identity of existence itself; what separates them is the illusion of what exists.
— Ibn Sab'in, *The Book of Total Comprehension*

The researcher is the cave of perfections, the essence of possibilities . . . With the primary researcher the factors involved in achieving perfection include changing times, transitory places, ephemeral constructs, and motivated students. The achievement of substance comes through the significances of divine possibilities.
— Ibn Sab'in, Commentary on Ibn Sab'in's "Testament to His Students"

Profound sea of intellect, all scented with musk,
Whoever enters it worthy need not fear drowning,
People of the Sufi path can appreciate the words of 'Abd al-Haqq.
— From the *Diwan* of Abu al-Hasan al-Shustari

1

ON THE OUTSKIRTS OF BADIS, a village of scattered houses and grassy expanses, I slowed my horse so it could recover its breath and relax a bit. The pilgrims were making ready to spend the night in a wide, desolate valley. I sat on a tree trunk watching the sunset and contemplating my present and future. If I had been able to do so, I would have asked someone else to tell me why I felt so exhausted. As it was, the selfsame voice that had often spoken at moments like these now decided to speak:

"Listen," it said, "as you can see for yourself, you have a light load to carry and a swift, regal steed beneath you. You're fulfilling the promise you made to catch up with the pilgrim caravan, the one you made with Ibn Khalas's squad at the door of your house. They allowed you a few hours to get ready. If their commander, Al-A'ma [the blind man] from Sicily, had not interceded on your behalf, they would have removed you forcibly at dawn. You made good use of that precious time to write a short note to your blessed wife, in which you proffered every conceivable excuse for leaving on the hajj in such a hurry and reassured her that things were fine. You asked her to return to the family home as soon as she could. By so doing, you explained why you had been willing to travel with very little baggage. In the margin you had written a note to Hamada, sending him your greetings and telling him to look after his mistress, Fayha'. You had also spent some time checking that everything in the house was as it should be and offering counsel and gifts to the servants. When it was finally time to depart, you had put your previous hesitation aside regarding the gold pieces from the king of Sicily and taken them with you, concealed in your baggage, all in the hope of returning them to King Frederic or, if that proved impossible, giving them to any needy people whom you might meet on the way. So, now that you have started your journey, albeit under compulsion, do you intend to pursue it to its final goal or will you be breaking your journey whenever you see fit?"

"The hajj is one of Islam's pillars," you replied, "an obligation for whoever is able to perform it. However, I will only undertake it when it is my own intention. You know the reasons for my exit from Sabta. During my exile, to the extent possible I am going to take an expansive view of things in terms of place and time: I may decide to stay in some cities that possess the necessary spiritual and pleasurable qualities; others I may pass by. Perhaps I will go to see the Hafsid ruler, Abu Zakariyya, to discuss matters in the Maghrib and Spain, but then maybe not. I may turn aside and visit the king of Sicily in order both to instruct and negotiate; there again, I may not . . ."

"So be it," said the fading voice, "bravo, by God, bravo! That way, you don't need to explain things to your beloved wife, who tends to get anxious and cry a lot."

Thus ended my thoughts, as it turned cold and night fell. I got up in order to go down into the valley, join the group, and show myself to the people who were expecting me. Once I had arrived and dismounted, some of the guards escorted me to the person whose name I had mentioned. No sooner had I entered the tent and my name been called than Al-A'ma from Sicily came over and offered me a warm welcome. He introduced me to the hajj caravan leader, his guide, his counselor, and some other people with him.

"Didn't I tell you all?" he said. "Ibn Sab'in, the saint of God, is a believer who keeps his word when he makes a promise."

He then invited me to share the evening meal with them. By way of excusing myself, I said that it was my custom to sleep on an empty stomach. I preferred to rest after the tiring day's journey, and made my way to a small tent close by.

Early next morning after I had performed the dawn prayer in the open air, my host invited me to his tent to have breakfast with him on our own. I noticed how skillful he was at pouring milk into cups and how he managed to name each kind of bread and the oil and honey he put on them as he graciously handed them to me. I attributed it to the skills that blind people develop. He then started describing the color and shape of the clothes I was wearing and congratulated me on their fine quality and the excellent way they matched my stature. He advised me not to pluck out the white hairs in my beard so they would grow to their full extent and not lead to the appearance of others before their time. All this amazed me, and I asked him if he had some kind of sixth sense that allowed him to detect so much detail.

He smiled. "Yes, saint of God," he replied in a whisper, "I use that sixth sense but also my naked eye!"

"And do you keep it open as well," I joked, "so you can ogle the women on the roof when you're doing the call to prayer?"

"No, no, heaven forbid!" he replied with a chuckle. "I only keep my eye open for His Excellency, Ibn Khalas the governor. He brought me from the court of the Hafsid Abu Zakariyya and hired me in his own service. He's the only one who knows that particular secret, and now you do as well. I'm sure you'll keep it that way. And now tell me some of your own secrets, so I can dig a hole for them inside my own heart."

"Since you're an agent for the governor," I asked with a wily chuckle, "what on earth can there be that you don't already know about me?"

"For example," he said, "are you planning to return to Sabta before going on the hajj? Do you intend to seek an audience with King Frederic and Sultan Abu Zakariyya?"

"God willing, I'll be returning to Sabta after the hajj, sooner or later," I replied resolutely. "And yes, I'm planning to meet the two monarchs, but only because such meetings will be to the benefit of Muslims."

My companion stopped eating and gave me a piercing stare from his one good eye. "I want you to treat any idea of meeting the Norman king as a complete impossibility," he said. "The reasons are complicated, and I'm sure that your broad intellect will be able to appreciate them. Previously we removed your request for such a meeting from the letter to the king, and confiscated your other letter to him from your envoy, Khalid of Tangier. With regard to access to the Hafsid ruler, you would have to face a thousand doorkeepers, the last of whom would be Abu Bakr al-Sakuni, who is the primary executive authority in the court. The only way you would be able to present yourself to the ruler would be over his dead body. He has every detail about you in his quiver, and his sleeves are loaded with reports concerning your deviant and heretical postures. I would strongly suggest that you make your way gently past Tunis, flitting as lightly as possible as you skirt the region and everyone who lives there. You won't be able to give any lessons or deliver any legal opinions. There will be no encounters with new recruits or gullible listeners. My best advice to you is to avoid unnecessary pitfalls and annoyances. As the saying puts it, you have to excuse the person who warns in advance."

In this piece of advice from Ibn Khalas's retainer I detected a direct warning.

"Once I get to Tunis with God's help," I responded by way of a challenge, "I intend to be very circumspect. But tell me, apart from pretending to be blind, what other secrets are you harboring?"

"You'll not be able to get me to share with you information that only my master the governor knows. But what I can tell you is that I'm on my way to convey to Abu Zakariyya Ibn Khalas's renewal of Hafsid control and to consult him on a variety of secret matters."

"My dear envoy," I told him, "you can assume that I share the same earnest hopes as Ibn Khalas when it comes to his wishes and aspirations regarding the Hafsid sultan."

"No, my good shaykh," he replied. "Politicians deal with matters of this world, while saints of God are concerned with those of the next. Every person is competent to deal with those matters for which he was created. What's more, my master doesn't like company or competition when it comes to politics!"

A drumbeat now announced that the caravan was about to depart. I got to my feet and stood in front of my host, saying no more for fear of bringing our discussion to an undesirable conclusion. He came over to me and clasped me to him with probing hands, while his servants prepared his riding animal. Whispering in my ear, he confided that a sign of how much he trusted me was that he was prepared to let me choose between riding with the caravan or else leaving it and traveling on my own. I told him that my intention was to head at speed for Bijaya. He then advised me to take the coast road by day so as to avoid the risk of being waylaid by bandits, not to mention holding on to my regal mount and the valuable baggage I was carrying.

I took some deep breaths of the air in the Banu Khalid mountains, keen as I was to build up my strength and follow the advice I used to give my own pupils and adherents with regard to keeping my nerve and staying on task. After preparing my horse for the journey, I sat down under an isolated, leafy tree close by, relishing its shade and pondering my state. By so doing I was hoping to turn into an ascending light that would serve a useful purpose. I pictured myself as a hovering angel, wings fluttering at times and outspread at others, while the wind beneath it pointed it in whichever direction seemed appropriate.

So there I was, a hovering angel weaving to and fro in the firmament of my own mind or floating on high in the realms of contemplation and observation, when I heard the tones of the muezzin calling people to prayer in Badis's single mosque. I went down there to perform the noon prayer. Once I had found someone to look after my horse, I mingled with the congregation. I was horrified to see some worshippers either sitting or prostrating themselves all the time and not changing their position either during the prayers or afterward. I looked for the imam of the mosque (who was stringing out the chanting of the verses), offered him my greetings, and asked him what was going on with these worshippers. He took me over to a corner and informed me that they were all drug addicts. Rubbing my hands together in dismay, I asked God to forgive them all. Just then a man grabbed me by the sleeve and asked me my name, where I had come from, and what was my destination. When I gave him a terse response, he accompanied me outside, asking me to explain a complex passage in the Qur'an as he did so; an itinerant jurist had talked to him about it a year ago, but had not come up with an explanation. It lay in the interpretation of the verse "Say, if the Merciful had a child, I would be the first of worshippers" [Sura 43, v. 81].

"God knows best," I said as I began my response, "but perhaps by the word 'worshippers' here is meant 'unbelievers,' since the Arabs are known to say, 'he denied me my rights,' meaning 'he disbelieved me.'"

I handed the imam some money to spend on those unfortunates. While he was thinking about my interpretation or contemplating my gift, I mounted my horse and took off apace toward the east.

■　■　■

From Badis, my first stop on the journey, I passed by Melila, Hanin, Wahran, and Tannis. In each place I stayed for a day or just a few hours in order to visit mosques and bathhouses, catch up on some sleep, and eat in some hostels. During my travels I almost came to grief in the desert region near Tannis when I was attacked by a group of robbers on horseback (who seemed to be uncouth Bedouin). I only managed to escape thanks to my magnificent Arabian stallion, which easily outpaced them.

In the city of Algiers itself I only spent a couple of days. At dawn on the second day I set out—as though impelled by some gentle, yet insistent force—and headed for Bijaya. I took the sea route so that I could both rest my horse and relax a little myself after the pressures of being permanently on the lookout for danger and the need to move at speed. While traveling by sea, I slept a lot and indulged in inward contemplation; I actually said and did very little. During my ruminations I thought about the huge number of concepts to be contemplated and the paucity of words to express them; about the human tragedy of sheer ignorance, idiotic feuding, and a failure to achieve any mutual understanding between peoples. Anyone who spotted me lost in thought and completely oblivious to my surroundings would certainly have imagined that I had somehow been brought low by either bankruptcy or despair. The truth of the matter was quite the opposite: my entire being and mental acuity was focused on the noblest and mightiest of ideas: prime amongst them was, of course, God, the steadfast creator of all, who envelops within His universal vision everything that is seen and unseen; it is toward Him that I strive to approach with my enlightened essence and laudable endeavors.

As the sailboat traversed the waves in much the same state as myself, it rocked me from side to side, and I was able to fill my lungs with fresh sea breezes. While I was in such a blissful state, how I wished for an angel to tear open my heart and purge it of all foul pollutants. Then I would have breathed in the pure scent of the blissful folk who are close to God's throne!

2

I ARRIVED IN BIJAYA in the evening and went looking for a hotel; I found one without difficulty. After the first night, I decided that I would extend my stay in this city; it felt as though I was tied to it in some way. After breakfast I made myself known to the warden of the hotel and entrusted the care of my horse to him. Then I headed for the nearest public bath to rid myself of the journey's grime. In the large city mosque I performed both the noon and afternoon prayers. While waiting for sunset, I took the opportunity to go and see the Pearl Palace, the architectural glory of the city, and the high mountains that surround it as its most obvious natural feature. I then did a tour through the quarters and markets, relying on being a stranger in these parts. I was completely fascinated as I infiltrated myself among its regular inhabitants and visitors.

In a central square people were gathered in groups, some of them to chat and exchange gossip, others to listen. There were bards and storytellers too, recounting tales of heroic sagas and literary salons; some of them were singing or chanting either accompanied by musical instruments or without. I was particularly attracted by one of them who sang the following ditty:

> Come hither and listen, be ye man or woman,
> Clever or stupid, from Bijaya or elsewhere.
> Let us begin by recalling the beloved.

Once he had finished, an incredible musician in the middle of the group began playing the flute, as though he were from the line of the Prophet David himself. He was an unbelievably skillful singer and drum player, one who could readily switch from poems and liturgies in praise of the Prophet to secular

Andalusian love poems. My, O my, what amazing talent he possessed, especially when it came to crafting his *envois* and *zajals!*

The story tells us that "whenever the Prophet of God witnessed a spectacle, he sat down." Following his example, I did exactly the same. I listened as the man recited some beautiful, flowing words, varying the beat of the drum from high to low as he did so. Within the circle of listeners individual voices were raised in appreciation, but then everyone chimed in: "Encore, Abu al-Hasan!" they yelled. With that, he started going around the circle carrying his instrument, as he chanted these lovely verses:

> Here's a shaykh from Meknes singing amidst the markets,
> What is there for me with people, and for them with me,
> Or for that matter, O master, with creation in general?
> The one whom we all adore is the Creator and Provider.
> Say not a word, my boy, unless you are sincere.
> Put down what I say in a notebook and write it to preserve my thoughts,
> What is there for me with people, and for them with me?

Voices of praise and admiration were raised, and another encore was demanded. The singer stopped chanting with his instrument and turned to normal speech, eyeing me every so often.

"Listen to my words, ye people, but this time without the envois and strophes of poetry. Here is a sacred waft of inspiration that has blown over me with the words: When the sphere is reiterated, it becomes fastened; nay rather, it turns empty and desolate. O those who aspire to more, move along with me and interlink. Among the living of the Creator and Lord, maybe you will rise up and benefit. Whoever has heavy feet, may he remain inspired by my Lord in vocation and garment."

As I retraced my steps, I kept thinking about the portions of this man's speech that I could recall. I was amazed by the sheer simplicity of his method and the mellifluous quality of his discourse. The assembled company had addressed him as Abu al-Hasan, and I wondered whether he was in fact Abu al-Hasan al-Shushtari, the Spaniard from Wadi Ash (Guadix) about whose career and poetry I had heard previously.

I passed by a perfumer and bought some scents and herbs, then a copyist so that I could check to see if he had on his shelves any texts with which I was not familiar. All of a sudden I felt a hand grasping my shoulder gently. Turning around, I discovered that the person in question was none other than the man who had been reciting at the assembly, along with his drum, his green coat, and his ruddy-cheeked complexion. He had a thick beard flecked with grey, and his body was slender and trim.

"I spotted you at my circle, Sir," he said in a mellow tone. "You look very like a person whom I have long admired in God Almighty, even though I have only seen him in dreams, someone I've longed to meet. Are you indeed the noble Sufi mystic, 'Abd al-Haqq ibn Sab'in?"

I nodded my head and confirmed that he was indeed Abu al-Hasan al-Shushtari. We embraced each other warmly, while he shed tears of happiness and welcome. He asked the amazed copyist to bring us some figs and yoghourt and introduced him to me, concluding with words of censure: "If you had any idea of the prestige of the person who is doing you the honor of visiting your establishment," he said, "you would be sacrificing a lamb and giving alms to the poor." The poor copyist was clearly embarrassed and offered me a basket of figs, saying that they were all he had. I took one with thanks, while Abu al-Hasan suggested to the copyist that he bring to his shop texts containing useful learning so that he might hope for a visit from me at some point in the future. With that he invited me to accompany him to his home in a nearby quarter. Saying farewell to the copyist, who vowed that I should take the basket of figs as a gift, we left the shop.

As we made our way through a number of markets, hands were extended toward my companion, offering him gifts of various kinds, all of which he declined. Here and there people kept asking him to entertain them, and he would respond by singing, "Let me be, let me be; for now I am enraptured by one whose very company delights me." With the market and its hubbub behind us, we made our way through a series of winding alleys and then a long, straight one that led to a desolate open space full of wild plants, thorn-bushes, and self-planted trees. Once across it, we reached the door of a modest abode built of grey stone that seemed to have come from the mountain that overlooked it. As my colleague proceeded to open the door without a key, I likened it to a fearsome cavern, suitable for worship and seclusion, but no place to live or spend the night. The simile I had invoked was confirmed when I glimpsed the room inside, which was totally bare of furniture or coverings of any kind; there were just a few scraps of cloth, books, candles on a table, and a water jar.

Abu al-Hasan's expression was one of serene contentment mingled with a certain pleasure and pride.

"Master," he told me, "this cavern is my refuge from both heat and cold, and I have other places like it, caves and houses, where I can invoke God in order to counter the whisperings of the devil and the instinct to sin."

I was unable to conceal my amazement and admiration. After a few confidential thoughts of my own, I launched into a paean of praise. "Praise be to the One who can transform conditions! This is a form of seclusion the like of which I have never encountered before, not least because the person involved is the scion of a prestigious and wealthy family. My brother, there's absolutely no doubt that you fully deserve the title of 'leader of the recluses.'"

He closed his eyes for a moment. "O you Ka'ba of all that is good," he went on happily, "all this is a boon from God Almighty and from you as well. You are my mainstay and my support."

I was utterly astonished at what he was saying and asked God for forgiveness. Without further ado, he invited me to complete my ablutions and perform the sunset prayers with him. That is precisely what we did. When it was done, we sat down on a mat with the basket of figs close by. Abu al-Hasan immediately took it upon himself to dispel the signs of amazement and anxiety that showed on my face.

"Master," he began gently, "for a while now I have been receiving news of your activities and perusing such pearls of your written works as I have been able to acquire. My source has been those of your followers who have moved from the cities of the Maghrib eastward and toward the holy cities of Arabia. The most recent was someone whom I met in Tripoli, named Khalid from Tangier. God reward him well, he loaned me the notes that some of your students have taken from your lessons and epistles. I spent three whole days making a copy of them so that I could return them to him before he moved on. Once I had finished making the copy, I hung a notice on my door to say that I was in seclusion. I then proceeded to study them carefully, memorizing parts and contemplating their meaning. By God, they managed to grab hold of the inner workings of my heart and to exercise my mind in ways that I had only previously appreciated at random. And then, while I was in Meknes al-Zaytun, I had a dream in which, as a condition for joining your mystical sect, you demanded that I give up all pomp and authority and rid myself of the world's trappings. Instead I was to wear a Sufi robe, take a drum, and wander around the market-places singing the praises of the Beloved."

Wonder upon wonder!

This man al-Shushtari was indeed one of God's authentic saints! Wisdom had come to him from gates that opened up to the heavenly spheres of inspirational vision and intuitional knowledge.

"God bless you, my brother!" I replied, wishing to learn more detail about his circumstances, "and I beseech God Almighty to let me stay in your own good graces. But what you heard me say in that dream is not the same as one person awake talking to another."

"My dear Pinnacle of the Faith," he replied immediately as he finished eating a fig, "does the process of being awake involve anything other than precisely those things you have written about and set down? Are not you the one who calls on people to rid themselves of the illusions prompted by various appendages and accretions and the general hubbub of others and opposites? All of that is part of the quest for the principal perfections, assuming the qualities of the beautiful names of God, the only ones that are genuine, through a linkage of the possible existent with the Necessary Existent and its absolute—namely God alone and no other entity! That at least is a small part of what I've been thrilled to comprehend from the realms of some of your epistles. I've learned such things in the way that I've described to you and memorized them as though they come directly from you to me or else have been revealed to me. Praise be to God then who has guided me to them and through them. And many thanks to you also and a fulsome reward."

I failed to find words with which to lessen the role that I seemed to have played in this man's decision to deny the world and seek something loftier, but I made up my mind to try.

"Abu al-Hasan," I said in as modest a tone as I could muster, "you are most generous in what you say. You ascribe to me a prominence that I don't deserve. Through God's aid you've indeed managed to rid yourself of worldly things in which you were steeped and have subjected the routine of your life and your personal preoccupations to a process of severance and abandonment, all with a view to concentrating on what needs to remain and reflects your real essence. However, if it were not for your previous proclivities and your desire to undertake the burdensome task of seclusion and aspiration to the lofty heights of truth, would the advice that I offered in your dream have been of any use?"

The person to whom I had addressed this question now handed me a fig, and I ate it. I took a second and then a third.

"Master," I heard him reply, "I'll not deny that your instructions to me in my dream reflected an inclination buried deep inside me. However, if it were not for my readings of your works and about you, that inclination would have remained hidden and inactive and I would not have come to the decision that I did, entrusted myself to God, and proceeded along that path. I'm older than you, but you're ahead of me in both learning and understanding. Your works have managed to rouse me from my slumber and ignorance. You're the one who's pushed me toward my dream and my ascent."

I tried to parry his praise, maybe for the last time. "The fact that I call on people to renounce worldly matters," I said, "does not mean that I need to claim the credit for it. It's true that, like you, I've renounced the world of pomp and authority, but, when I was a young man in Murcia, I lived a life of ribaldry and passion. In Sabta I've married a virtuous woman of high status and ambition, someone who's both influential and wellborn. Once I've completed the hajj, I wish for nothing so much as to return to her on the wings of affection and love."

I did not tell him about the purses of gold in my belt, nor about the splendid stallion quartered in the stables of my hotel. My companion remained silent for a moment, then stood up and indicated to me that it was time for the evening prayer. We both turned in humility toward the qibla, and, once we had performed the prayers, we read some verses from the Qur'an. That done, we both sat down again. A peculiar silence prevailed, and I would have assumed that it boded ill if Abu al-Hasan had not adopted his smiling visage as before.

"Lord of the Gnostics," he addressed me, "the course of renunciation is one of the fruits of struggle and aspiration. Only those who pursue the path of renunciation can achieve it. Don't regard me as an angel, for I'll never be one. Like you, I gained insight, albeit to the extent of your primary phase; I then moved beyond it to the second, operating on the basis of the noble Prophet's negative posture toward monastic life and bachelorhood. Yet I was to emerge from this phase with a bum's rap—widowed of a fine woman and divorced from another who was perverse and arrogant; nor did I have children with either of them. After that I did not try the marriage-market again; and thank God for what was written and decreed! So here I am; as you counsel in your *Epistle of Light*, I'm organizing my seclusion in such a way as to keep my soul far removed from evil forces that might destroy it, as distant as possible from family and other people. I use the lights of the faithful Prophet to guide me toward the absolute unity of existence. In my conduct I rely on two enlightened shaykhs: one from the previous century whose primary expression from the beginning till his very last breath was 'God is the truth,' namely Shu'ayb Abu Madyan,* the Great Sufi. In the present era, my shaykh is the person who is now sitting here with me; I am overjoyed to be talking to him and beg him to accept me as a student and follower."

I was at a loss and stared at the floor, thinking about what he had said but avoiding any hint of rejection or refusal. Abu al-Hasan was delighted.

"This is what Shu'ayb has to say on the subject," he shouted. "'A shaykh is someone to guide you by his ethics, support you by his contemplation, and illumine your inner world with his brilliance.'"

With that he embraced me and shed tears of gratitude and joy. I clasped his hand in order to calm his fervor, and in a moment he quieted down. He now invited me to share a modest hermit's meal with him, but I declined, noting that I had already eaten a lot of figs. I stood up to leave and asked my companion to direct me to the hotel whose address I gave him. Rubbing his hands together in sorrow, he jumped up and urged me to spend the night with him; he warned me that traveling back to the hotel on such a night was not safe. He promised to go early in the morning to bring my horse and belongings. By the light of a candle he accompanied me to another room and told me where to find blankets and a back door that led, as he told me, into a stable with a cow and other domestic animals and a variety of fruit trees and scented bushes. After praying for him, I withdrew so I could be on my own and get some of the sleep that I so badly needed.

3

NEXT MORNING I AWOKE to the cock's crow and the muezzin's call. I got up, did my ablutions, and prayed. There was no sign of my host inside the house. I sat there, thinking about a number of things, prime among them being the issue of my wife, whom I was longing to see, and of Al-Shushtari, this devout monotheist who aspired so fervently to attain the truth and could sing in a way that brought him close to God and that people appreciated so much. My whole being had become attracted to him, even though I had only met him a short while ago. What a wonderful holy figure he was, living in this era that was proving to be so parsimonious in its supply of figures who merited admiration and respect!

I stayed where I was until the morning sun was high in the sky. Emerging from the stable space I found myself in a field right at the bottom of a looming mountain. In it I found the animals that Abu al-Hasan had mentioned, creatures with which I was acquainted in some detail, a dog and cats that hissed at me. The explorer in me went behind a hovel and found a privy in the open air; after all the figs I had eaten the day before, I certainly needed it. I made my way up the mountain, following a marked path with various kinds of bushes and mulberry, olive, and carob trees on either side. Birds and cicadas were making a huge din. On my way up I met a man wearing a Jewish skullcap.

"Wayfarer," he said, "if it's Al-Shushtari's cell you are heading for, as I have done before you, then this path leads to it."

Al-Shushtari's cell! So here I was, standing in front of a stone hovel with this phrase painted on the door: "Only monotheists enter here!" Beneath it were the following words:

"'He is God only,' those are the words of my master, Ibn Sab'in. I recite it *ad libitum* to devotees":

In God men roam in love of the beloved,
God, O God, with me ever present; to my heart ever near.

My heart, bow down and rejoice; your beloved is here.
Be generous with your invocation of your Lord and recount the story.

Relish the occasion and live a charmed life among mankind.

With the words "In the name of God" on my lips, I entered the hovel; half of it was shady, and in that part was a water jar and a rug; the sunny half was full of anemones and a plentiful supply of other plants. What was weird was that, once you were inside, you could not hear a single sound of any kind.

I sat down on the rug and leaned my back against the mud-brick wall, relishing the absolute silence and trying as best I could to melt into it and bask in its peace. In behaving that way, my goal was to probe the depths of language, ritual, and song concealed within it. Let the truth be told: all I found there was the sheer truth, the kind that cannot be comprehended by description, causation, or understanding, the same kind that devoted seekers aspire to achieve through love and struggle, in the process eradicating their earthly desires and appendages as they seek the essence of the beautiful names of God and the wafts of eternity. All others, the great mass of humanity, simply meander around in the desert wastes of frivolity and fancy, buffeted by the dark forces of neglect and ignorance. I think that I pursued the flow of this silence through various stations and circles that swung between drowsiness and sleep, but then I suddenly woke up again. My astrolabe told me that it was almost late afternoon. I rushed outside. There I found myself face to face with Abu al-Hasan, clasping the bridle of my horse that had been loaded up with my belongings. With him was another man who had about him the look of a priest. My host looked at me with his fresh countenance and gave me the same greeting as his companion.

"My master," he said, "this mountain and its fresh air have clearly appealed to you and provided you with the serenity of this hermit's cell."

I returned their greetings. "You're exactly right, O cell-owner!"

"This priest and I," he went on, "have been waiting here until you finished and woke up. We too have been having our fill of peace and quiet. Now, Lord, it's up to you: do you want to spend the night up here, or accompany me wherever you wish to go?"

A Muslim Suicide | 271

I gathered that the silent priest needed to spend some time in seclusion in the cell, so I gestured to Abu al-Hasan that we should leave. We started on our way down on foot, while my horse enjoyed himself running around or chewing as much grass as he wanted. That done, he came sprinting toward us. All the while my colleague, who was clearly fascinated by nature, kept telling me about plants, insects, birds, and trees about which I knew absolutely nothing. As he sang the praises of their Creator he was able to assign each of them its name. He also drew my attention to the various dwellings on the mountain slopes and proceeded to describe yet another mountain high enough to be reachable only by predatory birds and certain categories of ape. Below it were the heights of Amsiwan and other promontories where he pointed out to me the fortress of the Banu Hammada and the vestiges of their now defunct kingdom. There was also the Almohad fortress and the mosque minaret. I was delighted to observe that, as the hills sloped down toward the seashore to the north, the city itself led toward some coastal plains with fields and orchards, not to mention valleys filled with trees and shady groves where apes and wild boar could be found. Abu al-Hasan finished by revealing the reasons for his delight at living in Bijaya, namely the extent to which God had endowed it with such natural wonders and a magical spiritual essence that was amply illustrated by its landscapes with their tiers and elevations.

I offered my blessing to God for having become acquainted with the one who had been able to use his knowledge and taste to describe such wonders. "This is what makes the genuine poet," I said, "that and nothing else. Someone who is familiar with the earth and what grows on it and who has learned the vast majority of the terms involved!"

The person I had extolled lowered his head modestly. "My lord," he replied, "my own knowledge is merely a small sample of your vast learning, a mere speck."

On our way down the mountainside my companion would occasionally stop in front of an aged oak tree, examine it for a moment, and then talk to it; at other times he would lean over plants or insects and say about the former that some of them had only recently arrived or sprung up, while concerning the latter he would note that they were the forest's memory and the shepherds of the ages. Once we reached the bottom of the mountain, he started rolling around in the dirt and grass, saying and chanting, "He is God" over and over again. As I watched in amazement, I envied him his courage in doing such a thing.

After washing ourselves in a clear spring, we continued on our way. Eventually we reached his house, and my generous host provided a nice stall for my horse, brought it some fodder, and then helped me unload my belongings. He then left me to arrange my things in my room while, as he intimated to me, he himself set about preparing an appropriate dinner; as he put it, one that would beggar description.

My host brought in a table and put it in the middle of the room between myself and him. By the light of a burning candle I could make out a *tagine** with strips of meat and slices of fresh egg and spices, the whole ensemble floating in a sauce with olive oil and wonderful herbs. Surrounding the dish were bread, cheeses, dates, and cups of milk. In presenting this spread to me, Abu al-Hasan explained that he only did so on blessed feast days and other significant occasions that were important to him. The opportunity to talk to me and share a meal was one such occasion. He then invited me to begin, praying that my stomach would accept the food proffered with blessed ease. Like him I said, "In the name of God," then started eating my fill of the tagine. I expressed my admiration for the one who had planned and cooked it. I noticed that my companion took less of it than I did, particularly since his desire to talk meant that ever since dawn that day he had not been able to fulfill some of his charitable works as he usually did. When I asked him about the exact nature of those activities, he paused for a moment.

"It's nothing more than God Almighty and His Prophet enjoins on us," he said somewhat coyly, "when it comes to offering help to those who are troubled and neglected. How numerous indeed are such people in these turbulent times when so many people are leaving our bereaved Andalus! To which I can add, master, my role as a mediator between people in order to resolve disputes and bring about reconciliation."

I expressed my gratitude to Abu al-Hasan for his good deeds, even though I thought to myself that they were clearly beyond his own means. It seems that he sensed that feeling on my part, because he decided to go into more detail.

"One of God's bounties to me," he continued, "is that he has made me one of his holy men who can give back what they have themselves lost. I collect wealth from the rich to give to the poor. Whenever the former prove to be stingy and tight-fisted, I put on an evening performance that sometimes consists of incantations and liturgies and at others of songs and recitation. Those events soften their hard hearts and open their hands so that they give enough of God's bounty to provide for the poor and needy. In all my efforts and mediations God is my helper and His visage is my permanent desire."

I now took advantage of the fact that my host's mouth was full. "Such conduct, my dear brother," I said, "is the very essence of the true believer. The path toward closeness to God involves offering service to His people; the quest for His delight demands help for the weak and poor."

He wiped his mouth and took a drink of milk. "My father—God have mercy on him!" he went on, "operated at the very highest ranks and levels of authority. He advised me to avoid contact with people and to stay out of the way of women. According to him, that was the way to retain a sense of self-respect and keep one's mind on the right path. When I was young, his only words of advice to me were, 'Don't go near the great mass of people; their ways of thinking and doing things are corrupt. Stay away from tyrants as much as possible. If you manage to place yourself beyond their coteries and modes of conduct, you will preserve both your soul and mind.' Even before being offered such advice, I had already been steering clear of tyrants. However, when it came to the mass of people, I did not follow my father's counsel, since I discovered that they constituted a domain where my natural abilities could be exercised. And, as you well know, master, there are many such people alive today, those who suffer ill at the hands of tyrants, their bodies and hearts shattered as they are deprived of their rights and senses. I get to meet all of them, whether they are free or reside in zawiyas, hospitals, or prisons. If you like, you would be welcome to join me tomorrow in my visits to some of them."

I listened to what this wonderful, saintly man was saying. "God willing," I responded, "we can indeed go together, although it would require me to postpone for a while my much-desired trip up to the cell on the mountain. Tell me about this cell that also carries your name."

"By God," he replied, "I've told people not to use that name, but to no avail. The phrase that I've painted over the doorway that you've read is of no use at all. The contents of the quotation are just part of the plentiful boons that you have provided for me. I put it over the doorway of every hut that I construct in the various Maghribi towns where I stay, be they in inhabited areas or in desert wastes."

I was somewhat overwhelmed by the fact that this remarkable man thought so much of me. "You even excel at house-building, Abu al-Hasan," I remarked by way of compliment.

"One of my students, Abu Madyan from Tlemcen, taught me how to do it. On windy mountains I construct them out of stone, but on plains and fairly flat hills I use wood, reeds, and palm leaves. God alone brings us success in all things!"

As night fell, we could hear the evening call to prayer, so we both prayed the obligatory prayers and added to them some other liturgies and intercessions. Once we had finished, my companion asked me a question, as to whether it was permissible to perform prayers some time after the time appointed or indeed to perform them all together at day's end.

"Dear brother," I said, justifying the practice and offering some explanation for it, "if prayer is the twin of thought and contemplation and the equivalent of good deeds and kindly words—be they recited or chanted, then each of us is involved in a continuous and constant process of prayer. Thus there can be no objection to performing the obligation whenever it is convenient to do so."

"My friend in all things," he replied enthusiastically, "you have spoken the truth so well! It's midnight now, so please provide me with some of your spiritual sustenance so that I can devote as much time as possible to perusing it."

I gave my companion a copy of my *Escape of the Gnostic*. I in turn asked him for some of his literary and popular poetry. He told me that some of it was in his memory, but there were other poems in his notebooks. I took some of the notebooks and said farewell, in the hope of meeting him again at dawn the next day.

When I lay down, I was not able to get any sleep because I kept thinking about my family and especially my wife, not to mention my students and this compulsory journey in which I was involved. It seemed to me that my sleeplessness was considerably alleviated by the fact that I had started reading some of the poetry composed by my wonderful, generous, and noble host. Sometimes I read strophic poems in the Spanish style, and at others I looked at more traditional Arabic poetry. Among the features that I noted were his sense of proportion in imagination, his sheer brilliance in embellishment, and the rare and wonderful gifts he offered in revelation. I found that I still needed to question this inspired poet about his references to drunkenness in some of his verses, specifically the particular and frank terminology he used. By the Arabic word *khamr* was he implying that kind of liquid "unpressed" or "not pressed by human agency," as used frequently by itinerant Sufis, or was it rather that—without resort to double-entendre or simile—he was going back to an earlier period of ribaldry in his life, the time when Abu al-Hasan would have drunk wine neat as the son of Spanish amirs?

4

NEXT MORNING I was awoken by the sun's rays shining on me, showing that it had to be almost midday. My host's notebooks were scattered all over the bedcovers and my own face; it may well have been their magic that managed to imbue me with a kind of figurative drunkenness that had allowed me to sleep so deeply. I collected them all and got up so I could check on things and cleanse myself before performing my prayers. All around me the cats, dogs, and chickens were now getting used to my presence. I washed my clothes and body, and then went out to look at a back garden where there were lemon trees and fresh-growing vegetables. I picked enough of each to satisfy my hunger, then left the hut in order to head for the city, where I planned to acquaint myself with its monuments, shops, and people.

Crossing the wasteland that separated my host's cell from the closest buildings that connected to the city center, I made my way across a market that seemed to belong to wool merchants, and then the main market known as the Qaysariyya, till I reached yet another market teeming with people, animals, and goods, which I was informed was the Bab al-Bahr market. There I bumped into the copyist-bookseller to whom Abu al-Hasan had introduced me earlier. I returned his greetings and asked him where the copyists' market was. He told me there was no such thing, explaining that people were far more concerned about what they would eat and wear and where they could live; they were totally uninterested in learning and those who practiced it. He then said a prayer of thanks to Al-Shushtari, who was providing him with some assistance so that he did not have to close his shop or fill it up with vegetables and ironware.

This brought to mind what my ascetic host had told me about taking money from the rich and donating it to people who were weak and poor. I could well understand his doing such a thing for this bankrupt copyist. I asked him where Abu al-Hasan was at this moment.

"Every Monday, Sir," he told me, much to my amazement, "you can see him at the head of a group of lunatics and people possessed. He does the rounds with them from Bab al-Bunud to Bab al-Marsa by the port. They all shout out, 'Ho, come with me, and you'll see!'"

And that is exactly what I did. It was only a few moments of walking and waiting later before Al-Shushtari appeared, just as my copyist companion had told me. He was striding along at the head of a group of people walking, some of whom were waving multicolored flags. I caught the following lines from the song they were chanting:

> Ye mendicant, hear what you should do;
> Meander in the world and show off.
> There is nothing in the world more comely than you.
>
> Forget about other people, and seek to understand the secrets,
> Clear the path before you, and you will see both past and future.
> The best of moments come when we are united with our true selves.
>
> Let your thoughts roam free and pursue their ease,
> The entire universe is at your disposal.

Along with my companion, I hurried over to another place where they were heading. This was their chant:

> Harken, thou best of creatures:
> Wander with whomsoever you will and remain untroubled;
> For you are both lover and beloved.

What a sight all this was! Men of all ages, some of them bare-chested and without shoes, all singing at the top of their voices, as they competed to repeat the chant of their leader or to accompany his own singing. For his part, once in a while he would beat or rap on his drum.

I felt a shiver of excitement coursing through me. Had I not been so worried about carrying my money-belt around with me, I would certainly have joined them and walked in the footsteps of the imam of the ascetics. Then I could have molded myself with their perambulation through the town, using their progress as a way of searching for a release from my own concerns and troubles and opening my heart to streaks of light and relief.

At this point I became aware once again of my copyist companion, who was amazed at the way I had succumbed to the experience of the moment. I advised him to go back to his home and place of work.

"What's the point of that?" he complained. "It's my fate to sit at home or in my copyist's store. My master, Al-Shushtari, has already put the notion into verse:

> O ye of feeble will, understand well the purpose of it all:
> How can anyone who stays idle possibly gain any control over things?
> Ascent belongs to the one who strives; for him perseverance is a habit."

I now took off and wandered around the port area. From there I made my way up and down, through alleys and across squares, repeating to myself Al-Shushtari's poetry that the group of madmen had sung during their tour of the town. I told myself how wonderful this new friend of mine was, seeing him as a remarkable talent and brilliant luminary. I kept wandering around like this till I found myself in front of a mosque door (it may well have been the major mosque in the town). I went inside and performed the afternoon prayer with the assembled congregation. That done, I went over to a shady corner where I could find some peace and quiet, recite some of my own prayers, and think for a bit. But, just as I was about to benefit from such activities, two men came up to me, leaned over, and spoke as though in unison.

"If I were you, Ibn Sab'in," they said, "I wouldn't stay too long in Bijaya. The best thing by far would be for you to speed on your way to the Hijaz."

The nasty, threatening tone that they both used and the fact that the whole thing happened so suddenly prevented me from responding or even trying to catch up with them after they had left. I just sat there for a while thinking the whole thing over and trying to link it to everything that had happened to me so far. Once I had made up my mind that there was indeed a link, I left the mosque with my head bowed and headed for the place where I was staying. Once there, I diverted myself by attending to my horse, gave him some more fodder and water, and fondled his head and mane, whispering words of comfort and reassurance as I did so.

Just as I was in the process of using this as a way of convincing myself to take things as they come, there was Al-Shushtari himself standing in front of me with a radiant smile. Kissing my shoulder, he gave me a warm embrace and then apologized for not waking me at dawn because I was so deeply asleep.

I told myself that now was the right time to tell this ascetic holy man about certain things and to ask his counsel about others. I invited him to come inside and sit down with me. Once he had watered his garden and tended to his various animals, he did so. Between us he placed something to drink and some pieces of bread, vegetables, and cheeses.

"So, Abu al-Hasan," I said as I peeled a cucumber, "you're good at growing things as well! I watched your work with the group of poor folk at noon today by the Port Gate. By God, the whole thing thrilled me!"

"My master, 'Abd al-Haqq," he replied after swallowing a mouthful, "every Monday I accept the invitation of a number of madmen from the asylum to do a tour of the town and sing with them. The whole thing ends with Sufi rituals and a ceremony in their residence. This practice seems to provide them some comfort and relief. Every Saturday I do exactly the same thing with prisoners; I have to take responsibility for them when I do so. With both groups I am trying to insert a small grain of charity into their lives and help them overcome their trials and tribulations. The chanting helps enormously in that particular regard. And success comes only through God!"

I extolled his actions in a spirit of genuine admiration and assured him that he fully deserved the title of "Pivot and Imam of the Ascetics." However, he hastened to remind me that whatever aspects of asceticism and mysticism he utilized had come from me, just the way a pupil does with his master.

At this point all I could do was to remove the money-belt from my waist and put it down in front of him.

"I'm not the way you think," I confessed. "Here I am carrying purses of gold coins! Will you relieve me of them and distribute them for charitable purposes? Then I can feel less guilty and relax a little."

He did not look the least bit surprised or taken aback. "This is the sentence's predicate, master," he responded, eyes lowered, "but what is the subject?"

I started telling my questioner about the purses' history and how they came to be.

"Now that the circumstances are clear," he shouted in delight, once the tale had been told, "there's no cause for surprise. This money of yours is fully earned; it is your legitimate property. Get rid of as much of it as you can for charitable purposes, but keep the rest for whatever the future holds. There can be no harm in that!"

My mention of Frederic, king of the Christians, and his gifts to me provided an opening for me to tell my companion about aspects of my life in Murcia. I chose to emphasize the more ribald aspects of my earlier years, the hope being that his sense of owing me so much as his master might be adjusted and diminished somewhat. That way, he would learn how my career had developed gradually over time, rather than envisioning me through his abundant love and good works. Instead he in turn, ascetic holy man that he had become, started telling me—and with no apparent embarrassment—about the reckless existence he had lived in the region of Guadix and in particular the village of Shushtar. He explained it all in terms of his having grown up in a wealthy and very influential family, something that became clear in the content of his classical poetry and colloquial verse.

This remarkable man continued to amaze me. "Even the daughter of the grape, Abu al-Hasan?" I asked with as much reticence as possible.

"Oh yes, master," he replied raucously, "in goblets and glasses! How much of it did I quaff in monasteries and taverns! And when it comes to stories about the evenings I spent with poll-tax girls, don't even ask. Such things are part of my secret life; only the Merciful Forgiver knows about them!"

This remarkable man had just reminded me of the times when I was young and reckless and used to consort with the prostitutes of Murcia, who were called "poll-tax women" because, as alien-residents, they were obliged to pay the poll tax to the authorities. Feeling bashful and not a little ashamed of the whole thing, I decided not to tell my companion about it. I also bore in mind the fact that his foreswearing of such activities had come about in Meknes and thanks to me because it was there that one of my students had provided him with copies of some of my epistles.

How amazing is the turn of events in this world of ours!

This worthy practitioner of good deeds was older than me. If I had gotten to know him earlier, I would certainly have been the one to ask him to forgive me for past indiscretions. He was the real ascetic, rather than me; he was the one doing good deeds and undertaking genuinely praiseworthy initiatives, someone about whom I could easily say exactly what Abu al-Walid ibn Rushd* [Averroes] had to say about Abu al-'Abbas from Sabta: "This man sees clearly that our life on earth is gauged by acts of generosity."

I decided to take advantage of the opportunity afforded by my friendly relationship with my companion to ask his opinion about my lost manuscript and my failure to get it back. What he had to tell me gave me some reassurance, but at the same time completely baffled me:

"My dear colleague," he said, "it may well be that you wrote it as part of a dream and lost it in the same medium. Aren't you the very one who, in his *Epistle of the Poor,* has this to say: 'You should know that the miserable person is one whose youth was spent in pleasure; and yet, after focusing all his energies on it, he discovers that its only legacy is regret. On the other hand, the happy man is someone who realizes that the days of one's life are merely a dream, whereas it is death that involves being awake. And as part of the reckoning comes the justification of his inspirations.'"

Yes indeed, I had written that or something very like it. But was that enough to remove all doubt and despair? But, rather than pursue the matter further, I decided to turn the subject to my life in Sabta. I told Abu al-Hasan about the city's most important groups and spoke briefly about my wife and my love for her. I told him about the people in general and personal acquaintances whom I had encountered in the city and on Jabal Musa. My companion was listening carefully to my description. Once in a while I had to provide a response to a specific question that he asked about a topic or person that had aroused his interest or curiosity.

When I had finished, he astonished me by making it clear that he had already perused some of the chapters in *Escape of the Gnostic.* I got the clear impression that he was the kind of devout person who manages to get by with a minimum of sleep. I decided not to overburden him by delving into some of the book's more problematic aspects: that once in a while the discourse would become diffuse and opaque, while certain sections might seem ambiguous and complicated. However, he anticipated me by giving high praise to the part of the chapter "Knowledge of the Reality of Things" that he had interpreted and understood for himself; also the section on the sciences. He went on to say that, where he was not able to understand, the only fault was in his own weak mental equipment.

"Whenever I read the work of a scholar whom I regard as one of my teachers," he said, "and realize that I'm getting absolutely nothing out of it, I find myself considering that particular zero from every aspect. All I discover is that the problem lies with me. That's what impels me to learn more in the hope that the person to whom I pose the question may be able to resolve the issue for me."

"My dear Abu al-Hasan," I said, "as far as I am concerned, your questions are most welcome. So ask away!"

He paused for a moment, so I took the opportunity to eat some dates. He asked me if I would mind if some students from his circle attended so they could profit from my learning; they were waiting in the stable. No sooner had I agreed to the idea than he clapped his hands three times. They all came in and greeted us, then sat down in a corner and started preparing pencil and paper so they could take notes.

Abu al-Hasan now turned to his question. "Master," he asked, "once when I was young, I felt unbearably depressed and out of sorts. I turned to the writings of Arab philosophers on the subject of the soul, hoping to find some means of support and cure for my condition. However, my quest soon resulted in complete failure; I seemed to be in one valley, as the phrase has it, while they were all in another. That is how I came to realize what the chief of the peripatetics had undertaken with regard to their views and realized that they were completely at a loss when it came to warding off sorrows. Master, I am completely unable to comprehend what the Muslim followers of Aristotle have to say on the topic; it all makes no sense. Instead I regularly resort to my drum and chanting; either that, or else I seek a safe haven in mystical writings on the stations and conditions of the path to God. So, tell me, are those followers really possessed of the kinds of qualities that you have noted and attributed to them?"

"As we all know full well," I replied, attempting to make things clear and simple, "verdicts on things are a subset of the way they are conceived. Both aspects operate in conjunction with the mind and its various abilities, levels, and categories. In such a context there's a huge difference between lower viewpoints and higher ones! The differences between them are like those between branches and roots or between segments and totalities. Thus, whenever I am standing, as it were, on the balcony used by someone who is a genuine and fervent observer— the status, shall we say, of lively, innovative learning that is in itself an emblem of lofty position, then I am able to see that our peripatetics worshipped Aristotle and made it their practice to follow his lead in absolutely everything. As a result where they were concerned, individual initiatives in creative thinking fell first into neglect and thereafter atrophied completely. However the most precious qualities that are needed involve a continual process of reexamining legal judgments and the use of creative ideas; and, as a direct consequence, a complete avoidance of traditionalist and sedentary attitudes. Ibn Rushd was totally in awe of Aristotle, placing him above everyone else and following in his footsteps to the ultimate degree. As a consequence, he believed that truth had reached its perfection with Aristotle, all of which led him to be blind to the fact that his number one teacher—Aristotle—failed to match the achievements of either Ptolemy or Galen—the latter in medicine and anatomy, the former in astronomy and his mathematically based theory regarding the galaxy. Ibn Rushd went so far as to tie himself up in knots over his own Aristotelianism, at least as he chose to see things. In his discussion of the earth's age, for example, he restricts God's knowledge to that of totalities and not partialities, and denies the possibility of the resurrection of individual souls and bodies. All these postures constitute assertions and arrogations, involving issues that Ibn Rushd adamantly refused to reveal to the general populace or discuss with them, a refusal that extended even to jurists, theologians, and mystics. The stated reason is that he regarded such ideas as the primary impediment to empirical truth. However, his famous definition unequivocally states that truth can never be opposed to itself, but rather accords with, and provides evidence of, it. Wisdom is the twin sister of law. But, beyond such troubling ironies as this, the actual situation is that these dilemmas and others like them are specifically ones that are difficult, if not impossible, to resolve empirically. If the human mind decides to broach such topics, it may well reach the extreme that most resembles a linden tree—producing blooms, but no fruit; or, if you prefer, like someone trying to rub oil on themselves from an empty bottle.

"Quite apart from all this, Aristotle himself places empirical logic in the specific context of mathematics and physics alone. In fact, even Ibn Rushd explains metaphysics by providing an explanation of what his great forebear and teacher meant: 'The essential has no proof, nor to that which is itself the essence; in other words, absolute proof. It is that which provides both existence and causality together.' I may be able to excuse Ibn Rushd, the renowned commentator, for trying to explain something that he does not fully understand, but I still have to express my regret that he fails to draw attention to another son of the same Spanish city, the great scholar Ibn Hazm, who, in his work, *An Approach and*

Introduction to Logic, discusses proof and principles of analogy. Such procedures may be valid for matters of physics, he says, but in matters of law all they can offer is deception and sheer nonsense. This then is the situation in this particular matter and others as well, including the ones you have mentioned. God alone knows how they are to be interpreted."

My companion was paying the closest possible attention to what I was saying, even more than the group of students.

"'God alone knows how they are to be interpreted,'" he repeated, as soon as he saw me taking a sip of my drink. "Master, I can recall that, when I was living in Guadix, I read Ibn Rushd's work entitled *The Decisive Treatise [Fasl al-Maqal]*. What amazed me most was the highly speculative way in which he interpreted certain verses from the Qur'an. I remember in particular his discussion of the third verse in Surat Al 'Umran [III]: 'Its interpretation is known only to God and those who are steeped in learning, saying what is reliable and everything that is with their Lord.' In that sentence Ibn Rushd is linking the phrase 'those who are steeped in learning' to the word *God* (may He be praised and exalted!), thus leaving the verb "saying" with no subject. In both syntax and sentence structure this is neither idiomatic nor correct. Isn't that the case?"

"Yes indeed, my brother, you are absolutely correct. Experts on the readings of the Qur'anic text are unanimous in their rejection of the idea of concluding the sentence after the words 'steeped in learning' and leaving out the rest, just as they are with other similar phrases from the text, such as 'woe to those who pray,' or 'do not approach the prayer.' In the eminent scholar Ibn Hazm's work that you have just mentioned, he had specifically referred to this grievous error some time earlier, in showing that it is crucial for seekers of the truth to follow the rules of grammar. He invoked the terrible tale that tells how a caliph wrote to one of his provincial governors with the following command: 'Count the number of transvestites in your community, using the verb *to count [ahsā]*.' Unfortunately the governor read the word wrongly, as *castrate [akhsā]*, and proceeded to castrate all the transvestites he came across. God alone possesses the power and glory . . ."

"Master," Abu al-Hasan now asked, "did not the great scholar Ibn Sina [Avicenna] express his utter aggravation at the dominance of Aristotelianism and the way it held sway over Muslim peripatetics . . ? Did he not say on the subject that 'throughout his career he has been devoted to what is past, not allowing himself any respite in which to revise his own thinking? Were he to do so, would he not come to realize that what the ancients have to say needs to be placed in a context that demands further investigation, or even reformulation and correction?'"

"Yes indeed, you're right. That particular sentence occurs in the introduction to his work *Logic of the Orientals.* For a while I was really thrilled and excited by it, believing, as I did, that our author's attachment to Plato would serve as the prelude to an entirely new and productive direction! But, like lightning that brings no rain, such feelings soon collapsed and vanished once I had actually perused the book with the attention it warranted. It was then that I became aware of the slavish way in which it replicates Aristotle; the same thing applies to the *Book of Cures,* where you will find Ibn Sina going so far as to adopt an assertion that the Greek philosopher had espoused fourteen centuries earlier in his *Politics,* namely that there exist people who are naturally and necessarily born to be slaves—from such notions we seek refuge in God, who liberates and honors mankind and creates them as people who can speak from a single soul; and we equally seek refuge in the chosen Prophet of God, his recorded practice, and the constitution as outlined in his sermon during the Farewell Pilgrimage."

At this point my companion surprised me by citing appropriate verses from the Qur'an, which he first recited in a melodious voice, then chanted, "O people, your Lord is one and your Father is one. All of you belong to Adam, and Adam is of dust. The noblest among you in God's eyes is the most pious. Arab has no superiority over non-Arab, nor white over black; it is only piety that counts." He then proceeded to chant the words of the caliph 'Umar, known as "the Arbiter": "When you enslave people whose mothers have given birth to them as free people"; and from 'Ali—may God ennoble his visage!: "People are of two kinds: your brother in faith or your peer in creation; never be the slave of someone else, for God has made you free."

The students all cheered and clapped. I too expressed my appreciation of the excellent way he had responded to my comments.

"Yes indeed, Abu al-Hasan," I said, "as the sayings put it, 'People are as alike as the teeth on a comb' and 'Women are the sisters of men.' That is precisely what the noble Prophet, indeed the Seal of the Prophets, declared. So in that spirit let us grant Ibn Sina a pardon for his posture in this regard, not to mention his excessive fondness for the pleasures of wine and diversion till he was struck down by colic, at which point his own medical knowledge was of no use and he died. We may perhaps seek some compensation for all this in the theological treatises he left us, by which I refer specifically to *Instructions and Indications*. 'God's for-giveness is broad,' and with Him is mercy."

My companion indicated that he endorsed my opinion and was eager for our discussion to continue, as though sleep had no dominion over him.

"Master," he went on, "I understand that Ibn Sina with his eastern wisdom provided us with a tendentious example to follow. In your view, does Al-Farabi provide us with the means to extricate ourselves from the dilemma and find a way forward?"

"Yes indeed, you can say that he set the way forward, and that's enough. From my perspective, in the Islamic context Abu Nasr al-Farabi is the peerless champion of all the philosophers. Even he may slip up when it comes to discus-sions of the material mind, the talking soul, and the fact that souls may remain in existence after the death of their bodies. The thing that I admire most about his career is that he devoted himself to contemplation and reflection and studiously avoided the attractions of courts and high places. Even there I have to admit that, for reasons known to God alone, he spent his latter days at the court of Sayf al-Dawla,* the Hamdanid ruler of Aleppo."

"As a consequence, master," Abu al-Hasan commented, "the only recourse we have in our quest for the higher regions is mysticism and the Sufi path."

"No, my brother," I replied, "not so. I have consistently refused to permit myself to conveniently gloss over the mistakes of the peripatetics, thereby for the most part disagreeing with Ibn Sina. I have adopted the selfsame policy and with even greater determination when it comes to people involved in theology and disputation. What is more, I have not excused jurists from my condemna-tions. For the most part they are pedants, only interested in details and ancil-lary matters. They weigh up today's events on the basis of yesterday, stunt Islam within the confines of the existent world, and deprive it of the benefits of inde-pendent thought and open-mindedness. In all this I have not been interested in placing the spotlight on Sufism or confining myself to such matters alone. After all, it is fine for Sufis to distance themselves from any process that involves the division of existence per se into logical attributes and postulates and the adop-tion of a whole variety of forms and statements in dealing with it. It is equally fine for them to devote their best efforts to religious exercises and initiatives as part of a quest for the Almighty and nothing else. All that said, my dear brother, I invite you to join me now in a search for something beyond basic Sufi practice—may the Almighty Judge never lower your status! Join me as we initiate a journey toward real inquiry and ultimate proximity. So come with me on a journey toward what is supremely beautiful and enduring, and you will truly gain the blessing of the One toward whom all ascents and heights aspire, namely God alone. 'The leaders, the leaders, they are closest to God.' This is the genuine choice and the genuine path."

Al-Shushtari's voice now rang out in Qur'anic chant. The students followed my lead, as with one emotion-charged voice we all whispered in utter humility, "'If he is one of those closest to God, then there will be for him rest, satisfaction, and a garden of delights'" [Surat Al-Waqi'ah (56), v. 89].

I chose this Qur'anic verse to bring the session to a close and told them all to go and get some sleep. We all stood up, and the students asked to come and see me again next day at noon. With a promise to let them do so, I said farewell to them one by one. With my host, al-Shushtari, I prayed the obligatory prayers; then we bade each other farewell. I now spent some time on my own so that I could cleanse myself and get some rest.

5

NEXT DAY AT NOON I met the students who had come the day before, and there were some additional ones as well. There was no sign of Abu al-Hasan either inside the house or among their number. I presumed that he had gone to do his own work and continue with his laudable activities. With the students I made my way up to his retreat house. Under some leafy trees I created a venue where we could all sit. I was eager to assess their intentions and get some idea about their abilities. With that in mind, I began by pronouncing the "In the name of God" and blessing the Prophet before proceeding as follows:

"Young men, the greatest boon to be gleaned from a contemplation of nature is that of being in touch with its Creator. There can be no exaggeration with regard to the constituent of one fundamental, nor any negligence regarding another. By way of illustration, no intellect will flourish unless it functions within the framework of human sentiment, nor can that same instinct blossom unless it is weighed on the scales of human intelligence. Straight lines and circles all lead upward toward each other. Nothing else exists apart from the Necessary Existent; no true reality can be embraced or have any validity unless it is through that existent and in it. How many forms of knowledge that fail to replicate the unity of the all-existing proceed to abandon us by the roadside, short of breath and with little nourishment, unsupported by any genuine inquiry and creativity! Albeit to a different degree, the knowledge-base of jurists, theologians, the majority of peripatetic philosophers, and others is of the same ilk. That is why I have promised myself that, when it comes to ideas and politics, I will never allow myself to be polluted by the actions of those who would create divides and fissures, people who prefer to submit to the forces of mere compliance and submission. In the same way I've decided, and to a degree even more intensely than previously, to devote my precious time to those figures, both past and present, who address themselves to the recesses of our consciousness and existence and who enhance their aspirations and imaginative instincts through wonderful, uplifting emotions and feelings and by proposing penetrating and insightful questions and ideas. In that way the passage of time will be able to scrape away all the leaden monotony of such static attitudes, so they can re-emerge fully alive, poised and ready to provide enlightenment on the broadest scale."

All of a sudden I stopped talking, and the students likewise stopped taking it all down. I waited for a few moments, assuming that they would ask me some questions and that would give me some idea about the extent to which they were responding and understanding. I would have convinced myself that I was shouting in the desert and beating a drum under water, had not a beardless youth stood up and asked to address a question to me.

"Master," he asked, "do you include poets in the group of people, dead and alive, about whom you have been talking?"

"Only as individuals," I replied, "and in accordance with their talent and reputation. Like all other groups, poets fit into different groups and classes rather than belonging to a single class or school of thought. People are classified by their actions and what they leave behind. Those are the only criteria that can serve as testimony either for or against them. That is God's law when it comes to His creation, and you'll never find any substitute for it."

The young man was silent for a moment, but then he started reciting a number of lines of poetry from the poetic heritage of the Arabs; the majority were by Ibn al-Mu'tazz.* I was amazed at his ability to memorize so much and to recall things with such conviction. I asked him why he was so fond of memorizing poetry, and he responded that he wished to become a poet himself. I then asked him why he liked Ibn al-Mu'tazz's poetry so much, and he told me it was because of the gentle quality of his verse and its accessibility. I complimented him on his craft and encouraged him to continue with his quest.

The other students were following this conversation between myself and their colleague who had memorized so much poetry with considerable interest.

"In olden times," I told them all, "a minor poet was someone who had memorized two thousand lines of poetry, while a real poet was supposed to have memorized much more than that. Major poets would have memorized the entire corpus of Arabic poetry. But you have to realize that mere memorization by itself is pointless and fruitless. In his poetry the poet has to be able to use his verses to enhance both intellect and feeling, at the same time giving the listener a good deal of pleasure and imbuing his best verses with his inner feelings and attitudes to life. He will then be able to endow the essence of his verse with qualities that will help avoid the kind of harmful frivolity that only manages to see everything the same way and destroy it. The quotation that you cited is actually borrowed from Abu Hayyan al-Tawhidi (may God perfume his memory!): 'The best discourse is that whose phraseology is delicate, whose imagery is refined, and whose beauty glistens. In the context of poetry it should seem like prose; in that of prose, it should seem like poetry.'"

Another student asked to speak, and I was delighted to allow him to do so.

"Master," he said, "I'm sure you are the kind of person who wants to see a question thoroughly explored. I have sat here listening as this student, Muhammad al-Zayyani, has recited some of Ibn al-Mu'tazz's verses about nature and similar topics. But he hasn't included even a single verse of the poet's obscene poetry! What do you have to say about such poetry and its author?"

"I assume," I replied by way of teasing my interlocutor, "that you have studied such poetry and the life of its author carefully?"

"No, Sir," he said, "I can't possibly do that. As we say in Bijaya, 'You can tell what kind of house it is by the doorway.'"

"But you should understand that a text has to be understood before you can pass judgment on it; that's a generally applicable principle. In any case, it's quite acceptable to utter a prayer for forgiveness. Now one thing that you all should know from the outset is that our poet, who was called 'prince of day and night,' was murdered by his servant, Mu'nis, and his colleagues who were palace pages. I will not conceal from any of you that, when I was young, I spent a lot of time reading Ibn al-Mu'tazz's poetry, which is highly accessible and an interesting blend of ancient and modern. That was one way in which I was able to enhance my own linguistic abilities. As I perused one poem after another, it became clear to me that this poet had made the most of his personal observation and indeed his own trials and tribulations until the Abbasid caliphate went into a decline, which would inevitably lead to a dire conclusion—one of the features of which became fairly obvious to him in not only the murder of his grandfather, al-Mutawakkil, and the deposition of his own father, al-Mu'tazz, but also in the increasing domination of the Turkish soldiery and their slaves. This poet-caliph, Ibn al-Mu'tazz, clearly did not like what he was seeing, and so early in life he decided to conduct himself in a way that ruined his possibilities as a political force and created an unbreachable chasm between himself and his right to the caliphal succession. The method he employed in order to register the clearest possible proof of his lack of leadership ability and political acumen was a truly debauched kind of Epicureanism and an ongoing quest for pleasures, both public and private. That applied to his conduct not merely in daily life, but also in his literary interests, in that he studied the poetry of his era in his book *Tabaqat al-shu'ara'* [The Classes of Poets], and also wrote *Al-Jami' fi al-ghina' li-adab al-khamr wa-al-sharab* [The Comprehensive Study of Lyrical Poetry on Wine and Drinking]. It was almost as though the poet had decided to divert his attention away from the constant threat of death all around him by indulging in every conceivable kind of excessively debauched escapade. Then there is the quotation attributed to him: 'If I am inevitably going to be killed, then let it happen when I am sitting amongst beauteous singing-girls and things that I relish.' In fact, his murder was of the most violent and atrocious kind: it was said that his testicles were crushed or that he was castrated—it really makes no difference. On the Day of Reckoning, Ibn al-Mu'tazz may well be asked about his life. I can imagine him replying, 'I'm no hero; I was forced.' Put another way, it was a matter of compulsion, not choice. Even though I may not have been happy about the way I behaved, I would still be unwilling to allow myself to take the place of the One who alone can pass judgment—He who is both Forgiving and Merciful. I would make do with uttering a prayer that Ibn al-Mu'tazz might receive his due share of pardon and forgiveness, like Abu Nuwas,* Ibn Sina,* 'Umar al-Khayyam,* and other sinners and reprobates. As God himself states in the Sura of Woman [Sura 4], 'God does not forgive those who associate anything with Him. But He will forgive anyone whom He wishes for offenses other than that.'"

I could not help thinking about the other things that Ibn al-Mu'tazz had said that I had omitted from my statement to the students: "I only composed poetry on the side; I never touched the daughter of the grape; I only consorted with women during my reckless youth when I spoke of passion—all that without any degree of exaggeration or addiction."

At this point a third student asked me for my opinion of Al-Shushtari's poetry.

"As you well know," I said, "our beloved companion Abu al-Hasan's poetry consists of some poems in colloquial dialect, and others in standard written Arabic. Neither language nor meter is complex, and they flow nicely. They stand liberated from the dictates of the rules of Sibawayh's* and Al-Khalil's* systems, and that allows them to seem both smooth and more pleasing. The imagery that he uses in his compositions is transparent and lucid in its effect and shows an excellent technique and accomplishment. The creative and attractive method that he adopts, the discourse shaped by circumstance and hard work, the unique ability to combine both aspiration toward the exalted beyond and a practical anchoredness in the world of mankind, all these qualities make me feel at one with the poetry since it responds to a natural urge within me and thus has a very positive impact. That feeling is even intensified when Abu al-Hasan invokes instinct and surmise to depict things that I find myself needing to formulate through prolonged examination and creative thought, namely the absolute oneness of existence and the process whereby the created entity rises to greater heights through a quest for perfection and a closeness to the Creator, who is no other than God Himself. How can I stop my entire inner self from catching fire and being inspired when I read lines from a zajal like these in Andalusian dialect:

> *Leave chance aside, strip away the ephemeral, and proceed to withdraw.*
> *Cut off all connections, and you will put on the garments of revelation.*
> *Aim for the Absolute Existent, and you will achieve revelation."*

At this point some of the students joined with me in the recitation:

> *You ply the fever-heat of secrets with sapless wine.*
> *And light shines on you; all diction is clear.*
> *Appreciate the arts; through synthesis aspire to escape to the heights,*
> *But then through analysis descend to your own self; for that is to be*
> *your limit.*

A voice was now raised—I could not tell where it came from, and other voices were raised to support it:

"These illuminations from Al-Shushtari, the imam of the Absolutists, are all the result of the influence of Shu'ayb Abu Madyan, the great Sufi leader, his blessings and generous gifts. Abu al-Hasan and all of us are disciples of that holy man. It is to him that we owe our Sufi allegiances. We still cling to the phrase that he constantly repeated until his dying moment: 'God is the Truth.' We all aspire to the paradise of Eden with all its blessings, the very thing that our revered shaykh promised us."

Suppressing my anger, I stood up and addressed the assembled company:

"Young men," I said, "I happen to know about this pious holy man from the previous century. In his asceticism and devotion to God's unity, he certainly achieved some wonderful things, but the differences of opinion that exist about him are the consequences of transmitters of accounts and former disciples of his. There are some wonderful tales about him, including the one about the gazelle that sought refuge with him and stayed in his cave in the desert near Fez. And there are others as well, but it's not clear if they are authentic. They were almost certainly fabricated by recorders and followers. But, whatever the case may be, no human being, no matter how sage and pious he may be, may promise a human being entry to paradise, nor may he guarantee anyone a place there. In that context, Al-Hasan al-Basri* went too far in his invocation of God's own words in the Qur'an: 'O My servants, enter paradise through My mercy and apportion it according to your deeds.' No, no! To God alone belong the keys to paradise and access to the next world. To Him alone belongs what is in the heavens and the earth; He alone is to be worshipped, and it is toward His noble and splendid aspect that humans are to strive. If it is paradise that you are after, then by all means make your way to the person who is buried in the mausoleum in Al-'Ubbad (in Spain). If on the other hand you aspire to the Lord of paradise, then come to me and to the absolute oneness of existence. You can use the phrase 'God is the Truth' provided that you are well aware of the meaning and implications of the phrase. 'God alone' is an alternative phrase that sits lightly on the tongue, yet weighs heavily in the scales of significance. Use it as a defense against noxious distortions and proclaim it in the face of every tyrant and every person who would try to provoke sectarian divisions. No other phrase can be more precious and effective during this era of petty kingdoms when our beloved Andalus is being torn apart by violent strife. Understand clearly what I am saying; if you do not, then the fault is yours. Those who warn others have their excuse."

Among the students some faces looked glum, while others were smiling. I made my way through the company in order to leave. Some of them followed me; they said nothing and were obviously thinking about what I had said. When we reached Abu al-Hasan's door, I suggested that they regard reading as an act of worship and thus to give it its due. I then said farewell to them one by one.

6

ONCE I GOT BACK TO MY ABODE, I spent some time thinking about the need to continue my journey and prepare my belongings. I was not willing to leave Bijaya under compulsion, nor did I wish to upset my distinguished host. However, Tunis was my next stop, followed by Egypt and Mecca the Venerable. In fact, Mecca was the place toward which I prayed and the direction toward which my gaze was directed now and always.

While I awaited Abu al-Hasan's return, I checked on my horse, who was obviously very pleased to see me, as was my host's dog. I gave them both something to eat and drink, and then checked on the cats and chickens and spent a bit of time with them as well. Turning to the garden, I watered the plants and picked such vegetables as were ripe and within reach.

While I was eating and collecting my belongings together, I heard the rustle of footsteps in Abu al-Hasan's room. I called out to him, and he came over at once. As he greeted me, he expressed the hope that he had not disturbed me in any way. I invited him to join me, and he did so. I was intending to tell him that I needed to move on from Bijaya either the next day or the day after. Instead he anticipated me by mentioning the Abu Madyan students who had attended my yesterday's session in the house as well as the second one up in the mountain retreat earlier that day. They had told him in the most fervid and eloquent terms that they were strongly attached to me. They had in fact asked him whether it was possible to be disciples of two shaykhs, one of whom had died some time ago—namely Abu Madyan, and the other who was still alive and functioning, namely the Pinnacle of the Faith, 'Abd al-Haqq Ibn Sab'in.

I realized that Abu al-Hasan had been informed about the way in which I had instructed the students to choose between the holy man of Tilimsan and myself.

"Abu al-Hasan," I told him, "the invitation I issued to the students up there in the mountains seems to me to be the same one I've been offering to you, albeit in a dream . . ."

"Yes indeed, you magnet of souls!" he interrupted me in sheer delight, "I have seen you in both my dreams and my waking hours, making me choose between paradise on the one hand and the Lord of paradise on the other. Now, and at a time more than at any previous one, I am proceeding in the direction of the absolute oneness of existence and the One and Eternal Lord. In that you are my companion and my guide."

We were both overcome, and not a word was spoken for a while. I noticed that this holy man who was undertaking so many praiseworthy activities was weeping copious tears. I asked him why.

"I am weeping," he replied, "because all around me I see so many people sound asleep and so few dreamers. I'm weeping because they're all huddled together in the dark like drug addicts, not experiencing the bright lights of the Prophet Muhammad (peace be upon him!) nor those of my Lord, the imam of the negators and the complete unity of existence. I weep too because I have not been able to fully comprehend some of the materials in *Escape of the Gnostic* and have thus been incapable of explaining it to the students."

As I responded to his comment, his tears came close to affecting me as well.

"Imam of the Absolutists," I said, "You can do things with people that I am unable to do. You arouse their consciences to the maximum extent possible and bring charity and good works into their midst. When it comes to obscurities in what I write, the blame can be laid equally on the era of severe decline in which we all find ourselves and on me personally. If the things that I have encountered in my travels had not caused my pen to dry up, I'd certainly have composed something else as a way of justifying what I've already done and lightening the reader's load by offering useful clarifications and revelatory illustrations."

"My dear Sir," he replied, "my own pen and paper are at your beck and call."

After a moment's pause for thought, I started to dictate:

"Abu al-Hasan," I said, "whenever I've written anything, I've always tried to be as concise and terse as possible. The reason is that I've always had an urgent sense of a shortage of time, something that has been part of my makeup since I was young. It has made me feel as though I'm under constraint, working as best I can to rescue crucial items of property that are in imminent danger of loss and destruction. Could those crucial items actually be a figurative way of talking about our beloved Andalus whose very pillars are in the process of collapsing, leading to a slow but inevitable fall? That at least may well be the most likely explanation and the one that deserves the closest attention. For that reason, no one should wonder at the frequency with which the phrase, 'For fear of prolixity,' occurs in all of my writings. The only justification I can offer is, as I've already suggested, my constant worry about the way in which collective time seems to be so restricted and claustrophobic. As a result, anyone with the requisite knowledge, insight, and understanding should not feel the need to indulge in excessive criticism of my dense and terse statements."

I paused for a moment, both to recover my breath and to allow my scribe to catch up.

"Among recent citizens of Andalus," I went on, "I'm not the only one to have had this insistent feeling. During a short sojourn in Cordoba, I happened to be visiting the bookstore of a Jewish merchant from the Tayyibun family and came across *The Summary of the Almagest*. I noticed precisely the same feeling in the author's, Ibn Rushd's, attitude, as if a fire had broken out in his house. That required him to provide a much-needed and useful summary, in terms of mode of composition, collecting a lot of information and then providing a précis. Even when dealing with the Burhaniyya, he eventually resorted to the same sifting process, subjecting the materials to severe editing and abbreviation—a sieve with very narrow apertures indeed. In making this comparison, I'm trying to allude to the possibility that, during Abu Walid ibn Rushd's time in Andalus—something he mentions only rarely—he may have sensed that he was experiencing within himself the crises and degradations of his own age, as he witnessed the gradual fading of the glorious times of the past and the end of an era. As evidence, we can point to his terse allusions to 'anxieties' and 'troubled times,' not to mention his unfulfilled promise (in spite of his long life) to write about this or that topic 'in much more detail.' He would regularly use the following expression: 'If God gives me sufficient time and I can rid myself of this lack of time.' In my own case, I'm not promising to write a more comprehensive or detailed work, something that I won't be able to do however long my life may be. The feeling that stays with me and that I've no power to overcome is best expressed in the prophetic *hadith*, 'Pens have dried up, and pages have been closed.'"

I stopped talking abruptly; it was as if my tongue had dried up as well. I signaled to Abu al-Hasan to stop taking notes, and he did so. I saw that he was looking in dismay at my packed-up belongings.

"What does this pile of baggage mean, my master?" he asked.

"My dear, generous friend," I responded, "the expectations of hospitality have long since been met and surpassed. Now it's time for me to move on."

"In this house there are no hosts or guests. When I'm not here, it's available for passers-by and people who have nowhere else to stay. However, if you've decided to move on, I'll certainly not stop you. I've always enjoyed travel myself. Fairly soon I plan to go to Fez and Meknes. And if you will permit me, I'll also go up to Sabta and Tangier and get some news about your family and loved ones. All being well, I'll bring you news of them all in Cairo."

I was so moved and delighted that I embraced him and kissed his head.

"I don't need to give you permission," I said. "In fact, I have a specific request. I'll not leave Cairo for Mecca until I feel sure that my family is safe and that I'll be able to return to them once I've performed the pilgrimage."

"With God's help your wishes will be fulfilled. I have to leave now to perform at a reception, and then again at a Sufi ceremony. Tomorrow morning, my beloved friend, give me whatever instructions you wish."

With that he said his farewells and left. I turned toward the qibla and devoted myself to prayers and supplications. That done, I finished packing my belongings, then lay down to get some rest. While I was dozing, I heard the guard dog barking. It stopped all of a sudden, and there was a scary silence. From the stable I heard a strange, troubling neighing from my horse. My nerves on edge and my thoughts racing, I rushed to the place where the noise was coming from. I spotted a shadowy figure hurrying away like lightning. Instead of running the risk of chasing after him, I decided instead to check on the animals. Thank God, the horse was fine, and I hurriedly brought him into my room, fondling his head as I did so; he seemed much more relaxed now. That done, I went to check on the dog outside the house; unfortunately what I found was its lifeless corpse lying at the base of the mountain. I dug a hole and buried it as quickly as possible so that I could go back to my room and take all necessary precautions. In case of emergency I kept a thick stick by my side. I assumed that the person who had killed the dog either intended to steal my horse or else had been sent by someone else to scare me into leaving town as soon as possible. I spent the rest of the night wide awake, part of it packing my bags and putting them on my pack animal, but also performing ablutions, changing clothes, and praying.

At daybreak Abu al-Hasan arrived looking delighted and fully alert.

"I can see that, like me, you haven't slept much!" he said as he embraced me and offered me a table full of milk and loaves of bread. "I hope, my Lord, that everything is fine."

I gave him a brief account of what had happened the night before. He did not panic or seem in the least surprised, almost as though he was used to such things or regarded the entire episode as something without particular significance or meaning. After having something to eat and drink, I stood up and told him of my intention to travel to Tunis by sea. I asked Abu al-Hasan if there was enough time to go and say farewell to his friend the copyist, and to visit a charitable house in Bijaya. He indicated that it was possible. We set out to visit these people, with my companion leading my horse behind him. When we reached the house, I asked for the warden, who arrived with warm greetings. I gave him two bags of gold pieces, asking him to spend them for the benefit of orphans. The man took them with a good deal of astonishment and proceeded to offer profuse thanks, while Al-Shushtari himself sang my praises. We left the charity pursued by a positive flood of fervent prayers from the warden, then made our way to the copyist's place. No sooner had we arrived than he greeted us warmly. My companion told him that I was coming to say farewell, and he wished me well on my travels. He entreated me to take two baskets of dried fruit, which he proceeded to pack in my saddlebags. I in turn placed a bag in his hand.

"One good deed begets another," I told him, "but it is the initiator who is the most generous. This is a gift from me. Perhaps you'll be able to use it for your own needs and those of your family."

"But make sure, Hamada," my companion added by way of a joke, "that you stock your shelves with beneficial knowledge and cut down on the amount of dates, beans, and lentils that you eat!"

The man looked at the contents of the purse and was obviously both stunned and delighted. As I said farewell and embraced him, he proceeded to raise his hands to the heavens, uttering prayers on my behalf and almost choking with tears. "May God be generous to you, Sir," he said, "grant you victory over those who oppose you, and preserve you for the ones you love and care for. God . . ."

We made our way through a market teeming with people and animals. Vendors and passers-by all begged my companion to chant one of his poems for them. Over and over again he had to say, "Leave me alone, leave me alone. I'm currently saying my farewells to someone who has claimed a predominant place in my heart!"

Once we reached the port, we discovered that the boat was ready to leave. All I had time to do was to add further to the tasks I had already asked Abu al-Hasan to perform in Sabta. I requested that he inquire as to the conditions of people in Andalus; the governor, Ibn Khalas; and the warden, 'Abd al-Barr al-Baradi'i. I also asked him to seek information about my students in Granada through their friends in Sabta. I handed him a letter addressed to them, a second one to the Sabta students themselves, and a third to my wife. I hugged him and whispered in his ear, "Beloved friend, no bond can be stronger than ours. We'll meet again at the Azhar Mosque in Cairo in four or five months."

His eyes welling with tears, he indicated that we would indeed be meeting again. At this point the captain yelled that it was time for me to get on board. Praying that my dear friend would be well, I said farewell and headed for a wooden cabin on the deck where I would be able to rest and relax. As the ship set sail, a sailor came over and collected the fare for the journey and a similar sum for taking care of my safety, tending my horse, and ferrying me in private quarters.

7

I SPENT THE ENTIRE VOYAGE tossing and turning, half awake and half asleep; night or day, calm or stormy seas, noisy passengers or complete silence—none of it made any difference. In my mind images and visions were all clashing against one another; all that remained were pictures of my beloved wife and close friends, chief among whom was Al-Shushtari, Imam of the Absolutists.

I have no idea how long the voyage lasted, but at one point the captain came over to tell me that we were reaching port. He also informed me that pirates had stopped the vessel and stolen most of the animals and property on board, my horse and belongings among them. When I looked surprised and alarmed, he made me realize that, like all the other passengers, I should praise God for saving me from a gruesome end and almost certain enslavement. I clutched at my money-belt and was delighted to find that it was still there. With that I disembarked. The angry and fearful expressions on the faces of the other passengers confirmed the captain's story. I was left to wonder at my own amazing ability to distract myself and disappear into other worlds.

I made my way on foot to the closest hotel in the city. As I approached the entrance, two men came up to me and asked me to accompany them to the house of Al-A'ma from Sicily. I had no choice but to go with them, particularly since I was eager to get some up-to-date news on events to the west. After a short walk I found myself facing my host, who was looking glum as he offered me a phony welcome. I sat down with him at a table full of eats and drinks and opened the conversation by asking him about Sabta, Ibn Khalas, and my family.

"Saint of God," he replied with a frown as he urged me to eat something, "things in Sabta are really bad. After we both left, there was a severe famine that killed off lots of humans and cattle. It had been preceded by a prolonged drought that had already led to a number of disturbances and two deaths. The news about Ibn Khalas is equally bad. He found himself beset by a number of intrigues masterminded by Abu al-Qasim al-'Azmi, all with the encouragement of Amir al-Murtada, 'Ali al-Sa'id's successor. The famine deprived him of all authority over the city, so he fled along with his family. God knows best, but people said that they had no idea where he went. In my opinion he probably took a boat here so he could seek the protection of the great [Hafsid] sultan Abu Zakariyya."

I interrupted his account to ask about my own family. His expression changed, and he looked a bit happier.

"Master," he went on, "your wife's fine. She's staying with her family in Tangier. Her only wish is to see your beloved visage once again. But you'll not be able to go back home until you have completed the pilgrimage, or rather until the rage of the new governor of Sabta has abated somewhat and the tribulations of Ibn Khalas's supporters come to an end. Both you and I are considered as being among the major escapees. So, Ibn Sab'in, be very, very careful! It would be absolutely fatal for you to consider returning to the Maghrib until the collapsing dynasty of the Almohads comes to its final end!"

From my facial expression it was not hard for him to deduce that I was both anxious and perplexed.

"For the next three days or so," he said, "you should stay here and not go out. After the tiring voyage you have just had, you can relax and get some rest. If you wish, you can go to the quarter's mosque, but only if you agree not to talk to the worshippers, give any lessons, or start any debates. The jurist al-Sukuni has his eyes firmly fixed on both you and me. If you do anything contrary to what I've just told you, I'm the one who'll be punished for it. Ever since I arrived in Tunis, this jurist has made it clear to me that a condition for his facilitating an audience with the sultan for me is that you should leave the city as soon as possible."

I realized that there was no point in arguing and indicated my agreement to the terms he had laid out. I now asked to spend some time on my own and was assigned a room. It was almost sunset, so I said my farewells, made for the room, and locked the door behind me. I did my ablutions so I could pray and bolster my sagging spirits.

Staying with my good friend Al-Shushtari had been both a boon and a source of relaxation, but this time spent with Al-A'ma from Sicily was anything but; I felt alarmed and scared. This man was a past master when it came to political intrigues and conspiracies; he could easily turn me in and cause my downfall. Not only that, but he could steal my money and spirit, all in return for a bit of favoritism that he might be able to glean from people who were eager to ensnare me and have my head. Indeed, the very next morning at breakfast, my host intimated to me that he had lost his eyesight when a saint of God who had been one of his enemies had called down a curse on him. If it were not for the fact that he was scared in case a similar disaster should befall him, he would certainly have stolen my money and handed me over to the most vicious of my enemies. I refrained from offering him my thanks so that he would not realize that I was actually poking fun at him. At the same time I decided not to tell him that I wanted to meet the Hafsid sultan. That was especially the case after he told me the following:

"The sultan rarely meets people who come to see him. That even applies to people like myself who have served him well and done their utmost to obey him and satisfy his interests. People say that it's because he's ill, or else there's another explanation known to God alone."

I told him that I had made up my mind to leave at dawn.

"That's a good idea, Saint of God," he said with a smile. "To make up for the things you've had stolen, I'll sell you my horse and other things you need. You can take a boat to Alexandria at dawn tomorrow. That's safest for both of us."

There was still enough of the day left to go to the *hammam* and wash myself. After that I headed for a nearby mosque to pray. But no sooner had I performed my obligations and made ready to leave than two men came up to me. They took turns slapping me on the face. "You heretic," they said, "you refuse to allow polygamy; you forbid cutting off thieves' hands and stoning male and female adulterers! You permit usury and other things forbidden by God! May the Almighty Judge curse your heterodoxy!"

I decided that it would be wise to restrict my reaction to giving these two provocateurs an angry stare and to leave the mosque with a straight back and firm resolve. After I had made a rapid tour of the city and undertaken certain specific tasks, I made my way back to the house. Once there I allowed my mind to wander and to contemplate a number of things, not least the huge chasm separating the current era with all its negative aspects from the ideal model. The possibility of a meeting with the Hafsid sultan, which I had envisioned as a means of helping the cause of Andalus in its current crisis, had now turned out to be a pipe dream, in fact the fourth in the category of sheer impossibilities. Any hope that I had had of spreading beneficial knowledge among students and ordinary people had now gone up in smoke as well. The only way I could find of surmounting the waves of constraint and sorrow was by reciting Qur'anic verses and prophetic hadith that can always give one a lift and provide nourishment. To these recitations I added some section from the *Book of Stations* [*Kitab al-Mawaqif*] of Al-Niffari and verses by my beloved friend Al-Shushtari.

Next morning Al-A'ma from Sicily accompanied me to the Tunis port. In return for a purse of gold, he gave me a horse laden with goods and cash, then entrusted me and my animal to one of the sailors. He bade me a fond farewell, but did not leave the dock until the boat that was transporting me to Alexandria was plowing its way through the waves.

8

DURING THE TRIP TO ALEXANDRIA I paid close attention to my surroundings; the calm seas and the sight of the wind-filled sails augured well. I made a point of spending time with my new horse so it could get to know me better. I also spent some time conversing with the other passengers and discovered that most of them were traveling from Andalus and the Maghrib, either to perform the pilgrimage, to engage in business, or else to look for somewhere to settle and earn a living.

In Alexandria I spent a couple of nights in a hotel so I could recover from the voyage and make preparations to go down to Cairo in a caravan that was leaving at dawn on my second day in Egypt. The journey went very smoothly, and the atmosphere on the way and at the stops was very pleasant and conducive. Seeing that the rest of the trip would be free of any dangers, I decided to do the rest of it on my horse so that I could get to Cairo as soon as possible and arrange my affairs there.

It was in the middle of the seventh century AH [thirteenth century CE] that I settled in Cairo. Sultan Thawran ibn Najm, one of the later Ayyubid rulers, was governing the country. His armed forces were busy preventing the rear guard of the Crusader army from occupying Damietta and the Syrian coastal region. In the city center, close by the Azhar Mosque,* I asked after Shaykh Abu al-Naja al-Nuʿman. Some merchants directed me to his house. When I knocked on the door, a voice shouted to come in. I crossed the threshold, tethered my horse in the yard, and headed for the place from which the voice had come. I found myself face to face with a man in Sufi garb who showed me to my room and welcomed me as a friend who was coming in the name of Abu al-Hasan al-Shushtari. That task completed, he disappeared.

The room contained a sufficient quantity of basic necessities. In the corner was a place to wash and a pitcher full of water. I took my belongings over there and did my ablutions before praying. I then had something to eat and lay down to recuperate from the exertions of the trip to Cairo. I must assume that I fell asleep almost immediately because I did not wake up again till a full two days after my arrival. While asleep I was beset by a number of scary dreams, but the only one I can remember came in three separate parts. The first revealed to me an enormous woman dressed in black, but that was all there was to see. With a brutally direct gesture she forced me to stand up and proceeded to berate me in an utterly boorish fashion:

"Hey you," the vision said, "you've assaulted me and done me wrong. I hereby command you to take your spike out of my flesh. If not, I intend to accuse you in court of destroying my honor and well-being."

"You're going to raise a case against me, lady?"

"Yes, I am. I'm going to drag you to court so I can have my revenge."

In my dream, how I regretted the fact that I wheedled my way out of this confrontation with such a provocative woman! I faced her down and delivered a haughty challenge to her threats: "Go ahead, woman, go right ahead, take me to court then!"

It would have been so much better if I had chosen instead to use a calmer manner and discussed with her exactly what might have been these supposed relationships between my spike and her flesh. How much I regretted responding so aggressively! Ripping off her shawl and veil, I found myself facing Hafsa, the maid, or rather what was left of her: a wreck of a woman, bald, with no flesh, eyes, or teeth, a mere shadow of a human being, moving to an inevitable decline and disappearance into the void!

The second part of the dream involved Hafsa as well, with her decomposing body, but I was visiting her in the insane asylum. This time, I was speaking to her nicely, using the gentlest of phrases. Even so, she turned away in disgust and made do with heaping reproaches on me: "Do you see what you have done to me?" she said.

Part three of my dream involved Hafsa still further. This time it was on a boat, and the sailors were cutting her up limb by limb and throwing the pieces to the fish. When the only part of her left was her head, she stared at me with her teary, bloodshot eyes and once again exclaimed, "Do you see what you did to me?" With that the men on the boat started kicking and throwing the head around, but they ended up throwing it into the sea.

These horrible visions plagued me for three nights in a row. The only difference was that, when I woke up, I could not remember any details; all that remained was the sense of terror. The only way I found of stopping the whole thing was to turn the entire night into antimony.* If you want honey, I told myself, then there is no avoiding bee-stings. To stave off the bad effects of such nightmares, what was needed was obviously periods of contemplation and study, a certain amount of time spent recording details of my travels, or even going out and finding out as much as possible about the situation in Cairo and the way people there lived.

When I first decided to go out and look around, the squares and districts around the Azhar Mosque and the shrine of al-Husayn* were teeming with people of all shapes and sizes, each one of whom contributed in one way or another to the general clamor and hubbub. It only died down when the muezzin announced the call to prayer and the day moved toward its close.

For days and weeks I alternated between my residence (where I never set eyes on my host) and the outside world, where I frequented the mosque a great deal. In Fustat* I wandered around on foot, exploring the gardens, alleyways, and markets. In the Mu'izz* quarter of Cairo itself I visited the seven gates of the city on horseback, with their openings toward the River Nile and the Khalij Canal.* When I reached Salah al-din's walls, it made me stop and reminded me of his glorious deeds. I then turned aside to take a look at the shrine of Sayyida Nafisa,* the mosque of Ibn Tulun,* and the Elephant Lake.* I also went to look at the monuments from the Fatimid and Ayyubid periods. Surely the only permanence belongs to the Necessary Existent, the light of the heavens and the earth!

After I had been in Cairo for five whole months there came the day when I really longed to see Al-Shushtari. I started asking some of the students at the Azhar and nearby residences if they had seen him. But, even though they all recognized his name and description and sang his praises, I found no trace of him. It so happened that a group of students made my acquaintance and followed me to the revered mosque. There they performed the afternoon prayer with me, then started asking me questions about Andalus and the Maghrib. They begged me to arrange a class for them; I could choose the topic or respond to some of their interests and concerns. I had to agree to their request, so I sat them all down in an isolated corner and made ready to address them. But, no sooner had I uttered the phrase "In the name of God" and offered blessings to the Prophet than a man came over and informed me that he was the mosque overseer. Without a license from the relevant religious authorities, teaching in the mosque was forbidden. That said, he went back to his place at the back of the assembled group and stood there with his guards watching.

The whole situation bothered me a great deal, especially since I noticed that there was a good deal of unrest among the group. Here and there I spotted some suspicious gestures being exchanged.

"So," I said as I stood up and addressed the students, "we've been prevented from speaking in God's own house, but God's earth is spacious enough."

"Yes indeed," people who could hear me repeated, "God's earth is spacious and wide."

The entire group followed suit, and some of them cited the hadith "A scholar who gives people the benefit of his wisdom is better than a thousand servants."

As I left the mosque, I was surrounded by the crowd. I walked at their head, asking them to proceed quietly and without fuss, since I was anxious to avoid confrontations with the police. I was also keen to avoid both banks of the Nile River because that was where astrologers, gamblers, entertainers, shadow-players, and fortune-tellers hung out, and I certainly did not want to attract stray indigents and beggars. For that reason I led this large crowd to the graveyard at the base of the Muqattam Hills. First I made them all sit on a piece of bare, flat rock; then I proceeded to deal with issues connected with their daily life and work, along with others that concerned more intellectual and religious matters. Some of them had questions concerning law, theology, philosophy, and Sufism, and I did my best to answer them as simply as I could. I brought things to a close by telling them about my theory concerning the true path to investigation and a closer path to God, linked to the conditions of detachment and abstraction that I deemed necessary for that process. I concluded by responding to questions they had concerning the conflict against the Crusader invasion. I told them that the fight against these invaders was an absolute obligation on all those who were capable of fulfilling the function, excluding the destitute, aged, and sick.

As the sun was setting, I stood up to leave. In the students' expressions I could see the light of appreciation and understanding; their warm and fervent comments competed in singing my praises. I advised them to return to their normal lives. Some of them took the trouble to warn me about some of the jurists and instructors at the Azhar. They told me that they had heard such people speaking in angry, condemnatory tones about me. "This man from Spain," they provided as an example, "has come to Egypt to corrupt our youth, just as he has done in the past in Murcia, Sabta, and Bijaya"; or, "this pseudo-philosopher is trying to put genuine and pious religious scholars out of a job by turning people against them. He must be stopped in his tracks." Having provided me with these details, they all said their farewells and ran to catch up with their comrades.

One old man, however, stayed behind and introduced himself as the keeper of the graveyard. He told me that he had much appreciated what I had to say, even though he did not understand all of it. He now invited me to spend the night in his house amid the graves of worthy believers. After a moment's hesitation I accepted his offer and followed him. I found myself in a large tomb lit by candles placed on tombstones; the walls were covered with cloths and rugs. He proceeded to tell me about some of the people who were buried there, one by one, all of them saints and holy men, although I had not heard of any of them. He offered me a piece of bread and some dates. He told me that he had things to do, and went on to say that I should not worry if a few vagrants came in to share my abode for the night. He then told me we would meet next morning, Friday, that being—as he informed me—the day for visits to tombs and charitable donations.

I sat on the floor, doing my best to control my anxieties about both the dead people inside the tomb and the living vagrants who would inevitably be arriving. If the latter group got a mere whiff of the gold I had on me, they would undoubtedly steal it and maybe kill me in the process. For their part, the dead would be rolling in their graves, furious at me for carrying so much money with me in their presence and keeping it hidden.

Prayer is the great antidote to such worries and tribulations!

I spent the first half of the night praying and performing extra intercessions and liturgies. If anyone came in, I paid no attention. I ignored all movements and mutterings, not to mention loud snores and farts. I stayed awake, without sleeping a wink, until dawn, when I performed my ablutions and prayed. When I had finished and looked around, I spotted the keeper right behind me, offering me his prayers and blessings. Standing up, I gave him some funds as a charitable gift, whereupon he blessed and thanked me even more. That done, I left the tomb. As the city of Cairo was waking up and the bustle of daily life was gradually returning to its quarters and alleyways, I made my way back to my quarters. I passed by a crop market and bought a sack of fodder, which I offered my horse as soon as I got to his stable, along with a pail of water. Once I was sure he was fine, I headed for my room, hoping to make up for the sleep I had missed.

At some point—it may have been between noon and sunset—I was awakened from my deep slumber by the din of people yelling at each other. When I listened to what was being said, it emerged that my host was uttering the strongest possible oaths to the effect that he had no intention of handing over anyone who was in his care, even if the governor himself showed up with his guards. With that, he locked the door and went back to his quarters, invoking God's aid as he did so. I gathered that the entire matter concerned me, so I immediately went to see him, greeted him warmly, and asked him what the story was. He told me that the police had come to take me before the chief judge for some particular matter. He had refused to respond to their demand and sent them packing. I thanked him and promised that I would respond to their request the next day before leaving Egypt. He made it clear to me that his offer of protection did not extend beyond the walls of his residence. He then handed me a letter, said his farewells, and left.

I lay down on my blanket. Opening the letter I read it through once and then a second time. It was from a merchant in Tangier to whom Al-Shushtari had given the charge of sending me information about my followers and family. The gist of it was that my beloved wife was fine. The man himself had met her in Tangier where she was staying with her uncle and Hamada. They were all in good health, and they all hoped that I would return to the Maghrib safe and sound. There was even a note from Fayha' herself, the light of my life. The letter also informed me that the house in Sabta was being looked after by Bilal and two servants, so everything was fine there too. The news about my students and friends was varied: some had died during the famine, while others had been scattered hither and yon by vicissitudes of this troubled life of ours.

I now made up my mind to continue my journey to Mecca and the Holy Ka'ba. I wrote a letter to Abu al-Hasan to that effect, on the assumption that he would find it when he stayed with Shaykh Abu al-Naja. That done, I ate something, prayed, and then fell asleep. When I woke up next morning, I handed the letter to my host and asked him for the address of the chief judge and the appointed time for the departure of the caravans for the Hijaz region in Arabia. He gave me that information, then wished me well. I was so impressed by his generosity and magnanimity that I handed him one of my purses of gold. He refused to accept it, saying that my need was greater than his. When I insisted that he take it, he still refused. As a compromise, I buried it in the ground and asked him to show Al-Shushtari where it was as soon as he arrived. He agreed to do that. After embracing him, I departed.

I left my horse at the tethering-post of the judge's residence and headed for his chambers. Some guards stopped me and asked for my identity. I made do with informing them that I was the person whom their master had sent to the residence of Abu al-Naja the day before. They immediately pointed me toward a hall facing an enormous door and told me to wait there. I started thinking about the questions the judge was going to ask and prepared short, pithy responses to them. Then I crafted some questions of my own that I would pose to him concerning major issues involving the Muslim peoples and matters concerning both present and future. I spent a long time waiting and was thinking of leaving and going my own way when a gruff voice instructed me to enter. I crossed the threshold and found myself in a huge chamber. On a dais a number of men were assembled, in the midst of whom was a man whose beard was as fulsome as his body, with broad shoulders and forehead. With a broad sweep of his cane he indicated to me to approach and sit down in front of him. After presenting my greetings, that is what I did.

"Ibn Sab'in," he said without further ado, "you are accused of major crimes, among them that the day before yesterday you caused the death of a man, maybe without intending to do so. This noble jurist, Qutb al-din al-Qastalani, will tell you about this tragedy and read you the text of the accusations."

This jurist's "ringing" name was by no means unknown to me already, he being—along with Al-Sukuni in Tunis, Abu al-Hamalat in Murcia, and still others in Sabta and other cities—a practitioner of intrigue and dirty tricks. They were all very willing to pollute themselves with the muddy waters of secular life and its ephemeral fripperies.

"My lord," I heard him say, "the evil repute of this man precedes him wherever he goes and stays. God protect us all, it reeks of evil and plays on the strings of misguidance and obstinacy. What he has to say about the One Existent is outright heresy and blasphemy. The way he is able to corrupt people who are naïve and minimally pious is both devilish and extraordinary. He uses magic and symbols to hoodwink people, using lengthy diatribes and erroneous heresies to lead them astray. Just to cite one example among many, he talks about self-denial and demands of his followers that they indulge in prolonged periods of asceticism, habitual recalcitrance, and outright denial of the rights of rulers and religious authorities. Indeed he takes it as far as complete stupidity and dangerous behavior. That is precisely what happened the day before yesterday. A poor student from Upper Egypt rejected his entire family and his profession and insulted a wretched, innocent young girl by breaking off his engagement to her. What is even worse than that is that one dark night he started taking all his furniture and possessions out of his room on to the roof and throwing them off. One heavy item happened to hit a poor believer who was on his way home from the evening prayer; he died instantly. When the police brought the culprit in for questioning, he was only wearing a loincloth. Asked why he had behaved this way, he replied, 'I wanted to deny myself, so I threw it all away.' He went on to say that, when he was throwing things off the roof, he was not doing it of his own volition, but under compulsion. As evidence, he cited the Qur'anic verse 'When you aimed at them, it was not you who did so, but God' [Sura 8, v. 17]. But God is surely far above such interpretations. When he was asked who had incited him to such acts of self-denial, he mentioned the name of the person now before us, 'Abd al-Haqq ibn Sab'in from the Maghrib (and people also say, from Spain)."

The judge sat there in his chair muttering to the other judges. He fixed me with a provocative stare. "So, you," he said, "what do you have to say by way of response?"

How was I supposed to respond to such an evil piece of sheer drivel? I decided that my response would be terse and to the point.

"Judge," I responded, "I categorically refuse to respond to such a tissue of nonsense; I see no point in debating a subject that has neither meaning nor benefit. Instead I seek refuge in God, the Lofty, the Protector, from corrupt and evil-intentioned jurists."

Al-Qastalani's features quivered, and he looked furious.

"Listen, you!" the chief judge boomed. "You have a choice: either you're going to spend a long time in prison, or else you're going to leave Egypt forthwith!"

"Don't worry, judge," I interrupted. "My horse and baggage are outside your door waiting for me. I clearly cannot return to this good land of Egypt again until such time as it can be rescued from the clutches of evil rulers and tyrants."

I did not even ask the judge for permission to leave, but simply turned my back on him, made my way swiftly out of the residence, and rode my horse to

Giza. However, once I got there, another horseman who looked as though he was a soldier came rushing up. He told me that Shaykh al-Shushtari was waiting for me at Abu al-Naja's place. He then disappeared as swiftly as an arrow from a bow. I had no doubt that he was telling me the truth, so I quickly turned around and headed back to Abu al-Naja's, my thoughts full of premonitions of bad news. Once I got there, I found my beloved friend, Abu al-Hasan, laid out on his back, surrounded by a cluster of men who were doing their best to help him and staunch the blood flowing out of wounds to his stomach and legs. I leaned over to embrace him; all I wanted to know was what exactly had happened to him. So that he would not tire himself, his companions responded for him. While he was serving in the Muslim infantry fighting against the Crusaders in Damietta, he had been wounded. The whole account amazed me; it seemed almost unbelievable. When I asked about Shaykh Abu al-Naja, they told me that he had gone rushing off to the front to take his wounded shaykh's place.

Among the people gathered around was a distinguished-looking man who took me aside and told me he was both a soldier and a doctor. He complimented me and told me that Al-Shushtari had said wonderful things about my talents and medical skill. He then gave me his diagnosis of Abu al-Hasan's condition and asked me to treat him. If I did so, he and his companions could return to the battlefront and help the war-wounded in Damietta. No sooner had I agreed than he handed me implements and medications, gave me advice and instructions, and then indicated to his companions that they should leave. With thanks they said their farewells.

I sat next to the injured man and checked on his condition. I took his temperature and checked his eyes and the color of his tongue. I noticed that he was extremely weak and tended to doze off. When he opened his eyes, he signaled to me that he recognized who I was. He tried to talk, but all that came out was a few isolated phrases. I made him stop so that he could give his heaving chest a rest and I could feed him some fluids. While I waited for him to recover some of his strength, I spent time praying and beseeching God on his behalf. From time to time I welcomed some of his students and disciples who came to visit him, but I did my best to make sure he was not unduly disturbed.

After three days he was showing more than usual signs of recovery, so I seized the opportunity to clean his wounds and treat his cuts and bruises. For that purpose I was helped by one of his disciples, who insisted on serving him both inside and outside the house. After a whole week, the holy man was once more able to converse fairly easily.

He started to sit up so he could pray, eat, and brush up. For my part, I seized the opportunity offered by the recovery of his vocal powers.

"So, Abu al-Hasan," I said by way of gentle rebuke, "you go off to fight the Crusaders, but you don't take me with you!"

He gave me a big smile, and his eyes gleamed. "My dear source of guidance after God himself," he replied, "everyone has to do what he is best made for. In a dream I felt summoned to perform a lesser jihad, so I responded. You on the other hand are involved in the much greater jihad, one involving the Mighty One God. Those who aspire in that direction are required by you to seek the loftiest heights and the elixir of blessed perfection."

Faced with the humility of this wonderful man, all I could do was to hug him and seek the perfumed blessings of his holy presence. I tried to cajole him into providing some details of the events in the battle in which he had participated, but he would only speak in short, image-laden phrases. The gist of what he told me was that, while he himself had been able to make a few penetrating thrusts, he himself had been hit twice, a glancing blow to his stomach and a much more serious one in the thigh. He finished by repeating the phrase "Reliance is on God alone and all praise is rightly due to Him."

Next day after the evening prayer a whole host of students and ascetics came to the house to find out how their shaykh was faring and to see for themselves how well he was recuperating. Soon the entire place was filled with people, and they all proceeded to seat themselves in a circle around Al-Shushtari's bed. They all shared the drinks and light snacks that were offered and conversed with one another. I got to hear a little bit about the shaykh's remarkable and courageous actions and also gleaned some words of praise about myself. All of a sudden there was complete silence, as a young man started chanting sections of the Qur'an in a beautiful voice. When he finished, the entire group chanted some paeans to the Prophet composed by Abu Bakr al-Natili from Granada and also some selected extracts from Abu al-Hasan's own poetry that were exquisitely lovely. In this wonderfully ecstatic spiritual setting my beloved companion managed to surpass me as he swayed and gave himself over to the rhythm, to such a degree that his eyes were flowing with tears. When the audience seemed to grow quieter, I watched in utter amazement as he got to his feet—apparently fully cured and inspired—and proceeded to recite a zajal poem that opens thus:

> *The word has reached me true*
> *And has infiltrated my secret haven,*
> *That the internal eye that sees*
> *Is the eye of the very essence of ideas.*

Every time his wonderful words referred to me, he would gesture in my direction and point with both hands. Once he had finished, he sat down again and gave us a superb rendition of some of the short suras from the Qur'an. Whenever he paused, everyone listening would pour compliments on him and offer prayers on his behalf. He then moved on to chant some Qudsi hadith.* The one that I liked best seem to encapsulate the essential core of my own ideas and method (as Al-Shushtari himself realized full well):

> *I am present in the thought of my servant and I am with him when he mentions*
> *My name. If he mentions Me in his own soul, then I remember him in a man-*
> *ner better than them. If he approaches within a single inch of Me, I am but a*
> *forearm's length away. If he comes within a forearm's length, then I am but a full*
> *arm's length away. If he approaches me at a walk, I come to him apace.*

He added to it another Qudsi hadith that has been very influential with those scholars who focus on God's unity. It begins:

> *The worshipper continues his course toward Me with supererogatory acts until*
> *such time as I come to love him.*

Our celebration continued to regale and enrich us with pearls and gifts like these until it reached its crowning moment—and both Abu al-Hasan and I participated in it with them all—in a wonderful Sufi *dhikr*, during which we all looked upward toward the One who was inspiring it and bodies and souls quivered in ecstasy. "Peace it is till the break of dawn." After which the entire group made its way to the Azhar Mosque for the prayer.

. . .

How wonderful Sufi ceremonies are! With Abu al-Hasan involved, they turn into a kind of prayer, of wisdom. Wherever he is involved, you can guarantee that they will be at their most elevated and superb. He insists that the ascetics involved should be able to indulge in some creative competition and defensive communication. One day, while I was in Bijaya, he confided certain information to me that shed light on the contents of his poem that begins

> Show respect at the gate of the monastery and remove your shoes,
> Give your greetings to the monks and linger with them a while.

"Saint of God," he told me, "no harm can come from listening to the chants of priests and deacons. However, if we fail to surpass them in stressing the unity of existence and its Creator, then we gain nothing. That requires of us the highest level of attention and exceptional kinds of music." It was absolutely typical of this brilliant man's humility that he added, "On matters of dancing and singing I have an eminent predecessor in Abu 'Abdallah al-Shawdhi al-Halawi—may God have mercy on him!"

I spent a further ten days in the company of this wonderful companion. During that period we got to hear of the martyrdom of Abu al-Naja on the field of battle at Damietta. We both mourned his loss, and Abu al-Hasan proceeded to tell me about his remarkable deeds. Among the things I learned was that for half the year this ascetic would refrain completely or at least substantially from talking; it had so happened that my arrival had coincided with that particular period. We were also receiving a number of reports concerning the ways in which Al-Qastalani was blackening my name in all kinds of circles and meeting places and trying to turn the sultan's coterie against me. These reports kept arriving in bits and pieces from followers and disciples in whom he had complete trust.

There came the evening when my companion broached the topic in some alarm.

"Dear holy man of God," he told me, "you've extended your stay here in order to take care of me and make sure I survived. Now that I'm feeling much better, I don't want you to get yourself in trouble on my account. The governor's and Al-Qastalani's spies are following you wherever you go. Last night during our Sufi ritual they infiltrated the group disguised in Sufi garb and followed the necessary rituals. Some of those present who were genuine Sufis wanted to throw them out, but I rejected the idea. I wanted them to see that our only goal was piety and good works. Fairly soon I'm going back to Bijaya where I can continue to train my soul in accordance with God's will and yours too, dear colleague. But you need to continue your journey to Mecca, the mother of all cities, that being your destination. I hope to be able to join you there when circumstances permit—once the current crises are coming to an end and glimmerings of better times are visible."

So it was that at dawn the next morning I got up and prepared my horse and baggage. All the while my companion was weeping and handing me books, folders, and addresses. As we embraced, I whispered in his ear, "You most blessed of sages, your eye always beholds what is right." I now headed for Giza in the company of some students. When we arrived, I bade them farewell, consigning to them the care of their revered shaykh. Near the pyramids I encountered a caravan that was about to leave for the south and came to an agreement with the head camel-driver on terms under which I would accompany them as far as 'Aydab on the west coast of the Red Sea. The deal involved my traveling in their number for part of the time and going ahead to find stopping places for them at other times. I would not be getting off my horse except to rest and sleep, sometimes in a religious hostel, other times in a hotel.

9

THE JOURNEY STARTED on the road from Minya to Bush Fadlas, where we had to stop for two days in order to buy fine-quality cotton very cheaply. From there we moved on to Minya ibn Khusayn, Manfalut, and Asyut, from where we crossed over to Akhmim Faqus. We used to stop regularly and take a rest, but during the exhausting journey to 'Aydab my horse died of thirst and exhaustion, so I completed the journey on a camel whose owner had died during a sand-storm. It so happened that the caravan was now joined by an official government party protected by armed soldiers, so the two groups joined together. That way the pilgrim group was able to help on matters of pious behavior, tending the sick and burying the dead after prayers had been pronounced over them. In all this I helped as much as I could and discussed with an expert on sea travel the best time to set sail. During this period, I was being called either Abu Hamada al-Ghafiqi from Sabta or simply Ibn Dara.

The party spent the better part of a month sharing the little water we had until it almost ran out and doing our best to cope with the trials and hardships that desert travel involves. By way of diversion they indulged in games of chess and stick-fights (where I had considerable success). Whenever things were espe-cially bad, they confronted the situation by reciting prayers and litanies. Some of them went almost crazy and started cursing the buffeting wind. I told them not to do that, citing the hadith that says, "Do not curse the wind, for it is the spirit of God, bringing mercy and trial. Ask God for its benefits and seek refuge in Him from its evil effects."

Early one morning, the desert wind calmed down and blew softly; the sea calmed down as well. Everyone agreed that now was the time to get on the ferry-boat and head for Jedda under God's protection. Thus it was that, after a day and night's voyage, we anchored in a port at evening time. Along with the other pilgrims I stepped off the boat in Jedda. There I spent the second half of the month Dhu al-Qaʿda along with a group from both the Maghrib and Egypt. We got to know each other well; most of them were rich merchants who were spending most of their time going about their own business. I only saw them at night when we would all try to get some rest in the light breezes that blew over the roof of the house that we had all rented. For my part, I spent the whole day reading and praying; for the latter activity I always selected smaller mosques where there was less noise, and where the heat and humidity were fairly low.

At the beginning of the month Dhu al-Hijja I made my way to Qurayn, the place where the pilgrimage to Mecca actually starts. In a religious hostel there I handed over my belongings (including my money-purse) to the shaykh. As the sun was rising I went to have a rest and dozed off for a while. Then I got up, washed, and performed the ritual ablutions. My intention was to perform an informal pilgrimage for my own enjoyment. So I donned the *ihram* garments and, immediately following the evening prayer, attached myself to a caravan of pilgrims whom I joined in salutations and prayers to God till we reached Mecca the illustrious at dawn. I immediately joined other pilgrims in the Abrahamic Shrine of the Kaʿba and performed the first part of the minor pilgrimage except for touching the black stone itself, which proved impossible because there were so many people clustered around it. I made do with offering a greeting. What I must also note is that women performing the circumambulation kept brushing past my hand as I headed toward the Zamzam* well. They all kept touching and kissing them, and one of them was bitterly complaining: "We poor unfortunate women cannot possibly get to the black stone, so our only consolation is in stroking the hands of someone who has managed to touch it." To complete my own minor pilgrimage, I drank some of the water from the Zamzam well and ran between Safa and Marwa as I paid my respects to the Kaʿba's black stone. I then had my hair cut, prayed the sunset prayer with the gathered crowd and the evening prayer with the Hanafi* group. Finally I made my way back to my residence in Qurayn, where I took off my ihram cloth and washed in preparation for prayers and then sleep.

Next day I moved to a place near the Kaʿba itself. Guided by the instructions that Al-Shushtari had provided for me, I went out of the Gate of Abraham to the residence of a renowned jurist from Meknes. Before his death he had served as the imam for the Maliki sect inside the sacred enclosure. I told the warden of the residence about my need for a quiet house for a time period that could well be a long one. I made sure to tell him who I was and to mention the name of the person who had sent me there.

No sooner had he heard the name Al-Shushtari than he got all excited. "A friend of my master and beloved friend Al-Shushtari," he exclaimed. "I'm at your service! If you wish, I can offer you the quietest room in my own house."

With profuse thanks I took my meager baggage and followed him to a two-room house: one on the ground floor that was dark and somewhat damp, and another above it with a roof on top. To the east you could see the Gate of Abraham (peace be upon him!) and the well that carries his name; to the west, an elegantly designed minaret. The warden enumerated for me the house's benefits in both cold and hot weather. "Only the most exalted folk ever stay here," he told me. I asked him how much the rent would be. "Only what you can afford," he replied as he left. "The servant can bring anything you need."

My inner self was delighted by this room; that I had managed to locate it so easily was clearly a good sign. Now that the fog inside me had somewhat dissipated, I decided to consider my current and future state. However, for someone in my position, such contemplation, however long and penetrating it might be, could never hope to find a solution to a multi-faceted problem or identify a way of opening doors with no keys. Thus it was utterly unrealistic to indulge in any deep thinking. My best plan was to make use of the current situation in order to bolster my spirits and improve my potential.

The muezzin announced the noon prayer, and I performed it on my own in the lower room. Once I had finished, I noticed that there was a black man, solidly built and immensely tall, standing behind the door carrying a tray of food. I invited him in. He put the tray down on my table and told me that his master, Yasir from Yemen, had told him to serve me and take care of my needs. After thanking him, I asked him what his name was. He told me it was Ghaylan, and he was from the Sudan. With that he said his farewells and departed.

On the tray in front of me was a selection of local food that looked really nice and certainly stimulated my appetite. Invoking God's name, I tasted a bit of it, then ate as much as my stomach could handle. Once I had had my fill, I spread out my various belongings in the two rooms and devoted some time to washing and brushing my teeth.

A Muslim Suicide | 319

Just before the afternoon prayer time I went out to perform the prayer in the sacred mosque with the Hanafi group right opposite the holy waterspout. As soon as that was over, I headed for a small mosque nearby to watch the flowing crowds all around me and the nonstop flood of people doing the circumambulation. I heard the sound of the muezzin at the Zamzam shrine raising his voice in a fervent prayer for some foreign potentate who, accompanied by his entourage, was performing the circumambulation. No sooner had he finished his task than I noticed a huge crowd of pilgrims spilling out of the Gate of Abraham. I was told that they were non-Arabic speakers who were crowding into the sacred enclosure through the other gates as well. They were all rushing toward the blessed waterspout, and the pushing and shoving rose to levels the like of which I have never witnessed in my life. A number of them fell to the ground, either badly hurt, dying of suffocation, or being trampled. Afraid to move, I stayed where I was, right next to the wall, but then I suddenly spotted the head of a young girl screaming beneath the pile of rigid, expiring bodies. Rolling up my sleeve, I plunged into the fray, grabbed her by the hands, and started pulling her out as though she were some poor animal ensnared in the fangs of a ravenous beast. Once I had her on her feet, I noticed that she had fainted, so I carried her to the closest rescue station, fully intending to hand her over to the doctor and his orderlies. However, I soon discovered that the place was absolutely teeming with the sick and wounded, all of them waiting for help along with their relatives. Any idea of pushing my way through to the actual diagnosis point was out of the question, so, when someone who looked like a manager came up behind me, I asked him to help me with this girl who was in imminent danger of dying. He responded in a gruff and surly tone that her condition was no worse than the majority of people who were waiting. With that, he disappeared without offering me any assistance. I now laid her out on a bench and immediately noticed that her pulse was getting weaker and her breathing was slowing down. I was afraid that she was close to death, so I started rubbing the edge of her heart and pumping it hard. I then put my mouth over hers, started pushing breath into her, and kept doing it until I detected a small flutter of movement, then breathing, and finally a return to consciousness. Some nosy people had been watching what I was doing. When they saw that it had worked, they launched into paeans of praise to God and told me that, with God's good graces, I had restored the girl to life. They assumed that she was my daughter, especially since they had seen her clinging to my arms and clothing. I now picked her up again and carried her back to my residence. I informed the warden what had happened to the girl (although she had yet to utter a word) and asked him to feed her and try to find out her name and general identity. Expressing his admiration for what I had done, he promised to do what he could. Then, with assistance from my servant, Ghaylan, he relieved me of all involvement with the girl. I now retired to my quarters to recover my breath and relax so that I could make a record of what had happened on this remarkable and frenzied day.

Next day at lunchtime the warden informed me that he had found out from the pilgrimage groups that she was from Khurasan and had now managed to restore the girl to her father and aunt. Her mother had died of suffocation in yesterday's mob scene. He told me that tragedies such as this happened every year during the pilgrimage season, something that caused us both to seek refuge in God Almighty from such calamities. I then told him that it was my intention to perform the pilgrimage rituals alone the next day at noontime. With great emotion he prayed that my pilgrimage would be blessed, fruitful, and well received by God. He proposed to me that Ghaylan, who was eager to perform the pilgrimage as well, should go with me, an idea that I accepted with great pleasure. After a moment's thought I then broached the topic of the money-belt full of gold coins around my waist, and he told me that I could either leave it perfectly safely in my room or else give it to him to look after. Without a moment's hesitation I handed them over to him, in compensation for which I gave him a purse full of cash to be used for expenses and charitable purposes. Before going upstairs to my quarters, I asked him if there was any news of our beloved friend Al-Shushtari, and he replied that the only information he had had come in the form of a dream, to the effect that all was well.

On the seventh of the pilgrimage month I headed for the ancient shrine of the Ka'ba; as the warden had requested, Ghaylan came with me. Yet again the streets leading to the sacred enclosure were teeming with people from all walks and cultures. This time I managed to perform all the rituals of the minor pilgrimage, since my enormous companion made it possible for me to actually touch the black stone. This time, however, after I had completed the circumambulations, only one woman reached over to touch my hand and kiss it. That done, I allowed Ghaylan to perform his own pilgrimage rituals. I asked him to select someone who could make the preparations for our full pilgrimage and agreed with him that we would meet at dawn the next day by the waterspout. In this sacred spot I now prayed the afternoon prayer on my own, then added my own voice to those who were pronouncing their prayers and requests. When the time came for the sunset prayer, I performed it there along with the entire gathered assembly, then the evening prayer as well (for which I joined the Hanafi community, most of whom were Persians and Turks—I could tell that because one of them spoke to me, and his faulty Arabic was both obvious and amusing).

I found that I had time to wander around the enormous expanse of the sacred enclosure and to look at some of its architectural features. I walked slowly toward the lighted candles and lamps, looking closely at the adjoining alcove and the plethora of columns that carried the weight of the extensive convex roof. I paused by a number of gates that I had not noticed previously: the Gate of al-'Abbas's Dome and that of the Jewish Woman's Dome to the north, and that of the Zamzam Dome to the east. I then went out to the exterior enclosure, paused to look up at the seven minarets, then turned aside to the Dome of Inspiration, that being the haven of Our Lady Khadija*—may her memory be blessed! Being so close to her in this holy spot, I decided to go over to a corner and sit down, my eyes closed and my mind lost in thought. At times I thought of that holy lady with all her wondrous acts, while at others I worried about my beloved wife's, Fayha''s, safety—may God keep her alive for me and make it possible for me to return to her safe and sound!

On the morning of the eighth day of this blessed month I accompanied Ghaylan and a whole group of other Muslim believers up to Mina, where we spent the night. Next morning came the ritual of standing at Mount 'Arafat, then on to Muzdalifa, and then on the tenth back to Mina, at which point stones were hurled and animals were sacrificed. I performed all the rituals, as did Ghaylan, for whom this was his first-ever pilgrimage. He copied me in everything I did, and paid no attention whatsoever to the instructions from the person whom he had hired to serve as our guide. Once we had completed the rituals, he went away and came back with his head completely shaved. He begged me for the privilege of cutting my hair, and I allowed him to do so before we returned to the Ka'ba in Mecca to perform the farewell circumambulations in preparation for reassuming our normal way of life at dawn on the following day. I spent whatever time there was left to relax and take things easy, strolling my way around Mina, looking at the sights of Mecca itself, and visiting my own residence. Every time Ghaylan, the new pilgrim, had the chance, he thanked me profusely and offered prayers and blessings on my behalf in his colorful Sudanese accent. Yasir, the warden, who had performed the pilgrimage so many times that he could not even count them, also thanked me profusely and showed me his particular brand of Yemeni hospitality.

On the very last day of the pilgrimage month, I spent an entire day walking around and exploring. When I returned to the house, I found the Khurasani girl and her father waiting for me, duly attended by the warden. I greeted them warmly in response to their greeting—including my sorrow over the death of the man's wife, but I barely had time to sit down before he launched, albeit in a very fumbling Arabic, into a string of expressions of gratitude to me for saving the life of his only daughter, the apple of his eye. Pointing to the heavens above, I told the man that it is God who determines who is to live and die. He was anxious to reward me with a whole host of sealed purses, but I turned down his generous offer, citing the Qur'anic verse "Nay rather, I shall not ask you for a reward for it, save love for those near and dear" [Sura 42, v. 23]. The man then invited me to dine with them the next evening, just managing to say in Arabic, "You dine with us." Suppressing a giggle, the warden corrected him and told me that this generous man wanted to invite me to dinner with him and his family. In my mind's eye I now saw the image of Fayha'. I asked her what she thought, and she responded with a gesture that was unambiguous. So with the appropriate words of thanks and apology, I declined the offer. The man now told me that in two days' time he was returning to his homeland. He expressed the hope that we would meet again on some future pilgrimage. As we all stood up so they could leave, the girl grabbed my hands and started kissing them and weeping copious tears. She clung to my clothes and refused to let go, uttering phrases in her Persian dialect as she did so. It needed her father, Ghaylan, and Yasir to break her free and carry her to her camel litter outside the door. With that I took advantage of an opportunity to spend some time on my own, close to the Dome of Inspiration, where I allowed myself to ponder the fate of that strange teenage girl from Khurasan.

The next day I stayed put in my lower room. Apart from my normal activities, I was interested to read *Information about Mecca* by Abu al-Walid al-Azraqi.* Maybe I could slake my thirst by learning more details about the city where I would be residing for a period yet to be determined. Once in a while I put the book aside and started recalling some of the notes that my wife, Fayha', had sent me before we were married and that I had memorized by heart, word for word, sentence by sentence. In doing so my purpose, as on previous occasions, was to pass the time pleasantly and provide encouragement to my very soul.

Just before sunset the warden arrived carrying a load of sacks. He apologized profusely for disturbing me.

"My master," he said hesitantly, "here are your purses; I'm returning them to you now. These other sacks are gifts from that foreign shaykh. He brought them yesterday morning and asked me to give them to you."

I sat the man down, anxious to calm any worries he might have. "Is that all there is to it, Yasir?" I asked.

"My lord, the rest of it's even better!"

"Fine, so tell me, then you can relax!"

"That man from Khurasan told me how you had saved his daughter with God's permission. He translated for me the Persian phrase she kept repeating in your presence. She wanted more of your breath so she could fully recover and be completely well. A few people have been talking to me about you; they look on you as a saint who can perform wondrous deeds. I see now that they're right. However I'll keep on turning them away so long as you don't give me other instructions."

I asked for God's forgiveness. "Yasir," I told him, "you can tell such people that I used medical methods to cure that Khurasani girl. There was nothing miraculous about it. And please give those sacks to charities in Mecca. That's a much better idea!"

"You speak the truth indeed! I'll provide you with details of their dispensation as soon as possible."

"Is there anything else?"

"Master, I shouldn't be keeping your purses. There's a hole under your bed where you can keep them safe."

Taking back the purses, I said a fond farewell to him at the door.

10

DURING THE FIRST SIX MONTHS of the following year I divided my time between visits to the sacred enclosure of the Ka'ba and the library of the Maliki residence and familiarizing myself with the buildings and monuments of Mecca and the surrounding desert. Whenever time allowed, I liked to climb the mountains that surrounded the city: Mount Abu Qubays, and specifically Mount Hira' and Mount Thawr.* Scrambling up these mountains became a form of physical exercise that allowed me to check on my pulse and breathing, and therefrom my ability to withstand hardship. One mountain was actually called Mount Thawr [Bull] because, as the saying put it, only a bull could climb it. When I reached the top, I paused for a while to look out over Mina and the southern part of Mecca. After that I was delighted to be able to go into the blessed cave up there and spend as much time as God permitted, seeking the boon of the noble Prophet who had spent time there and hoping to inspire a downpouring of mystic illumination. I used to do the same thing in the Hira' Cave,* which had its own blessed associations.

As the old saying puts it, be alive during Rajab and you'll witness something wonderful!

By now I had been staying in Mecca for three years. Could there have been a more peculiar story than the one about the Egyptian lady who was residing near the sacred shrine? The warden of the Muwaffaq hostel came rushing over to ask me to come to her residence; she was extremely weak and was having trouble breathing. Once I had checked on the condition of the patient, who was lying on her bed, I discovered that she did indeed show some alarming signs: emaciation, pallor, and a sickly appearance. Her chest was heaving up and down, and the choking sounds coming out of her mouth sounded for all the world like a death rattle. I told the warden to bring a bowl, water, and herbs. No sooner had he left that she opened her watery eyes, pointed to my mouth and hers, and indicated that what she needed was mouth-to-mouth resuscitation. After a moment's pause I did as she asked, but I stopped as soon as the warden came back with the things I had requested. I prepared a potion whose formula I knew and boiled it in hot water. I gave it to her to swallow slowly. A few moments later I was on the point of leaving, but watched as the woman sat up and gave me a warm smile. She told me she was hungry. The warden was amazed and delighted. "A miracle, by God," he said as he went out, "a veritable miracle!" I stayed and sat by her side, but the only communication we had was through our eyes. Once the man had come back with a tray of food, I departed, pursued by the warden's praises to God and the patient's glances.

What was so amazing was not the events that I have just described, but rather what she confided in me when I responded to her request and went back to check on her condition. Her face was radiant, and she looked in every way restored to health. I sat with her in a shady garden while the warden went back and forth offering his services.

"Good Sir," she told me in a muted tone, "I have been residing here in Mecca for more than a year now. My only guardian and helper is God Almighty. My family is in Egypt; some of them, my father and husband, are now dead, while others are in the waiting mode. I noticed you performing your first minor pilgrimage ritual; I was among the women who touched and kissed your hand. On the second occasion I was lucky enough to be the only woman who did so. Watching you performing the circumambulation on both occasions, I admired your appearance and was overwhelmed by your dignity. But there is no cause for alarm or concern. After all, the very model for all Muslims, men and women, the Lord of creation and the prophets has said, 'While circumambulating the Ka'ba, I happened to see a woman whose appearance pleased me.' Beyond that, I saw with my own eyes the way you rescued that girl from Khurasan and restored her to life through your own pure breaths and the assistance of God Almighty."

She now paused for a moment, as though she were making ready to tell me something momentous. I too remained silent, unable to decide the best way of responding to her remarkable story. However, what she went on to say only increased my feelings of uncertainty and bafflement.

"Good Sir," she told me, her eyes closed and her cheeks blushing, "I am in love with you through God. All I ask in my loneliness is that you keep me company to the extent that you wish and guide me along the path of righteous Sufi belief. My dearest wish is that you should accept me as a disciple, one who will be obedient and cause no problems. I faked my illness so that I could get to see you and share my devotion and thoughts with you. Is God prepared to renounce one who seeks access to Him through one of His holy men? O Lord, if I have committed a terrible sin, then You are generous in understanding and forgiveness. So there it is. You have been my goal all along, and you are the arbiter. So please tell me what you think, or else reflect on it for a while and then get back in touch with me in whatever way you see fit."

How was I supposed to respond to this woman, when my mind was churning in sheer amazement?

"Handmaid of God," I stammered in reply, "I will certainly have to think about your request. If it takes me a while to respond, then it will be because of some impediment that God alone will be able to remove."

I asked her permission to leave, then said my farewells and departed.

■ ■ ■

Almost three months went by following this amazing and baffling conversation. During that time I only met a few people and debated issues with them. I also performed my third minor pilgrimage. As I circumambulated the Ka'ba and ran between Safa and Marwa, my mind was completely focused on the One Existent. I was assessing my own inevitable attraction toward his illumination through the Unity of the Absolute Existent. After that I took advantage of the final ten days of Ramadan to isolate myself, spending part of the time in my house and part in the all-blessed Hira' Cave.

On the morning of the feast at the end of the fasting month I purified myself, then joined the other people in the residence for their celebrations. On the second day of the festivities, the Egyptian lady came to visit me again in the evening, and I received her in the garden. Our company also included Ghaylan, who insisted on plying us with yoghourt and sweetmeats of various kinds. It was a short meeting, during which we exchanged names and words of congratulation on the feast and also on our health and well-being. I did not want her to feel I was being rude or mean, so I made a point of sounding both sincere and warm in my greetings. As she stood up to leave, she whispered in my ear, "'Abd al-Haqq, you know where my house is."

Yes indeed, I certainly did know where this noble lady, whose name was the same as my mother's, Umama, lived. But how on earth could I go there without arousing all kinds of suspicions and chit-chat?

How nice it was for this woman to be in love with me through God and for me to share the same sentiment with her! And equally nice to seek consolation in the line of poetry by Imru' al-Qays*:

> She was our neighbor when we were both strangers in the land;
> Every stranger is thus related to other strangers.

But what was supposed to happen if this entrée proceeded to a point where I was no longer in control or where the consequences would be bad? That is precisely what had happened years earlier with Maymuna, my elder brother's divorced wife, and with many others whom I do not even remember. This was a tricky question, one that I had posed to the image of Fayha', my wife, as soon as I had met this strange lady from Egypt. The gestures that I had got back counseled extreme caution. However, when I sought her advice again, her face was shrouded in a veil of total silence and rigid neutrality. As I pondered the situation, I decided that what it meant was that Fayha' was leaving the decision entirely in my hands and giving me complete discretion in the matter.

So be it!

However, I have a personal problem, one that I must try to solve, or else it's going to totally preoccupy my attention. The issue concerns monogamy: that I'm married to one woman and only one, Fayha', my very life and the sweet perfume of the monotheistic phase in which I am living and functioning. O God, please resolve this problem for me, unravel my uncertainties, and show me the path that You prefer me to follow!

I kept repeating that prayer beneath the sacred waterspout and in every single holy spot that I visited; in my prayers, litanies, and supplications; sitting and standing, every single place I went. But days and months went by without my getting any answer or even part of one. No light shone on the topic, not even the glimmer of one. All praise be to God who decides and predestines!

Ah me, how days and seasons can weigh one down when there is no certain news about one's homeland and family!

By now I have been in Mecca for more than five years. There's no news about either my students in Granada or my family in Sabta and Tangier. My only consolation lies in the fact that I've received a letter from Al-Shushtari in which he tells me that he is settled back in Bijaya and trying to recover from his various health problems. He tells me that he is hoping to join me in Mecca soon. Part of the letter includes a poem that begins

> *I see someone who asks of us more, not mere happiness,*
> *With his ideas he has fired an arrow that has transcended Eden itself.*

There are other verses too in which he lavishes on me the kind of praise that I pray to God to justify their author's good opinion of me, if only to a certain extent. I will also admit that I got a good deal of consolation from the series of meetings that I used to convene with some students on the roof once a week at lunchtime. The person who was most assiduous in proposing the idea and organizing the session was none other than Yasir from Yemen, the warden, who spared no effort to get things ready and provide all the necessary facilities to make it successful. Among those who used to attend the sessions on a regular basis was that strange Egyptian woman whom I continued to address as Sitt Umama.

I was very careful to make sure that the meetings with this woman in the garden, all within the general context of those lessons, were overseen, indeed overlooked, by the warden in person. I wanted to avoid any suspicion. In my fear of God I asked Him to keep me safe from the temptations of the Devil and the lusts of the flesh. Our discussions were usually somewhat sorrowful, but were nevertheless pleasant enough; there was no dissimulation or formality involved. She would ask me a question about the law, and I would give her a legal opinion; she would ask me to explain some Sufi principles or about previous female ascetics, and I would respond. When she inquired about my family, I told her that I loved my wife deeply and was very attached to her, to which she responded by wishing us both health, long life, and the opportunity to live together once again. Once in a while she came to ask to borrow some of my books or to give me some spiced coconut honey or sweetmeats that she herself had made, prime among them being some special pastries.

Thus I used to spend my days teaching, worshipping, and reading. Whenever I felt weak or ill at ease, I used to go out on exploratory walks around Mecca and the neighboring areas. I walked for miles, and on each occasion I used to turn off by the Mountain of Light; part of the time I would simply sit on the flat stone, but I would also squat in the blessed cave as well. Just listen now, Al-Shushtari, as I briefly talk about this particular spot (and I'll be able to expand on this description when we meet, either in this place or somewhere else):

As I've already told you, my pens had all dried up and my pages had been folded away. However, at this particular place and time, I've started composing again, but based on tablets whose origins lie inside me and whose branches are in my mind. The pen that I am using is subtle, precise, and clear, to the point of being almost invisible. The ink that flows from it could just as well be coming from the Red Sea itself, so plenteous is it, or from some abundant underground well. What I compose is a vast flood, but, when I go back to my private quarters, all I can remember is the headings. Some of them observe my transformations from the onward rushing violence of time to my desire for the clear truth, while others raise high the standards of my defiance and ascent to flutter obstinately in the breeze.

This then was my way of life, with its burning, ascendant motto: anyone who would advise people to continue the struggle and ascend ever upward without doing such things himself is a craven hypocrite. Knowledge is an indication of lofty goals. In the firmament of love one will find nourishment for life and the path to well-being. Those are the things that I have talked about and taught to others. There can be no going back, even if all manner of catastrophes, disasters, and squabbles should gang up against me. My success comes only through God; it is toward Him that I strive and to Him that I turn for consolation and help.

As the sixth year of my stay in Mecca drew to a close [1258 CE], news arrived of the terrible destruction that Baghdad had suffered at the hands of the Mongol hordes under Hulagu Khan.* Everything had been destroyed: crops, property, children, families. The collapsing fortunes of the Abbasid caliphal dynasty had finally been crushed. As a direct result, huge numbers of refugees made their way to the Hijaz region of Arabia, as they tried to escape almost certain death. The city of Mecca received a large number of such people, and Muslims rushed to offer them all the assistance that they could: shelter, food, and medical services. I was among the group charged with medical matters and offering care to the wounded and traumatized. The majority consisted of wounded men, but there were women, children, and old folk as well. At the hospital I did my best to treat them with drugs, plant remedies, and comforting words. The majority of people I dealt with in this way were orphans, widows, and bereaved women. They all had their stories about the utter barbarity of the Tatars and their deliberate terrorist policies involving mass murder and total destruction of everything.

On the third day of my work at the hospital as a doctor and assistant dealing with all the sick and wounded, word reached me that the governor of Mecca, the noble Lord Abu Numa, had arrived. When I looked around, I spotted an imposing figure, with a thick black beard, tall stature, and broad shoulders, coming in my direction, surrounded by his guard. He came over and greeted me, then leaned over to talk to me.

"May God reward you well for coming to the aid of these poor people. Ever since you arrived in Mecca, I have been hearing about your activities. As you know full well, this era of ours is fraught with problems. People in authority like me need the counsel of holy men of God who are loyal. It is even worse to cause a true scholar such as yourself problems than to disturb someone praying humbly to his God. My residence is always open to you, whenever you choose to visit."

He said all this with a spontaneous humility. He now left to resume his visit to the sick and inquire after their state of health, so I duly exchanged farewells with him.

Just before I went to sleep, I recalled the way in which the warden had sung the praises of the governor of Mecca and his senior sharifs. My first instinct, however, was not to forsake the protection of Ibn Khalas in Sabta in order to enter that of Abu Numa in Mecca, even though the latter was clearly more upright and morally sound than the former. My purpose in coming to Mecca had been spiritual; I had no desire whatsoever to get involved in politics and power games.

However, I had no time to refine or consider this instinct in any depth, so I decided to put it aside so that I could devote my attentions to my normal activities, they being the things that I really wanted to do: tending the sick from Iraq in tent-camps or hospital buildings; making my excursions to the mountains and valleys; and teaching an ever larger number of students. In addition to all that, there was also the time I spent in the gardens by the blessed stream of Solomon or in the cemetery at the Bab al-Mu'alla where the tombs of some important figures from the early period of Islam were to be found. Every time I heard that a group of pilgrims had arrived from Andalus and the Maghrib, I made every conceivable effort to get whatever news I could about both regions. Nothing I gleaned from such conversations suggested that there was any cause of joy or hope: Al-Murtada, one of the last would-be Almohads, was now essentially restricted to Marrakesh and a few of its surrounding territories. The Zanati Marinids, with their weak doctrinal background, were bolstering their dynasty with Abu Yusuf al-Mansur.* The overall collapse of Muslim power in Andalus now meant that the region around Granada and its functions was all that remained. Faced with the tyranny of the Nasrid dynasty and the hardships of daily existence, people were living a life of permanent fear. Power and authority lie only with the Creator, the Lord of mankind.

One day in the following year, I was rushed at noon to Governor Abu Numa's palace, with the urgent request that I treat the wounds that he had received during a surprise raid by some Bedouin in the desert outside Mecca. When I reached his bed and checked on his condition, I found that he was almost unconscious. His face was covered with bruises, making clear to me that he had some minor fractures at the front and back of his skull. I began my treatment by cleaning him up with water and powder. When he came round, blinked his eyelids, and started breathing a bit more normally, I asked the servants to bring me some materials that I specified. I made a gypsum cast and placed it on his bald head, my hope being that after a while it would help the bones to reknit. That done, I decided to return to my residence, but I instructed the chamberlain that it was essential that his master have complete rest for seven whole days.

How can I possibly avoid expressing my admiration for the way Abu Numa behaved so modestly with people and took good care of the poor and sick, not to mention the way he insisted on giving them a model of behavior by showing bravery and initiative in conflict? Such a leader certainly has no comparable figure in Andalus today, which is ruled by pathetic cowards?

A week later I decided to go back to the palace and check on his condition. He received me in his council chamber at once, and with a warmth that drew the attention of his chamberlain and aides. He started expressing his enormous gratitude to me, while I accepted his words with what I hoped was the appropriate level of humility. He pointed to the cast on his head.

"So, holy man of God," he said with a smile, "I've done nothing for a week as you advised. When are you going to rid me of this helmet?"

"Not until it's done its work and I've checked on you, Sir," I replied. "I'd say, a least a month."

"A month or more! No, my brother, please take pity on me, and bear in mind the number of responsibilities I have."

"There's nothing to stop you working, provided that you support the cast with a turban or hat of some kind. You will still need to avoid any situation that involves tension, worry, riding horses, and fighting."

The governor looked down for a moment, then asked his retinue to leave.

"What you advise is obviously the wise thing to do," he said. "May God never disable your right hand! Your counsel is worth more to me than refined gold. I do wish you would give me your advice on other things too; at the top of the list, religion, politics, and strategy. So now Baghdad has been destroyed by the Mongols, and the Abbasid caliphate is breathing its last. If we decide to ally ourselves with the Mamluks as a way of getting rid of the Tatar menace, are we liable to be moving out of the frying pan into the fire? Or, beloved of God, do you have some other way of looking at it?"

I got the clear impression that the governor knew the correct answer full well, but his question was a way of testing my knowledge of politics and recent events.

"May God support you with His knowledge, Sir," I replied. "The steel of Mamluk power is the only force that is able to confront the Mongols. Their leader, Al-Muzaffar Sayf al-Din Qutuz,* and his peer, General Al-Zahir Rukn al-Din Baybars,* have given us sufficient evidence of their ability to defend Islam's interests and territories. In that way, they are the contemporary replica of the Seljuk* and Ayyubid forces in times past. If we are to confront the dangers posed by Hulagu Khan and his hordes, we have no choice but to rely on the Mamluks. Quite apart from the basic logic of that decision, the entire matter rests on the principle that any decision has to be based on what is reckoned the most appropriate, that being a governing principle even when the person involved is a manumitted slave. The same thought occurs in the sermon that Muhammad, our Prophet—prayers and blessings upon him—delivered on his farewell pilgrimage [632 CE]: 'No Arabic speaker has precedence over a non–Arabic speaker; no white person has precedence over a black. Precedence can only be based on belief in God.' There are many similar references to be found in the Qur'an, the text of all texts, and in other source works."

I noticed that my interlocutor was looking very tired. Suggesting that he needed to pray and get some rest, I asked his permission to leave and departed with expressions of support and prayers for his continuing recovery.

Just before the end of the first week of Rajab, Yasir the warden handed me a letter from my beloved friend Al-Shushtari, which he in turn had received from a Fez merchant on his way to the Hijaz and Syria. After reading it, I felt relieved and happy. The writer was able to reassure me about the health and safety of my wife and Hamada, who were both in Tangier. Al-Shushtari told me that he himself hoped to be with me, God willing, fairly soon. That afternoon, just after the prayer, I received a visit from Sitt Umama, accompanied by the warden. I shared with them my delight at the news in the letter I had received, and they both shared my feelings and blessed my good fortune. My servant, Ghaylan, meanwhile, was making it his job to provide our table with all kinds of food and drink. I asked the lady how she was feeling, and she replied that, thank God, she was well, almost as if the contagion of my own happiness and well-being had spread to her as well. We then started a discussion of divine love as seen by Rabiʿa al-ʿAdawiyya, and of self-obliteration and permanence in the career of Al-Hallaj. As the hour for sunset prayer drew close, she bade me farewell, much affected by our discussion. I hurried to the sacred enclosure to do my ablutions and pray.

One Monday morning at the start of Shaʿban, I went to Abu Numa's palace at his request. He bid me a profuse welcome. No sooner had I joined him at a table loaded with food than he pointed pleadingly at the plaster cast on his head.

I decided to tease him a bit. "It should probably stay on for another month, Sir," I said with a smile, "so that the cast can bear fruit . . ."

"Bear fruit, you say!" he interrupted me in alarm. "No, Ibn Dara, that's not what you should be saying. Rather, so the lice can build a nest in what's left of my hair!"

"Good news, then!" I replied. "With God's help, it's release that's coming, not lice!"

I indicated to him to lie down on his bench. I ordered a servant to bring some liquids that I specified. I then tried, ever so gently, to get the cast off, but without success. I whispered in the governor's ear as he lay there that his crown was refusing to break its vow of loyalty to its master.

"Then tell it to start a rebellion!" he joked back.

With that I moistened the edges with warmer water till it felt soft and malleable. I removed it ever so slowly and started rubbing the entire skull with cotton swabs dipped in ether. The fractures had clearly healed completely. I put some caster oil on his head and pressed down, but the governor showed no signs of pain whatsoever. With that, I told him that he was fully cured, whereupon he embraced me and offered me profuse thanks. He now sat up and took a deep breath. One servant proceeded to spray us both with perfumed water, while another filled a brazier with aromatic wood.

"Now, my savior and physician," he said, "pray to God to give me the strength to run the city's affairs properly and to solve issues that are still pending. About a month ago, when you spoke to me about the two Mamluk leaders, Qutuz and Baybars, and praised their prowess, their army had already advanced into Palestine and amassed at 'Ayn Jalut* in the Nablus desert region. Were you aware of that?"

I shook my head. "How could I possibly know that," I asked in amazement, "when my purpose in coming to Mecca was entirely devotional? I have absolutely no involvement whatsoever in politics, let alone military matters!"

"In that case, you have the gift of foresight! Now I can tell you what has actually happened. There was an enormous battle between the Tatars and Mamluks, with both sides armed to the hilt. They both used infantry, cavalry, and artillery. Everyone in Egypt, Syria, and the Hijaz was hoping and praying that God would put a stop to the Tatar advance by granting victory to the Mamluks and their allies."

"Amen, amen! O God and Lord of mankind! A Mamluk victory would certainly be the lesser of two evils, although it would obviously strengthen their hold over the Hijaz and even encourage them to set their sights even farther afield. That is the way victorious armies normally behave!"

I stopped talking in order to encourage the governor to share with me his concerns about the Mamluk sultan and their armed forces.

"I'm convinced," he told me tersely, "that the Prophet's descendants here will not suffer any harm from the Mamluks, even if they do assume power and take over from the Ayyubids."

"I pray to God Almighty that He spread the standards of peace and tranquility over all His servants and spare them the consequences of hatred and enmity."

I made do with this one prayer, and my colleague responded with his own "Amen." I decided to keep my own concerns to myself, leaving it to the passage of time to reveal whatever unforeseen or concealed factors might also be involved and to make clear what would inevitably take place. Even so, he did not miss the dour expression on my face.

"I beg you," he asked in a confidential tone, "in the name of God and the sanctity of the Prophet's family, to share with me what troubles you. Is it the same thing that's troubling me as well?"

"What's that, Sir?"

"That the Mamluks, like their predecessors, will try to hang on to the illusion of the efficacy of the Abbasid Caliphate and try to revive it, however rotten it may be . . ."

"That's precisely what worries me," I replied. "For some time now the Abbasid caliphate has lost its authority; its flame has simply gone out. If a dynasty from this generation decides to cling to its coat-tails, then it can only be for some very particular reason, such as exerting authority and control under the guise of canonical law and the usual justifications based on practice."

"So we clearly share the same views on this subject. Tell me then, holy man of God, which dynasty is there—even if it is in the Maghrib—where legitimate authority and religious leadership are to be found. I will then pledge fealty to their ruler as caliph."

"In our era," I replied without the slightest hesitation, "only the Hafsids in the western regions of Islam—they being heirs to the Almohads and a branch of their noble family—fit that category. Were you to bolster their cause by an expression of fealty and were other sharifs in the Arabian Peninsula and their parties to follow your lead in doing so, their prestige and status would be greatly enhanced. They would be able to unite peoples and regions in the cause of defeating the Christian forces in both the east and in my own long-suffering Andalus."

"God grant you light!" he replied. "Write for me a letter of fealty that I can send urgently to Muhammad al-Mustansir ibn Abi Zakariyya,* the Hafsid ruler. Success comes only through God!"

I did not respond to his request, as a way of showing that I needed to think some more about the entire matter, and in an atmosphere far removed from any demands for rapid action. We now had a conversation about personal matters and our own lives. It became clear that the governor already knew some details about my way of life, but he now asked me to give him some more details about my written works. Just before the noon prayer I asked his permission to withdraw, and he accompanied me to the door.

"Don't forget about that letter," he whispered in my ear. "And don't forget to come and visit me."

With that I made my way through halls and courtyards accompanied by two guards. My movements were closely watched by senior officials and aides, but I decided not to bother myself with worries about their significance.

I spent the rest of the month of Sha'ban dealing with the increasing number of students, offering sessions on the bases of religion and Sufi ethics. Their questions and requests for elucidation also required that I address other ancillary topics. I held the sessions either in the library of my own residence or in the Muwaffaq hostel, also on two occasions in a portico of the Ka'ba Shrine itself. Truth to tell, among the students in Mecca I did not encounter any who were the equals of my students in Murcia and Sabta. They did not possess the same level of intellectual curiosity, breadth of vision, and ability to absorb ideas. The only exception to this was actually Sitt Umama, even though in recent times she had been less assiduous in her attendance.

I did not forget about the letter of fealty that the governor had asked me to compose. Indeed, I sat down on an irregular basis and composed different segments of it, all in anticipation of the time when I would bring the whole thing together. I chose appropriate verses from the Qur'an to go along with the opening of the two suras, Al-Fath and Al-Dukhan. When it came to other source works, I found some support in Muslim,* who says, "The Prophet of God—on him be peace and blessings—said, 'At the end of time there will come a caliph who will share wealth without counting it.' Abu al-'Abbas al-Hamadhani* went further and gestured with his hand toward the Maghrib." I went on to cite another text from Baha' al-din al-Tibrizi in his epic work: "If the fire of the Hijaz goes out, the caliph of Baghdad will be killed. In the Maghrib the rule will remain strong and will extend its word into different regions. Its name will be proclaimed in the pulpits of the Abbasid caliphs, and great benefit will accrue from its passage to the land of India." In order to talk in more precise terms about al-Mustansir's claims, I included the following passage: "I have cited these things so that the ruler— God provide him support!—may realize that he is the one to whom reference is being made and that he is being charged, through God's own power, with the reform of what has become corrupt. In these times of ours there can be no Caliph for the Muslim community other than the person whom we have indicated." I specifically mentioned the Almohads and "their mighty human leader, enabler of the Almohads over the other heretics, mainstay and backbone of the faith, maintainer and propagator of the Islamic religion, and leader of the community of faithful believers in prayer, all in imitation of his father, himself a leader in prestige and glory."

I had to include some words of praise for the Prophet's family in the person of 'Ali ibn Abi Talib—may God honor his visage!—so I copied al-Hudhali's* statement about him: "He is the Imam, and in him are to be found four aspects (and he possesses them all, even if aspects of anthropomorphism and causality are removed): namely, learning, prudence, fortitude, and noble family."

As I sat there, thinking about all the ideas churning around inside my head, I decided to include some of my own opinions, which were certainly extremely forthright and daring, to the point of constituting a real risk in the uncertain times ahead: "Perhaps the factors that founded and raised the Islamic faith from the eastern regions but then proceeded to destroy it can be restored from the western regions without the need for transfer. Anyone who believes in God and His angels, books, and prophets is obliged to ensure that his goals are not changed and that he does not make do with merely hearing his praises sung. An entire people's limbs have been trammeled by chains of polytheistic worship. It is oppression that has inevitably led them to destruction at the hands of the Turks."

When the month of Sha'ban was almost at an end, I had completely finished the letter, a process that involved condensing its content and fixing its sequence. I did all that without in any way lessening the blunt and direct message in many of its sections. I made a point of specifying the place where it had been composed: facing the Ka'ba on the western side of the sacred enclosure. I assumed that the sender of the letter would add the date and his own seal. All that completed, I put the letter under my pillow and waited for Abu Numa to ask for it.

I spent the first third of the fasting month of Ramadan secluded in my residence, in the sacred enclosure near the Ka'ba, or in the blessed cave of Hira'. Wherever I happened to be and in whatever state, I only had one aim and one desire: to achieve the state of closeness to the One Necessary Existent, in all His abundance and eternity, that being God alone. In that process I relied on a continuing quest, as I practiced my rituals and climbed upward along the paths of transubstantiation by means of the beautiful names of God, they being the absolute and the ideal. When I had some verbal inspirations that emerged from these gifts of seclusion, I recorded them on imaginary pages, using the same pen that I described earlier. But this time there was a difference, in that I remembered some of them by heart and wrote them down in my room as a text with the title *An Epistle on the Illuminations of the Prophet.*

A few hours before the celebration of the Night of Power, the governor sent for me. I concealed both the letter and my epistle in my sleeve and went to our rendezvous. He had hardly welcomed me to his residence before he asked me anxiously about the letter.

"Which letter, Sir?" I asked him, pretending not to remember.

"Good grief, Ibn Dara!" he yelled. "I mean the fealty letter."

"Oh, forgive me," I said. "The Devil himself made me forget to give it to you. Here it is, and I also include an epistle about your ancestor, the chosen Prophet. It too is my own composition."

Sitting up, he urged me to come closer. He then started reading both texts out in a muted voice. Once he had finished, he drew me toward him.

"You've done a superb job," he said. "May your pen never go dry! The letter needs no emendations, whether omissions or attachments. In it I express my willingness to offer fealty to the Hafsid ruler known by the name Al-Mustansir as caliph of Islam. As for the epistle, I am prepared to offer my fealty to you as a holy man of God. From now on, please serve as my personal shaykh and religious guide."

When my latest disciple leaned over and embraced me warmly, I was overwhelmed. At that precise moment the chamberlain came in to announce that it was time for the evening prayer. My host stood up at once and asked me to follow him in the company of the Prophet's descendants and his aides. Once we reached the sacred enclosure on foot, we prayed there with the assembled congregation. That was followed by the rituals of the holy Night of Power, the imam's sermon, and recitations of prayers and prophetic eulogies. Every so often, the Zamzami official would raise his voice in prayer for the governor, the people of the Prophet's family, and the community of Muslims as a whole. All these ceremonies were performed in a wonderful atmosphere of holiness, illuminated by lamps and candles, and refreshed by perfumed sprays and purified incense. Throughout it all, I felt that every single cell and bone in my body was turning upward to the heavens in prayers that would be answered in this holy location. My primary wish was that God should look after Fayha', my very life and foundation in a world of troubles and disasters, present and to come.

When the festival arrived, I charged Yasir with distributing my alms and then decided to convey my blessings to the governor himself after the congregational prayer. His palace was full of people, but he spent a few moments alone with me. He told me that a delegation on his behalf was now on its way to Tunis to present the fealty letter to al-Mustansir. I praised the initiative and congratulated the governor for organizing it.

Both of us then joined the larger company. The conversation involved some members of his own retinue and others who had come from Syria, and concerned the continuing clashes between the Mamluk and Mongol forces and the obvious superiority of the former over the latter when it came to military prowess, strategic planning, and experience. Abu Numa was very keen to hear which of the two I expected to be the victor. I suggested that the Mamluks would emerge the winners, with the proviso that the reports of clashes so far were accurate and that there was an exclusion from consideration of unforeseen factors. This was also the opinion of the governor and the assembled group. However, I went on to point out that no throne was wide enough for two victorious leaders to sit on: inevitably one of them would demand obeisance from the other, while the second would have to submit or else suffer the fate of either exile or assassination. As a consequence, there would then only be one leader who could exert his authority as he saw fit.

At this point some voices were raised in favor of Qutuz for the fine achievements of his career; they all devoutly hoped that he would emerge as the sultan. I took the opposite view, expressing my opinion that Baybars was far more likely to be the one to assume power because he had already shown his leadership abilities in the conflicts with the Crusaders in Egypt. He had defeated them at Al-Mansura, imprisoned their king, and only let him go after a large ransom had been paid. His sword was far more effective when it came to killing his enemies and indeed his rivals. The elite and the populace in Egypt both referred to him as "the Conqueror." All this was quite apart from his renowned talent and influence in matters of leadership and the military.

As the group broke up, the governor leaned over to me. "Holy man of God," he told me as he bade me farewell, "if your assumption is correct, I'll have to pay you whatever you ask. If, on the other hand, you're wrong, you'll owe me!"

"That's not a legitimate bet!" I whispered jokingly.

On my way to the sacred enclosure I pondered the fact that his firmly fixed opinion may have been the same as my own, and yet he was tagging me along so as to be able to cajole me into doing what he really wanted through actual help or in some other kind of service.

Back at the residence I shared lunch with Yasir, Ghaylan, and some other residents. We discussed whatever interested them; sometimes the topic was secular, at other times religious. Before I went to my quarters, the warden handed me a sealed letter from Sitt Umama. In it she offered me her blessings on the festival day and went on to inform me that she was moving to Medina so as to allow my thoughts to reside exclusively with my beloved wife and to remove all possibility of suspicion or malicious gossip. She concluded her message with expressions of fulsome prayer for myself and my wife and appended her new address, duly sealed with expressions of love and respect. I will not conceal the fact that, when I finished reading what she had written, my heart shrank a bit and gave a little shiver.

At the beginning of the month Dhu al-Qa'da, Ibn Bartala, the leader of the governor's delegation to Tunis, came back and provided me with an enthusiastic description of the way the caliph had welcomed the fealty of the people of the holy family and their mighty leader. He went on to describe the sermons in mosques that had accompanied their reception and the celebrations that had been attended by both the elite and the general populace. Ibn Bartala finished by noting that it had been a totally remarkable day. He then proceeded to recite to me several paragraphs from the letter the Hafsid had sent, praising the Prophet's family and lauding their governor, Abu Numa.

At the end of this same month, news arrived of the victory that Qutuz and Baybars had scored at the Battle of 'Ayn Jalut. The Mongol commander, Altunbagha, had been imprisoned and killed, and the Mongol army had retreated from Syria and Iraq as well. Mecca, the cities of Arabia, and others as well were all overwhelmed by feelings of joy and relief. Everyone could now take a deep breath, as they praised God and offered Him thanks for enabling them to emerge victorious after so much hardship. At the hands of His servants, the Mamluks, the Mongols had finally been driven back. The Zamzami official, preachers, and pilgrims to Mecca in general all offered fervent prayers of thanks to the Mamluks and their redoubtable commanders.

It was only a few days after this notable victory that what I had already predicted actually happened. Baybars had Qutuz, his rival, murdered, thus adding to the list of his victims (among whom in recent times had been Al-Malik Turan Shah, the Ayyubid). He was thus able to claim the sultanate for himself exclusively. God alone is the victor!

11

A WONDERFUL DAY to be recorded in letters of gold: the tenth day of Dhu al-Qa'da in the year 660 AH [1262 CE]. In the evening the warden Yasir came up to my room and told me to accompany him at once; my eyes would be delighted by what he had to show me. I followed him, albeit with a certain concern since I was worried that Sitt Umama might be involved. However, no sooner had he opened the door to a room opposite the garden than I set my eyes on my beloved friend Al-Shushtari, lying in bed. He managed to sit up, albeit with a good deal of effort. We embraced each other warmly and shed some tears. After such a prolonged time apart, I was delighted to see him again, so delighted in fact that, like him, I could not stop crying. Beyond that, I was distressed to find him in such poor health, obviously a direct consequence of his heroic participation in the fighting against the Crusader forces at Damietta.

I began by asking him how he was.

"Saint of God," he sobbed in reply, "the fact that you were so far away was the only thing that kept me feeling miserable. In fact, I still managed to be with you several times in my dreams and debated matters with you. Not only that, but I also mentioned you, with all due humility, in some of my poems. As I told you in my letter, your wife and family are safe and sound in Tangier, God be praised! All they're hoping for is your safe return and the possibility of seeing your luminous countenance again when the clouds thrown up by your enemies have finally dissipated along with the political machinations of the people who wish you ill. Concerning your students, I have only learned a very little, and even that is not very reliable."

"But what about you, Abu al-Hasan?"

"You can see for yourself. This Muslim is in bad shape. My bones are weak, and my hair has turned white. I need a cane to walk. But, in spite of everything, my enthusiasm is still as strong as yours, full of aspirations—thank God!"

I urged him to get as much rest and sleep as he could, otherwise he would wear himself out talking and answering questions. I instructed Ghaylan to do everything necessary to arrange his quarters and carry out whatever functions Al-Shushtari might need. It was sunset on the following day when the holy man woke up again. I paid him a call after evening prayer and found him much recovered and fully ready to sit up and chat.

Ghaylan came in, greeted us both, and placed some food on the table. I asked him if he would like to perform the pilgrimage again this season, adding that, with God's aid, I intended to do it myself along with my companion. Ghaylan's eyes sparkled as he responded that he would indeed like to do so.

"My dear colleague," said Al-Shushtari, "I've been away from these blessed regions for a very long time. I'm longing to perform the pilgrimage and stand at 'Arafa. To be able to perform my last pilgrimage in the company of a beloved colleague such as yourself is an additional boon."

"So then, Abu al-Hasan," I responded gently, "we'll perform the pilgrimage together. And, God willing, there'll be others to follow."

We prayed the evening prayer together on the roof. Once that was finished, we sat there under a sky glittering with pearly stars and exchanged information that each of us thought was important. Al-Shushtari told me that the death of Ibn Khalas, governor of Sabta, had been confirmed; he had drowned while escaping to Tunis. He had vigorously objected to the general tyranny and corruption of his successor as governor, whose evil conduct was only rivaled by the boorish and uncouth governor of Tangier. By now, the Almohad sultan had completely abandoned all interest in Andalus and was completely preoccupied with protecting the few cities still under his control from the ever-growing power of the Marinids. Hearing all this, I begged God to show some of His kindness.

For my part, I told Abu al-Hasan about Sitt Umama, my Meccan students, and my meeting with Abu Numa and my favorable impression of him. He shared my opinion and confirmed my intuition about this sharif's leanings toward Shi'ite belief and his general support for ascetics and mystics. Abu al-Hasan then went on to tell me somewhat bashfully that in Bijaya he had married a worthy lady whose company and assistance he sorely needed today. I offered him my blessings on his marriage and prayed that both of them would be happy and healthy.

As night pursued its relentless course, we moved to a discussion of Baybars and his defeat of the Mongol armies. We both agreed that this sultan's primary demand would be to be made caliph now that the Abbasid dynasty had collapsed. In doing so, he would have to rely on the opinions of pedantic jurists who were as lily-livered as they were unprincipled. This Mamluk would then proceed to impose Sunni doctrine, relying in doing so on spear tips and sword blades. Invoking God's mercy and sympathy, we asked ourselves how it was that, every time extraordinary caliphs or remarkable generals made an appearance on history's stage, they decided to impose religion by force, either imprisoning or else killing off all liberal thinkers who derive their inspiration from the spirit of God and the pure scent of discretion and ease. Both of us cited the names of Mu'tazilites* and others who had been killed during the controversy over the created nature of the Qur'an. Abu al-Hasan made an emotional reference to Abu Mansur al-Hallaj, while I raised the fate of Shihab al-din al-Suhrawardi, known as "the slain Sufi," intending, as I did so, to ask my colleague about an issue that had been bothering me from time to time.

"Abu al-Hasan," I said, "I've memorized this saying of al-Suhrawardi: 'If there is something in existence that does not need to be defined and explained, then it is clear. Nothing in existence is clearer than light, so, of all things, it needs definition the least. (End of quotation).' With that in mind and in direct opposition to it, darkness—taking into account Al-Suhrawardi's comment (he being the shaykh of the Illuminists)—is too broad to be encompassed by a definition, to such an extent that there can be no end to its parameters and thus no specific definition and no determination of its precise dimensions."

For a while my companion stared at me pensively, suggesting that either he had fully grasped what I was aiming at or else was encouraging me to continue and clarify what I meant.

"My dear colleague," I went on, "when discussing the topic of death, there are people who talk about it in lofty, abstract terms. They find it most appropriate to invoke all kinds of figurative language, such as the journey, the end of a time-span, or transfer to the love of God. They cover up its tragic aspects with such expressions as 'delayed, but not overlooked,' or 'when it happens to everyone, it is not so cruel.' Other people treat death as a matter to be hushed up and hidden away, as though it were something private and unmentionable. Still others choose to decline the death verb in the first person, using expressions of relief and even welcome. Some people are panic-stricken, while others laugh defiantly. On this particular subject I myself have not settled on one view or another; or, more accurately, it depends on the circumstances involved. Like some compulsive traveler I move from one camp to another. That at least was the way I used to consider the issue until a point a while ago when the thought of the possibility that I might die at the hands of Sultan Baybars began to preoccupy my mind, as it must have done Al-Suhrawardi, who was killed by Salah al-din the Ayyubid (albeit in very different times and circumstances). 'Every soul tastes death.' In any case, I pray to God that he will protect me from an evil end at the hands of the forces of compulsion and intolerance."

My interlocutor remained silent for a while, then fixed me with an affectionate and sympathetic stare.

"Holy man of God," he said, "may I be made your ransom! By God, I have watched as the Angel of Death has snatched away souls in whole clusters. He has looked straight at me. 'Your turn soon!' he's threatened. At the Battle of Damietta I was hoping for martyrdom with every thrust I made, but my prayers were not answered. It was as though Izrail, the Angel of Death, was not interested in me and kept pushing me aside for some other time. So here I sit before you, still alive, albeit with a body that is sick and decrepit. I have no idea how I'm going to die, but what I do know for sure is God's own words: 'God will not grant any soul a delay when its time has come.'"

I made clear that I agreed with him, regretting all the while that I had even raised the subject. As we concluded our conversation, it was obvious that we were in agreement.

"Let's go and prepare ourselves for prayer."

We headed for the ancient house of Abraham, did our ablutions once again, and prayed some extra prayers along with the assembly of Muslim believers. We then sat down in an alcove and whispered some other parts of the Qur'an and litanies. Once we had finished, each of us returned serenely to his normal level of consciousness. I surmised that my companion was doing as I was, namely engaging in sacred and lofty thoughts about the passion of Abraham, the faithful companion and pioneer monotheist, and the tears of Hagar, mother of Isma'il and our female ancestor. Maybe, like me, he was also considering the way that change and the passage of time had affected his life. At any rate, the two of us stayed there till dawn, at which point we performed the prayers.

When the pilgrimage season arrived, I took Abu al-Hasan early to Mina, accompanied by a group of his followers and my servant, Ghaylan. They all took turns in helping my companion perform the familiar rituals, all of which showed convincingly that Abu al-Hasan was really weak and incapacitated (even though he himself put on a brave front in order to convince us all of the opposite, something that only made him even more tired). By the waterspout and at 'Arafa he performed his prayers in a voice so low that no one could either hear or understand them.

When the pilgrimage season was over, I was delighted that the holy man of love and generosity was still alive and breathing. He spent several days resting, all the while receiving my students and his beloved friends. Once his health had recovered somewhat, he convened a chanting and recitation session on my roof. How we all enjoyed his rare and unique gift on these occasions! He used to chant two suras, "The Light" [Nur] and "The Merciful" [Rahman], and other parts of the text in a melodious tone that made our bodies shiver with excitement. Tears regularly flowed from people's eyes and coursed down cheeks and lips. When he chose to sing some of his zajals in praise of the Prophet and other holy narratives—as he had done previously when we had been together in Cairo—everyone began to accompany him (as best they could), either vocally or with gentle clapping or beats on drums and tambourines. Some people were even tempted to stand up and perform the Sufi dance, repeating the phrase "God is aliiiiiiiive . . ." Both Ghaylan and Yasir danced, and they did it superbly.

In such an august and wonderful atmosphere of devotion, we all relished each and every moment and bathed in its wondrous light till dawn. At that point we all stood up, duly enlightened and excited, and went to perform the prayers in the great mosque.

We also held sessions like this one in the Valley of Solomon's Spring, which was about a day's journey from Mecca itself. Abu al-Hasan had had another hut built there, modeled on the one in Bijaya. The valley was surrounded on all sides by orchards and fields that had been put there by highly experienced Moroccan peasants. For such occasions the peasants prepared a variety of dishes, mostly consisting of vegetables, as a way of honoring their shaykh, Al-Shushtari, and his companions, I being one of the most prominent among the latter group. They also took part in the Sufi rituals, dancing and singing. In the open air amidst plants, torches, and tents, the sessions were even more spectacular for being conducted in a fertile valley, full of wonderful aromas and scents. In such an environment Abu al-Hasan began to recover his health; or perhaps he was managing to supplant the weaknesses of his bodily frame with heavenly light, in that his entire spirit seemed to be aglow with a sublime, holy essence. As each session drew to a close and the group rose at dawn, I watched as he rolled his body in the dust. "One piece of dust hankers for the other, my beloved friend!" he told me. I would simply stay there, watching him with all due affection.

We used to hold our sessions in the Valley of Solomon's Spring or the Meknesi residence once or twice a month. Between such occasions days and seasons passed by with their usual daily concerns and religious rituals. Once Abu Numa had discovered that I had no desire to attend his parties and ceremonies, he requested that I meet him in private. He asked me about Abu al-Hasan. I gave him a short summary of his life and made it clear that he really needed time on his own to recover his health. Abu Numa asked for my views on matters relating to people in Mecca, the Prophet's family, and ways of improving the pilgrimage season. My responses reflected whatever my mind told me was best. When it came to discussing the best posture toward Sultan Baybars, I gave terse answers or asked for time to think about it. When I was alone with Abu al-Hasan, I asked him what he thought about the Sultan Baybars question. His reply was to the effect that I should be very economical in my contacts with the sharif of Mecca and the Shi'ite people in the city. Furthermore, if Baybars were to come to the city in order to check on things, I should hide somewhere safe.

One morning when the weather was moderately warm, my companion expressed the desire to visit the Hira' Cave. At noontime he mounted a compliant mule and rode off with me. By nighttime we had reached the Mountain of Light (Al-Nur) region. I hurriedly tied up the mule and gave it some food and drink. I then carried an exhausted Abu al-Hasan up to the cave. Once there I handed him his blanket and lit some candles so we could emulate the practice of the Prophet, lord of the messengers and model for monotheists. We spent most of the night this way, not closing our eyes and only using gestures and glances to discuss the cave and its contents. We went back down to our residence immediately after performing the dawn prayer, our souls deeply moved by the experience and filled with a spirit of joy and sanctity.

I accompanied Al-Shushtari on many other visits both to the cave and to the Valley of Solomon's Spring. In the valley we used to spend the night, either in his hut or in a tent. During the daytime he introduced me to the Maghribi peasants one by one, beginning with their chief, Hamada the Zanati. He made a point of extolling my virtues to the skies, then gave me the benefit of his wide knowledge of the vegetable and fruit species that they were cultivating so expertly—species that were previously unknown in the Arabian Peninsula. All I could do was to congratulate these folk for their skill and ask God's blessings on them. They in turn thanked us profusely and asked my colleague and me to pray for them and their families. We both proceeded to do just that, both together and separately.

When the weather was really hot in Mecca, I used to convene sessions for students and followers in the orchards of the valley, with Abu al-Hasan in attendance. The topics of those lessons would involve questions that they posed to me or that I would direct at them. The majority concerned matters of jurisprudence and Sufism. The sessions used to begin between afternoon and sunset prayer times, and some of them extended into the evening. We would continue them, spending pleasant hours performing litanies, Sufi rituals, and recitations. On one occasion I preferred to dismiss the group so that I could spend some time alone with Abu al-Hasan and ask him about Sultan Baybars. That was because the sultan's shadow had recently started to insert itself into my dreams.

"Abu al-Hasan," I told him once we were left alone, "in my dreams I keep seeing Baybars issuing threats against me.

"'I'm told,' he keeps saying, 'that you've blasphemed, if I've understood things correctly, by claiming that the Prophet Muhammad, Ibn Amina, exaggerated widely when he said, "I am the seal of the Prophets." What is your response to this charge?'

"I have then replied, 'That is not an idea I've ever expressed. I might have misquoted someone else, or else while I was daydreaming or asleep. In any case, there's no harm in denying its validity once I acknowledge it when I'm fully conscious!'

"'You're wrong,' he goes on. 'The whole thing has now spread far and wide.'

"'As I've already told you,' I reply, 'I've explained the context and amended the text. Now that the circumstances have been explained, there's no cause for surprise.'

"'And who can vouch for the fact that you've only proclaimed such things in dreams?'

"'God and His apostles,' I've replied. 'If I dreamed that I wanted to kill you, would you punish me simply because of the dream?'

"'Is that what you really want?' he asked.

"'Life, O Sultan, consists only of dreams. Only God knows how to interpret them.'

"'Take him away and slit his throat so we can be rid of him.'"

Abu al-Hasan gave me a sympathetic look. "Holy man of God," he said, "may I be your ransom! Don't bother about predictions you see in your dreams. You need to concentrate on the danger signs of your wakeful existence! If the Mamluk sultan comes to Mecca demanding your head on a plate, don't seek refuge with the sharif, with Abu Numa, or even in the cave on the Mountain of the Bull, which is already renowned for hiding the Prophet of God. Go to my hut and spread word that you've gone back to the Maghrib. That's a subterfuge of the kind the Prophet himself used, and it's one you'll need to use till the danger period is over. These Maghribi peasants will be your protection; they would not betray you for any amount of money. Now, Ibn Dara, get up and let's go and pray at Abraham's own house."

As usual, this beloved colleague managed to restore my confidence. I stood up and embraced him. "You're absolutely right," I whispered in his ear.

At the conclusion of the third year of Al-Shushtari's residence in Mecca, he started to look much better.

"Abu al-Hasan," I used to say to him, "it's all a sign of good things to come!" whereas he would reply, "Or maybe one last burst of spirit!"

He made up his mind to travel to Medina for a month, although he categorically forbade me to go with him, knowing full well that the governor of that city was an enemy of mine. At the end of Dhu al-Qa'da, he returned to Mecca. His health had greatly improved; by now he had recovered a good deal of his enthusiasm and energy. He urged me to join him in performing the pilgrimage ceremonies for that year, and I welcomed the invitation. We performed the rituals in the company of the large group of my students and his followers. But no sooner were the ceremonies over and the festival celebrated with the arrival of the month of Muharram than my companion told me with a certain degree of alarm that he had to return to Bijaya. He had had a dream in which his poor wife was begging him to return to the Maghrib as soon as possible.

How could I possibly do anything but agree with his decision to return to his homeland and family that was longing to see him? If circumstances allowed me to do the same, would I hesitate for a single second? At this point I recited his wonderful lines, while he accompanied me:

> O night, be you long or not, I am bound to stay awake.
> If my own moon shares the night with me, I will not stand watch
> over yours!

The difficult parting took place in the middle of the month of Safar. My only consolation was that Abu al-Hasan promised to return whenever he could, bringing with him news of my family and loved ones. He then urged his students to keep me company and follow my example. When the time came for the Jedda caravan to depart, I embraced him, my eyes brimming with tears.

"My master, haven of all that is good," he whispered in my ear, "no bond can be stronger than ours!"

Everyone now crowded round to say farewell to the shaykh, their voices uttering fervent prayers and their hearts bursting with fierce emotions. Behind me, a whole group, the majority of them from the Maghrib, recited some of Abu al-Hasan's wonderful verses:

> Ye mendicant, hear what you should do;
> Meander in the world and show off.
> There is nothing in the world more lovely than you.

> Forget about other people, and seek to understand the secrets,
> Clear the path before you, and you will see both past and future.
> The best of moments come when we are united with our very selves.

> Let your thoughts roam free and pursue their ease,
> The entire universe is at your disposal.

The fact that Al-Shushtari had now departed from Mecca did not escape Abu Numa's notice. It was just a few days later, right after sunset on a steaming hot Friday afternoon, that he sent for me. He received me in a small lounge that was extremely sparsely furnished. I got the impression that he wanted to check on my health and activities; no one else was included. All that separated us was a small table, with some dried fruit and yoghourt on it.

"When two holy men of God get together," he began by saying, his face wreathed in smiles, "both governor and sultan get ignored! Al-Shushtari has managed to preoccupy your time and energy. There's nothing I can do when you're devoting yourself to the things and people you really love. If it weren't for the fact that I've been incredibly busy myself, administering the lives of the Prophet's family, arranging housing and water facilities during the pilgrimage season, not to mention forays against thieves and highway robbers, I would have demanded my own time and share of enlightenment from you!"

I tried to appear duly humble as I made a point of showing the governor how embarrassed I felt by his words of praise.

"Your campaign, my Lord, against those who would defile this sacred territory," I said by way of focusing on one of his major points, "pillagers and thieves that they are, is indeed a campaign in the cause of God Almighty. Pilgrimage caravans from a wide variety of lands have to cross dangerous terrain in order to reach the Hijaz. That terrain is full of pitfalls and dangers, and sometimes there are all kinds of taxes and major expenses involved too. The situation is so bad now that in the past several major scholars from Andalus have issued legal opinions annulling the obligation to go on the pilgrimage at all. Among intellectual leaders who never went on the hajj to Mecca are the philosopher judge Abu al-Walid Ibn Rushd and his colleague Ibn Tufayl, and the astronomer Al-Bitruji.* There are many other names as well. Ibn Jubayr* did complete the pilgrimage, he being a well-known traveler from the same region and period, and he suffered very badly in the process. In his book *Travels* he makes a point of registering his own annoyance. The passage, if I recollect it correctly, says, 'If there is a land that needs to be purified by the sword and washed clean of its filth and dirt with blood duly spilled in God's own cause, then that land is the Hijaz. At the moment, they don't seem to be bothered about the negative effects on Islam and the fact that pilgrims are liable to be robbed and injured.' This has been the situation until fairly recently. Now, thanks to the efforts of the sharifs in Mecca and all Muslims with your qualities, things are gradually improving."

The governor paused for a moment's thought.

"During your trip to get here or your time in Mecca," he asked, "have you been attacked?"

"No, I haven't. That is thanks to God's good grace and Al-Shushtari's letters of introduction. Also my caravan was protected by a troop of armed guards."

"By the Lord of the Ka'ba, I will not rest until I make it possible for pilgrims to come to the holy cities on a blessed mission, traveling safely and residing here in comfort. That's a promise I've made with myself. All the governors of the other cities in the Hijaz are doing the same thing. Success comes only through God! But what is really troubling me, and I can see no way out, is that Sultan Baybars is insisting that I swear fealty to one of his cronies who, it is alleged, is a descendant of the Abbasids, named al-Mustansir Billah, that being, of course, a direct imitation of the name of the Hafsid ruler to whom I have already sworn fealty, as you yourself suggested. As a scion of the Prophet's own family, I am totally unwilling to break my oath or indulge in any kind of dissimulation. You are a sage advisor in matters of religion and this world of ours, so what do you advise?"

I said nothing for a while as I tried to think of what to say.

"In view of your noble sentiments," I responded, "the appropriate answer involves adhering to the pledge you've already made and not giving way. Your noble status is one that I respect, and Baybars will never be able to do anything about it, however much he tries to interfere."

"I'm not worried about my own reputation. What bothers me is your position in Baybar's eyes. From now on, you're under my protection even more than before. Don't leave Mecca, or else no one can say what might happen. My protection only covers the city, not outside it, even Medina where the authorities are already furious with you."

"I already know that, Sir. And you can add the minister of Yemen, al-Hashwi, who loathes me, even though his master gives me all due honor and respect. God alone has the power and might!"

"My council has been purged of all those who resemble this stupid minister, chief among them being my chamberlain, 'Abd al-Muhaymin al-Khazraji. Everyone opposed to you is also opposed to me. I'm on my guard all the time and never allow myself to slack off. I'm attaching three guards to you, who will guard you night and day. They'll bring you any news about Baybars and his spies. With God's help, they'll protect you against their evil intentions."

"I beg you, Sir, spare me guards and detectives. My reason for making such a request is that at some point everyone in life will meet their end. Fate does not brook any caution!"

"From one point of view you're right. But I'd remind you that we're all enjoined not to expose ourselves deliberately to perdition. Baybars will undoubtedly be on his way here to perform the pilgrimage very soon. He'll be bent on searching you out and bringing you before him. You know full well why."

"At that point I'll take all necessary precautions. I've a number of hiding places in the desert around those holy sites."

"But you'll need to stay well clear of the famous caves and the sacred sites. Make sure you choose somewhere that's known only to God and don't come back until the danger is past and the storm has blown over."

The muezzin now announced the call to evening prayer. My host insisted that I lead the prayer, so I did so. Once we had finished, he accompanied me to his garden. While we were walking, he asked me what was my dearest wish. I said nothing.

"Isn't it to have your wife join you here?"

"Of course!" I replied at once. "But how can that happen?"

"I'll send someone to ask Al-Mustansir to grant that favor. I think he can do it. If not, how can his caliphate possibly have validity and how can anyone from east to west swear fealty to it?"

At that point a strange idea occurred to me: could it be that the letter of fealty that I had written was merely a pretext the governor had used to respond to my obvious desire to bring my wife and very life, Fayha', to Mecca?

"In my view," I replied somewhat hypocritically, "it's not a good idea to involve the caliph in matters that are beneath his dignity. Maybe he can't be bothered . . ."

"To the contrary," he interrupted firmly, "I'll use this request to assess his prestige and rulership qualities. By the Lord of the Ka'ba Himself, the Creator of male and female, if he doesn't respond to my request and refuses my initiative, I intend to break my vows of fealty to him. Let me take the matter in hand, and we'll see what happens. Now let's go to dinner."

I reminded him that, in accordance with Sufi practice, I preferred to sleep on an empty stomach. Saying farewell, I departed.

Oh my, how that idea began to churn inside me; it seemed to have drifted up from some secret lair, from deep-buried recesses in my soul. Beginning with that very night it kept haunting me, seething and heaving, provoking all kinds of ideas and surmises. The only way I found of suppressing or pushing it all aside

A Muslim Suicide | 353

was by reciting intercessions and going out to perform the prayers and talk to people.

About a month later the governor called me to a meeting in his alcove within the sacred mosque. He told me that he had indeed sent someone to ask that my wife join me here. I acknowledged his gesture and thanked him profusely for it. We then both performed the afternoon prayer with the congregation. When the prayer was finished, the governor added a prayer that God would grant me my dearest wish before the beginning of the year's pilgrimage season.

12

I NOW SPENT THREE WHOLE MONTHS living on tenterhooks, all the while recalling my own share of this lower world and displaying my fervent love for it. A little while later Abu Numa was able to give me the glad news that his envoy had been successful with Al-Mustansir: my wife would soon be leaving by ship along with pilgrims from Tangier and Granada. From now on, in my prayers and devotions my only request was that God would grant her a safe passage and spare her the travails and dangers of the journey itself. I began to recall the days of my life that I had spend in her care and protection; glowing images suffused my sight and soul, full of light and emitting wafts of perfume and beautiful garlands of flowers. Clasping those thoughts to myself all day long was enough to bolster my heart long enough to endure the trials of waiting.

A month and a half went by. Such was my love for my wife and my yearning desire to see her again, she being mistress of my body and soul, that I counted the passage of time in heartbeats. I decided to bolster my patience by performing the minor pilgrimage and standing on the Mountain of Mercy, invoking all kinds of prayers that would engender a favorable response and good outcome. That is how I came to compose the *Epistle at 'Arafa,* all of it in accordance with the statements of various schools and accepted traditions. For students I convened a number of sessions on the topic, in which I expounded on the work's major themes and explained the work's goals. I pointed out that the process of standing at 'Arafa was a gesture of wisdom, not merely an act of worship. I summed up the whole thing by saying, "The day spent standing at 'Arafa represents continuation of the relationship, severance of the appurtenances of causality, departure from the humiliation of pernicious phenomena, and entry into the higher world by means of essence. It is there that one glimpses the first signs of the ultimate, is exposed to the fragrances of the good works of the one who gains cognizance so that he may perceive and be perceived."

The students made many copies of the *Epistle* and circulated it to pilgrims and people praying in the Great Mosque and at some of the entry gates. Some copies fell into the hands of the usual set of jurist pedants, who proceeded to read it with their feeble eyes and intellects, not to mention their poor and outmoded methodology. It managed, not surprisingly, to get on their nerves and provoke their extreme anger. They all went to see the governor to complain and showed him a copy of the *Epistle,* pointing out passages that they considered deviant and blasphemous. When the governor looked at the text for himself, he told them to stop disparaging a holy man of God. He likened them to someone whom I actually mention in the epistle itself, looking out on the world from a concave fortress so that all he can see is whatever is directly facing it. Hatred, the governor reminded them, only engenders troubles. He went on to suggest that they follow the path of tolerance rather than the opposite, of lofty goals rather than paltry ones. With that he sent them away, duly humbled. Someone whose information was entirely trustworthy shared this account with me, all of which only increased my admiration for the governor.

With the arrival of the month of Rajab I was hoping dearly for the fulfillment of that amazing event, than which there could not be anything sweeter and dearer to my heart: to see my wife standing before me, to hug and kiss her and share those bonds of marriage that God and religion have declared permissible. During that month, never a day passed without my washing myself in either the Jamal al-din or the Mayyanshi baths, putting on some perfume, and donning my very best clothes. I would leave it to Ghaylan and Yasir to clean the house and prepare for my reunion with my wife. I would then hire a camel and head out of Mecca to the north toward the port of Jedda. There I would ask for the captain of the boat in which my wife was traveling. No one knew of his whereabouts. I kept on searching and making inquiries, but without success. I even gave my wife's name to the person in charge of receiving pilgrims. When I eventually returned to the residence at night, my hopes dashed, I would start to panic. I endured a thousand kinds of agony, and only intercessions, dreams, and constant prayer enabled me to overcome them. Both Yasir and Ghaylan realized full well what I was going through. They both advised me to relax at home. They volunteered to take turns traveling to Jedda to check on things.

But at the end of Rajab there came the day when I received the most unbearable news conceivable. At midday both men came into my room, their faces glum and utterly miserable, followed by a group of other people. From them I learned that my dear wife had died; they offered their sympathy and condolences. I looked like someone whose tongue had been cut out or who had swallowed steel; my only response was with eye movements and gesticulations. The captain of the vessel and its pilot both told me about the journey and the difficulties they had faced. They particularly emphasized the efforts they and the women on board had made to save my wife; she had been struck down by a fever, and it had reached its most intensive stage in the boiling heat of 'Aydab, that unlucky spot. But God had decided to take my wife to Himself, along with five other victims. They handed me the death and burial certificate before departing along with the group of other people, all of whom also expressed their sorrow and condolences.

No sooner had they left than both Ghaylan and Yasir burst into tears. I meanwhile was trying to get my tongue to work, while simultaneously holding back my own tears and preventing myself from feeling giddy. They then took me into the garden, where a host of mourners, students, and disciples were gathering, people I knew and others I didn't.

Just after noon, a group of sharifs arrived, with Abu Numa at their head. They all offered me their condolences, while Yasir was yet more affected by the fact that the governor and the sharifs had come to see me. He and his assistants did their level best to offer a welcome to the mourners according to custom and tradition. Just before the afternoon prayer, everyone left for the sacred enclosure in a procession that I myself headed, accompanied by the notables of the city. Their leader held on to my arm and from time to time whispered words of sorrow and sympathy into my ear. Once the ablutions and prayers were over, we were summoned to the prayer for the departed. The ceremony was conducted in a reverential manner. When it was completed, I told my distinguished companion the governor that I dearly wished to return to my residence and rest. He suggested that he would accompany me on a trip to visit my late wife's grave and gave me a choice of two dates. "The best charity is that which comes soonest," I said, quoting the old proverb. With that, we embraced, and everyone went their own way.

Once back at my residence, I locked the door and lay down on my bed. Now the tears came, and I started sobbing quietly, fully aware that there was no way of salving my shattered soul and broken heart. I felt absolutely terrible and was unable to sleep, except perhaps for the occasional nap. This went on for two days or more, at the end of which Yasir knocked on my door to make sure I was still among the living. He told me that the governor had been asking for me. I decided to get up, wash, and pray. As I left the house, I acknowledged the condolences of a new set of people, including students and disciples. I first checked on the date and time, then headed for the governor's palace, where I found Abu Numa waiting for me.

As I walked toward him I offered my apologies, but he gave me a warm and sympathetic welcome. He took me to a back courtyard where a troop was ready to leave. We both mounted horses and headed for the Jedda port surrounded by armed guards. Once there, we boarded a boat along with our mounts, bound for 'Aydab. When we arrived, he headed for the cemetery to the south of the town that had been designated on the death and burial certificates. The five members of the guards split up to look for the other victims who had been buried here, and I trusted my heart and instincts to direct me to the place where my late wife was buried. I walked very slowly, followed by my companion who had made this trip possible. When I stopped, I took a look at the letters inscribed on the grave to my left, and there indeed was my wife's grave. Without tears or panic, I leaned over the soil and inhaled the blessed scent of the precious one it contained. The sharif did likewise. I then pronounced some short verses from the Qur'an and prayers invoking God's mercy on the pure spirit of my wife, asking that the Creator grant her entry into the broad expanses of His paradise. All around me, the sharif, his guards, and some local indigents kept repeating their amens and invoking phrases appropriate for the place and occasion. Both in the cemetery and by the gate I handed out as many alms as I could, as did the governor himself. With that we returned to Mecca. During the return journey the governor asked me about the idea of building a tomb for my late wife, but I declined his offer, saying that I thought it better for her grave to be just like the majority of other believers. Apart from that conversation, the governor and I remained silent for the rest of the journey.

I spent the rest of the month of Sha'ban alone in my residence. Ghaylan and Yasir did their best to make sure that my seclusion and devotion to both worship and rest were not disturbed. Truth to tell, during my time alone I was exploring entirely new and unknown terrain since I was gradually increasing the doses of some herbal substances so that I could get more and better sleep. The time I spent asleep during this particular phase and in my current mental state was filled with terrifying and totally abnormal visions. They were of such a kind, that, had I chosen during my periodic intervals of wakefulness to put on paper the kinds of things I could remember from these nightmares, I would have confirmed for sure to both politicians and jurists that I was indeed an infidel, someone who deserved to die.

With the arrival of the fasting month of Ramadan I decided to spend it in Al-Shushtari's hut. My primary goal was to rid myself of the flood of nightmarish visions I was having and also to strengthen my ties with the Maghribi folk in the Valley of Solomon's Spring. That is precisely what I did, but only after informing Yasir of my plans, leaving some of my belongings with him, and using his expertise to leave Mecca without my students and visitors being aware of it.

When I reached my destination on horseback, I was given the warmest of welcomes by the peasants. I explained my situation to them and made it clear that all I needed was seclusion and the opportunity to worship. They all expressed their condolences on the death of my wife, and in a spontaneous and sincere way that brought tears to my eyes. They all swore the most solemn of oaths in the name of God and his holy men, with Al-Shushtari in the forefront, that they would protect me and keep my secret safe, even if a tyrant or legal authority inquired after me.

Al-Shushtari's hut here was like the one he had built in Bijaya, the only difference being that I had this one to myself and did not have to share it with either a Christian or a Jewish ascetic. Within its walls I found peace and quiet. I only left it once in a while in order to take a stroll or eat breakfast and chat with my guardians. As a way of preventing the nightmarish visions from overwhelming me, I slept as little as possible, but the amount of time I stayed awake at night meant that, during the afternoons and at twilight time, I felt a powerful urge to take naps. When that happened, I used to have a number of daydreams, but, when I woke up, I could only remember snippets of two of them, although both augured ill.

In the first I saw myself sitting down with Abu Hayyan al-Tawhidi, accompanied by another man who looked both wise and august. Al-Tawhidi kept leaning over and reciting prophetic traditions to me, all without attribution as was usually the case with him. He would tell me that some of them were examples of *hadith qudsi*,* while others were ones that the Prophet had dictated to him in dreams. I then watched as he turned to his companion. "So it's wrong, Sophocles," he said, "to follow your views and state that man desires to live long even when he simply shifts from one misery to the next. I have to tell you clearly, as an old man with a decrepit frame and bent back, that your views are lacking in precision. Like me, you yourself will not be spared the impositions of a long life nor will you see any more benefit from this mistaken view than anyone else. Quite to the contrary, miseries accumulate and beset mankind, no matter what the age or time."

In the second dream I saw a woman who looked exactly like me. She refused to acknowledge the fact that I had already forgotten the one thing that I had considered the most precious thing in my life.

"What's that?" I asked her.

"Good grief," she responded, "the manuscript—your lost manuscript!"

I told her that I had long since despaired of ever locating it and refused to bother about something that no longer had any point.

"But your long lost manuscript's in my hands," she said. "I'm prepared to give it back, but on one condition."

"And what's that?" I asked her.

"That you change your religion, and become a Jew."

"I belong to a faith that represents the seal, substituting the general for the particular, and even the One and Only God for the Trinitarian views of the Gospels. All that makes it unnecessary for me to bother about coincidentals, even if they include my manuscript."

The fields and orchards all made it possible for me to gradually dismiss these nightmares and daydreams. I decided to extend my stay so I could allow my spirits to recover from the strains and miseries to which they had been exposed and renew my sense of expansion and security. I spent my time on a number of different activities: contemplative prayer and a decision not to write anything (except with that unseen pen that operated in the imagination); learning about certain horticultural and irrigational skills from my expert guardians; teaching their children language and grammar rules; and occasionally resolving disputes that arose. All that was in addition to the walks I took in the area and its surroundings. I used to walk somewhere and sit on the roots of flowering trees. Once in a while I would emulate Al-Shushtari, my beloved friend and host, by rolling in the grass and earth; at others, I would imitate birds and domestic animals by sharing their sheer delight in life. Finally I would head for Solomon's Spring, drink some of its water, and wash myself.

However, no one should imagine that I ever forgot about my dear wife who had died on her way to Mecca. While I was staying in these regions, I would often visit her grave in my imagination and spend as much time as I could clasping at its soil, bathing it in tears, and implanting my fervent kisses on it. It would have been my dearest wish to find an entryway so I could be with her, thereby joining her in proximity to God Almighty and the havens of that wondrous eternity.

13

FIVE MONTHS LATER Yasir came out from Mecca to inform me of something that was almost inevitable: Abu Numa and my disciples were insisting that I come back. What is more, Sitt Umama had returned to the city and kept asking for me. Yasir asked me if I would in fact come back, then handed me a letter from my students and another from my dear friend Al-Shushtari. Both of them offered their condolences on the death of my beloved wife.

At sunrise the next morning, I said farewell to my Maghribi guardians, but not before they had received a promise from me to come back at the earliest possible opportunity. I returned to my residence in Mecca as fast as my horse would allow. Yasir and Ghaylan both welcomed me profusely. I washed, prayed, and changed clothes, then headed for the governor's palace, eager to find out what had led him to summon me back. When I arrived, he greeted me warmly and, with a minimum of questions, assured himself that I was well. For a while he spoke about his concerns and responsibilities: making the road to Mecca safe for pilgrims, preparing things for the pilgrimage season, and implementing various measures to control the flood of visitors so as to avoid troubles and disasters. I shared with him my view that there should be some limit to the number of visitors to the holy shrine at any one time and some organization of the way in which they moved in groups through the various stages of the ritual. In particular, there was a pressing need for more guards, doctors, and medical technicians. On that count he agreed with me and promised to do whatever he could.

"But then," he sighed, "what are we to do when so many pilgrims hope to die and be buried in this blessed territory?!"

In my own mind I resented such people, but what I loathed even more was the idea of those nasty, murderous thugs who waylaid pilgrims—may their efforts and pilgrimages find no such blessings! For a few moments my companion said nothing, as though he were preparing to tell me something momentous, the real reason for summoning me. The gist of it was that every indication suggested that Al-Malik Al-Zahir Baybars was planning to perform the pilgrimage this year. He therefore encouraged me to take all necessary precautions and to avoid all the usual hiding places, beginning in Dhu al-Qa'da until such time as the danger was past. That was particularly necessary, he went on, because Baybars had learned the identity of the author of the letter of fealty to the Hafsid caliph, al-Mustansir.

I calmed the governor's concerns about my precautions and plans, offered him my prayers of thanks, and then left with a show of determination.

So here we were in the first day of the month of Jamadi al-Akhira in the year 667 AH [1269 CE]; in other words, five months or less before Baybars would arrive. I decided to spend the time between my residence, the Hira' Cave, and Abraham's Shrine. At times I would be instructing students, while at others I preferred to be alone and spend the time in pleasant contemplation. When I returned to the Meknesi residence, it was to find Yasir waiting for me. He indicated Sitt Umama, who was awaiting my return in the garden. No sooner had I moved toward her than she jumped up, kissed my shoulder, and offered me condolences on the death of my wife, her voice full of sadness. In order to calm her down, I offered her my thanks, then led her back to where she had been sitting. I asked her how she was, but her only response was to lean over—her eyes still filled with copious tears—and to tell me, "God help you, Sir, in the loss of your beloved wife. Only someone who has also lost an irreplaceable loved one can truly appreciate the pain you must feel. Promise to take me to her grave so that I can beg God's mercy on her pure soul. If you agree, then let it be soon, the last Friday of this month." I signaled my acceptance of her suggestion, then accompanied her to the door, feeling deeply affected.

Immediately after dawn on the appointed day, I charged Ghaylan with accompanying the lady on the caravan to 'Aydab, while I would join them at the cemetery in that unlucky town. Thus it came about that, just a few hours later, we were standing together at the graveside of my beloved wife, Fayha', begging God to have mercy on her and praying fervently. When it was time to go back, my female companion asked for a little more time. I watched in amazement as she proceeded to throw herself on the grave, embrace it fervently, and utter uncontrollable sobs, moistening the soil with copious tears. At the same time she kept repeating typically Egyptian prayers, the like of which I had never heard before. For a few moments, Ghaylan and I just stood there, mouths agape, not knowing what to do. At that point the sun was right overhead and beating down on us. The lady now begged me to let her spend the night in the company of Fayha' and her pure spirit, but I firmly rejected the idea. I stood her up, clasped her to me, and headed for the exit so as to put a distance between her and the grave. She kept on crying, but then fell silent. At the cemetery gate I handed her over to Ghaylan to take back to Mecca and the Muwaffaq hostel. Meanwhile I mounted my horse. In the light of what had happened on this truly amazing morning, I let both it and my emotions have free rein.

Before the end of Rajab, what had been becoming more and more likely actually happened. Using a dogged insistence that was impossible to resist, both Yasir and Ghaylan urged me to act—namely to marry Sitt Umama in accordance with all the rituals enjoined by the faith, God, and his Prophet. The whole thing was done with a minimum of fuss or ceremony so as to reflect the more intimate joys implicit in the occasion. The actual ceremony of the wedding night took place at my residence, and a day later the bride moved to a life of security beneath my own roof. There I spent a period of almost two months in her amiable company. When the month of Ramadan was almost at an end, I suggested that we spend the festival period at Solomon's Spring, although I did not explain to her what was the real reason, the compulsory factor, that required me to go there. She seemed pleased by the idea and readily agreed.

Just before we left, I told Yasir why I needed to get out of Mecca. He swore to keep my secret to himself and to take care of my residence. I asked him to purchase a mule for my wife, put some of my own belongings on his own riding animal, and ride with her to a place he knew well. I would go ahead of them a little way. Yasir realized the purpose of the plan and agreed to make the necessary arrangements so things were as safe as possible. And that is precisely what happened—all thanks be to God as is due!

I was delighted to be back once again with the Maghribi peasants and staying in Al-Shushtari's hut. I was equally delighted that Sitt Umama was with me as both wife and companion. I was happy to see how much she enjoyed the orchards and the generous people who maintained them. I told Hamada the Zanati, their leader, and his confidants that I had married Umama and gave them a few details about my new wife. They all congratulated me and offered their blessings on our marriage. They then took both Sitt Umama and myself to a big tent with furniture and all kinds of coverings. News of my marriage soon reached the women, and they arrived to take Sitt Umama away to their own quarters, about which men know absolutely nothing.

On the Night of the Festival itself, I caught the sounds of women singing poems and ululating, then watched in the candlelight and lamplight as they encircled my wife and in sight of everyone led her to my tent to the accompaniment of blessings and expressions of joy. At the threshold of the tent, they all sang and danced. The point of all this, I gathered, was that they were bringing Sitt Umama to me as a pure, new bride in accordance with their customs. My assumption proved correct in that, no sooner had they left us alone, than the tent flap was lowered and they all departed quietly.

Sitting by my side, my new wife was almost dizzy with the overflow of emotion and bashfulness. Her full body was regaled in a flowing white gown that exuded a gentle warmth and a lovely musky scent. Her lovely face was glowing; it was as though the women had used some holy waters to recreate her beauty anew, so that this woman from Egypt had responded willingly to the hands of the women from the Maghrib. All praise be to God for his beneficence and generosity!

The second wedding night was even better than the first!

All praise to the One who can reinvigorate the veins after they have atrophied and revive the senses when they have grown lethargic! You can bear witness, Sitt Umama, can you not, that I have not forgotten my share of this lower world, as the Lord of mankind has commanded and recommended . . .

Next morning my wife woke me up very gently, albeit with the help of the cock's crow and the sound of activity outside our tent. Both of us looked incredibly happy.

We both took deep breaths and ingested the fragrance of plants and crops all around us. After washing ourselves and doing the ritual ablutions, we prayed the dawn prayer, then made ready to join the rest of the group and participate in the festival celebrations. While I headed for the men's group and their leader, Hajj Hamada, some women arrived to take Sitt Umama off to their section. The men all offered me their heartiest congratulations and good wishes, then insisted that I had to sacrifice a lamb that they were offering as a celebration of my marriage and my presence among them. All I could do was to accept their offer, and I did so amidst a positive hail of shouts of "God be praised" from the men and ululations from the women, while the children made their own din.

When the time for the noon prayer arrived, I served as imam for them all in the open air. That done, we all moved to the chief's tent, where the festival feast had been laid out. Everyone took as much as they wanted; in fact, encouraged by my host, I ate more than I should, even though I made an effort to eat less by asking them all a variety of questions. I wanted to know where they all came from and what their ancestry was. I discovered that they were Arab Amazigh [Berbers] who through a process of intermarriage had become a single unified tribe, which explained why they came from various locations. I was told that some of them were from the fertile Moroccan coastal region, which explained why they were now living where they were and knew about plowing, crops, irrigation, and harvesting. They each took it in turn to address my curiosity by providing particular details, with their leader offering the most information of all.

For my part, I started reciting various Qur'anic verses and hadith relevant to the topics, duly explaining their significance in terms that they could understand. They offered praise to God and prayed also for his Prophet. They were equally complimentary about my own learning and the way I could invoke such a wide variety of knowledge and explain things so clearly. We continued in this fashion until the time for afternoon prayer arrived, which we all performed in a spirit of mutual affection and serenity. With that done, I asked Hajj Hamada's permission to rest.

There was no sign of my wife in my tent, and I fell into a long, deep sleep. When I eventually awoke, it was to find Sitt Umama by my side, softly whispering my name with affection and warmth. I gave her a hug, and she rested her head on my chest.

"The way these Moroccan women keep treating me with such warmth and generosity is truly amazing," she told me happily. "Here we both are, living with these wonderful people in these gorgeous pastoral surroundings! It feels as though I'm either a genuine princess in a dream or else in paradise!"

Those words of hers suddenly reminded me that I had been having a dream about our stay in this beauteous paradise. It had only been ruined when soldiers had arrived to take me away and kill me. I came back to my senses to hear my wife breathing deep sighs.

"You certainly are a real princess and more, dear lady!" I said.

"And you are my guide and the source of my good fortune!"

She sat down, lit the lamp, and then proceeded to show me the bottles of perfume, kohl, and new clothes that the Maghribi women had given her as gifts. She asked me if I was going to sit with the men and chat.

"No," I told her with affectionate longing, "tonight is our night. Tomorrow can wait."

When I woke up the next morning, my tongue was still moist from repeating the prayer that I must have invoked just before going to sleep and probably during it as well: "O God, the One, the Worshipped, please allow my wife to remain with me and do not bring a dire punishment."

This then was the way I managed to spend several wonderful days with my wife. She passed her time with the women and looking after me, while I spent mine looking after her and attending to the needs of the group—leading the prayers, chatting with them, offering advice on issues they raised, and teaching their children. I also spent some time alone, contemplating and reading some of the materials I had brought with me. I only wrote in my mind, using that invisible pen.

One morning at the beginning of Dhu al-Qaʻda, my wife and I got up full of energy and went out for a walk in the surrounding fields. Here and there we spotted guard dogs, but they did not snarl or bark. Breathing in the pure air, we decided to extend our walk. As we passed by the animal pens, I started telling my wife about the lofty palm trees and their luscious fruit hanging down. I also described the other crops for her and detailed the beneficial health effects of each one. For her part, she kept praising the Creator and pointing out the vegetables and aromatic plants with their particular scents.

"Just look at the vegetables in front of us," she said, "and the carrots and cabbages over there. Eggplant as well! See the roses and ben, not to mention the myrtle, jonquil, and jasmine! My dear, how delightful are their scents and blossoms for both eye and nose, in fact all the senses combined!"

Like my delighted companion I could only marvel at the wonders of nature and be deeply affected by them.

"Umama," I said, "the essences of these plants and scents all aspire to their Creator, blossoming and flourishing so that they may receive wafts of divinity from light, dew, butterflies, and bees. Every single pulse you see comes only through the Spirit of the Truth."

We continued enjoying the magic of our stroll through nature till we had gone way beyond the hedgerows of figs and straw. Just then, two men caught up with us and asked us to go back the way we had come. The chief of the group was waiting for us. I left my wife and went over to greet him. His smiling response was mixed with a certain level of concern and aggravation. He accompanied me to my tent and sat down to have some breakfast. He handed me the present that he had been carrying under his arm: a brocade kaftan, a woolen undershirt, undergarments, headcloth, and shawl. I thought the gift was far too much, but I could do nothing but accept it. I thanked him and offered prayers for him, his family, and his tribe as a whole. I then asked him what the problem was.

"It's all fine, beloved of God," he replied kindly. "If you're not aware already that you're under my protection, then be aware of it now. Don't go outside the bounds of our territory, or else my guards will bring you back the way they did a few moments ago. If you want to go for a walk, it's better to take some of my men with you, but not your wife. My own shaykh, Al-Shushtari, committed you to my care, and the sharif of Mecca has also told me about your situation. My loyalty to both those men requires that I make sure that you are safe and sound."

I immediately understood what my breakfast companion was telling me, and promised to take all necessary precautions.

"Tell me, Hajj," I asked him, "has Sultan Baybars already arrived in Mecca, or not yet?"

"People say he's going to arrive either in the middle or toward the end of Dhu al-Qa'da. But his spies and agents have already arrived to make preparations for him to perform the pilgrimage and meet his other demands. He intends to grab the Hijaz and the holy territories and demand that the sharifs join his cause. He has also declared his intention of arresting you, holy man of God."

I was amazed that he knew so much about me. The only source of such information that I could think of was Governor Abu Numa or one of his confidants. My amazement was even greater when I heard him say the following:

"The contact between me and the governor is Yasir from Yemen, the warden of the Meknesi residence. A few days ago, Baybars's spies harassed him by asking a lot of questions about you. They did not get what they were looking for. He comes here in disguise either at night or by day to tell me anything new regarding Baybars, who's after your head."

"Then what's to be done, brother Hammuda?"

"The governor and warden are both agreed that you need to restrict your movements to this area and not beyond. When they both give the word, you and your wife are to disappear from view."

"But where can we hide?"

"Holy man of God," he replied, "your hiding place is right under your feet. Come with me, and I'll show you."

We both stood up, and my companion lowered the tent flap. He pulled my bed board back a little and removed some soil with his powerful hands. An iron door appeared, which he lifted up and put to one side.

"This is our underground storeroom," he said as he lit a candle, "so here's your hiding place. Come with me."

Following in his footsteps I descended a ladder leading to a wide cellar. When he lit some lamps, I could see bedding, floor covers, and furniture in the middle, while in the various corners were piles of sacks that, he told me, contained foodstuffs stored here for use during drought years. He showed me where the bathroom was and a hidden opening with a tunnel that led to another cellar with an exit into the desert.

The cellar had enough light to see by, and the air was breathable; there was certainly enough food to last for a while. On the back wall I noticed some weapons hanging, along with baskets of onions and garlic. Turning away, I offered words of admiration for this remarkable place. I then followed my guide back up the ladder. While he was replacing the soil and bed board, I declared myself completely satisfied with the plans. With that, he said his farewells and departed, assuring me all the while that only his very closest aides were aware of the cellar's existence.

Someone who is totally accustomed to spending time alone will never find disappearing for a while all that difficult. The slogan adopted by Shaykh Ibn al-'Arabi was mine as well: "Seclusion brings with it knowledge of this world of ours." But how was I going to explain to my wife, Umama, what I would have to do in order to avoid imminent danger?

At night I allowed her to recount to me what she had been doing that day and what she proposed to do with the Maghribi women the next day. When she had finished, I decided that I had to tell her what the situation was with me and what I had to face. I whispered to her a brief but frank summary of things. When I finished, I was delighted to see how easily she had understood and how readily she agreed.

A Muslim Suicide | 369

"A good wife sticks with her husband through thick and thin," she told me.

I was as pleased and relieved to hear it as I was when she told me that we had to be steadfast in resisting such trials and tribulations. Just before we gave ourselves up to slumber, she swore to me that what I had told her would remain a secret buried deep inside her heart.

In the ensuing days I stayed inside my tent, only leaving it when it proved really necessary. Umama busied herself with the usual chores and continued that way. When the first day of the pilgrimage month arrived, I was awakened by someone calling my name at the door of the tent. I had no doubt that it was my host, so my wife told me to hurry up and get ready. I went outside to check, and there was Hammuda, the head of the tribe, holding a huge basket full of food. He told me that Sultan Baybars had arrived in Mecca and urged me to go down into the cellar. He asked my permission to open it up, then proceeded to do so with great skill, apologizing to my wife all the while and urging her to grin and bear it. Just a few moments later, my wife and I, along with our belongings, were safely ensconced in our new abode. Our guardian had already lit the lamps and proceeded to hand over the basket, sacks of dates, dried fruit, a pitcher of water, oil, and honey. Before retracing his steps, he assured us that we would only have to stay down there for the pilgrimage season, no longer—God willing.

Umama now went to explore the place and its various corners and checked on the sacks and pitcher. She came back smiling. I decided to see how satisfied and happy she actually was.

"It's a cave," I said, "with no daylight and no sky above!"

"You proponent of seclusion and the ascetic life," she replied firmly, "do you really need those kinds of things? All you need to do is to close your eyes. In your mind's eye you can see light to envelop you and skies to give you shade. So now we can both close our eyes down here and seek peace and contentment."

O God, grant us both a sleep of reason, not like that of the Seven Sleepers of Ephesus* or that of the dead!

God answered my prayer. When I opened my eyes, it was to see Umama cooking food in a corner that she had turned into a kitchen. When she brought over the dishes, I asked her if this was breakfast or lunch. "Neither," she replied, "it's almost dinnertime." I checked my astrolabe and found that it was not working. That may have been because the cellar was too deep; I estimated about fifteen meters. Our stay in this cellar was going to be something the like of which I had never experienced before: no way of telling the time; only candlelight; and no heavens above. But, praise be to God, we had enough food, water, and air. My wife made me relax, and I enjoyed both keeping her company and drawing close to the Necessary Existent, invoking to the extent possible His blessed beautiful names.

I did my ablutions and washed, and then sat around a low table with Umama. I ate her food and praised her cooking—with its authentic Egyptian touch, but suggested that it was lacking certain necessary spices. She thanked me for my compliments.

"My dear husband," she asked me in amazement once she had finished eating, "you are clearly gifted in the realms of learning and Sufism, incredibly so. But I also observe that you are equally skillful in matters of politics and government. Otherwise why would the Mamluk Sultan Baybars resent you so much that he wants to catch you?"

I was aware that my interrogator already knew a few details about Sultan Baybars's life and admired him, as did I.

"My dear lady," I replied as briefly as possible, "major politicians and rulers are never happy simply to control the reins of authority. They've always wanted religious scholars to do their will as a way of enhancing their prestige and efficacy. If any religious scholar chooses to object to the process, their enforcers proceed to bully the scholar in question until he changes his stance and does what he is told; either that, or else he is exiled or murdered. The vast majority of religious scholars give up and go along. Only a tiny minority ever hold fast and stick to their beliefs. Through God's power and will, I'm one of that tiny minority. I've used outright rejection as my strategy, but without needing to die for it. That's why I'm now in hiding, the idea being that Baybars won't be able to do to me what Salah al-din the Ayyubid did to Al-Suhrawardi, for example (and there are many others as well)."

"So, my dear heart," she said, "you are refusing to die a grisly death! Here you are with me in this cellar, enjoying our legitimate pleasures and eating my *ful mudammas** and other dishes! This is a boon from God that the Mamluk Sultan cannot even imagine."

I laughed, and she laughed with me.

"Now our God has a claim against us!" I said in a more sober tone.

"Indeed he does," she replied. "But what prayer are we supposed to pray, when we don't even know what time of day it is? What is your opinion in view of this unusual situation?"

"No, you tell me what you think."

For a moment she stared at me in amazement. "Women have no role in such things," she said.

"Yes, they do," I replied. "You have knowledge, intelligence, and sincerity, even though our scholar-pedants may hate the very idea. Don't you remember the hadith of our noble Prophet concerning 'A'ishah,* mother of the believers: 'Take half of your religious beliefs from this Himyari woman!'?"

She paused for thought, then bashfully expressed her opinion with lowered eyes.

"In view of the requirements of this situation, you most just of people," she said, "we should combine the five daily prayers into one late at night, just before we begin to feel sleepy."

"By God, that's the correct answer," I said. "With a little bit more study and effort, I can give you a certificate in Mecca as an interpreter of religious doctrine. Now get up and wash, then finish the other things you want to do."

As I lay down on the bed with my eyes open, I uttered words of praise to God as I invoked devotional thoughts and gave more focused thought to what I might do in this cellar to use the time more profitably. Some ideas began to take shape in my head, and I made up my mind to clarify them as soon as I woke up the next day.

I was brought back from my contemplations by the sound of Umama's voice, waking me up again before I fell sound asleep. I proceeded to lead the prayer with my wife, who was now my companion in this cellar and my period of hiding. She would be keeping me company and using her care, joy, and innate sense of fun to lighten the burdens that I was feeling.

Next morning the first thing I did with my wife was to use some sacks and curtains to cordon off a corner for myself. In it I put a bed board, a table, and the poetry and other books that Al-Shushtari had given me. Among them was an incomplete copy of the *Kitab al-I'tibar* by the prince of Shayzar, Usama ibn Munqidh*—may God give us the benefit of his memory! From now on I started spending a lot of time reading and whispering the Kawthar litany. Umama meanwhile was spending her time memorizing the Qur'an, doing household tasks, and using incense to lessen the humidity in the cellar.

In a place where no light penetrates and no sound disturbs the silence, it is good for the soul to immerse itself in its interior world. In that world I was the monotheist existent, the tester and observer. I had both roles to play and postures to maintain, the keys to which in my current situation involved as much as I was able to remember. My entire life bubbled and rose before my eyes with images and memories, taking me back to different periods and places, events and faces, all of them intertwined and interconnected. One might say that they provided a snapshot of what I had been and the point I had now reached. As I delved into my memories, famous dead people came to occupy a prominent place and lofty station, headed, of course, by my wife, Fayha', who had been my very life and the lovely facilitator of my closeness to God Almighty.

I spent several days—I estimated them as six—either in my little corner or in communion with my wife. On the seventh day in the evening I heard Umama utter a cry as I sat in my closet. She had seen a basket lowered with a rope from the cellar entrance. I inspected the basket's contents and discovered food, water containers, and a note from Hammuda. He told me that "troops from Sultan Baybars had come to the encampment three times; they had searched everywhere and asked about you, holy man of God. I denied all knowledge of you, and so did the other members of the tribe. With that they went away. Through God's power, the ordeal will soon be over!"

"Our ordeal will be over soon, Umama!" I yelled to my wife. "Very soon."

She looked delighted at the news, although a cough kept preventing her from saying so. I gave her some honey mixed with oil. With God's help the cough became less severe. The next day, being the one when pilgrims go up to Mina, I invited my wife to do a virtual performance of the pilgrimage rituals, and she proceeded to join me, exactly like Al-Hallaj and others who were not able to perform the pilgrimage itself. When we had finished, we recited the name of God many times, then spent the tenth day relaxing, and making up for the food and sleep we had missed.

The next morning, a table was lowered that for both of us was a festival in itself. We put on the finest clothes that we had been given as gifts by the generous folk above us, performed the festival prayers, and then took turns reciting muwashshahahs and songs. Then I did what I loved to do so much, namely pacing and strutting up and down the cellar, followed by my wife, who perfumed me with incense and sprayed scented water over me. She was ululating and praising the fine clothes I was wearing. She also offered prayers of protection on my behalf against those who kept conspiring against me and all my enemies. We spent some remarkable hours this way, during the course of which I was able to extricate myself from all thought of the devious tactics of those enemies and to confront the challenges involved with a spirit of pure joy and lofty intent. From morning till night that particular day was filled with happiness and precious moments of sheer enjoyment. The feeling only came to an end when our eyelids started to droop, and we performed the five prayers together.

Very early in the morning I was awakened by the sound of my wife's coughing hard. I lit a candle and noticed that she was looking very pale and breathing with great difficulty. It was clear to me that honey and oil were not enough to deal with the situation; what she needed was fresh air. I shinned up the ladder and started knocking hard on the door, asking for someone to come and help. It was not long before Hammuda was looking down at me anxiously, wanting to know what the problem was. I told him that my wife was not well, so he brought two women and told them to them get my wife out of the cellar as quickly as possible and help her in any way they could. It took only a few moments for one of them to check on my wife and give us the good news that she had completely recovered. I took a deep breath, then asked my colleague, once I was back inside the cellar, whether I too could come out into the fresh air. He gave me the choice, but told me that, if I came out now, there was still a distinct danger, whereas if I could stand staying in there a couple of days more till Baybars and his army had left, it would be better. Any danger to which I might be exposed would also inevitably involve the people who had been so generous to me and had protected me from hunger and worry. Bidding my companion farewell once again, I told him that patience and endurance were my decision and my best weapon—may God protect you and your people from all harm!

I lay down on my bed and focused on the hole covered by a curtain, wondering to myself what lay behind it and where it led. While I was indulging in such thoughts, I fell into a deep sleep and only aroused myself from its restless moments after an indefinable period. As a way of using up time and confronting the unknown, I decided to follow an idea that had been dogging me for some time. I got up, grabbed a lamp, and put a dagger in my waistband. Making my way through the hole, I entered the tunnel, sometimes crawling like an animal, other times upright like a human being. After a good deal of effort I reached another wide cellar. My lamp showed that there were cracks in the ceiling through which a certain amount of light was visible, although it was partially hidden by spiders' webs. I also spotted a swarm of bats hanging from the ceiling; that made me stop moving about so that I would not disturb those blind creatures and other night animals that I could not even see, all of which would create a disturbance and bring undesirable consequences. When I listened, all I could hear was the echo of horses' hooves above me. At this point I decided that I should go back the way I came, but, before I got there, I lay flat and held my breath, as though I were in a grave or over a precipice. When I started breathing once again, I recognized it as being a welcome differentiator between life and death! I started moving again. No sooner had I reached the hole in the wall and pulled back the curtain, than I found myself face to face with Hammuda and Yasir, who both helped me to get out. In order to calm their concerns, I told them I had just needed to get some more grain, basing myself thereby on God's own words in the Qur'an: "God has made the earth for you a wide space so that you may follow diverse paths in it."

I cleaned myself off and changed my clothes. When I went back to the two men, they were both smiling broadly. I asked them what news there was, and they both shouted with glee that Sultan Baybars and his army had finally left for Egypt. I embraced them both warmly and praised God for releasing me from my troubles. I asked them what day and time it was, and they told me it was afternoon in the middle of the pilgrimage month.

"Now, Sir," said Hammuda, "it's time to go back up into the fresh air, unless of course you prefer to stay here in the cellar."

"By God," I replied, "you've have been most generous, sharing both the surface and subterranean aspects of your region. Fresh air is exactly what I need. Then I'll be going back to my residence in Mecca."

Yasir agreed with my plans. He started collecting my possessions and carrying them back up to the tent above us. We spent some time resting and had lunch together, all the while exchanging sentiments of affection and promising to meet again. Meanwhile the men were putting the baggage on the pack animals, while the women surrounded Umama and wept at the thought of her leaving them. I stood up and said farewell to everyone, one by one, especially their chief, whom I thanked profusely for all he had done for me. That done, our little caravan moved off, duly followed by prayers and good wishes.

14

WHEN WE DREW CLOSE TO MECCA, Yasir took over and led my wife and myself by a quiet and uncrowded back way into the city, leading to our residence. He then turned his attention to unloading the animals and transferring our baggage. I was very glad to be back, and my wife encouraged me to relax and spend some time on my own while she undertook the necessary household tasks and prayed. Having tried in vain to stem her flow of joyous tears, I left her on her own.

Ah, prayers!

I had no idea how many of them I had missed, but all I could do now was to perform as many of them as I could and more. Thus it was that, in addition to the normal prayers, I performed liturgies and extra readings till nighttime came and my wife let me know that we needed to get ready for bed.

Next morning, I decided to find out as much news as I could. Ghaylan welcomed me with open arms; in all likelihood he had known nothing about the reasons for my prolonged absence or even where I had been. Yasir surprised me by handing me a letter from Al-Shushtari. In reading it I learned that he planned to come back to Mecca as soon as his health permitted. Yasir handed me a medium-sized purse, telling me that it was a gift from the pilgrim whose daughter's life I had saved. When I looked inside, it was to find a whole pile of gold coins and jewelry. I told Yasir and Ghaylan to take their due share of the gold pieces and to distribute the rest as alms. I gave Umama all the jewelry. I asked Yasir for news of Abu Numa, the governor. Had he been asking for me? He replied that the governor had been away from Mecca for some considerable time, touring the cities in the Hijaz. His chamberlain and a small group of sharifs were acting in his place.

I now eagerly headed for the sacred enclosure of the Ka'ba and spent the entire day inside, praying, contemplating, and talking to whoever happened to approach me for alms, assistance, or legal advice. It was not long before a cluster of students gathered around me, praising God for my safe return and begging me to resume my classes as soon as possible. I promised them to do so and told them to read certain source-works that I named for them. A little while later, I joined the congregation in performing the evening prayer. As it came to a close, I noticed a neatly dressed and respectable-looking man directly opposite me. He responded to my greeting and sat down beside me. I remembered that he was Shaykh Safi al-din from India; I had met him two years or more ago in Mecca. He had borrowed a copy of *Escape of the Gnostic* from me, along with some of my epistles, saying that he would want to discuss them with me once he had read them. Now he offered to give them back to me, but I let him keep them as a gift. I invited him to walk with me outside the mosque, and he readily and joyfully agreed.

As we were walking amid the hubbub of the city's streets and squares, he started citing the text of complete pages from my works, particularly those concerning inquiries into the modes of knowledge of the true nature of things. I let him talk as much as he wanted, hoping to avoid any kind of argument—something that at this juncture I certainly did not need. But he soon paused for a moment and unloaded a whole series of questions and comments that showed clearly how enamored he was of the philosophical side of things and particularly Aristotle and his school. When he asked me to justify one parameter of philosophy and no others, I had to respond.

"When you have reached the age that I have and are in the situation in which I find myself," I said, "philosophy involves a concern with death and rediscovery of those divine recesses hidden within me. I am that Possible Existent, a part of the Necessary Existent, He who is eternal, possessor of the beautiful names and the heavenly kingdom."

"But then what?"

"That's it! Time, place, and circumstance do not allow for anything else."

The man was perplexed and asked me to elucidate.

"My dear Safi al-din," I told him, "if you are in quest of a philosophy that differs from what I have presented and extolled here, then seek it where you wish and delve into virgin fields, such as history, its events, eras, and vicissitudes. In order to do that, you should leave Mecca the honored city and the Hijaz in general. If you find my lengthy stay here peculiar, then you need to understand that

Mecca and its noble Ka'ba are my final resort in life and my enduring residence. In no other place within Islam's dominions will I feel protected and safe."

My companion leaned over and embraced me, showing me that he had fully understood what I was saying. With that, he said farewell and retraced his steps.

At home I found Umama waiting for me at the dinner table. No sooner did I set eyes on her than she started nervously peeling off her jewelry. She asked me whether it was permitted for a devout woman to bedeck herself in costly rings, armlets, bracelets, and necklaces. I told her that it was perfectly fine, as long as they were not being used for public display and vanity. I told her the story of the man who had given me the jewelry and purses of gold and followed it with the story of my correspondence with King Frederic. That gave me the opportunity to tell her where I had hidden the purses of gold that he had given me and to encourage her to use the money as she saw fit. She was duly amazed by both stories, and by the second one even more than the first. With that she proceeded to shower praise and prayers on me.

The month of Muharram in 668 AH [1269 CE] arrived, and days went by without any particular problems, as they had in previous months. Every time I thought about my wounded soul or felt nostalgia for my homeland and loved ones, I would seek distraction by going about my routines and visits. Whenever time permitted, I would teach the students and talk to residents and visitors to the Meknesi residence, usually sitting in the garden. I also sat with my wife and told her what was going on; for example, the fact that Abu Numa, the governor, had been away for a long time. Her gentle conversation used to calm me down and help me endure my adversities.

With the advent of Rajab, Abu Numa's absence moved out of the realms of astonishment to become a genuine mystery. No one whom I questioned had any idea of his whereabouts. All I could gather was that he was determined to fight the highway robbers and perform other worthy activities in Medina to the north, along with some other cities in Yemen where Sultan Baybars had managed to sow discord and strife. When it came to the governor's coterie—with their new chamberlain at the head—they chose to respond to my inquiries about their leader with reluctant and gloomy expressions. All of which made me decide that I would not set foot in the palace again unless the entire situation was much clearer.

Here was a case where I had no way of finding out anything about it, either its preliminaries or the current situation. Since I am not someone to indulge in secrets or to involve myself in conspiracies and plots, and am certainly not one of those juridical authorities who is prepared to make blanket decisions, this situation suggested to me that the best thing to do was to wash my hands of it completely and wait to see what transpired. In that way I could adhere to my own beliefs and the ethical principles that I hold dear. So, as the pilgrimage season arrived, then the festival, followed by the month of Muharram in the following year, that is what transpired. There was still no news of Abu Numa, apart from the rumor that he would be coming back soon.

In fact, it was not until the middle of Jumadi al-Ula that it was finally confirmed that he had returned to his palace and was staying in his residence and council chamber. For my part, I too stayed in my residence and my usual haunts, waiting until such time as the governor took the initiative of inviting me to pay him a visit.

Indeed an emissary from Abu Numa arrived at my house in the afternoon of a day at the end of Rajab, giving me the choice of either accompanying him then or else going on my own after evening prayer. I chose the latter, with the idea of organizing a number of issues in my own mind and going to our appointment under cover of darkness. And so it was. The governor welcomed me profusely, then sat me down beside him at a table filled with food. He seemed much the same as before, although he looked thinner and tired. I thanked God for his safe return to his base.

"And I in turn," he responded in his usual loud voice, "thank God Almighty for saving you from Baybars's clutches. I watched as he searched everywhere for you. At times it even seemed as though his only reason for undertaking the pilgrimage at all was to take you prisoner; either that, or else his own obligations would not be complete unless and until he caught you. When he failed to find you and eventually left, he encouraged his troops to provoke as much dissent and strife as possible among the rulers of the Arabian Peninsula and even the Yemen. It was the absolute necessity of eradicating these disputes and restoring some semblance of order among these people that has led me to spend so much time away from Mecca, quite apart from the normal campaign against smugglers and highwaymen. I think I've succeeded in doing all that, although I had to return quickly to Mecca in order to put down a conspiracy here launched by my chamberlain. I've now dismissed him just as I did his predecessor. Thank God, things have now returned to normal. That explains why, dear holy man, I've only been able to invite you here today!"

As my companion was talking, I commented approvingly on all his endeavors and prayed to God that he would continue to be victorious and successful. I felt a strong urge to ask him about my own situation and the future, with Sultan Baybars still intent on pursuing and imprisoning me.

"What amazes me," I said, "is that the Mamluk leader seems so intent on capturing a harmless person like me and watching my every move, when he has previously shown great mercy to his diehard opponents and dealt with them fairly gently! It all reminds me of Salah al-din al-Ayyubi who killed Al-Suhrawardi, the proponent of Illuminism, and yet, when he captured Jerusalem, he dealt kindly with the Crusaders, those consumers of Muslim flesh, and spared them any thought of detention or vengeance. I wonder, governor, did Baybars negotiate with you about my situation?"

"As far as possible, I steered clear of the subject. I only met him once, on the day he arrived. He asked me whose claim to the caliphate was legitimate, and in self-defense I replied that it had to be the Abbasid who was now under his control. He asked me about you, and I told him—this is exactly what I told him—'He may well have gone back to the Maghrib, or he may have died.' Apart from that, I only saw him again for a few moments when he was leaving."

"I don't want to cause you any more problems than I already have," I said after a few moments' reflection. "What do you advise me to do?"

"I promised to protect you," he replied, "and I'm not going to break that promise. My best advice to you is to go into hiding."

I raised my eyebrows in surprise.

"I would suggest that you send your wife to Egypt," he explained, "till everything blows over and the situation improves. By going into hiding, I mean that you should keep changing your address. Whenever you go anywhere, say you're going somewhere else. By indulging in both subterfuge and sheer patience, you're replicating the behavior of the Prophet himself."

With a smile I offered prayers to the Prophet, then stood up to bid the governor farewell. He gave me a warm embrace, warmer than he had ever done before.

I got the impression he was saying farewell for the last time. Trying to control my emotions, I departed with firm step and lofty intent.

"God protect us from anything even worse," I muttered to myself.

I now spent seven whole days, day and night, explaining my current plight to my wife and convincing her that she should go to Egypt ahead of me. I would join her whenever I could. She tried to persuade me that we could both go to Upper Egypt; we could stay at a farm belonging to her aunt and enjoy some peace and quiet there. I opposed the idea, saying that I would be much safer staying by the sacred enclosure than I would be in coming even closer to the lion's jaws.

At the end of Rajab, my wife suddenly started gathering up her possessions, teary-eyed. She apologized for seeming so reluctant and stubborn, but justified it all by saying how much she loved me and how worried she was on my account. I got her to stay with me for three more nights, then asked Yasir to accompany her to Jedda and arrange for her to cross to Egypt as comfortably and safely as possible. When the morning of her departure arrived, I handed her the purses of gold that I still had hidden, but she refused to take them, saying that I needed them much more than she.

A warm embrace, overpowering love, uncontrollable feelings, and copious tears. God, the Truth, alone has the power and majesty!

15

WHEN SITT UMAMA LEFT, I spent the entire time till the end of Sha'ban secluded in my residence, performing various rituals and devotions, looking out for early signs of danger, and surrendering to a variety of daydreams and nightmares. Some of the memories were packed full of disturbing images while others were calmer and more comforting. They would emerge from the deep recesses of my memory, gleam brightly for a moment, and then disappear again deep into an abyss. How could I possibly hang on to such memories and even record them when my hand felt almost paralyzed and my entire body was weak and out of sorts?

Since I was spending so much time in seclusion and eating very little, Yasir took it upon himself to serve me instead of Ghaylan. Every time he brought me food or information, he would ask me anxiously how I was. I would try to calm him down and eat as much as I could.

"Sir," he told me one evening somewhat diffidently, "I'm stopping your students from coming to see you and telling them that you're away. I'm doing it because you need to be safe, and I realize that you want to stay in seclusion. That's particularly the case since I've noticed some strangers among them, and I'm not too happy about their being here. I think it would be a good idea for you to move to Al-Shushtari's room where I can keep my eye on you. There's a hiding place in it that no one knows about except me. By the right of the One who has life and death in His hands, I'll never allow you to fall into the hands of any tyrant, even though he may pluck my eyes out or cut off my limbs."

I shook the man's hand and offered prayers of thanks to him. I agreed to go along with his plan and asked him to offer my apologies to the students. Before leaving, he handed me a letter that he said he had received from a traveler whose name he did not reveal. I opened it, hoping dearly that it might be from either

Abu 'Ali al-Nasir or Khalid from Tangier and his wife, 'Abla. However, I discovered that it was from the Sufi poet Najm al-din ibn Isra'il of Damascus. He had prefaced it with a wonderful poem in which he extolled me and my religious position. I did not respond to his letter because I felt exhausted; indeed I found it impossible to write anything at all. God is witness to what I am saying, He being the most merciful of all.

So on the third day of Ramadan I moved to my new quarters. Once there, I felt a new sense of security under the protection of that holy man, Al-Shushtari—may God cure him and grant him what he wishes and desires! Quite by chance, I found the small dagger that I had hidden in my trouser belt when I was hiding in the cellar in the orchards by the Solomon's Spring and once again hid it in my belt in case of unforeseen problems. In this room the hiding place consisted of another cellar, this time smaller than the other one; no one could possibly notice the entrance unless they were shown where it was. Acting on Yasir's instructions, I had to use it twice during Ramadan: that happened when there was a hue and cry by the door of the residence, and it emerged afterward, so Yasir informed me, that the noise was caused by my own students and followers. I also took to going out to the sacred enclosure at night; I did it three times in all, accompanied and protected by Ghaylan.

On the Night of Power, which, as the Qur'an says, is "better than a thousand months," I made my way alone to the Ka'ba shrine. I did the circumambulation in disguise and ran between Safa and Marwa. My prayer was that my Lord, even in this final struggle, would enable me to strive toward the best arrangement possible, my primary state, and then He would still think well of me. My other prayer was that my Lord would afford me a gentle entry to the process of eliminating all trace and memory of my existence, through my love and devotion to Him, the Necessary Existent, the Absolute. There would be no slips of the tongue, no rantings and ravings, and no cursing the fate that is, in fact, God in person, something the Prophet of Islam had specifically forbidden.

On the first day in the month of Shawal I woke up early to find myself bleeding from the nose, something that I took as a symptom of my blood being purified and cleansed. I spent several hours on my back, trying to stop the nosebleed with rags and using some of my potions to staunch the flow. But when I had managed to stop it, I started to shiver. A fever crept its way through my joints, followed by a migraine that was more painful than anything I had ever experienced before.

Just when things reached their peak, Yasir asked to come in. I did my best to welcome him with a big smile so as to conceal from him the state I was in. I asked him whether any of my followers had asked after me.

"One of Abu Numa's messengers whom I recognized came to see me," he answered hesitantly and with obvious reluctance, "and told me that his master was traveling. But, before he left, the governor had instructed him to tell the holy man, Ibn Sab'in, that his son, Hamada, had been put in prison in Egypt. Unless Ibn Sab'in came to Cairo very soon, his son would be killed. The governor—descendant of the Prophet himself—advised Ibn Sab'in to show the necessary endurance in the face of such adversity."

So here is yet another terrible blow I am facing!

Hamada, who is just twenty-five years old, is now in the tyrannical clutches of those Mamluks loyal to Baybars.

So the Mamluk sultan now summons me to Cairo. But how can I possibly go there when my entire body is weak and in great pain? Even if I could, there is no way that I could save the poor boy from a dreadful fate.

Your sympathy, O Lord, Your sympathy, please!

I asked Yasir to bring me some herbs and liquids that I named, and he did so. Once he had done that, I asked him to stop keeping watch and not to be alarmed if he did not find me at home. Entrusting my papers and epistles to his care, I asked him to tell people that I had decided to move to Basra on my way to India. I instructed him to spend the rest of the gold money in my purses on the needy. When I hugged him, he was in tears. I told him not to knock on my door unless I called him. He left for a moment, then with apologies poked his head around the door and told me that one of the students whom he had stopped coming in to see me yesterday had claimed to be one of my Andalusian devotees, named 'Abd al-'Ali al-Nasir. He went on to tell me that, after he had failed to get to see me, the student had said he would be going to visit the Prophet's mosque in Medina.

Yet one more piece of news assailing me like a thunderbolt!

So my beloved student al-Nasir had been there, just a few feet away on the other side of the door. And yet fate had decided to keep him away from me and prevent me from seeing him and giving him a hug.

O Lord, Your sympathy, please!

Galen,* Al-Razi, all the physicians of Islam, please help me!

If any of you know how to make me well, please do it with my thanks. If not, then I'll have to leave my health in the hands of fate and wait until the heavens lower a rope and open a gate to the galaxies of heavenly existence.

My potions and medicaments managed to lessen some of the pain I was feeling, but only some. At least it was enough to enable me to get some sleep—undisturbed some of the time, but restless at others. When I became conscious again, I could recall some of the visions I had seen but not others. I can vividly recall one of them: my late wife, Fayha', appeared to me, riding a splendid and richly caparisoned horse. She leaned down with outstretched hands and begged me to mount the horse behind her. But when I tried, my legs would not move. I found myself stuck in a slimy marsh with fetid water. The only way I avoided asphyxiation and drowning was by waking up in a panic.

In another dream Shaykh 'Abd al-Kamil from Meknes, my companion in the time I spent in the zawiya on Jabal Musa in Sabta, appeared.

"Do you remember me?" he asked.

"How could I not remember you?" I replied. "Had it not been for the mention of your name, I would not have been able to stay in the Meknesi residence in Mecca for so long!"

"Leave this ephemeral world now," he said, "and come to the eternal existence. This is where you'll find the genuinely pleasant life, boons and comforts the like of which no eye has ever seen, no ear has ever heard, and no human heart has ever thought of in the lower world. Did I not tell you that I would enter heaven through its wide gate? So come along. Your own gate may be even wider and larger . . ."

There was still another vision, but I can only recall a few nasty fragments of it. The young boy, Hamada, is screaming and shouting for me, begging his Creator to help him. A group of sordid Mamluks are toying with him and committing serial acts of sodomy on him.

I was flat on my bed for several days, and my health went from bad to worse. Sometimes I was bleeding from both nose and mouth; it was almost as though the blood intended to drain away completely. When I realized that my medicaments were not having any effect on my worsening condition, I gave up and took a large dose of herbs that I knew from experience would be able to tranquilize me. I hid the rest of the potion in my belt alongside the dagger.

I now decided that my condition might improve somewhat if I took an exploratory stroll around some of the quarters of Mecca at dawn. So I washed and did my ablutions, perfumed myself, and donned my nicest clothes. I stole out to the stables, got on my horse, and let it wander wherever it wished. As it ambled slowly around the city, I realized that we had reached the southern slopes of Mount Abu Qubays,* so I took the opportunity to bid farewell to the house where the Prophet had been born. I then turned in the direction of the Bilal Mosque and prayed as much as I was able, all in preparation for a visit to Medina in spite of the known enmity of its governor and all its juridical authorities. But the path in front of me seemed to have been cut—taunting me with the name of my beloved student 'Ali al-Nasir. The very idea seemed to me even more impossible than clearing a virgin forest or fertilizing a rocky mountain, not least because the midday sun was beating down and I was starting to bleed again from my nose and mouth. I decided to retrace my steps. As I was approaching the outskirts of Mecca, the pains in my head and body suddenly became worse than ever before, and I had no alternative but to swallow the rest of my herbal potion. My hope was to be able to endure the agony I was feeling. Staring at the sun high in the sky, I continued on my way, chanting as loudly as I could:

> Ye poor, hear what you should do;
> Meander in the world and show off.
> There is nothing in the world more lovely than you.
>
> Forget about other people, and seek to understand the secrets,
> Clear the path before you, and you will see both past and future.
>
> For me the very best of times come
> When I am gathered together with my own self.

When I reached the places where people were gathered and crowding around, I got a cupper to shave my head completely, then exchanged my fine clothes so I could disguise myself in a *jallaba* and headcloth, and set my horse free to wander wherever God willed. That done, I made for the Ka'ba shrine and circumambulated the black stone several times till I started feeling giddy. I lay down for a while near a pillar and lost consciousness for a while. When I came round, I discovered that my mouth had a gold coin in it; some rich foreign pilgrim had obviously put it there as an act of charity as they usually do with poor, needy folk who are sleeping in the mosque. I took the gold coin and put it in another sleeping ascetic's mouth. I then headed for a fairly deserted wall in the outer courtyard and sat down in the sun with my back leaning against the wall. The pain now eased somewhat. Using whatever level of consciousness remained, I started to review my life in the context of its imminent erasure amid the whirl-winds of oblivion.

In my estimation some small portion of my life would linger; maybe nothing more than that. In any case, here is what I would say to anyone who does remember me and writes about me:

Whatever else you forget, do not forget that, to the extent that I could, I encapsulated myself in the processes of growth and ascent to loftier planes. If I did manage to transcend my lower existence, then, by God who is the Truth, my only motivation was a sensible and individual desire, one with no equal: to speed my journey toward the Necessary Existent and to find perfection in the glow of divine abundance.

Through my cloudy vision Baybars now appeared, looking like a savage ghoul with a vicious, angry countenance.

"You heretic," he was yelling, "don't think you're going to escape my punish-ment. When you did those circumambulations a while ago, you looked just like donkeys around a mill-wheel!"

"Most people are like that, if you only knew," I replied, facing him down. "They claim to be carriers of the Qur'an, but in fact they have no awareness of it nor do they understand it. The simile used in the text of the Qur'an is exactly applicable to them: 'The example of those who were given the Torah but then did not carry it is like the donkey carrying texts.'"

With that, the Mamluk sultan issued his orders: "Grab this unbeliever. Grab him and kill him!"

Time went by, although I have no idea how long. Gradually the shapes of people and objects turned into blurry images of a kind I had never experienced before. I closed my eyes so that I could protect myself and think about some-thing else. Before long I watched as two octopus-like arms, long and powerful, stretched downward toward me and started lashing me with heavy blows. When they had finished, they were replaced by scorpions, vipers, and hornets, which started stinging me all over. They were followed by scavenger birds that kept pecking and gnawing at me.

Just a rainbow's distance from death, I was bleeding all over when Baybars reappeared, this time at the head of an army that was marching toward me.

"So, you renegade," he yelled, "you disobey me and write that anyone who does obeisance to Turks is only motivated by grief and idolatry. Take him away and kill him . . ."

I had neither breath nor energy to respond. I took out my dagger to defend myself. With that the soldiers surrounded me and started pounding and throttling me. Their leader grabbed my right hand, which was holding the dagger, and slit the veins. As I breathed my last, I kept repeating:

> *A Lord ruling, a servant dying, a vision looming, a truth proceeding,*
> *and you thus being;*
> *A Lord ruling, a servant dying, a vision looming, a truth proceeding, . . .*

Appendix · What Some Writers Have Said about Ibn Sab'in

O Ka'ba of all that is beautiful, my pillar,
> *Goal of constancy, you are my means to the beyond.*

O my treasure, my haven of belief,
> *The very mention of you is for my heart the best of*
sustenance.

With your heart you have attracted the whole of humanity.
> *You are indeed the very magnet of souls.*

By your proximity you have guided them,
> *Thus does the effective heir take over.*
> > —Al-Shushtari, in praise of Ibn Sab'in, *Diwan*
> > [Collected Poetry]

■ ■ ■

Ibn Sab'in was more knowledgeable about philosophy than Ibn al-'Arabi. In theology, both of them sought information from the same source, namely al-Juwayni, the author of the *Irshad,* and his followers such as Al-Razi. Ibn Sab'in was a major heterodox figure, a polytheist and magician. He was by far the brightest and cleverest of them all, and the most knowledgeable in matters of philosophy and philosophical Sufism.

> —Ibn Taymiyya, *Al-Rasa'il wa-al-Masa'il* [Epistles and Questions]

■ ■ ■

Ibn Sab'in studied the ancients and philosophy. As a result, he was to a certain extent heterodox in his views and composed in that vein. He was expert in the interpretation of symbols and made full use of this skill to hoodwink stupid rulers and wealthy people.

> —Ibn Kathir, *Al-Bidaya wa-al-Nihaya* [The Beginning and End]

▪ ▪ ▪

Ibn Sab'in was a person with a strong ancestral link to his home town. He grew up in great luxury and in a prestigious environment, the spirit of which never left him. He was handsome, attractive, and open-hearted, with a princely guise to him.

> —Lisan al-din ibn al-Khatib, *Al-Ihata fi Akhbar Gharnata*
> [A History of Granada]

▪ ▪ ▪

When it comes to books that contain these erroneous beliefs and copies of them that may be currently available to people—such as *Fusus al-Hikam* [Bezels of Wisdom] and *Al-Futuhat al-Makkiyya* [The Meccan Conquests] by Ibn al-'Arabi, *Budd al-'Arif* [Escape of the Gnostic] by Ibn Sab'in, and *Khal' al-na'layn* [Removal of Shoes] by Ibn Qasi, the decision regarding such works and their ilk should involve taking all copies and putting them in the fire, then washing one's hands so that all traces of their contents are erased. It is, of course, in the general interest of the community of the faithful that all bogus beliefs should be eliminated. It is the obligation of those in authority to burn such books as a precaution against corruption of the public mind and likewise to remove all copies that people may own so they can be burned.

> —Ibn Khaldun, *Fatwa fi Shifa' al-Sa'il Li-Tahdhib al-Masa'il*
> [A Legal Decision Regarding the Cure of the Questioner
> with a View to Instruction Regarding Questions]

▪ ▪ ▪

Concerning Ibn Sab'in I heard that he slit his wrists and allowed the blood to flow until he died.

> —Ibn Shakir al-Kutubi, *Fawat al-Wafayat* [Record of Deaths]

▪ ▪ ▪

I heard Shaykh al-Abili talking about Qutb al-din. He said that, in the seventh century, three great scourges occurred within Islam: the school of Ibn Sab'in; the Tatar conquest of Iraq; and the practices of the Assassins.

> —Ahmad ibn al-Maqarri, *Nafh al-Tib 'an Ghusn al-Andalus al-Ratib*
> [Waft of Scent Concerning the Lush Branches of Andalus].

Translator's Afterword

THIS MARKS THE THIRD TIME that I have embarked upon the difficult task of translating into English a novel by the Moroccan writer Bensalem Himmich, currently the minister of culture in Morocco (2009). The first two novels were both prizewinners in their Arabic form: the first (in order of publication in Arabic) was *Majnun al-Hukm* (1989; translated as *The Theocrat*, 2005), winner of the London-based Al-Naqid prize for fiction—an account of the reign of the controversial (and probably schizophrenic) Fatimi caliph Al-Hakim bi-Amr Allah (d. 1021); the second, winner of the Naguib Mahfouz Prize for fiction, was *Al-'Allamah* (1997; translated as *The Polymath*, 2004), an account of the latter years in Cairo of the great Arab historian and historiographer Ibn Khaldun (d. 1406). More recently still, Himmich has been awarded a second Naguib Mahfouz Prize, this one awarded in Cairo by the University of Cairo (2009).

In using the adjective "difficult" to describe the process of translating Himmich's novels into English, I am not specifically referring to the admittedly complex interpretive task associated with the transfer of any literary text from one cultural environment to another; that much is a given. What I am referring to is the fact that many of Himmich's novels are rich and carefully constructed investigations in fictional form of an entire period within the premodern history of the Islamic world writ large and of its intellectual and textual heritage. The creation of the appropriate fictional context for such investigations involves, it goes without saying, a number of factors: first, a profound knowledge of the repertoire of relevant historical and literary sources in Arabic and their replication—either directly or via imitation—in the novelistic text itself; then a series of narrative strategies in order to provide a variation on the normal demands of a chronological presentation of events and characters; and a style that is replete with the

391

complex lexicon of the various spheres of knowledge and research that are involved. In every case, the detailed descriptions of particular events and personalities and often extensive discussions of their implications also allow the reader to gain insights into other issues with much broader ramifications. In the case of the novel about Al-Hakim bi-Amr Allah, for example, we are dealing with the issue of contacts and conflicts between the Shi'i and Sunni communities of Islam during the tenth century CE and the origins of the Druze sect. With the novel about Ibn Khaldun, we are invited to listen in on a series of discussions between the theoretician of history and his amanuensis regarding his earlier work on the cyclical nature of events, the *Muqaddima* (Introduction) to his work of history, *Kitab al-'Ibar* (Book of Exemplary Lessons), and to consider various adjustments to the theory in the light of the chaotic events in Northern Africa and Spain during the course of the fourteenth century, to which Ibn Khaldun himself had been a witness and occasional participant. And, behind and beyond all these events and personalities, there lies the implicit topic that, in one way or another, can be seen as subsuming them all: the nature and legitimacy of authority, its use and abuse—that indeed being a topic the relevance of which is by no means a matter of interest in the context of the premodern history of the Arab-Islamic world alone.

In the current novel, the "hero" is Ibn al-Dara from Murcia in Al-Andalus—Islamic Spain—or, as he becomes known (and/or notorious), Ibn Sab'in (1217–1269 CE). As shown above regarding the other novels of Himmich that I have already translated, the confrontation in this novel between Sufi mysticism and philosophy on the one hand and literalist Islamic orthodoxy (and fundamentalism perhaps) on the other is once again not merely a topic for historians concerned with the premodern ages of Islam. Throughout his career, Ibn Sab'in finds himself surrounded by admiring students and challenged by literalist theologians and jurists who regularly incite the local political authorities against him. All of which turns Ibn Sab'in's life story into a lengthy travel narrative, one that, like many others, involves the Muslim obligation of the *hajj,* the pilgrimage to Mecca in the Arabian Peninsula, but in his case also a journey that is the direct consequence of political pressures, however much it may also represent a primary goal of his aspirations as a devout Muslim.

His life story begins in Spain, in the southern coastal city of Murcia (also the birthplace of another renowned Sufi figure in Islamic history—indeed perhaps the most renowned of all, Ibn al-'Arabi [d. 1240 CE]). Muslim rule in the Iberian

Peninsula as a whole, nominally under the distant suzerainty of the Almohad dynasty in their Moroccan capital city of Marrakesh but actually controlled by a number of local client (petty) dynasties, is in the gradual but inexorable process of collapse in the face of the ever-encroaching forces of the Christian *"reconquista."* That is the historical backdrop against which the novel's events as a whole are set, as the puritanical instincts of the Almohad dynasty's founders and propagators have gradually given way to a widespread quest for luxury, to rampant corruption, and—most directly relevant to the case of this novel's primary character, Ibn Sab'in—to an intolerance of radical thought and heterodox views, particularly those involving philosophy and Sufi ideas and their combination. In other words, we are here presented with a direct illustration of (and perhaps an inspiration for) the theories concerning the cyclical nature of tribal hegemony that were later developed by Ibn Khaldun and discussed (as noted earlier) in Himmich's earlier novel *Al-'Allamah (The Polymath)*.

The character of Ibn Sab'in, as developed in this novel, is to rue the fate of his native "Al-Andalus" throughout its narrative, but his initial preoccupation is with something else that is close to his heart, a manuscript in which he has elaborated his early ideas but which has been lost. His desperate search for it, in its physical form and within his own memory, provides a wonderful novelistic device, one that demands reflection on his current thinking and an elaborate process of considering who might have stolen it. Bearing in mind the quotation cited at the conclusion of the novel from the later scholar and statesman Lisan al-din ibn al-Khatib (d. 1374 CE) in his history of the city of Granada, namely that Ibn Sab'in was "handsome, attractive, and open-hearted, with a princely guise to him," it is not surprising perhaps that the people whom he suspects as possible thieves are mostly women that he has known in his younger days, indeed women of a wide variety in terms of origins and religious affiliations (or lack thereof)—that being, of course, an apt reflection of the diversity of Andalusian society in the thirteenth century. However, it is not only women that Ibn Sab'in attracts with his "princely guise," but also an increasingly large group of disciples and students. As word of his preaching spreads, with its vigorous advocacy of the need to incorporate into Islamic beliefs and practices independent thinking that is based on the study of philosophy and a quest for the transcendent, so do the local authorities—with Ibn Sab'in's own brother as their emissary—become sufficiently alarmed to demand that he either recant or move elsewhere. Reluctantly leaving his loyal disciples (and women friends) in Murcia behind, he begins what are to become his lifelong travels, by way of a short stay in Granada, to North Africa and the city of Sabta (often now written as Ceuta) and its most characteristic geological feature, Jabal Musa (Moses's Mountain), from the heights of which one can stare across the straits at that other rocky outcrop, Gibraltar (Jabal Tariq, named after the Amazigh general who led the Muslim forces across the straits in 710 CE). Indeed, Ibn Sab'in spends many hours staring wistfully across the water at his beloved Al-Andalus, which is being relentlessly lost to Islam thanks to the incompetence, corruption, and sheer venality of its Muslim rulers.

Once settled in Sabta, Ibn Sab'in takes up residence on the mountain in a "zawiya" (a term that I have retained in the translation because no single word in English can cover its multiple functions: part shrine and mosque, part hostel, part retreat-house, and, in this case, provider of shelter for the indigent and insane). His reputation as a teacher has preceded him, and once again he becomes something of a magnet to those members of the local community of Muslims, and particularly young Muslims, who are in search of an alternative to prevailing orthodoxies. The continuing crisis in Spain even leads him to engage in a fascinating correspondence with King Frederic of Sicily, who is shown to have a very open mind about Muslim-Christian relations and even seems inclined to support the Muslims in the conflict against his fellow Christians in Spain. Ibn Sab'in also forms a close relationship with Ibn Khalas, the governor of Sabta, who is duly impressed by the Sufi philosopher-theologian's wide learning, and in matters of both religion and medicine. However, it is another close relationship in Sabta that is to have a lasting impact upon Ibn Sab'in's life. A very beautiful and wealthy woman, Fayha', invites him to visit her opulent residence and makes it clear that she is in love with him as both a person and a spiritual guide. The two are married, and Ibn Sab'in moves from the mountain zawiya into his wife's home, to which a private closet has been added for his own use. They live a very contented life together, and Ibn Sab'in now hopes that he has found a haven of stability where he may continue to study, teach, worship, and contemplate. However, the admiration of Ibn Khalas is not sufficient to protect him from the increasingly pointed attacks from orthodox cronies dispatched by the Almohad authorities in Marrakesh, and eventually Ibn Sab'in is firmly instructed by the governor to move on. In this case, that implies undertaking the pilgrimage to Mecca and remaining out of the region until the political situation stabilizes (presumably as a result of the downfall of the Almohad dynasty). With a heavy heart Ibn Sab'in says farewell to his beloved wife, sending her to stay with her relatives in Tangier and not realizing at the time that he will never see her again.

The travel toward Mecca takes Ibn Sab'in first to the city of Bijaya (known in French as Bougie), and it is there that one of the most important relationships in his life is to develop. He meets the renowned Sufi poet Abu al-Hasan al-Shushtari (d. 1269 CE), a virtuoso singer, poet, and musician in addition to his role as a devout ascetic. The two men form a lifelong bond. The extract from one of Al-Shushtari's poems devoted to Ibn Sab'in that Himmich cites at the conclusion of this novel is evidence enough of the total affinity that connects the two prominent Sufis, with Al-Shushtari regarding Ibn Sab'in as his spiritual mentor:

> O Ka'ba of all that is beautiful, my pillar,
>> Goal of constancy, you are my means to the beyond.

> O my treasure, my haven of belief,
>> The very mention of you is for my heart the best of sustenance.

Since Ibn Sab'in is forbidden to return to the Maghrib (or, at least, without placing his life in great danger), it is Al-Shushtari whose journeyings back and forth across North Africa keep his friend in touch with his wife, colleagues, and students in Sabta, Tangier, and Spain.

The continuing journey toward the goal of the Hijaz in Arabia and the Ka'ba shrine in Mecca now takes Ibn Sab'in first to Tunis, from which he is ordered to depart in short order, and to Cairo, where, after staying in a local Sufi hostel and gathering—yet again—a group of students around him, he is gruffly interrogated by the presiding judges of the city and told to leave. However, placing his own life in danger, he stays on in order to treat the terribly wounded Al-Shushtari, who has joined the Muslim forces fighting the Crusaders at the Battle of Dimyat (English Damietta), part of what is generally known in Europe as the "Seventh Crusade," led by King Louis IX of France (1248–54 CE). However, once Al-Shushtari is sufficiently recovered, Ibn Sab'in joins a caravan heading south toward the port of 'Aydab, where he will find a ship to transport him across the Red Sea to Jedda and then Mecca.

It is in Islam's holiest site that Ibn Sab'in is to spend the remainder of his life, although, needless to say, he continually aspires to return to his beloved Maghrib.

His hopes of any return to his native Al-Andalus seem to have long since been crushed. The era—indeed the thirteenth century CE in general—is fraught with conflict: the ongoing reconquista in Spain, the equally ongoing series of Crusades, and, most recently, the Mongol armies' steady advance across Asia. In 1258, the Mongols sack Baghdad amid scenes of barbaric cruelty, in the process bringing to an end the 'Abbasi caliphate, which, since the mid-tenth century, had served the community of Muslims as a kind of spiritual figurehead but one with no real political authority. As the Mongols continue their westward march, it is the army of Egypt, led by the famous hero of Arabic lore Al-Zahir Baybars, that is to confront the Mongols and eventually defeat them at the Battle of 'Ayn Jalut (Goliath's Spring) in 1260. Ibn Sab'in, as we have noted above, has already been subjected to a kind of "inquisition" at the hands of the Islamic orthodox establishment in Cairo, so it is not surprising that the victorious Baybars, now ruler of Egypt, comes to Mecca in the wake of his triumph with the twin purposes of performing the pilgrimage and putting a definitive end to Ibn Sab'in's "heretical" preaching and writing.

Ibn Sab'in's prolonged stay in Mecca has been much facilitated by his friend Al-Shushtari, who has arranged for him to reside in a local hostel for Maghribi residents and visitors. From there, he is able to perform the major and minor pilgrimages on a regular basis, to explore the city and its environs, to observe the habits of pilgrims from different parts of the Islamic world, and to teach students in a variety of locales within the city and in its environs. Once again, his reputation as a scholar, physician, and radical thinker has preceded him, and he earns the respect of the governor of Mecca, who accepts his medical and spiritual advice while offering him as much protection as he can. It is the governor with whom Ibn Sab'in discusses the impending threat posed by the Mongol invasion and the vexed question of allegiance, now that the 'Abbasi caliphate in Baghdad has collapsed. In Egypt Sultan Baybars has accepted the validity of the claims of a young 'Abbasi "survivor" of the Mongol massacre in Baghdad, but Ibn Sab'in persuades the governor of Mecca (who is thus leader of the sharifs—descendants of the Prophet Muhammad himself) to declare his allegiance to Al-Mustansir, the Hafsid ruler in Tunis. With the advent to Mecca of Baybars himself, both the governor and Ibn Sab'in find themselves on the wrong side.

Yet another pattern from Ibn Sab'in's life journey repeats itself in Mecca, in that a beautiful Egyptian widow, Umama, visits him in his residence and declares her admiration. He is clearly much attracted to his devoted and lovely new disciple, but the image of his wife, Fayha', continually appears before his eyes. However, when Fayha' dies of a fever during her long journey to join her husband in Mecca, he finally acknowledges the suggestions of his companions that he is really obliged to marry the Egyptian widow who has remained loyal to him for such a long time.

Among the communities with whom Ibn Sab'in has become acquainted during his prolonged stay in Mecca is a group of Maghribi Amazighen who have established for themselves a complete encampment outside the city where they can practice their agricultural skills. It is among them that he and his new wife spend their honeymoon, and it is in their secret subterranean storeroom that they spend the entire pilgrimage month while Baybar's forces scour the city and countryside searching for him. Once Baybars has finally left the city after failing to achieve his goal, Ibn Sab'in and his wife emerge from their hiding place to much rejoicing. And yet the situation is still not safe. He decides to send his wife to Egypt for her own safety, and, upon hearing that his sessions are being infiltrated by spies, moves his quarters to live the lonely and secluded life of a bachelor once again. He becomes severely ill and endeavors to treat himself, but without success. Bad news piles upon bad news: his son has been imprisoned by Baybars in Cairo; and one of his Andalusian students who has traveled all the way to Mecca to see him has been turned away. As the fever associated with the disease worsens, Ibn Sab'in starts seeing nightmarish visions of Baybars, threatening him with death. In a massively controversial and defiant gesture, he staggers his way to the Ka'ba shrine. In a virtual coma, he lies against a wall and, at least in this novel, feels his wrists being slit . . .

This summary of Ibn Sab'in's life journey, as told in this novel, has illustrated the skillful way in which its primary "character" is placed not only into a turbulent temporal context, as noted above, but also into a physical and theological frame of reference that serves to introduce the reader to a highly important and controversial intellectual, the enormous breadth of whose learning and interests was characteristic of his time, and especially of Andalusian culture during several of the seven centuries of the Islamic period in the Iberian Peninsula (eighth to fifteenth centuries CE). Reflecting Ibn Sab'in's own intellectual and spiritual predilections, the text is full of debates and statements, for example on philosophers—Greek and Arab, poets, religious beliefs, and legal practices, and, above all, powerful statements concerning the pursuit of the Sufi path toward the transcendent, the "Necessary Existent," to which he refers throughout the text. Everywhere that Ibn Sab'in resides, he is met with, on the one hand, the fervent admiration of those Muslims who believe in the dynamic nature of discussions of phenomena and the placement of religion and sacred texts within that frame of reference, and, on the other, the dogged and often pedantic resistance and outright opposition of religious scholars and jurists with whom the rulers of the time seem to surround themselves. Such is Ibn Sab'in's intellectual ability that he is always able to best these pseudoscholars by pointing out the ways in which they are distorting the meanings of texts (or even the texts themselves). However, as he discovers at every turn, that is of no help when orthodoxy and political power combine to squelch debate. Among the eminent contemporary and subsequent textual sources on the subject of Ibn Sab'in cited by Himmich at the conclusion of the narrative, that of Ibn Taymiya, the renowned Damascene scholar of the thirteenth/fourteenth century CE, is of major interest in this context:

> Ibn Sab'in was a major heterodox figure, a polytheist and magician. He was by far the brightest and cleverest of them all, and the most knowledgeable in matters of philosophy and philosophical Sufism.

Even from Ibn Taymiya, a major conservative figure who advocated a return to the Qur'an and Sunna as sole sources of Muslim belief and a purge of other extraneous elements, including many aspects of Sufism, there is a grudging respect for the sheer power of Ibn Sab'in's intellect.

Ibn Sab'in lived in a period of profound change in the Islamic world. His journey from Murcia to Mecca is certainly a physical one, but it is also a vivid example of intercultural and intercommunal relationships in the inexorable process of breakdown. Once again, Himmich seems able to make use of the historical novel to revive a period in premodern history in order to confirm George Santayana's well-known quotation that "those who do not know history are condemned to repeat it." Or perhaps, *"plus ça change, plus c'est la même chose"* . . .

In conclusion, a few words concerning the translation. I can begin with the English title, which is not a translation of the original. Behind that choice lies a story. I mentioned at the beginning of this afterword that I have previously translated two of Himmich's other novels. I happened to meet him at a Cairo conference while I was completing my translation of the second, now published as *The*

Polymath. He informed me that he was already well involved in a new novel about the Sufi philosopher Ibn Sab'in, and was proposing to call it *Al-Intihar bi-jiwar al-Ka'ba* (Suicide Inside the Ka'ba). I suggested to him that, while that was certainly an exciting title (and indeed one that reflected historical accounts of Ibn Sab'in's death), it was also not a little provocative and even controversial in contemporary terms. I do not know what happened in the intervening period before the novel was finally published in 2007, but the eventual title, *Hadha al-Andalusi* (literally, this Andalusian) seemed to sway perhaps too much in the other direction. At any rate, I can report that it is at the author's specific request that this translation into English reverts to his original ideas concerning the title of this novel. With regard to the text of the novel itself, Ibn Sab'in is portrayed, with complete historical accuracy it would appear, as a widely read and intensely devout Muslim with an ongoing interest in philosophy and a permanent quest for the loftier planes of mystical inspiration and communication with the beyond. Sufi discourse in Arabic, with its particular lexicon and elaborate modes of expression, shares many of the qualities of the poetic, not least in its multivalent significances. In this translation, as in my previously published translations of Himmich's other novels, I have followed the balance suggested by the ideas of the German philosopher-theologian Schleiermacher (d. 1834), who expressed a clear preference for a view of the translator's activity as being one of acquainting the reader with the unfamiliar and foreign rather than attempting to adapt or alter the cultural significances of the original text so as to conform to the reader's "horizon of expectations" (to use an expression connected with Reception Theory). At the beginning of this afterword, I talked about Ibn Sab'in's use of "a style that is replete with the complex lexicon of the various spheres of knowledge and research that are involved," not to mention Himmich's craft in imitating it. With that in mind, my translations of Ibn Sab'in's ecstatic utterances (and even his reflections on them) attempt to capture as much of the phraseology and imagery of the original text as possible. The resulting English versions will certainly confront the reader with the unfamiliar (except perhaps those who have read the thoughts and poetry of Hildegard of Bingen, for example, or Julian of Norwich). As is usually the case with Himmich's novels, there is a veritable host of references to places, battles, texts, and authors, and I have provided a glossary to assist those readers, who, like me, see the historical novel as not only a pleasant introduction to the premodern world but also as a reminder of what has been and might yet be.

Glossary

NOTE: In this glossary we have aimed to assist the general reader by listing the names of prominent scholars as they are presented in the text of the novel. Thus, for example, "Al-Shushtari" appears below under the name "Abu al-Hasan al-Shushtari." Cross-references are provided to the name(s) by which such figures are more commonly known.

'Abd al-Rahman III (899?–961): The Umawi amir who declared himself caliph in 931 and made Cordoba his capital city. The palace of Al-Zahra' outside the city is a reflection of the heights to which he brought learning and culture during his lengthy reign.

'Abdallah Musa ibn Ishaq ibn Maymun (1135–1204): The renowned Spanish-Jewish scholar (Moshe ben Maimon), known in the West as Maimonides. Rabbi, philosopher, and physician, the turbulence of his times took him from his native Spain, via Morocco, to Egypt. His *Guide for the Perplexed* is one of the major works on the reconciliation of religious belief and philosophy.

Abu al-'Abbas al-Hamadhani (863–944): A renowned Shi'i scholar on prophetic traditions.

Abu al-'Abbas from Sabta (1129–1204): Moved from his native Sabta to Marrakesh and became highly revered as a Sufi ascetic. Initially residing in a cave outside the city, he later moved to a hostel and madrasa constructed for him by the Almohad ruler Ya'qub al-Mansur.

Abu 'Abdallah al-Shawdhi (also known as "Al-Halawi"): A prominent figure in Spanish Sufism from Seville who was most influential in Ibn Sab'in's early development.

Abu Da'ud (817–888): A famous collector of hadith from Khurasan and author of *Sunan Abi Da'ud,* one of the canonical collections of prophetic hadith.

Abu Dharr al-Ghifari (d. c. 652): An early convert to Islam, highly regarded in the Shi'ite community because of his opposition to the caliphate of 'Uthman ibn 'Affan, the third caliph.

Abu al-Faraj al-Isfahani (897–957): The compiler of one of the greatest collections of Arabic poetry and literary biography, *Kitab al-aghani* (The Book of Songs), long since acknowledged as the major source for information and anecdote about poets, poetry, and performance in the classical period of Arabic poetry.

Abu Madyan: see Shu'ayb Abu Madyan.

Abu al-Hasan al-Shushtari (1212–1269): The renowned Sufi poet and singer, who became a disciple of Ibn Sab'in and who is to play a major role in the narrative of this novel.

Abu Muhammad 'Abdallah (d. 1227): The Almohad ruler who succeeded his assassinated brother, 'Abd al-Wahid, in 1223. His brothers conspired against him during his reign, and he was eventually put to death by drowning in 1227.

Abu Nu'aym al-Isfahani (d. 1038): A prominent Sufi master and transmitter of prophetic hadith.

Abu Nuwas (756–814): One of Arabic's most colorful poets, whose poetic persona—amplified in the tales of *A Thousand and One Nights*—is difficult to separate from his actual life. He was famous for his wine poems and his *ghazal,* addressed to lovers of both genders. His collected poetry *(diwan)* may be the first to have been organized according to subgenres rather than other more traditional methods (such as end-rhyme).

Abu Qubays: A mountain running north to northwest outside Mecca.

Abu Talib: The uncle of the Prophet Muhammad and father of 'Ali.

Abu Tammam (d. 845): one of Arabic's most renowned poets, remembered for the originality and complexity of his poetic imagery and the adverse reactions of the critical community to his works.

Abu al-Walid al-Azraqi (ninth century): The author of a description of Mecca and its environs, entitled *Akhbar Makka.*

Al-A'mash (680–765): Otherwise known as Sulayman ibn Mihran, a collector of hadith and a specialist in the recitation of the text of the Qur'an.

'A'isha: Daughter of Abu Bakr (who later became the first caliph of Islam), and wife of the Prophet Muhammad.

Alexander legends: Stories concerning the life and exploits of Alexander the Great, the king of Macedon, began to appear in Greek from the third century. The story of "Dhu al-qarnayn" (two-horned one), linked to an episode in the romance, appears in the Qur'an (Sura 18, The Cave).

Alfonso VI (1040?–1109): King of Leon and later of Castile, both a learned man and a vigorous defender of Christian Spain. While an advocate of relations with the Muslim rulers of Spain, he opposed the invading Almoravids (q.v.) and was defeated by them in 1086.

'Ali ibn Abi Talib (c. 599–661): The cousin and son-in-law of the Prophet Muhammad, caliph between 656 and 661, and, following his death, the foundation figure of Shi'ite Islam (originally "Shi'at 'Ali," 'Ali's party).

Ali al-Sa'id: One of the Almohad rulers of Morocco (and Spain) who ruled from 1242 until his death in 1248.

Alif-lam-mim: These are some of the so-called "mystical letters" found in the text of the Qur'an. Several suras of the Qur'an begin with this and other combinations of letters of the alphabet, and there are a variety of interpretations as to their significance. James Bellamy has suggested, for example, that they constitute abbreviations of the "bismillah" (in the name of God) formula.

Al-Mansur, Abu Yusuf (d. 1199): The Almohad ruler whose reign marks the climax of Almohad power. He conducted successful campaigns against the Christians in Spain and his rivals in Morocco before retiring to Morocco and bequeathing authority to his son, Muhammad.

Almohads: In Arabic, "Al-Muwahhidun" (those who support the unity of God), the Amazigh dynasty that gained control over much of North Africa and Spain in the twelfth century, making Seville their capital from 1170 onward. Their period of power came to an end with the Battle of al-'Iqab (q.v.).

Almoravids: In Arabic, "Al-Murabitun," a term derived from the word *"ribat"* (monastery, fortress). They were an Amazigh dynasty that, having brought much of northwest Africa under their control in the eleventh century, were invited to assist the last of the so-called *taifa* kingdoms, of Seville, in resisting the Christian armies of the north. In 1091 the last of those rulers, Al-Mu'tamid of Seville, was deposed, and the Almoravids ruled Spain from their capital in Marrakesh until they too were ousted by the Almohads (q.v.) in 1147.

Antimony: Also known as "kohl" in Arabic, in medieval times it was believed to have medicinal properties for the eye.

Aristotle: Among the Greek philosopher's works, the following are specifically identified in Himmich's text: the *Categories* is a title given by his followers to one of his major studies on logic; *On Generation and Corruption* is a text concerning the causes for the generation and disappearance of phenomena based on empirical observation; *Meteorology* is a text discussing the environment and climate.

'Ayn Jalut: see Battle of 'Ayn Jalut.

Ayyubid: The Bani Ayyub, a dynasty of Kurdish origins that ruled over Egypt and much of Syria in the twelfth and thirteenth centuries.

Azhar Mosque: In Cairo, built originally by the Shi'ite Fatimids in the tenth century CE, it subsequently became a major center of Sunni learning.

Al-Azraqi: see Abu al-Walid al-Azraqi.

Badis: A thriving port on the North African coast.

Banu Ahmar: The rulers of Granada until its fall in 1492, who gave their name to the city's most famous monument, the Al-Hamra'—"the red" (Alhambra).

Banu Hud: One of the so-called *taifa* kingdoms that ruled the Zaragoza region of Spain between 1039 and 1110. In opposing the Almoravids, they sought the aid of the kingdom of Castile and were forced to pay tribute.

Banu Nasr: see Nasrids.

Battle of al-'Iqab (Las Navas de Tolosa, July 1212): A turning point in the history of Islamic Spain, in that the Christian forces of Castile, Navarre, and Aragon united under the command of Alfonso VIII and inflicted a crushing defeat on the Muslim Almohad army.

Battle of 'Ayn Jalut (Goliath's Spring): The crucial battle in September 1260 in which the Mamluks of Egypt, under the command of Al-Zahir Baybars, defeated the Mongol armies.

Baybars: see Al-Zahir Rukn al-din Baybars.

Bishr al-Hafi (767–840): The "barefoot," one of the earliest of Sufi masters.

Bismillah: The formulaic utterance "In the name of God, the Compassionate, the Merciful."

Al-Bistami, Abu Yazid (804–874): An early Sufi master who emphasized the ecstatic nature of the process of cancelling a concern with this world as a means of communication with the transcendent.

Al-Bitruji (d. c. 1204): A major Arab astronomer who composed *Kitab al-Hay'a* (Book of the Planetary System).

Brethren of Purity (Ikhwan al-safa'): A group of esoteric philosophers who gathered in southern Iraq in the tenth century and produced a series of epistles *(rasa'il)* on a variety of topics.

Al-Buni, Ahmad ibn 'Ali (d. 1225): A Sufi writer who concentrated on the mystical value of individual letters in the Arabic alphabet.

Buraq: The name of the miraculous horse on whom the Prophet Muhammad is said to have left Mecca and gone on his "night-journey" into the heavens. One of the suras in the Qur'an *(Al-Isra')* is named for this event.

Elephant Lake (Birkat al-Fil): A lake in the middle of Cairo in premodern times, around the shores of which notables constructed their mansions.

Al-Farabi (d. c. 950): One of Islam's greatest polymaths. Of Persian origin, he wrote works on philosophy and music among many other topics. Among his many works on philosophy is the one mentioned in this novel, *The Collection of Opinions of the Two Sages, Plato and Aristotle.*

Fernando [Ferdinand] (III) of Castile (1199–1252): From 1217 king of Castile and later Leon (1230), he was responsible for the Christian capture of many prominent Andalusian cities, including Cordoba (1236) and Seville (1248).

Frederic of Sicily (1194–1250): The Holy Roman emperor who lived much of his life in Sicily. He warred against the papacy and was excommunicated. One aspect of his considerable erudition seems to have taken the form of a willingness to engage with the Muslim scholars of his day.

Ful mudammas: Perhaps Egypt's most characteristic food dish, consisting of fava beans, lentils, onions, and tomatoes.

Fustat: The oldest inhabited part of Cairo, lying to the south of the main part of the city.

Galen (129–?217): A pioneer in Greek medicine, whose work on anatomy was to remain current until the medieval period in Europe.

Al-Ghazali (1058–1111): One of the most renowned of scholars within Sunni Islam. Learned in many sciences, his major work, *Ihya' 'Ulum al-Din* (The Revival of the Religious Sciences), was an enormous labor of synthesis, bringing together analyses of every aspect of the study of religion.

Hadawa Brotherhood: A Sufi sect, often suspected of using hashish as a means of achieving a state of ecstasy.

Hafsids: The Banu Hafs, who, splitting off from the Almohads (q.v.) in the thirteenth century, established their own dynasty based in Tunis. They were particularly welcoming to Muslims fleeing the reconquista in Spain.

Al-Hakam ibn 'Abd al-Rahman (915–976): Known as "al-Mustansir," the son of 'Abd al-Rahman III, the founder of the Umayyad caliphate in Cordoba, Spain.

Al-Hallaj, Abu Mansur (c. 858–922): One of the most famous of all Sufi mystics, who was executed on orders of the Abbasid Caliph, Al-Muqtadir, after he had declared "Ana l-haqq" (I am the Truth) during his ecstatic trances.

Hanafi: The name of one of the four major schools of Islamic law, named for Abu Hanifa (699–765).

Al-Harawi, 'Abdallah al-Ansari (d. 1089): Born in Khurasan, 'Abdallah al-Ansari al-Harawi was a Sufi jurist and hadith scholar. His *Manazil al-sa'irin wa-zad al-'arifin* (Stations of the Wayfarer) discusses the stages on the path to transcendence.

Al-Harrali (d. 1240): Like Ibn Sab'in himself, a mystic born in Murcia, he was known as both a commentator on the Qur'an and as a mathematician specializing, among other things, in the numerical values of letters.

Al-Hasan al-Basri (642–728?): An early supporter of the doctrine of free will (as opposed to those who advocated predestination), he lived an ascetic life that was to be a model for the emergence of Sufi ideas concerning the need for withdrawal from earthly concerns.

Hatim [al-Ta'i]: A renowned poet of pre-Islamic Arabia who was proverbial for his generosity.

Hawqala: The formulaic utterance "There is no power or ability save with God."

Hira': The name of a cave outside the city of Mecca where Muslims believe that Muhammad received his first revelation.

Al-Hudhali, Abu Bakr (d. c. 775): A hadith specialist from Basra, often cited in connection with anecdotes concerning 'Ali, the Prophet Muhammad's cousin and son-in-law.

Hulagu Khan (c. 1217–1265): The commander of the Mongol armies that invaded the Middle East and sacked the Abbasid capital of Baghdad in 1258. The invaders were eventually stopped in their advance at the Battle of 'Ayn Jalut (q.v.) in 1260.

Al-Husayn (626–680): The grandson of the Prophet Muhammad, martyred at the Battle of Karbala'. The mosque named for him in Cairo stands at the entrance to Khan al-Khalili, the city's famous bazaar.

Ibn Adham, Ibrahim (d. 777): Originally a member of the royal family of Balkh in Khurasan, Ibrahim ibn Adham abandoned that life to become a renowned Sufi figure.

Ibn al-'Arabi, Muhyi al-din (1165–1240): Like Ibn Sab'in, a native of Murcia in Spain. Also like Ibn Sab'in, he eventually left Spain and moved to the east, initially to perform the pilgrimage to Mecca. One of the most famous scholars in the history of Islam, his works include *Fusus al-hikam* (Bezels of Wisdom) and *al-Futuhat al-Makkiyya* (The Meccan Illuminations).

Ibn al-'Arif al-Sanhaji (1088–1141): A Sufi scholar of Moroccan origins who gathered a large following during the Almoravid period (q.v.). Like Ibn Sab'in himself, he was accused of heterodox beliefs by the authorities in Marrakesh.

Ibn Bajja (d. 1139): Known in Europe as "Avembace," he was born in Saragossa and became a major intellectual figure, being not only a political adviser but also an astronomer, philosopher, musician, and poet.

Ibn Baqi (d. c. 1145): An Andalusian poet famous in particular for his strophic poems in the muwashshah (q.v.) form.

Ibn Da'ud al-Zahiri al-Isfahani (c. 868–910): Author of *Kitab al-Zahra* (Book of the Flower), an early poetic anthology on the theme of love.

Ibn al-'Farid (1181–1235): The most famous of the Sufi poets who wrote in Arabic. His *khamriyya* (wine poem) uses the symbolism of the wine poem to express the quest for the transcendent that is the primary quest of the Sufi devotee.

Ibn Hazm (994–1064): A famous Muslim poet, philosopher, and controversialist, who is best known for his study on love, *Tawq al-Hamama* (The Neckring of the Dove).

Ibn Jubayr (1145–1217): A renowned Andalusian traveler who wrote an account of his travels from his native Spain to the Arabian Peninsula.

Ibn al-Mar'a (d. 1214?): From Malaga, Ibn al-Mar'a, one of Ibn Sab'in's teachers, was a jurist and theologian of the Maliki school of Islamic law.

Ibn Masarra (883–931): A major figure in the foundation of Spanish Islamic philosophy and its relationship to religious belief. Like his successor, Ibn Sab'in, and others, he suffered greatly from the attacks of orthodox scholars during his lifetime.

Ibn al-Mu'tazz (861–908): Abbasid caliph for a single day before being assassinated, he was a major poet and critic. In addition to his major contributions to various genres of Arabic poetry, he both wrote *Kitab al-Badi'* (Book of Tropes)—an analysis of poetic devices—and compiled *Kitab al-Shu'ara' al-Muhdathin* (Modernist Poets) in which he advocated the value of many of his immediate predecessors and contemporary poets.

Ibn Qasi, Ahmad (d. 1151): The initiator of a revolt against the Almoravids (q.v.) and author of *Kitab khal' al-na'layn* (The Removal of Sandals), the title of which is a reference to the Qur'an (Sura 20) and the story of Moses. A work of esoteric wisdom, it was a source of inspiration for the great Spanish Sufi scholar Ibn al-'Arabi.

Ibn al-Ramimi: The ruler of Almeria in southern Spain who was ousted from his position by Ibn al-Ahmar, the Nasrid ruler of Granada, in 1238.

Ibn Rushd (1126–1198): Known in Europe as "Averroes," Ibn Rushd was one of the most prominent scholars in Spain during the Islamic period. He composed works on philosophy, theology, poetics, and music, as well as on the natural sciences.

Ibn Sahl (1212–1251): A renowned Spanish poet of Jewish origins, known in particular for his love poetry. Following the capture of Seville by the Christians in 1248, he moved to Sabta.

Ibn Sina (980–1037): Known in Europe as Avicenna, Ibn Sina was one of the most renowned philosophers in the history of Islam. Besides a number of works on philosophy and logic, he was also renowned for his studies on medicine, including *Al-Kanun fi al-Tibb* (The Canon on Medicine) and *Al-Shifa'* (Book of Healing).

Ibn Tashufin, Yusuf (d. 1006): The commander of Almoravid (q.v.) armies that, having subdued much of North Africa (and established a capital in Marrakesh), crossed the straits at the invitation of Al-Mu'tamid and defeated the Christian armies under the command of Alfonso VI. The Almoravids remained in control of Spain until they were ousted by yet another invading force from North Africa, the Almohads (q.v.).

Ibn Tufayl (c. 1105–1185): A scholar born in Guadix who is remembered primarily for his philosophical narrative *Hayy ibn Yaqzan*.

Ibn Tulun (835–884): Ahmad ibn Tulun, originally appointed governor of Egypt by the Abbasid caliph, founded the Tulunid dynasty that ruled the country in the second half of the ninth century. His mosque is one of the most elaborate surviving monuments of the period.

Ibn Tumart (c. 1080–1130): An Amazigh scholar who became the founder of the Almohad dynasty (q.v.).

Ibn 'Umar (614–693): As his name implies, 'Umar was the son of the second caliph, 'Umar ibn al-Khattab, and a famous collector of hadith.

Ibn 'Umayra (1186–1259): A Spanish poet remembered in particular for his poetry of nostalgia for the Spain that had been lost to the Christians.

Ibn Zuhr (1113–1198): Member of an illustrious family of physicians, Abu Bakr ibn Zuhr became well known as a poet, serving as physician to the Almohad court of Ya'qub al-Mansur in Marrakesh.

Idris al-Shafi'i (767–820): The founder of the one of the four major schools of Islamic law, his *Risala* (Epistle) is a major source for the prioritization of authority in determining matters of Islamic jurisprudence, involving the Qur'an and prophetic hadith as sources, and analogy and consensus as methods.

Al-Idrisi: see Al-Sharif al-Idrisi.

Imru al-Qays: The semi-legendary pre-Islamic poet and composer of one of the seven (or ten) renowned long poems known as the *Mu'allaqat*.

Al-'Iqab: see Battle of al-'Iqab.

Jabal Musa ibn Nusayr: The mountain adjoining Sabta that is named for Musa ibn Nusayr, the governor of Africa who dispatched Tariq ibn Ziyad across the straits in 711 CE.

Jihad: A concept within Islamic doctrine that implies "[spiritual] effort, initiative." The usual English translation of the term ("holy war") is in fact a concept of Christian origins and is not a valid translation of the term.

Khadija (c. 555–619): The Meccan woman who became the Prophet Muhammad's first wife. During her lifetime he married no other woman.

Khalij Canal: A canal that used to run through central Cairo, but is now covered over (Port Sa'id Street).

Al-Khalil ibn Ahmad of Basra (c. 718–791): One of the early polymaths in Islamic history, the author of works on music and prosody and the compiler of one of the first dictionaries of Arabic, *Kitab al-'Ayn*. His metrical system was to become the standard for the analysis (and indeed the definition) of poetry.

Al-Khidr: A mysterious figure who appears most prominently in the Qur'an, Sura of the Cave (Al-Kahf, Sura 18), where he places Moses into a series of complex situations. Al-Khidr is also a major reference point in Sufi literature.

Al-Ma'arri (973–1057): One of Arabic's most famous poets. Blind from the age of four, Abu al-'Ala' al-Ma'arri became renowned both for his philosophical poetry and his often heterodox and antiestablishment religious opinions.

Maghrib: Literally "the place where the sun sets, the West," the term "Maghrib" was originally applied to the lands to the west of Egypt as they were converted to Islam in the seventh to eighth centuries. In more recent times, the word refers to the region and nations of Northwest Africa—Tunisia, Algeria, and Morocco—and, more specifically, to Morocco.

Maimonides: see 'Abdallah Musa ibn Ishaq ibn Maymun.

Malik ibn Anas (711–795): A foundational figure in the study of Islamic jurisprudence and founder of one of the four major "schools" of Islamic law. His most famous work is *Al-Muwatta,* a major collection of prophetic hadith. The adherents to his school of law are known as Malikis.

Malik ibn Dinar (d. c. 748): A disciple of the renowned theologian Hasan of Basra (642–c. 728), regarded as a reliable transmitter of traditions.

Mamluk: Literally "owned, slave" the name of a dynasty that ruled Egypt and its environs from Cairo during the thirteenth to sixteenth centuries. It was a requirement of the dynasty that the ruler had to have been born a slave.

Al-Ma'mun (1186–1232): Abu al-'Ula Idris, the Almohad ruler, who was born in Malaga in 1186 and lived much of his life in Spain, where he was forced to negotiate with the Christians in order to obtain their support against the rival Banu Hud (q.v.).

Maqama: The name of an indigenous form of short narrative composed in the highly ornate style known as *saj'* (rhyming and cadenced prose) that came to prominence in the tenth century (with Badi' al-Zaman al-Hamadhani [d. 1008] often described as its initiator).

Marinid: An Amazigh dynasty that took over control of the Maghrib from the Almohads in the thirteenth century and ruled the region till the fifteenth century.

Misriyya: In Morocco, the Misriyya is the name given to a single room on the upper stories or roof of a house.

Mountains of Mecca: The holy city of Mecca is surrounded by mountains. Among the principal ones mentioned in this text are Abu Qubays, running north to northwest; Thawr (Thour) to the south of the city; and Al-Nur to the east, where the cave of Hira', the site of Muhammad's earliest revelations, is to be found.

Al-Mubashshir ibn Fatik (d. c. 1087): A Syro-Egyptian scholar who compiled a collection of ethically based maxims under the title *Mukhtar al-hikam wa-mahasin al-kalim.*

Muhammad ibn Sharaf (d. 1068): A poet from the Tunisian city of Qayrawan who moved to Spain.

Al-Muhasibi, al-Harith (781–857): Prominent Sufi teacher and philosopher in Baghdad. His *Kitab al-tawahhum* (Book of Imaginings [of the last days]) is one of his best-known works.

Al-Mu'izz (930–975): A Fatimid caliph who gives his name to the quarter of Cairo around the Azhar Mosque that was constructed in the tenth century when Fatimid authority was transferred to the city.

Muslim ibn al-Hajjaj (c. 821–875): The compiler of one of the two major collections of *sahih,* those reports of the Prophet Muhammad's statements and actions that were considered to be maximally authentic and applicable.

Muhammad al-Mustansir ibn Abi Zakariyya (Hafsid ruler, d. 1277): The second ruler in the Hafsid dynasty in Africa (Tunis), who was closely involved in the conflict against the Crusaders and who provided (as the account in this novel suggests) an alternative power center to that of Baybars, the Mamluk ruler of Egypt.

Al-Mu'tamid ibn 'Abbad (1040–1095): Renowned Hispano-Arab poet and ruler of Seville who, having at first supported the Almoravids (q.v.) in their fight against the Christians, was deposed by them and ended his life at the Almoravid stronghold of Aghmat in Morocco.

Al-Mutanabbi (915–965): Literally "he who claims to be a prophet," Arabic's most famous poet of the premodern era. He is as well known for his ringing odes in praise of Muslim rulers as he is for lampoons deriding those who failed to acknowledge and reward his talents.

Mu'tazilites: Literally "those who went into seclusion," the term used to describe the group of rationalists who questioned orthodox principles such as the uncreated nature of the Qur'an and predestined evil. The doctrines were adopted by the Abbasid caliph, Al-Ma'mun (786–833), and tested on the theologians of the time through the "examination" process known as the *mihna,* but were later rescinded during the caliphate of Al-Mutawakkil in 848.

Muwashshah: A type of strophic poetry that emerged in Spain during the Islamic period and spread eastward.

Al-Muwatta [75]: The famous manual of jurisprudence written by Malik ibn Anas (c. 711–795), who gives his name to one of the four major schools of Islamic law.

Al-Muzaffar Sayf al-Din Qutuz (d. 1260): A Mamluk ruler in Egypt who was heavily involved in the fight against the Mongol invaders, but who was assassinated by his rival, Baybars, following the Battle of 'Ayn Jalut (q.v.).

Nasrids of Granada: The Banu Nasr came to power in Granada following the disastrous Battle of Al-ʿIqab in 1212 (q.v.). Building up Granada as a major cultural and commercial center, they remained in power until the Christian armies of Castile and Aragon captured the city in 1492.

Al-Niffari, Muhammad (d. 965): A famous figure in Sufi writing and thought, the author of the *Kitab al-Mawaqif* (Book of Stations) and *Kitab al-Mukhatabat* (Book of Conversations).

Al-Nur: A mountain to the east of Mecca, where the cave of al-Hira', the site of Muhammad's earliest revelations, is to be found.

Porphyry (c. 234–305): A student of Plotinus. His most famous work is the *Isagoge*.

Proclus (412–485): A Neoplatonist philosopher and commentator on the dialogues of Plato. The Arabic version of his *Elements of Theology* was translated into Latin as *Liber de Causis*.

Pyrrho (c. 360–270 BC): A Greek philosopher who is credited with being the first of the Skeptics.

Qudsi hadith: While hadith are reports on the statements and behavior of the Prophet Muhammad during his lifetime, the Qudsi hadith are considered to be the actual statements of Muhammad.

Al-Qushayri (986–1074): A renowned Sufi scholar whose most famous work is *Risala ila al-Sufiyya* (Epistle for Sufis).

Rabiʿa al-ʿAdawiyya of Basra (717–801): Revered as one of the earliest Sufis and an exponent of the concept of divine love, something that she expressed in her poetic output.

Raquta: Now Ricote, a village to the northwest of Murcia.

Al-Rashid: The successor of Abu al-ʿUla Idris al-Maʾmun (q.v.) as Almohad ruler (1232–42).

Al-Razi, Abu Bakr Muhammad ibn Zakariya (865–925): Known in Europe as "Rhazes," Al-Razi was a pioneer in the study and practice of medicine. His nine-volume work, *Al-Hawi,* is a comprehensive manual on medicine.

Riyad: The traditional Moroccan residence, centered around a courtyard open to the sky with a fountain and (often) various fruit trees. Around it on three sides are tall-ceilinged rooms. There are usually two other floors above the ground-floor level where different generations of the family will live.

Salah al-din (Saladin, 1138–1193): An illustrious leader of Muslim armies against the invading Crusaders.

Sayf al-Dawla al-Hamdani (916–967): The ruler of the Hamdanid dynasty, whose court at Aleppo was to attract a number of renowned figures, including the philosopher Al-Farabi and the poet Al-Mutanabbi.

Sayyida Nafisa (d. 824): A descendant of the Prophet Muhammad through his grandson, Al-Hasan. She remains highly revered in Egypt, and her tomb-shrine is in the City of the Dead, south of the Ibn Tulun mosque.

Seljuks: The dynasty of Turkish-Persian origins that took control of the secular aspects of the eastern Islamic domains in Baghdad in 1057. It was their capture of Jerusalem that instigated the First Crusade in 1096–97.

Seven Sleepers of Ephesus: A legend mentioned in Sura 18 of the Qur'an, whereby a group of young people in Ephesus were entombed in a cave (they are often known as "the people of the cave") and woke up centuries later in a very different (Christian) era.

Al-Shadhili al-Ghumari (c. 1196–1258): Born in the Ghumara region of Morocco, he was the founder of one of the major Sufi brotherhoods, the Shadhiliyya order. Later in life he moved first to Tunisia and thence to Egypt, from where his influence spread. The *ahzab* (litanies) are among his relatively few published works.

Al-Shafi'i: see Idris al-Shafi'i.

Shaqura: Now known as the Segura, the river that runs through the city of Murcia.

Al-Sharif al-Idrisi (1100–1166): The geographer who traveled widely before settling in Sicily, where he wrote his famous study *Kitab Rujar* (Book of Roger), named for King Roger of Sicily.

Shu'ayb Abu Madyan (1126–1198): Widely regarded as a foundational figure for Sufism in Spain, much revered by his successors, including Ibn al-'Arabi. Like Ibn Sab'in he left his native Spain (Seville in his case) and moved to Fez in Morocco, then undertook the pilgrimage to Mecca. Unlike Ibn Sab'in, he was able to return to the Maghrib, where he died.

Al-Shushtari: see Abu al-Hasan al-Shushtari.

Sibawayh (760–c. 793): Author of the most famous work on Arabic grammar, known as *Al-Kitab*.

Al-Suhrawardi (1155–1191): A renowned Sufi scholar and founder of the school of philosophy known as "Ishraqi" (Illuminist). He is often referred to as *"Al-Maqtul"* (the slain) because he was executed on orders from Saladin's son, Al-Malik al-Zahir.

Surat al-Duha (the Forenoon): The 93rd Sura of the Qur'an.

Tagine: One of the most characteristic dishes in Moroccan cuisine, a mixture of couscous and meat, fish, or vegetables, often blended with fruit and cooked in a vessel with a domed top that is called by the same name.

Tariq Ibn Ziyad: The renowned Amazigh ("Berber") general who led the Muslim forces across the straits in 710 CE, passing the rock that was later named after him "Tariq's Mountain" (Jabal Tariq, Gibraltar).

Al-Tawhidi, Abu Hayyan (c. 930–1023): A scholar renowned for both his literary talents (especially as a prose stylist and compiler of anecdote) and his philosophical and mystical writings.

Theologia: Attributed to Aristotle but in fact a compilation of extracts from the *Enneads* of Plotinus.

Thawr (Thour): A mountain to the south of the holy city of Mecca.

'Umar ibn al-Khattab (c. 590–644): The second caliph in Islam, also known as "Al-Faruq" (the arbiter).

'Umar ibn Khayyam (1048–1123): Renowned in the West through Fitzgerald's translation of his *ruba'iyyat* (quatrains), Khayyam wrote poetry in Persian, but was in fact better known in his own time as an algebraist.

Usama ibn Munqidh (1196–1288): Scion of a nobly Syrian family, he was a chronicler of the Crusades. His autobiography is entitled *Kitab al-I'tibar* (Book of Admonition).

Uways al-Qarni: Born in the Yemen, he converted to Islam during the time of the Prophet Muhammad and was martyred at the Battle of Siffin in 657.

"Woe for al-Mu'tasim" ("wa-al-Mu'tasimah!"): A proverbial expression coined in the name of the Abbasid caliph Al-Mu'tasim after a disastrous defeat of Muslim forces by the Byzantine army in early 838. The defeat was swiftly avenged at the Battle of Amoreum in the same year.

Ya'qub al-Mansur (c. 1160–1199): Almohad ruler who inflicted significant defeats on the Christian armies in Spain during his reign.

Yusuf ibn Tashufin: see Ibn Tashufin.

Al-Zahir Rukn al-din Baybars (1223–1277): The redoubtable general of the Mamluk armies who not only defeated the Crusaders' forces under Louis IX of France, but also defeated the Mongol armies at the Battle of 'Ayn Jalut in 1260. He went on to become ruler of Egypt and surrounding areas as the Mamluk dynasty extended its sway.

Zajal: A type of strophic poetry that emerged in Spain during the Islamic period and spread eastward.

Zamzam: The name of the well inside the sacred enclosure in Mecca. It is associated with Abraham, for whom God provided water to slake the thirst of his son, Isma'il.

Zanati: The Zanata tribe along with the Sanhaja and Masmuda were major African confederacies of Amazigh ["Berber"] tribes. They are used by the historian Ibn Khaldun (d. 1406) in order to illustrate the virtues of the tribal life of the desert in the process of developing a sense of group solidarity.

Zanki (Zengi, 1085–1146): An illustrious leader of Muslim armies against the invading Crusaders.

Zawiya: A word that, in the Maghribi context, means a small mosque and shrine, but that might also include an adjoining hostel for visitors and—as in the case of the one on Jabal Musa in Sabta—an asylum and hospital.